HAPPENSTANCE

JOEL AUSTIN

ISBN: 9798640101195

DEDICATION

For the amazing women in my life.

ACKNOWLEDGMENTS

A big thanks to my Dad for being the first reader and to Jake for diving in without hesitation.

A NOTE TO THE READER

I want to extend a huge thank you to all my readers. Your support is marvelous, and it keeps me going. I do have one request, if I may be so bold.

If you enjoyed the book, please leave a review on Amazon. It is an immense help to me.

Additionally, you can follow me at www.joelaustin.online. I have periodic book giveaways and free stories. Hope to see you there.

Cheers!

Joel Austin

CHAPTER ONE

NORTHERN CALIFORNIA

The cigarette wouldn't light. Rain had rendered it into a useless, soggy cylinder. It had been coming down steadily for over an hour. Nothing torrential. Despite the leaves overhead, dampness had burrowed through his coat. The seasons had changed. Summer had set, replaced by the sodden cold of fall.

Unsatisfied by the first attempt, he dropped the saturated Lucky Strike without a second thought and withdrew a fresh one from the pack. It lit without issue, a lone orange glow in the night, and he inhaled with gratitude.

Glancing at the phone, more out of habit than any rational reason, yielded nothing but the time. Two hours had passed without a word. Arriving early had been part of the plan. No sense in cutting it close. Habits were often hard to break, but circumstances could change or even bend the need for consistency. The man he was waiting for was punctual and habitual, yet capable. That much was clear. The eyes gave it away. Eyes that had seen things and done things. Stained by deeds of the past.

There was a certain kinship in that regard between him and the man. Only he hadn't quit and left the life behind. His past wasn't so easily shed. No. There was family and history to consider. You can't outrun the past. That was certain. The shadows of his family were too long. Casting aspersions, they fall upon those who strayed. Quitting was not an option.

At a quarter to seven, the phone rang. A trill beep in the damp air absorbed by the leaves underfoot.

"Yeah," he answered with some annoyance.

"Just left. Ten minutes out."

"Okay."

Turning to the two men nearby, he motioned up the road, "Ten minutes. Cut it down."

The chainsaw roared to life as the bigger of the men set to work cutting down a young oak growing out from the shoulder of the road. The tree was a known dimension. Its vertical height translated into a complete blockage of the road. He liked the choice. It was a solid tree. Not too big to move, but large enough to prevent a detour.

Another cigarette was lit off the end of the second. More deep breaths. Then the tree cracked and fell. A muted pop lost in the rain. More or less, it landed as planned.

Five minutes remained. The men gathered like some brutish huddle. He sent a skinny accomplice with a shotgun across the road. A blocking maneuver of sorts, not that he expected the man to run. Maybe fight, but not flee. Quitting had been one thing, but that seemed like a moral or philosophical choice. Fleeing a fight was something else entirely.

In the distance, a lone engine whined. Small and foreign, not like the big throaty domestic sounds. With a thumbs up, the men moved into position near the road, hiding behind whatever seemed to fit. He grabbed the old Colt 1911 pistol from his jacket and pulled the slide slightly back, reassuring himself a bullet was chambered and ready to fire.

The old Toyota truck arrived abruptly, announced by the squeal of tires fighting to find traction. Headlights cut distinctive arcs through the darkened mist. Cones of light that petered out, overpowered by the millions of droplets wafting in the air.

The door opened, and a man got out. He couldn't see the driver's face, but the truck was right, his build was too. Moving in from behind, he could see the man stooped over the fallen tree, sizing it up. In measured steps, he moved forward. He wasn't over fifteen away when the man stopped fussing and stood up. Twisting his head without moving his torso, the driver glanced backward and scoffed

"Figures."

"Lieutenant," he replied with a raised pistol.

SAN FRANCISCO AIRPORT

The flight was late. The announcer said delayed, but Captain Frank Sherman thought otherwise. A delay was, by definition, the making of something late. A direct flight would have been on time, but that did not exist. Fourteen hours of travel was bleeding into sixteen, expected to be eighteen.

He dialed Lieutenant Tillerman's number from memory. His friend would be waiting in the parking lot in front of the small regional airport. Common courtesy, he thought, not that the Lieutenant had ever minded a delay.

No beeps, rings, or elevator music. The call went straight to voicemail. Tillerman eschewed technology, but Sherman had never known the man not to answer. It was the one abiding trait that never ceased to amaze. In all those years the Lieutenant missed one call, and he fell off the wagon to make it happen.

Sherman dialed again, but only heard a generic female voice reciting a number. A seed of worry grew in the recesses of his mind.

The bartender looked his way, and Sherman nodded. It may have been morning on the West Coast, but he was still on Azerbaijan time. Four hours later than London, the last city under his feet. As far as his body knew it was twelve hours later than the clock hanging above the taps. His way of rationalizing a second beer at eight in the morning.

"You keep rubbing that chin like you lost a friend," said a nearby patron. It was true. Sherman kept checking his face where his beard had been, as if it would magically return.

"It hasn't seen the sun in fifteen years," he replied.

"Fresh start or a clean break?" asked the man.

Sherman pondered the question for a moment, "I'm not sure yet. Let's call it a short-term separation."

"Hard to run away from what you know," replied the man as he raised his glass.

"Ain't that the truth," responded Sherman before finishing his beer.

Eighteen hours, not fourteen. Definitely late.

"Now boarding United flight 8475," blared the speakers with a touch of static. The announcement mentioned nothing about the delay. No apologies.

Sherman meandered over to the small gate hidden in the far corner of some backwater terminal that only carried regional passengers. A dozen people milled about. All of them had resigned themselves to their fate. Acceptance was the key to traveling. No point in fighting the system. It won a long time ago.

He recognized a few of his fellow passengers from the bar. Like minds, he thought.

Outside the window, a small twin turboprop was fueling up. A puddle hopper. Sherman liked the small planes, it felt like real flying. Closer to the military mentality; bumpy with no frills.

He called Tillerman one last time. Still nothing. The seed was sprouting.

The flight attendant went through her spiel: buckle up, exits, seat cushions that float. Sherman thought of the imaginable bodies of water they could crash into between here and there. None of them were survivable. Besides, there was no way that someone could hold on to those things for very long. Arms through some loops, hugging a cushion in near hypothermic temps. Thirty minutes, maybe an hour tops, before their muscles gave out, and they sank. Might as well be useless, he thought.

Taxiing and takeoff took another twenty minutes. The large commercial fleets dwarfed the miniscule plane. A speck on the vast runway.

By the time they reached cruising altitude, the flight attendant had about five minutes to hand out drinks and pretzels before the pilot announced their descent.

"Welcome to Cumbre County Regional Airport. The current weather is fifty-two degrees with a chance of rain. Thanks for flying United."

Sherman shook his head and disembarked down the ramp straight onto the tarmac. No fancy walkway to the terminal, no frills. With no bag other than the small pack over his shoulder, he took the exit straight into the parking lot. The Lieutenant always parked in the shade of an old live oak, but the space was empty. Nothing.

A lone cab waited at the curb. Some old Crown Vic long past its prime. The hand-painted letters on the sedan were slowly fading, and the phone number was only six digits long.

The old man in the driver's seat nodded as Sherman walked up.

"Where to son?"

"You know South River Road?" Sherman asked.

The old man nodded and motioned for Sherman to get in.

"Third house past the creek," he instructed.

"Sure thing," said the driver as he dropped the old car into gear. It squeaked into drive before rumbling down the road.

CHAPTER TWO

The driveway was steep. More rise than run, as his father used to say. Old oaks and chalk-colored sycamores encroached on the roadway. The trees stretched around the Lieutenant's house like open arms. A river was back there somewhere, masked by a facade of leaves and bark.

The cab stopped at the bottom of the hill. Sherman looked at the meter and handed the driver thirty dollars.

"You know him?"

Sherman smiled, "Something like that."

"Odd fellow. Really keeps to himself," added the driver, relishing the opportunity to share some gossip.

"The army always thought so," replied Sherman.

"You boys served?"

"He did three tours in Afghanistan and Iraq. I never left."

"Hell of a war, that one," mused the cabbie.

Sherman nodded at the man old enough to be his father, "Nam?"

"Summer of '69 to '70."

"Right in the suck."

The cabbie grunted, his eyes staring into some distant battlefield where the screams were still very much alive.

Sherman squeezed his arm, "Thanks for the lift. Keep the change."

"Thanks, good luck to you," said the cabbie, back in the

present. He handed Sherman a business card.

Sherman looked at the rectangular piece of paper in his hand. "See you around, Mr. Brummet," he replied.

Sherman slung his pack and trudged up the rather steep driveway. Half rotten leaves, still slick from a recent storm, squished under his boots. An earthy aroma of decay hung over the property. The humidity was thick, but Sherman felt invigorated. He had spent too much time in the desert.

Tillerman's truck was missing. Not parked in the driveway like usual. Sherman didn't like it in the least. Something felt wrong. His gut had known from the first missed call. Now his brain was catching up.

The house was modest. A single story, but not as rambling as a ranch. Green siding a few shades darker than forest covered the exterior walls. It was earthy and grounded amongst the trees. Not hidden, but not a showy announcement of wealth or prestige. The previous owners had left it in its original state more or less. Limited in updates but well maintained.

The porch out back was the actual reason Tillerman bought the place. The seclusion didn't hurt, but the entire town was a few steps from nowhere. Sitting on that porch with the trees practically on the deck, the sound of the river a constant reminder of the water, could ease the weight of many a wrong. Not forever and not for those deeply buried sins, the ones singed like a brand into the very soul. Sherman wasn't a metaphysical man, nor a gambler, but he bet the Lieutenant suffered from the latter sin. The town, the house, was the closest Tillerman ever came to a salve.

There was only one bedroom, built as it was for a retired couple. Despite the ownership change, it still served its original purpose. This was the Lieutenant's retirement. An escape or atonement from the past, the war, and the man he had been. That past was out of sight, discarded like an old shirt, but not forgotten.

Sherman never begrudged his friend's choice to leave the army or run away to the mountains. Loyalty was never the quality in question. Some were good at killing and some could handle the aftermath. Tillerman could "do" but not cope. Sherman managed both.

He tried the front door. Locked. Peeking through the windows, nothing looked amiss. Everything was neat. Perfectly stacked magazines and clean counters. No clutter at all. Disorder wasn't in the Lieutenant's vocabulary.

There was a spare key hidden in the backyard under a slowly decomposing bag of dog shit. The Lieutenant owned no dog, but that didn't matter. No one would lift a bag of crap to look for a key.

Sherman let himself in and looked around. No sign of his friend or where he went. The fridge was not full, but not empty. Leftovers and the odd ingredient remained. Remembering an ongoing test, he hunted down a bottle of bourbon the Lieutenant kept in a kitchen cabinet. It was still there.

Years ago, when Sherman helped him sober up, the Lieutenant brought home a bottle of Bookers one night. Sherman almost broke his jaw, but Tillerman insisted he needed it. Not to drink, but to remind him of lost time. Despite his misgivings, Sherman allowed it, and he had been drinking and replacing that bottle ever since. It was mostly full, just the way Sherman left it nine months earlier.

"At least you're still sober," he muttered before grabbing a glass from the drying rack.

Sherman poured out two fingers and gave the golden-brown liquid a good sniff. It smelled like a lot of things, places and times. Some bad, but most good. With nothing to do, he headed out to the back porch to grab a seat on a rocking chair.

The Lieutenant had taken up woodworking to pass the time, and it turned out to be a calling. Sherman ran his hand over the smooth oak armrests and smiled. The man had a talent.

As the hobby turned serious, the Lieutenant had built it into a business. It gelled with the hipster, crafty, homemade crowd. In combination with GI money, he had bought the house on the hill and an old truck.

The pickup was manual and lacked any frills. Sherman sympathized with the compulsion for simplicity. The truck, the wood furniture, the lack of television. It made sense to him. Technology's inexorable march across society had left many a solitary being wanting for a bygone era. The same could be true of the battlefield. Sherman wondered how long until he was superfluous. Fifty years? Sixty? His money was on less than forty.

Two fingers had turned to three when Sherman heard the front door open. He smiled and wandered inside, half-expecting some bizarre story about deer hunting with a knife. The smile quickly vanished.

Standing in the doorway were two local sheriff's deputies. For a tiny town, they represented about half of the law. Sherman had met them in passing more than once over the years. He had been visiting Byron Mills for over a decade, and he considered it more home than not. Over all those years and interactions, he had never come away with a positive impression of the law.

Sherman had taken the two men by surprise. It was clear from their expressions of shock they were not expecting anyone.

He glanced at the name badges while making a stand in the living room. Sherman didn't plan to give any ground to the interlocutors. "Can I help you Deputies Barrios and Simpkins?" he asked.

Deputy Barrios shot him a contemptuous look and demanded, "Who the hell are you?"

Sherman remembered the man. From what the Lieutenant had recounted, Barrios was a man with a mean streak that grew quickly after high school when the weight of his shortcomings brought down whatever high horse he rode.

"Someone standing on private property," responded Sherman, not intimidated by the two deputies.

Simpkins took his turn at the bad cop. "Look asshole, identify yourself now while you're not under arrest."

Sherman was sensing a theme. All bad and no good. "Alright, no need for the idle threats. My name is Frank Sherman, I'm an old friend of Lieutenant Tillerman."

"Nothing idle about the situation, Frank," spat Barrios while taking a step closer. He pointed a thick finger at Sherman's chest to emphasize the point.

"Call me Sherman and you still haven't explained why you entered my friend's house without a warrant."

Simpkins laughed, "Your friend is dead. We don't need no warrant."

Sherman sighed, but he didn't feel much surprise. On some level, he already knew it, but hope had kept him waiting on that porch.

"Shit," he finally said solemnly, "what happened?"

"Got drunk and wrapped his truck around a tree," answered Barrios, barely concealing his glee in breaking the news.

Sherman blinked in amusement at the outright lie. At the audacity of it. No true alcoholic like the Lieutenant would fall off the wagon and leave a bottle of their favorite bourbon untouched. Not a chance.

"When did it happen?" probed Sherman.

"Early this morning on Upper Mill Road."

The location rang a bell. A narrow road with tight corners, but not enough straightaways to pick up speed. It would be hard to generate enough force to do actual damage unless someone was trying.

"And you're here to... what? Make sure he didn't have any pets?"

Barrios tilted his head to the side as if to think, "Uh, yeah. Common courtesy."

"How thoughtful," said Sherman, "that must be dog food you've brought." He nodded at the grocery bag Simpkins was carrying.

"Ya... Yeah," stuttered the simple man.

"You can leave it there." Sherman pointed to a nearby table.

"Well, I don't see no dog," said Barrios smiling "We wouldn't want to waste any more taxpayer dollars."

"Whatever you say, sheriff."

Barrios turned back to face Sherman, suddenly remembering the powers imbued by his badge. "I think it's time you left," he sneered.

"Not gonna happen."

The deputy's mirthless smirk stretched further, and he took a step forward. His hand rested on his pistol in an attempt at intimidation.

Sherman couldn't have cared less, "And I'll need the key you stole to get in here."

Barrios lost it completely. No one had challenged him since he got the badge. Everyone agreed and complied with his demands. His entire ego rested on that crutch of power. Sherman was challenging the sand beneath his feet.

"Fuck you, asshole," Barrios roared back. Spittle clung in the corner of his mouth.

Sherman rolled his eyes in contempt.

Barrios grabbed the collapsible baton from his belt and extended it with the flair of someone who practiced in front of the mirror. The smile on his face laid bare the twisted joy he found in the movement and sound. Pure egotistical power. The kind only a badge or uniform can provide.

Sherman knew the look. He had seen in the shaming yells of drill sergeants and the nonsensical orders of commanding officers. Staring it in the face once more, Sherman couldn't help but laugh at the unfolding drama. Despite his size, Barrios looked like a man who hadn't fought someone willing to strike back in years. For too long a badge had cloaked his ego in the backwaters of California.

"Try it," said Sherman, igniting a rage summering just below the deputy's thin skin.

Barrios reared back with the baton and advanced towards Sherman, who was still holding his ground in the living room.

"Goddamnit Barrios," boomed a voice from the front doorway. "Knock that shit off now!"

The deputy's face almost froze, like a kid caught watching porn. He stood to attention with an expression full of fear and seething anger. Sherman relaxed his stance, but knew he had made an unwelcome enemy in town.

In strode the portly sheriff of Cumbre County, with all the pompousness such a position granted. He was a sizeable man who the Lieutenant described as a three-high stack of whiskey barrels. Sherman guessed the description also described the man's internal state. Smooth and complex, but also volatile.

"Captain Sherman, my apologies. It's been a long night and my deputies acted out of turn."

Barrios raised his eyes at the mention of rank and the admonishment from his boss.

Sherman remained stoic, "Sheriff Reinhold. I'd say it was nice to see you, but the circumstances are shit."

"I assume they told you what happened."

Sherman nodded.

"My condolences, Lieutenant Tillerman was an honorable man and an upstanding citizen."

It almost sounded sincere, but the Sheriff was a consummate snake oil salesman. Everything came out sweet, but the bite was real. Sherman had met many men like him across the world. Afghan warlords, Iraqi ministers, tribal leaders, jihadi recruiters. All of them could lie and swallow their words as truth.

"Thanks, sheriff," replied Sherman, trying to hide his sarcasm. "Do you know what happened?"

Reinhold looked at his deputy holding the bag, "I guess he fell off the wagon. Went out drinking and then driving."

Sherman nodded along with the lie.

"Went up Upper Mill, lost control of the truck and crashed into that old oak near Mr. Mosley's farm."

"The one almost in the road?" asked Sherman, making

sure he could picture the place.

"The same."

Sherman sighed, "What a waste."

"We'll leave you be. The boys just wanted to make sure the house was okay while we contacted the next of kin."

Sherman smelled the bullshit, but played dumb. "As far as I know, he had no immediate family. Raised by the state and then the army."

Reinhold nodded, "Like I said, we'll leave you be until probate clears."

"Okay then."

The Sheriff motioned for the two deputies to leave. Barrios shot Sherman a look dirty enough to be evidence in a murder trial. Simpkins just nodded and walked out, taking the brown paper bag with him.

Sherman closed the door behind them and watched them walk down the driveway. Once they crested out of view he bolted out the back door and into the dense thicket of oaks, sycamores, buck brush and redbuds next to the house.

Silently he weaved down the hill towards the road. The soft damp leaves muffled his footsteps. Earthy forest scents and fall humidity filled his nostrils. It felt so natural, and Sherman moved without thinking.

The police cruisers sat across the road, about thirty yards away. The men were talking.

"You idiot," said the Sheriff. "What were you fucking doing?"

Sherman couldn't hear the response, but he saw Barrios shake his head and shrug.

"You're lucky he didn't take that baton and smash your little fucking pea brained skull in," continued Reinhold.

"Fuck that," said Barrios, loud enough for Sherman to hear.

"That guy," said Reinhold, pointing up towards the house, "has probably killed more men than you've pissed off."

Barrios was shaking his head again, "I'd stomp that Ranger."

"As usual, Barrios, you've massively understated the fucking problem. Rangers get killed; ghosts don't die." The Sheriff shook his head at the insolence of his deputy. "Get in the car, we need to clean up this mess."

With the cars out of view, Sherman leaned against the smooth trunk of a sycamore before heading back up to the house. Gone were the sweet odors of earthly decay, overpowered by the stench of wrongdoing. His creeping suspicion of foul play had bloomed into a fully formed fear.

Sherman sat back down on the porch, whiskey in hand. "Lieutenant, what did you get yourself into?"

CHAPTER THREE

By two o'clock Sherman knew that he needed to sober up. The cops had come and gone, leaving behind the bitter taste of suspicion. Whiskey had helped, but its appeal rested on a bell curve. Sherman was rolling down the backside and picking up speed. A gallon of water and a walk seemed like the solution.

Heading straight out the backdoor towards the river, he found a suitable spot to consider unfolding events slightly downstream. It was quiet, save for the noise of rushing water. Years ago, he had visited the same sandy alcove during the height of summer. The heat had driven him into the water like a hippo heading home. He had emerged healed. Not in the biblical way. It was no baptism, but it was all he needed. Absolved from the gnawing guilt and fear in his chest. Years had passed, but he could still feel that moment of liberation.

The preceding week had taken a toll. It had spilled blood. Too many died. The violence spanned a generation with his own father at the center of it all. He had come back to Cumbre County to get away from the killing, to reset and heal. Turned out it was an inescapable vortex, and he was being sucked back in again despite the distance.

Sherman has lost friends before. More than he cared to count, but that was over there. Different rules and mindsets applied in the sand. This time it was here, and it was personal. Someone had killed his best friend.

He skipped a rock across the swimming hole and pondered the current situation.

The Lieutenant was an alcoholic. That much was true. Sherman doubted he tumbled off the wagon, but it wasn't beyond the realm of possibility. Relapses happen, that was just a fact of life. Tillerman had several before it stuck. What did that leave?

A man, ten years sober, gets loaded a few hours before picking up his only remaining friend from the airport. He gets so drunk that he wraps his truck around a tree. On a road, that if Sherman remembered correctly, dead ends near a pile of rocks. It was a stretch, but plausible for an alcoholic.

That was before the cops showed up. He could almost give them the benefit of the doubt. They show up and notify next of kin, make sure they leave no pets unattended. Small town nice. But what was in the bag, and why did Deputy Barrios lose his temper when confronted?

Sherman skipped a few more stones and considered the plausible answers. He wasn't a cop, never had been, and he didn't deal with common criminals. What he knew was killing, including the essential covering your tracks part. That is what it felt like. A cover-up.

That meant the bag had evidence destined for the Lieutenant's house. Evidence that he prevented from being planted. The Sheriff had mentioned cleaning up a mess. Sherman mistook that to mean the altercation with Barrios. Perhaps he had meant the missed opportunity to put something incriminating inside the house.

The answer hit him on the third skip as he watched the water ripple. Sherman felt stupid for not thinking of it earlier. Booze. They were planting empty bottles of alcohol. The bag was the right size. It would have easily fit two bottles of whiskey.

"Fuckers," he muttered to the river.

The gallon jug of water was empty. So was the deepest of the whiskey haze. The anger remained. Unbridled.

Sherman rarely displayed anger, not genuine anger. He was a great operator because he remained calm and collected under duress. The shooting would start, and his mind would flip a switch. Everybody would try to kill him, and his mind was processing tactics and angles. No anger, no hate. Emotions cloud your judgment and that was his greatest asset. Fighting in the Middle East for the last fifteen years had taught him many things. The first of those was don't lose your head. Yet there he was, sitting by the river, barely below the legal limit and angrier than ever.

He called his commander. Major Sanders was his name. They had served together since the army assigned Sherman to JSOC. That was ten plus years ago. The Major was about the only person left in the Army that Sherman implicitly trusted. The number was not in the phone, and he would delete the record after the call ended.

"What happened?" The Major's question cut to the point. Sherman had only just left the theater. A call so soon meant trouble.

"Lieutenant Tillerman is dead," he answered. A bit of that anger crept into his voice.

The Major drew in a deep breath, "How?"

"The local cops say drunk driving accident."

"You don't sound convinced."

"Not in the least. The locals are dirty, no doubt. They showed up at the house to plant some empty whiskey bottles. Didn't expect me there."

"They're still breathing?" It was a fair question.

"Until I learn they're complicit," replied Sherman.

The Major grunted, "Different rules on the home field. I can't help if things go south."

"Understood. But I have a favor to ask."

"Go ahead." The Major was all business, all the time.

"Check the metadata on the Lieutenant's phone," said Sherman as he rattled off the number.

"Timeframe?"

"Last forty-eight hours."

"Copy. Good hunting." It was the same phrase the Major used in-country. A fait accompli for that to come.

Sherman skipped one last rock and walked back to the house. He needed to take stock of the situation. If the sheriff kept his word, which Sherman had no reason to believe, he might only have a few days. Best to sort it out before probate closed, and he got kicked to some motel.

He was standing in the kitchen, lost. "Where do you start?"

During previous visits, Tillerman stocked the fridge. Not with beer, but plenty of food. He checked. It was bare save for some leftovers.

"So, he never made it to the market."

Sherman had called around 5:00 pm local time. On paper his flight landed 7:00 am the next morning. The market closed at 10:00 pm. That left plenty of time for the Lieutenant to pick up provisions the night before. But he didn't. That left a five-hour window from Sherman's call to the market closing. Five hours wasn't long.

His head hurt a little. Maybe from the booze or the travel or the shock. Probably a combination of all three. He rubbed his temples hard enough to erase the last few hours. It didn't work. He was still in the kitchen, and his friend was still dead.

"Don't assume," said his inner cynic. It was right. Recreating those five hours was the key to understanding what happened.

He tried to remember what the Sheriff had said. Something about a late night. The memory was a little hazy.

If the Lieutenant died late the previous night or early that morning, then what the hell happened?

He walked through the rest of the house. It was orderly and clean. So was the workshop out back. No signs of a struggle. No broken glass or blood.

A scenario was forming. One that Sherman understood.

His friend left for the store, probably around 7:00 pm when the evening rush had died down. The Lieutenant wasn't too fond of crowds after Afghanistan. It would have been dark by then. Having been party to a few renditions, Sherman knew night was the best time to take someone. He usually came by helicopter and death followed, but this wasn't there and the road into town was full of blind curves and sharp bends. During that drive, his friend ran into a blockade of some sort. Maybe a motorist in distress or a fallen tree. Anything to get him out of the truck. Then it happened. Sherman wasn't sure how or why, but he didn't think the Lieutenant died then. No. Persons unknown took him.

The inexorable logic didn't surprise Sherman. They had lived violent lives and despite the distance from any war, the Lieutenant had died from that same violence.

It would have been a tidy little bow covering the crime. But then he walked in and mucked it up. Sherman knew he was a loose end now. A liability. He smiled, they did not understand what was coming.

Sherman placed a call. The cabbie answered on the third ring. It was almost 7:00 pm. Late for a small town.

"Hello," he asked, not recognizing the number.

"Mr. Brummet," said Sherman, reading the name on the card. "This is Frank Sherman. You dropped me off this morning on South River Road."

"Ah, Mr. Sherman. I didn't recognize your number. What can I do for you?"

"I'm looking for a ride back into town. I apologize if I'm interrupting a meal." It was a small-town apology. Seven in the evening meant most people were well past dinner.

"Not at all. I can be there in twenty minutes. Same spot?" replied Brummet.

"Thank you kindly," said Sherman before hanging up.

The Lieutenant didn't own a gun. He had seen enough in Afghanistan. Sherman knew that and didn't bother looking for one. That didn't prevent him from wishing for one.

What Tillerman had was knives. Part of the self-reliance,

anti-tech stance he had taken. Sherman picked a fixed blade tactical variant from the work shed. Matte black with a five-inch blade. It looked vicious in a practical, no nonsense, and morbid sort of way. Despite his abhorrence towards the war, the Lieutenant never got over his taste for other forms of bloodshed. He had started too young to go back; they baked it into his DNA. Since the Lieutenant used it for hunting, Sherman reasoned he could.

He left out the back door and circled down to the road through the woods. It was mostly night. Those few minutes where twilight succumbed to darkness. Sherman had borrowed a forest green jacket hanging in the closet. All he had was a red parka and that wouldn't do for sneaking around at night.

Standing in the woods near the road, Sherman waited and listened. The river burbled in the background, cicadas buzzed in the black envelope of night, but nothing human. Nothing sinister.

Brummet pulled up the cab on-time. Punctual. Sherman liked him already. If a man emerging from the darkened woods frightened the cabbie, he didn't show it. He merely nodded as Sherman got in the back seat.

"Evening," said Brummet.

"Thanks again and sorry for the short notice," replied Sherman.

"It's your dollar."

Sherman laughed, "Fair point. Look, I've got an odd request."

Brummet eyed him through the rear-view mirror, "Listen, I don't need more trouble in my life. No drugs and no girls."

"It's your car friend. I just need someone to drive me around, make a few stops."

"Nothing sketchy."

"Just looking for answers," said Sherman.

"Alright then, where to?"

"That's the thing, I'm not sure yet. Let's start by heading

to the market." There was only one market in town, and no one referred to it by any other name.

Brummet turned the cab around and headed back into town. The Lieutenant had chosen a remote road outside an insignificant town. It had some charm. Most of all, it had the river and the mountains. Trees, lots of trees, saturated the entire area.

"If you don't mind the intrusion, Mr. Sherman," said Brummet, looking back, "why do you need me?"

"No need for formality, Sherman is fine."

Brummet nodded, "The name is fine for me."

"My friend, the Lieutenant, is dead."

Brummet took a deep breath. "I'm sorry to hear that. What happened?"

"I'm going out on a limb here, but you seem like an upstanding guy. They say he crashed his truck on Upper Mill road, drunk as a skunk."

"Not buying it?"

Sherman grunted, "Let's just say I'd like to see the truth be told."

"Small towns reluctantly tell the truth, especially to outsiders," said Brummet. It was true. Places like Byron Mill operated almost tribally. An us-versus-them mentality. The outsider is guilty until proven otherwise by deed or death.

They drove on for a few minutes until something on the road in front of them caught Sherman's eye. "Stop there," he said, pointing to a set of skid marks on the road.

Brummet came to a stop in front of two small black smears on the road. They had just come around a tight bend and the sight lines were minimal. Not quite a blind corner in daylight, but close at night. Crickets chirped in the mild darkness. Cool air hugged the ground, intent on staying put, and blackberry bushes lined one edge of the road.

Sherman stood in front of the cab, casting a silhouette across the pavement. The skids marks were from braking. Heavy up front and fading with distance. Whoever drove the vehicle wasn't going fast. The marks were short and abrupt.

"You okay," yelled Brummet from the cab.

Sherman flashed a thumbs up, "You mind waiting a few?"

"Your dollar."

Off to the side of the road, next to the slowly growing carpet of sycamore leaves, Sherman searched the ground with a small flashlight he found at the house. He was looking for something off. The marks could have been from anyone, but the spot was too good. His gut told him this was the place.

Two trees back, he stopped. Dropped casually on the damp leaves were several cigarette butts. Lucky Strike brand. The car door closed, and Sherman turned to see Brummet following him into the woods.

"It might be best if you stayed in the car," said Sherman.

"I turned off the meter," he replied.

"Why?"

"I've seen this before. Ia Drang Valley. July of '69."

"Ambush?" asked Sherman, wondering if the man agreed.

"Cut my company to pieces. Lost my best friend that day. Twenty feet away from me and I couldn't help him. Tracers so thick they looked like a fireworks show."

"A hard bend in the trail?"

"Yes sir, just like this one. Charlie just appeared out of the jungle."

Sherman nodded towards the cigarettes, "Anyone live around here?"

Brummet squinted into the night, "Not really. A ranch up the road, but nothing on the other side."

"So, what's back there?"

"Bureau of Land Management open space and a fire road."

Unused land. Little regulation or oversight. No prying eyes. A perfect spot to take someone.

To Sherman's right was a downed tree. Someone had

hauled back into the woods. A telltale smattering of broken limbs left in the wake.

Sherman gestured towards the tree. Brummet looked at it and then back at the road before nodding in agreement.

If there were blood stains or signs of violence, Sherman didn't see them. Crouching down, he looked at the foot traffic still present in the dirt and leaves. Not a lot of men. Less than six, he guessed.

"You said you're still in the service, right?" Brummet asked with a good deal of recognition in his eyes.

Sherman nodded.

"And what unit are you with?"

"Something under JSOC."

Brummet raised his eyebrows, "Special Forces."

Sherman shrugged.

"And your friend? He was too?"

The man was taking a circuitous route with his questions. "Yeah," replied Sherman.

"And he could handle himself then?" he continued.

"Your point being, he went quietly," concluded Sherman.

Brummet laughed, "Yeah, I see you're a step ahead."

"I don't know about that, but I agree with your idea. Overpowered?" Sherman shrugged at his own question.

"Or," said Brummet while scratching his beard, "he was incentivized."

"You're a devious man, Mr. Brummet. What would get him to go quietly?"

Brummet shrugged, "I didn't know the man."

"Maybe I didn't either." Sherman said, looking out into the forest. "How much do I owe?"

"I'll start a tab."

"Kind of you. Are you free around nine tomorrow morning?"

"I can be."

"Good. I'll see you then."

Brummet looked confused, "Are you walking back?"

Sherman just flashed him a thumbs up and walked off into the soft, damp embrace of the night. It left Brummet shaking his head and wondering who he was helping.

The fire road was not far away, and the boot prints were obvious. No one was covering their tracks. No one expected someone to look.

He found the tire tracks maybe a few hundred yards from where he left the cabbie. It wasn't far from the river, which the locals called a fork, but this far back it was its own entity, not yet sullied by other waters. Grass covered everything there. Thick and verdant, save for a deep brown scar from truck tires. It was conspicuous and lazy.

Sherman looked at the impressions. Four parallel lines heading towards the river. Two trucks seemed reasonable. Good to have backup. But the lines were too neat.

"Dually," he said into the stillness.

Following the tracks was easy. They were a veritable four-lane highway, even with a bare crescent of moonlight. Life filled the small valley. The air was thick with dew and heavy with nature's nighttime hum. Contrasted against the desert heat and bone-dry air, this felt like home.

The tracks led Sherman to an old wooden bridge across the river. The fire road lay on the other side. Tire tracks ended on one side of the bridge and then mingled with a dozen more on the other. He gazed up into the hills for a moment, contemplating where the road traveled. Somewhere up into the pines and redwoods.

From where he stood, they could have taken the Lieutenant up into the hills or to the other end of town. Sherman guessed the latter. If the cops had staged his accident a few hours later, it made little sense to drive a doomed man up and down the mountain when a more direct route existed. He allowed himself the potential to be completely wrong.

The house was around five miles upriver. The walk, he reasoned, would give him time to think. Time to plan.

"Who drives a dually?" The question kept coming back.

CHAPTER FOUR

Sherman was barely in the cab and already asking questions. "Who uses that fire road?"

Brummet looked back, a bit confused by the question. "A veritable smorgasbord, I guess. Outdoorsy folks. Drunk high school kids. Forest service. Oh, and the loggers."

"Loggers?"

"Yeah, Uncle Sam opened up a few parcels up there. No clear cutting. Selective cutting, whatever the heck that means."

"Where does it start?" asked Sherman.

"The road?"

"Yeah."

"Upper Mill Road is the primary entrance. That chunk connects across to it," answered Brummet.

Sherman stared out the window in silence.

"What did you find last night?" Brummet asked, breaking the stillness in the car.

"Tire tracks leading to the fire road."

"And that means something to you?"

"Cops said the accident happened on Upper Mill Road."

"Oh," added Brummet.

"Yeah."

"Coincidence?" asked Brummet in a voice tinged with a fading hope.

Sherman locked eyes with the man in the mirror.

Brummet needed no further clarification.

"Okay. What now?"

"You know anybody who drives a dually?" Sherman felt the man was trustworthy enough to let him in on that clue.

Brummet chuckled at the expansive answer. "A few dozen suspects I imagine. Most of the ranchers, all the rednecks, the Sheriff and his deputy. To name a few."

Sherman paused, "Which deputy?"

"The one with the temper. Got that Mexican name, but he's white."

"Barrios," said Sherman.

"Yeah, him."

"Know where he lives?"

"Close to me."

"Let's start there," said Sherman.

"Your dollar."

The old sedan floated as much as drove down the road. Brummet had the habit of swaying in his seat, turning the steering wheel as he went. The old boat never reacted to the tiny changes, content as it was to carry on. It wouldn't turn unless heavily prodded.

A bright red dually sat out front of the house, gleaming in the morning sun from a recent wash. Water pooled in the driveway and brown streaks of dirt stood in contrast to the black asphalt. No police cruiser meant Barrios was at work. Sherman debated whether he should stop and have a look inside but decided against it. It didn't matter now. Barrios was guilty in his mind. He had passed the judgment, there was no turning back. Only the sentence remained.

"Thanks, Brummet, let's head over to the sheriff's office. I have a few questions for the man."

"Reinhold?" asked the cabbie.

"You know his story?"

"Family has been in town since the gold rush ended. His brother runs the candy store by the Mill."

"What's your take on him?"

Brummet shrugged his shoulders, "Not much to say."

"Nothing nice, I assume."

Brummet shrugged again in apparent agreement.

Sherman scratched his slowly returning stubble. Shaving it had felt cathartic, a shedding of skins. But that was days ago, when the blood was not yet dry. Now the dog inside him had a new bone and was ready to bite down hard.

Brummet turned on the highway that ran through town. Byron Mills didn't have a Main Street. No quintessential prairie feel. They lost such tidiness crossing the Rockies. What it had was a strip of shops along the main road leading into the mountains. A long narrow valley heading up or down depending on your proclivities. A road on the south side and a river to the north with shops sandwiched in between. The homes fanned out from there. Nestling in smaller valleys and flats. Most sat along some tributary or creek, and the names lent themselves to such descriptors. North River Road, South River Road, Mineral Creek Drive, and so on. California sprawl for none of the stereotypical reasons.

What drew people there remained a mystery to most visitors, but there was an undeniable appeal. Far enough away from something major to keep the average vacationers away, but with enough natural beauty to keep tourism dollars flowing. It made sense, the call of the wild, the freedom, and the nearby extractive industries that provided decent jobs. The true uniqueness, what he really understood and what pulled in the Lieutenant, was the people. They didn't particularly care what you did or where you came from. They were cordial enough to strike up a conversation outside of the pizza parlor, but didn't ask questions beyond the weather. Everyone seemed to value space and privacy. Warm but distant is how Tillerman had described it many years before. Sherman appreciated discretion, but right now he was looking for answers and wasn't stopping with the temperature.

Most everyone already knew about the Lieutenant. Word travels fast, even for a town teetering on the digital age.

Some locals recognized Sherman without the beard. Others saw an average stranger.

Brummet pulled into the gravel parking lot of a nondescript building, save for a small sign announcing its use by the Sheriff's department. Sherman raised an eyebrow and shook his head.

Brummet answered the unasked question, "It used to be the visitor center."

"Not so welcoming now," noted Sherman.

"The internet ruined it. No one needs advice from an actual person anymore." Brummet raised his hands in resignation.

"I imagine this won't take too long," Sherman said as he exited the cab.

"I'm gonna go grab a coffee, you want one?"

"Gladly."

"Black?"

"Splash of cream." Sherman liked to drink it right away. Black meant hot. Hot meant waiting. His patience did not extend to caffeine.

The bell over the door rang as Sherman entered. One of those jingling sounds that reminded him of something out of an old western. Judging from the look on Barrios' face, it might have been a high noon duel in the making. Sherman looked right through him, making sure the deputy knew he didn't give a damn.

Sheriff Reinhold looked up from his morning paper as Sherman walked up. His deputies were all standing, chins at the floor, looking guilty.

"Captain Sherman," boomed the Sheriff. "What can I do for you?" He gave his men a look that said get busy.

"Good morning, Sheriff, I had a few more questions about the Lieutenant. Do you have a few minutes?"

Reinhold motioned toward his office, "Of course. Come on in. Coffee?"

"I'm fine," answered Sherman, taking a seat.

Reinhold sat down in a big executive leather chair, leaned

back, and threw his cowboy boots up on the desk with a thud.

"What can I do for you captain?"

"No need for rank. I'm on leave."

"I like to keep things professional when necessary."

Sherman nodded, "In that case Sheriff, I have a few questions regarding the death of Lieutenant Tillerman."

"I assumed as much, shoot."

Sherman smiled at the word, already convinced it would come down to that. "What time did it happen?"

Reinhold shrugged, "County doc says around nine."

"When did you find him?"

"Around ten. One of the local boys up there called it in."

"Which boy?"

Reinhold stared at Sherman but said nothing. It wasn't a surprising move. The Sheriff didn't have to divulge that info, and for his part Sherman wasn't expecting him to.

"I'd like to see the body."

The thick-set man scratched his chin and raised his ten-gallon cowboy hat. "That is reserved for next of kin."

"You show me the next of kin and I'll back down. Until then, I'd like to see my friend."

Reinhold grunted, aware that no one was coming for the Lieutenant, "Alright captain, he's down in Spartanville. We don't have the facilities in Cumbre County, but I'll call ahead."

"Much obliged. Last thing, I'd like to look at the truck."

The Sheriff raised an eyebrow at the entirely predictable question, "Truck is over at O'Toole's place. Take as much time as you need."

The old BP service station rang a bell. A ramshackle town of broken and wrecked cars cut into the hillside. The more cars he acquired, the farther back they dug. A complete history of a town parked on the side of the road.

"Thanks for your support Sheriff, I appreciate it," Sherman didn't mean a word of it and doubted the man sitting across from him did either.

"Captain, I'm glad we can help give you some closure over this terrible accident."

The last word hung in the office for a moment, like bait carefully skewered on the end of a hook. Unwilling to bite, Sherman merely smiled and walked out past a glowering Barrios.

Brummet was in the parking lot drinking his coffee on the hood of the old sedan. Disheveled but somehow stately in his advancing age.

"Since you're not in handcuffs, I assume that went well."

"Very cordial," replied a smirking Sherman.

Brummet handed him a coffee, "Now what?"

"O'Toole's is on the way out of town, right?"

Brummet nodded.

"Okay, then the Spartanville morgue."

"Your dollar. That's an hour drive."

Sherman shrugged, "Put it on my tab."

The first leg was short from the middle to the edge of town. Brummet pulled the car up to the service station and got out. Tom O'Toole was sitting on the bench. His grease stained green pants and matching jacket looked untouched by detergent. He smiled as Brummet got out. Sherman could tell from one look that he was a genuinely friendly person.

"Hey Tom, how's it going?" asked Brummet.

"Can't complain, still have my health. And you?"

"Oh, nothing but problems and no solutions."

The two men shared a laugh over their commonality of years. Sherman guessed they were both late baby boomers.

"Tom, I want you to meet Mr. Sherman. He was a friend of the Lieutenant."

O'Toole extended a gnarled hand, "Damn shame about Tillerman. I always liked the kid." Sherman almost winced with the handshake. Despite being twice his age, the mechanic still had the grip of a pneumatic vice.

"I appreciate that, Mr. O'Toole."

"Call me Tom."

Sherman smiled and nodded, "I'm was hoping I could look at his truck."

O'Toole nodded towards a hunk of scrap metal in the corner.

"Hit that tree hard, must have been in quite a hurry."

Sherman looked at the remnants of the truck. A semicircular cavity in the front mirrored the shape of the tree. The radiator was in the middle of the engine compartment with everything else pushed back accordingly. No airbag had deployed, despite the assurances written on the steering wheel. Whatever had happened required a tremendous amount of force.

Sherman turned to Tom, "You ever seen anything like this before?"

Tom scratched his head and nodded, "A few crashes like this up in the mountains. Maybe a logging accident or two."

"Anything on Upper Mill Road before?"

"No. I'm impressed that he got that much speed. It ain't exactly Daytona up there," replied O'Toole.

Tom was expressing the same feeling Sherman had when he first heard of the location. The road meandered and so did the drivers. A slow back and forth of the steering wheel. One way and then the other, like a boat rocking in a gentle swell. A few kids drove fast on it, but the locals took their time.

Sherman had to ask, "Anybody hit that tree before?"

"Oh yeah, the Mitchell boy nearly killed himself a few years ago coming back from the bar."

"But he didn't?"

Brummet cut in, "No, he broke himself damn good, but nothing time couldn't heal."

Sherman circled around the truck to look in the bed. Speckled with sawdust and odd bits of excess wood, it contained nothing unexpected. A few nails and screws rattled about the metal floor. Packed into one corner was a random mix of trash and sawdust blown there by the wind. Sherman grabbed a handful and let it fall through his fingers.

Thoughts of the end filled his mind. The terrible facts of violent lives. Torture was a possibility, and he shuddered at the thought. To make it through the war and be murdered by, well, who? There were always more questions than answers.

Most of the dust fell back in the truck and his hand was empty now save for a cigarette butt jammed between two fingers. Sherman blinked for a moment in disbelief. Brummet looked his direction, and he held the stubby cylinder up for the cabbie to see.

Brummet cocked his head to one side with an expression of resigned acknowledgement. Fears were confirmed, but the evidence was still building.

"Thanks Tom, I think I've seen enough."

Nodding with understanding, the old man said, "Let me know if you need anything else."

"Morgue?" asked Brummet.

"Afraid so," replied Sherman.

Getting out of town required an hour long drive out of the foothills and into the northern reaches of the Central Valley. The smog filled breadbasket of the state. Home to almost all the production and none of the wealth. Dotted with roadside fruit stands and women selling bunches of freshly cut flowers. The heart blood of every piece of fruit, nut and vegetable sold from Florida to Japan.

Cumbre County was too small to enjoy the ease of its own morgue, much to the chagrin of Reinhold. This left him at the whim of the neighboring Dawson County and its sheriff.

Despite the diversity of its founders and the eclectic past it enjoyed, the county seat got stuck with the very mundane name of Spartanville. Most residents assumed it was on account of the rather scarce amenities at inception and not any relation to the martial city-state of yore.

Any geographic limitations imposed by the mountains and valleys of Byron Mills melted away. This was flat land. That forty-foot-thick expanse of topsoil between the Sierra

Nevada and the coastal range. Bountiful, loamy and, unlike much of the state, water rich. Rivers flowed into rice paddies and other intensive crops. Hot, but not dry.

Spartanville lay on the eastern edge of a railway spur and owed its location more to the Union Pacific than any logical or geographic feature. Thirty thousand large according to the previous census, it had nothing substantial to brag about. It was a town full of farmers and middle America folk, just like all the others who didn't live in Frisco or LA. California was more than a coastline. Most of the state was inland, far from the politics or vagaries of its more famous cities.

Brummet pulled into the county complex. It was a three-story building surrounded by a few trailers designated as temporary offices some twenty-odd years earlier. Nothing but their permanence remained.

The morgue was in the basement of the main building. Hidden in plain sight, like most unceremonious aspects of our existence. The coroner sat behind a small metal desk near the entrance, busily filling out forms and charts. Sherman knocked as he entered and the man, who was in his early thirties, looked up at the visitor.

"Mr. Sherman?"

"Sherman is fine. Thanks for letting me in today."

The coroner shrugged, "Not exactly Chicago here."

"Thanks just the same, Doctor...?"

"Murray."

Sherman nodded

"Come on back," said Murray.

The center of the operation was two stainless steel tables and a wall-sized refrigerator. Each square door could hold a single body. Three doors high by three doors wide. Nine corpses. By Chicago standards, that wouldn't last a work week. By Afghanistan standards, it wouldn't last a day. Sherman had seen that filled in the blink of an eye. In the time it took for electricity to travel down a copper wire buried in the sand and ignite the bomb hidden underneath.

Death was no stranger for either man. Both dealt with it daily. For the doctor, it was a clinical relationship. One layer removed from the personal. The dead stayed at the office. For Sherman, it was different. He dealt with and in death. The doctor only saw the end state, after the fact. Sherman was involved, if not culpable, for the entire process. They were living and after they weren't. There was no layer to remove, no distance to create.

Murray opened door number six according to the black stenciling and unzipped the white body bag. No ceremony, no attempt to hide the mundane details of human demise.

Sherman looked at his friend and thought back to all those moments of danger. The bullets that missed and those bombs detonated a moment too late. All that luck, that karma, gone over what? Some pettiness in Northern California?

Dark blue bruises covered his forehead and surrounded a deep laceration running from eyebrow to eyebrow. As Murray unzipped the bag more bruises were evident on the chest and torso. Fist sized evidence of violence. All the fingers and toes were accounted for and no nails were missing. No signs of electricity. Beaten, but not tortured.

Sherman turned to Murray, who had been watching as he walked through some macabre mental checklist, "What killed him?"

"Blunt force trauma to the forehead, causing hemorrhaging in and around the prefrontal cortex," answered the coroner with certitude.

"From?"

"The car crash."

Sherman eyed the man intently. He wasn't sure if the junior doctor was in on the cover-up or not.

"I didn't find any perimortem injuries, so all the damage was done relatively close to death."

"And his blood alcohol level?"

Murray went back to his desk for the chart, "0.27%."

"Damn, surprised he found the ignition, let alone the

clutch."

The coroner shrugged, "A man of his size, maybe his tolerance was high."

"Ten years sober," replied Sherman without taking his eyes off the body.

"What did you say?"

"He was clean for ten years, then in one night he falls off the wagon and gets loaded over three times the legal limit but manages to drive."

"Maybe he got kicked out of the bar. The bruises on his side are consistent with a fight."

Sherman nodded, "Any defensive wounds?"

Murray hesitated for a second, "No. Cops found the truck around a tree. It doesn't take a detective to figure this one out."

Sherman wanted to call bullshit on the deflection but held his tongue. Sharing unfounded accusations with someone related to law enforcement was pointless.

"Thanks Doc, I think I've seen enough."

"No problem, sorry about your friend."

Sherman nodded again and walked out

"Well?" Asked Brummet after he gotten back in the car.

"Doctor says head trauma killed him."

"From the accident?"

"That's what the report will say, but he took a beating beforehand and drank a gallon of whiskey."

"Wait, wait. Start with drinking. What was his level?"

"Point two seven."

Brummet's eyes widened, "Damn, I'd have to try real hard to do that."

"Precisely."

"You think it wasn't his choice?" asked the cabbie.

"I have a hunch he had help. Probably the same friends who roughed him up."

Brummet nodded, "Right, the beaten part. Now what?"

"How many bars are in town?"

"Two and the logger place at the end of Upper Mill."

"Thirsty?" asked Sherman. "I'm buying."
"When did thirst have anything to do with drinking?"

CHAPTER FIVE

Beer two edged into a third while a basket of twice fried onion rings slowly disappeared, leaving only a puddle of grease as evidence. Sherman and Brummet sat on stools at the bar chatting with the bartender, a man named Ross. Brummet had stopped the cab at the first bar for those heading west to east.

The Riverfront Bar and Grill was a town staple, serving up all manner of fried since the post-war forties. Like most things in Byron Mill, the best part of the place was the view out back. Drinking on the deck, the conversation flooded by the sound of rushing water, kept the coffers full even in the off-season. Most of the regulars were out there, despite the overcast sky.

Sherman wanted to know if Tillerman recently patronized the place, and Ross seemed the likeliest source of that intelligence. Brummet had kindly broken the ice, and the conversation had veered towards the accident.

"Damn shame about that," said the bartender.

Sherman asked, "Did you know him?"

"The wife bought a chair from him last year. Gave us the locals discount."

"Yeah," said Sherman laughing, "his motto was 'it's only money.'"

"Superb craftsman too, that chair is a work of art."

"Did he ever come in here?"

Ross raised his eyes with intense thought, "No, I don't think so. Mostly kept to himself, but shit, so does most of this town,"

Brummet raised his glass, "Cheers to that."

Sherman checked out of the conversation after that, and his eyes wandered. Eight people were inside now, not counting themselves. Plus another six out on the deck. He couldn't help but know; a consequence of too many years watching out for the next bullet.

Most of the crowd was there when they arrived, save for two surly outdoorsmen types who walked in twenty minutes after and were now playing a game of pool with a can of Natural Light in hand. They were years younger than the rest of the crowd. Not part of the retired cadre that frequented the bar on weekday afternoons. Something about them was odd. Not in the town's context, but in their attitude.

Sherman's back was to the pool table, but the men were visible in a giant vintage Grain Belt Brewing mirror hanging behind the bar. He could see them playing poorly and drinking slowly. Neither of those things made sense. Those who drink and play pool in the middle of a workday do one of the two well.

City folk would have called them rednecks because they lacked nuance with the subject. Barrios was a redneck. Those two were more pragmatic and less showy in their convictions. Hillbillies or hicks or some other word that Sherman couldn't recall.

Brummet had just finished discussing the finer points of stringing barbed wire with Ross when Sherman gave him a nudge.

Nodding towards the mirror he asked, "You know them?"

Brummet glanced up for a moment, "Those Yokels? Not really. Logging boys, I think."

"Yokels?"

"Hill folk."

"Gotcha."

"Something wrong?" Asked Brummet.

"Not yet, but they're not here to play or drink."

Brummet raised his eyebrows in confusion.

"I'm gonna step out the side, if they follow me, go start the car." Sherman paid the bill and exited through the side door into the gravel parking lot that served as a gathering place for the local drunks once the bar closed. Most slept it off in a truck bed or backseat. The Sheriff looked the other way when it got rowdy and left them alone.

There was a small storage shed used for used fry-oil storage to the left after exiting. Sherman circled the small structure after he walked out and listened. Boots crunching on the gravel followed the distinctive slap of an old wood screen door. Sherman came around behind the two men who were scanning the parking lot.

"You lose something, boys?" asked Sherman.

Both men swiveled quickly and cleanly at the sound of his voice. Neither showed any surprise or distress at the unexpected. The nonchalant reaction of those at ease with the unknown. Sherman took notice. His gut said they could fight, but his brain wasn't in the mood to find out.

With a laugh verging on a sneer, the bigger of the two spoke first. He wore an old stained flannel. Nothing hipster about it. "Nah, we found it before, we can always find it again."

"Friends of yours?" Brummet said as he pulled up.

The two men drove away in an old green Chevy, "Looks that way," replied Sherman as he watched the truck drive off.

"Nice chat?"

"Exuding hospitality from the barrel of a pistol."

"I didn't see any guns."

"The one with the army jacket had it stuffed in his pants behind the back."

"Damn, I guess I wasn't paying attention."

Sherman shrugged, "It's a curse."

"Probably not your line of work. Where to now?"

"Another drink at another place?" asked Sherman.

Brummet nodded with satisfaction, "Good plan."

Getting to the next bar took them by the town's namesake. The mill was only a rapid downstream from where the two forks of the river met. Built back when it was still under Spanish control, it had a brief flash in the pan during the gold rush. Prosperity didn't last, but the loggers stayed. Timber, good timber, was always in demand. More so with the post-recession housing boom.

Snaking further east up the river, they passed the commercial heart of the area. There was the small market stocked well enough for the locals. The owner's mail-order bride made excellent pies. She was Latvian or Ukrainian, depending on who you asked. No one would ask the woman herself, but they all ate the pies. The town was very progressive in that sense. No pastry discrimination at all.

The pizza parlor, drug store, and Mexican restaurant all shared the same building. The former occupied the entire second story. It used to be some big-name bank before the Dot-com bubble burst and corporate America retreated to the big cities. What remained of the vault got converted into a small arcade. Relegated, as it was, to guarding the loose change of ten-year-olds. The pizza wasn't half-bad either. Sherman enjoyed the garlic bacon combo.

"They serve beer too," interjected Brummet, "if you want to check off all the potential relapse spots."

"Tillerman didn't like to drink in well-lit places. He preferred his booze and bars some shade of brown."

"Next place fits the bill. All wood and smoke, well, minus the smoke these days. God damn government impinging on our rights."

"I didn't take you for a smoker," said Sherman.

"I'm not, dirty habit, but it's the principle of the matter."

"Public health?"

"Ugh, not you too."

Sherman laughed with mock indignation while Brummet

grumbled under his breath about some liberal conspiracy.

The Falls Restaurant and Bar was written in large gold cursive lettering across the sign by the road. Compared to the last place, it was the paragon of fine dining in town. It had something to do with the order of booze versus food within the name.

"See what I mean," said Brummet as they walked inside through a heavy wooden door. The interior decorator had a taste for turn-of-the-century boardrooms. Even in the late afternoon it was dark and heavy with little direct light.

Sherman nodded, "I like it already."

Tables took up most of the space. Two tops and four tops. The bar itself hid around the corner from the main entrance. Nothing big. A dozen stools and few tables. A young couple were busy flirting on one end, so Sherman and Brummet sat down on the other. An old man and an old soul had no need for the pettiness of youthful love.

"Mr. Brummet, what can I get you?" asked a voice from behind the bar. It was youthful and southern, carrying those vowels just a little higher and farther. Sherman could barely make out an outline in the low light. A fleeting figure busy shifting bottles around.

"Hey Ruby, I'll have the usual."

"Sure thing, darlin' and for your friend?"

Sherman smiled, "Bourbon, if you have it."

"What else is there? Top or bottom?" replied the woman with a coy smile. Her black shirt was a few buttons short of closed. She was pretty in the conventional sense, but it was her attitude that Sherman found intriguing.

Avoiding the up-sell was standard practice, but Sherman liked her already. There was something tangible in that accent that he couldn't shake.

"You choose," he answered.

Ruby smiled back, "Bookers it is."

She came back with two fingers of whiskey and a Bud Light. Sherman shook his head at Brummet.

"What brings you in today, fellas?"

"Your lovely smile," quipped Brummet.

"Ah, fuck off," said Ruby while batting her eyes.

"Actually, it's a somber occasion. Mr. Sherman here lost a friend."

"Sorry to hear that. Someone local?"

"Yeah, Tillerman."

Ruby gasped and put her hand to her chest, "Oh Jesus."

"You knew him?" Sherman asked.

"Yeah, he was a regular."

The world suddenly seemed much smaller. Sherman could feel his chest tighten at the thought of his friend lying to his face about being sober. Anger bubbled slowly to the surface, followed by all the questions. Was he wrong about it all? Was this just some sordid conspiracy theory run amok? Occam's Razor, the simplest explanation, is usually right.

"What was his poison?"

"Oh, Tillerman chased the girl, not the bottle. Usually club soda, maybe a pop."

Sherman sighed with relief and surprise, "Which girl?"

"Ashley. One of the other bartenders. Shit, I bet she doesn't know."

"Is she working tonight?" asked Brummet.

"No, she went to visit her mom on the coast," replied Ruby before moving off to check on the young couple.

"Relieved?" asked Brummet.

"In a conflicted sort of way," answered Sherman.

The cabbie nodded in understanding.

"If he could avoid drinking here, I'm convinced he didn't just fall off the wagon somewhere else," added Sherman.

"Seems fair. I take it you didn't know about the girl?" Brummet asked.

"Nope, but we hadn't talked for a good nine months."

"Another tour?"

Sherman scoffed at the idea. "They don't even have those anymore. You're in it or you're not. Just one merciless unending fight with the occasional intermission."

"This ain't the draft, why not quit?"

"And do what? Flip burgers or manage a Walmart?"

Brummet shrugged, "What's wrong with that?"

"Nothing, but it's not for me. Maybe other people, just not me."

"I've seen that look before," Brummet said, pointing towards Sherman's eyes. "When all that shit you've seen cats its way out."

Sherman scratched at the slowly returning stubble and the inevitable return of the Special Forces operator.

"You've hit the nail square. This was supposed to be a reset. I came here to visit a man who got out. To check in on that side of myself, to look in the mirror and decide if it suits me."

He looked out the window towards the river roaring some thirty feet below, "That is my healing water. Now," he swirled the whiskey around, "this will have to do."

"There's a place for us all. Sounds like you haven't found yours, yet."

"Or maybe I have, and I keep leaving it."

"Here?"

"No," said Sherman, shaking his head. "The war."

Brummet raised his eyebrows in disbelief, "Ain't like my war then."

Ruby came back to check on them, "Another round fellas?"

Sherman was staring at the wall, really at the chalkboard on the wall. It was small and divided into three columns. All three had names in them. First came a name, then another, and finally a beverage. Ruby followed his gaze.

"You can buy a friend a drink. They collect it next time they're in. A little gimmicky, but the thought is nice."

"I think I will have the second glass," replied Sherman as he pointed towards the fifth name on the list. "That's me."

"You're Frank Sherman," said Ruby with more

statement than question.

"Afraid so."

"Jesus, have I heard some stories about you. Your friend told some crazy shit in the last few months."

This piqued Brummet's interest, "Oh, do tell."

Sherman gave him a look, but Ruby obliged despite his unspoken objection.

"Told me how you dragged his ass for ten miles off some god-forsaken mountain with fifty Taliban on your heels."

Sherman laughed, "That's a good story, but it was one mile and there were only eight of them."

"Still sounds scary to me," replied Ruby.

Sherman shrugged, "Didn't have a choice. There was only one way out."

"And the rest of your team?" Asked Brummet.

Sherman finished his bourbon in a single swig and stared at the empty glass, "Dead."

"Christ," said Ruby with a touch of empathy, "that's fucked up."

"What else did Tillerman say?" Sherman wanted to change the subject. Talking about that side of him, about the past, brought him no joy. Most people didn't know, couldn't know, what it was like.

Ruby smiled, "Said you were a solid guy, a man with principles."

"I don't hold a light to him."

"Maybe not, I just met you," came her reply as she walked into the storeroom.

As the conversation shifted towards the unfortunate specifics of history, Sherman took his bourbon to the patio. Some thirty odd feet below roared the relentless churn of whitewater. A smoky veil of night covered the valley, and the smell of oak lingered in the air. Sherman felt somehow intrusive, like an uninvited guest lifting the covers on that which should not be seen. Was it too much to talk with Ashley? The Lieutenant had kept that hidden for a reason. Perhaps, wondered Sherman, if some secrets were best kept buried.

"You hiding?"

A smile crept across his face at the sound of the southern drawl with its extended I's. "Guilty as charged."

Ruby joined him against the railing, "He meant a lot to you."

"About the only friend I had left."

"Brummet told me he crashed on Upper Mill."

Sherman nodded, "Drunk as a skunk."

"But he was still on the wagon," said Ruby with a touch of surprise.

"You knew he was an alcoholic?"

"Sling booze long enough and you get a sense for people. Tillerman just had this look whenever whiskey got poured. You can't unlearn that need."

"Cops disagree, as does the coroner. If he didn't have it in town then where?"

"Home?" she guessed.

"Nope. Bottle of Bookers was still intact."

"Not at home then. Um. Only other place is The Crosscut, up in the trees."

"Guess that is my next stop," he added.

Ruby giggled, "A clean-shaven boy like Tillerman wouldn't exactly blend in there. Even your stubble might be offensive."

"Rough crowd?"

"They know little but fighting and fucking," replied Ruby.

Sherman had to ask, "Speaking from experience?"

"Well, aren't you direct, Mr. Sherman," her voice rising with the contraction.

"Mr. Sherman is my father. Frank or Sherman will do fine."

Ruby smiled, "My mother always said I had her sister's taste in men."

"I take it she isn't happily married."

"No, on both accounts. She was unhappily married to a

real brute of a man. Mean streak about as wide as he was tall."

"And that ended how?"

"Poorly for him. My auntie got fed up one night and shot him with an old smokeless while he slept. Ended up pleading down to some lesser offense before the trial, but still be wearing that prison orange."

"Seems like a low bar to undershoot."

Ruby shrugged, "I've had my moments, but enough about me. Start talking, Mr. Enigma."

Sherman glanced at the bar. "Shouldn't you be working?"

"Nice try, Frank. Nobody inside but Brummet and he knows where we keep the beer."

"What do you want to know?"

Ruby flashed a smile of delight, "Let's start with a gimmie. Where are you from?"

"Here and there."

The smile wilted into a frown, "Care to elaborate?"

"I grew up in the Army. Lots of places, lots of towns, a few countries."

"Hmm. When did you join the Army?"

"One month into college, September 2001."

"Oh," she said, her voice sort of training off with the thought. "And what does your unit do?"

"Classified."

"You fucker," said Ruby as she punched him in the arm. "Some open book you are."

"Consequence of the job," he mused.

"Likely story. I'll tell you what, let's make a deal."

"I'm all ears."

"You're gonna need someone to get you through the door at the Crosscut. I'll be your fixer, but you're gonna answer some questions as payment."

Sherman didn't need the help, nor was he particularly worried about getting into or out of the bar, but he liked Ruby. That alone was worth a few questions, and maybe the help would save someone a few broken bones.

"Deal."

"Great. I get off at midnight. Party should just be kicking off."

"Perfect, but you'll have to give me a ride home."

A quizzical look crossed her face before connecting the dots, "You're staying at his house?"

"For now. Cops gave me until probate closes. I figure that should be sometime next week."

Ruby nodded, "Sure, I'll give you a ride."

The bell hanging over the front door jangled loudly and Ruby excused herself to deal with a new customer, Sherman stayed on the deck, soaking up the sound of rushing water and the sweet smell of wood stoves. Up in the mountains a few stray lights twinkled through the smoky haze, solitary and defensive on their high perch.

Brummet smiled when Sherman finally walked back inside and joined him at the bar.

"She's something else, right?"

"Ruby?"

"Who else?"

"She has character."

Brummet laughed, "Every guy that comes in here thinks of nothing else, but you're the only one I've ever seen her talk with."

"I'm just a puzzle that needs solving. She'll lose interest soon enough."

The old man just shook his head, "Fine. What's the plan now?"

"Ruby offered to protect me at the Crosscut."

"Oh. That's kind of her. Does she know what you do?"

"No, not really."

"Just wondering who she is protecting, them or you?"

"A warm intro is better than no intro. Might save me some trouble."

"You're right there. Those boys ain't exactly hospitable to strangers."

"Yeah, you two make it sound like Fallujah."

Brummet laughed, "No, they keep the guns outside. The worst you'll have is a knife fight."

Sherman nodded at the joke, realizing that it was no laughing matter. The knife in his pocket reminded him of all the other times he had used one. It may have been a cavalier comment to Brummet, but the memories and scars Sherman carried were anything but trivial.

The Crosscut sounded like a place of violence, filled with hard-edged men. No doubt there was some kernel of truth in those stories of ugly deprivation, but he doubted anyone there had seen the aftermath of an IED or the bloodied fingertips of a torture victim. Unless there was a connection to Tillerman's death. In which case, perhaps the patrons were more depraved than he imagined.

"I'll take my chances with the knife," he finally replied.

"God help them," said Brummet as he stood up. "I take it Ruby is giving you a ride back."

Sherman nodded.

"Call in the morning or if you need bail."

Sherman smiled, "Will do. Thanks for today."

"It's your dollar," he said as he walked out the door.

Sherman turned to the menu and ordered a steak. Continuing to drink for another five hours until Ruby's shift ended was a terrible idea by itself. Couple that with some hard-nosed assholes and it bordered on a disaster. Sobering up seemed like the best bet. So that is what he did. Steak and water until midnight while sitting at a corner booth in the bar.

Midweek wasn't too busy, so Sherman didn't feel like he was taking up valuable real estate. The sign outside said, 'Prime Rib Tuesday' and it filled the place with locals pursuing some weekly ritual. Habits and happiness. The correlation was obvious.

Slowly the hour hand wound its way around the pale white interior of the cuckoo clock sitting in the corner. The steak and water chased away whatever haze the whiskey had brewed. Sherman was working his way through a second cup of coffee strong enough to strip paint when Ruby walked over to his booth.

"You ready?"

"For the interrogation?"

"And the adventure," she replied with a smile.

In the parking lot, Ruby walked over to an old Jeep Wagoneer. Sherman reacted with a bit of surprise, expecting something sporty and red.

Reading the look on his face, she said, "My dad had one. I guess it is a bit of nostalgia."

Sherman shrugged in understanding, "Mine drove an Oldsmobile."

Ruby giggled at the simplicity of his answer. Somehow it conveyed all that she needed to know about his father in a single sentence.

"What color?"

"Army issue green."

"The apple didn't fall very far, did it?"

"Not far enough."

Ruby turned the key and the old V8 rumbled to life. She eased the stick into reverse. At 4,500 pounds, the Jeep was more tank than truck. With all that weight, it never got past third gear as they worked up into the mountains.

The road was not flat. Nothing more than a thin serpentine ribbon of degrading asphalt barely wide enough for a single car. Unlike most, it was best driven at night when the pale-yellow cones of light shining around the corner announced a fellow motorist. So sharp were some corners that during the day one relied solely on the brake pads and awareness of the other drivers. With remarkable speed the road separated from the river, leaving it below to wash over its increasingly rocky course.

Ruby knew the route well enough to speed up it, but kept the Jeep slow enough to maximize her question time.

"Alright mister, let's have it," she said with a grin.

"Deal's a deal. Fire away."

"Only child?"

Sherman nodded.

Ruby made a face as if it confirmed all her suspicions. "And you moved around a lot?"

"Here and there. Mostly stateside, some overseas."

"Nerd or jock?"

Sherman paused for a moment, "Neither I guess, but if you have to pigeonhole me, nerd is closer."

She eased the Jeep around another tight S-turn, "Care to explain?"

"I was outdoors most of the time, but nothing as formal as sports. Old-fashioned stuff, you know. Hiking, hunting. Shit like that."

"No video games?"

"You say it like an accusation of guilt."

"Just fucking with you. I assume all boys like games and porn."

"That's a given."

Ruby laughed at Sherman's pensiveness, even if she couldn't tell if it was genuine or not. "Enough simple stuff. You joined after 9/11, why not before?"

"I was rebelling, in an odd way, by going to college. My old man pressured me to enlist right out of high school. Follow in the footsteps of my forefathers. Serve my country. Honor and duty. All that bullshit."

"Wait, you don't believe in that? Isn't that like ice cream and apple pie to you Army boys?"

"Wrong generation."

"Then why join? Why not stay in school and stick it to your old man? Doesn't sound like you two got along."

"Not at all, he was a first-rate asshole and shitty father, but he got one thing right."

Ruby interjected by paraphrasing Edmund Burke, "Don't idle in the face of evil?"

"Nothing so philosophical. I wasn't cut out for school."

She laughed hard enough to swerve a bit, "Sorry, sorry, don't stop."

"Truth is, he was right."

"You seem like a sharp guy, so was it the booze or the girls?"

"Don't get me wrong, the beer, the girls and booze took their toll, but," Sherman trailed off.

"But what?"

"How do I explain it without being some highfalutin asshole?"

"Don't use fancy words is always a good start."

Sherman rolled his eyes, "They had this entitled ambition of a better future, but no one would risk anything outside of an opinion."

"You sound bitter."

He shrugged. "Realistic. My roommate cared about his hair and which sneakers got him the most ass."

"Sounds like every other nineteen-year-old male. So what, you didn't care about sex?"

"Not enough to change shoes."

"A gentleman and a scholar, I see."

"Turns out that I don't care about a lot of things."

Ruby nodded her head and said, "I get that, I do. Sometimes I look out over that bar and wonder what is driving all those people to get all that stuff."

"Anyway, I watched the towers fall from the couch of my dorm room and the next day, a Wednesday, I went into the recruiter's office."

"Just like that? Never looked back?"

"Not long enough to see anything but dust."

Ruby carved the Jeep through another S-turn while taking up ninety percent of the road. Sherman guessed they were close. His internal map said two miles left.

"Tell me about this bar. What kind of adventure am I in for?"

She laughed, "Nervous?"

"Professional skepticism," Sherman answered.

"Total shit hole packed with drunks, angry men and angry drunks."

"And how do you know the place?" he asked.

"Oh, I may have dated the bartender for a while."

"Recently?" Sherman wanted to know how fresh the wounds were.

"As of last week," replied Ruby a bit sheepishly.

"Am I here to make him jealous or get punched in the face?"

"Don't take it personally."

Sherman raised his hands in some unseen frustration, "Take what personally?"

"Ya know. The trash talking and name calling."

"I'll try to keep my vanity in check," he replied, not holding back the irony smeared across his face.

CHAPTER SIX

Ruby swerved to avoid hitting two guys in chainsaw pants beating the snot out of each other on the side of the road. The neon glow of a giant Pabst sign illuminated the fight with blue hues that turned their blood-stained faces black. Sherman thought it was a fitting introduction to the Crosscut. By now he expected nothing less.

Gravel crunched underneath the heavy wheels as Ruby pulled into the crowded parking lot. The bar was a single-story affair, not much bigger than an old ticky-tacky bungalow. Twice longer than wide, with the character of an hourly motel. It had windows in the past, but plywood had superseded glass as the material of choice. Hinges from a long since forgotten screen door remained attached and the front door had a single bullet hole through it.

Sherman stuck his pinky finger in the hole and guessed .357 Magnum. Not that the powder charge mattered, but the clientele seemed the type for oversized guns and egos.

Ruby pushed through the door and into the blare of heavy metal music and the sour stench of stale beer on carpet. The place was filled from one end to the other with all types—tall Nordic looking guys with thick blonde beards specked with sawdust; hard-nosed cowboys waiting for a chance to hijack the jukebox; bikers proudly displaying club emblems across their leather jackets; meth cooks; pot growers; the place had them all.

A man with ox-wide shoulders stood by the door. He smiled when he saw Ruby, but the corners of his mouth flattened then sank as Sherman walked into view. He moved his seven-foot frame towards the door.

"Gerhardt, he's with me," said Ruby to the bouncer who shot back a disappointed frown.

"That is what I'm afraid of. Gunnar won't like it and I don't need no trouble." Gerhardt turned his head and looked down at Sherman, "You're not here to make trouble, are you tiny man?"

"Nothing to damage but my liver."

Ruby smiled at the towering man, "Best behavior, I promise."

Gerhardt motioned towards Sherman to raise his arms. Ruby's friend or not, he still got searched. The guy was built like a series of interconnected boulders stacked into human form. With hands the size of basketballs, each pat rocked Sherman back and forth like a small boat in rough seas. He hid the grimace everyone felt after walking through the door. Upon finding the tactical knife, Gerhardt opened it with a nonchalant flick of his wrist and smiled. The matte black blade seemed to vanish into the dimly lit air as he moved it around, feigning a slicing motion.

"You know how to use this thing?"

Sherman answered, "Just for show and apples."

Gerhardt rumbled with laughter, "I hope you're wrong about that. Go on."

Sherman pocketed the Lieutenant's knife and worked his way towards Ruby at the bar. Everyone noticed him enter, dozens of eyes darted around projecting something between menace and indifference. A few bumped hm with their shoulders out of some masculine show of force. Sherman rolled with each attempt, letting the men stumble past.

A black leather jacket was offering to buy Ruby a drink when Sherman finally reached her. Biker patches wasn't something that he studied in the Special Forces, but both groups were armed gangs, and they shared a linguistic fraternity. The three skulls emblazoned above the club's name spoke loudly and proudly of a body count. A calling card of violence to warn or impress the crowd. Sherman knew the man wasn't alone.

Ruby smiled when he arrived. The jacket's owner did not.

"My new friend here was just offering to buy me a drink."

"Let me get the first round," offered Sherman hoping to diffuse any tension.

The biker grunted and nodded towards a tall bartender that Sherman assumed was Ruby's recent ex-boyfriend. He was not happy to see her.

"Pretty boy here is buying a round."

Gunnar looked Sherman over like a butcher does a hog, "Whiskey or beer?"

"Both," replied Sherman.

The bartender turned without acknowledgement and grabbed three bottles and glasses.

"I think he likes me," whispered Sherman in Ruby's ear.

She smiled and whispered back, "Good of you to stay positive."

Gunnar returned with their drinks, "Thirty bucks." He pointed overhead to a sign that read 'No Fucking Plastic'. Not that Sherman ever expected the place to take Visa.

Peeling off two twenties, he handed them over with a nod to keep the change. Gunnar flared his lip in disgust but kept the money.

"To bitches and blades," yelled the biker before pounding the whiskey and beer in short order. Sherman stopped at the whiskey, which was shit, but Ruby went along.

"Just catching up," came her reply when he looked over.

Sherman shrugged with indifference, "Who should we ask about Tillerman. I need to know if he was here."

Ruby smiled and leaned over the bar, allowing her arms to push out her cleavage to the point of almost spilling the banks of her bra.

"Hey Gunnar," she yelled across the bar.

With a scowl, the bartender walked over and leaned forward enough so that their noses were nearly touching.

"What!" he groaned.

Ruby was enjoying the exchange and whatever had caused the breakup was not amicable.

"My friend wants to know if Ashley and her beau were drinking here recently."

Gunnar scoffed and glared first at Sherman and then at Ruby. The anger was genuine and deep, like a festering wound only the innocent receive. Sherman wondered what a strange, twisted triangle he had bumbled into.

Finally, the bartender stood up, "Nah, I haven't seen Ash in a week, but Army boy was here on Friday or Saturday."

"Drunk?" Sherman asked, hoping for a no.

"Still on the wagon, drinking the free club soda. Wanted to talk with the old man. Now, if y'all can get the fuck outta my face, I have drinks to pour."

As Gunnar walked away Sherman turned to Ruby, who was getting a perverse but not undamaged satisfaction out of the exchange. "Who is the old man?"

"Oh, Ashley's daddy owns the place," she said casually.

"And why would Tillerman want to talk with him?"

"I haven't the faintest idea."

Not knowing who anyone was in town felt unsettling to Sherman. From a quick count on the way in, there were at least four dually trucks in the parking lot. Any one of them could have been involved with Tillerman's murder. At least it convinced him of the outcome. If the Lieutenant was still sober after dating a bartender, he made his wagon of sturdy stuff. The only way off was a strong push from someone else.

Ruby was fast engaged in some conversation with the leather jacket and his friend who had seen her cleavage trick with Gunnar. Neither would remember her eye color, so focused was their attention on her other traits. From what Sherman could tell, she had them wrapped around her finger like mesmerized little boys. The night wasn't yet old, and the place remained packed.

Scanning the room came naturally, no different from looking for an IED in Iraq. It's the little clues that count. A piece of paper a bit too new or a rock slightly askew. Slight differences meant life or death. Years of living at the edge had taught him as much. The look on a suicide bomber's face differed from the guy aiming to shoot you in the back. Different purpose, different goal, different eyes. There was a lot of contempt, but no outright malice. Everyone knew him as a stranger and not as a threat, which brought some level of comfort and disappointment. Sherman wanted to know Tillerman's killers, who they were, what they looked like. Their habits, their schedules. When they shit, what they ate. Knowledge was more than just power; it sharpened the spear itself.

Sherman was no longer home. His mind had traveled back to the battlefield, to some baser state. Stripped of those social norms so deeply ingrained in civilized folk, he operated on instinct and experience. That chunk of his brain where every solution was permissible regardless of the ends or the means. Where everything was a problem waiting for solution. Sherman could feel the shift, but he didn't fight it. After all these years it was his natural state, his equilibrium. A singularity of purpose boiled down to him or them.

Running his hand over the slowly returning stubble, he wished for its swift return. For the mask that had become his face.

"I'm gonna grab some air," he told Ruby. She smiled and waved, barely exiting her conversation with the bikers or detecting his lie.

Stepping back out the front door and around the side led Sherman to a large dirt patch. Metal folding chairs lay scattered about in some random pattern. A few got used by those unable to stand, but most of the dozen patrons congregated around an old oil drum repurposed as a fire pit. Most gazed at the fire, some smoked, some drank, and the rest did both.

Sherman ambled over, beer in hand. Some faces looked up as he approached, their features hardened by the flickering light. Though they saw an outsider, none said anything. The mountain air was chilly at night, but it felt bracing compared to the heat of Jordan or Syria. With each exhale, he watched the steam form like proof of continued existence. After all the years, the death and blood, he was still breathing and the one who left it behind was not.

Smoke from the fire and cigarettes hung over the dirt patch like an early morning bank of fog. Sherman glanced at the smokers. Nearly all had Lucky Strike. They probably sold the brand behind the bar or from some old vending machine. Multiple dually trucks and an entire room full of the same cigarette brand made his clues almost worthless.

A grove of redwoods stood like giant sentinels staring down at the unruly crowd. The flames amplified the red hues of their bark. Shadows wobbled against broad trunks and in that moment came a strange sense of calm and stillness that took Sherman back to a distant childhood memory.

Camping years prior in a spot not so dissimilar, alone with the trees swaying in the wind, their tops seeming to bend beyond any breaking point. Although he couldn't place the year it felt defining, one of those core memories that surfaced in times of uncertainty. A light in the dark, back when he craved that sense of purpose. A path to walk down and run across with head held high. Such a noble path wasn't real. It was an egocentric dream filled with hot air but unable to rise. Youth conjures up such notions because it needs the energy to grow and thrive. Only age dampens such heat.

Twenty years later Sherman felt in awe of that memory. At the audacity of his former self to think he alone mattered. At the wonderful selfishness it entailed. The mystical grandeur of that age brought some measure of hope to his bleak world of perpetual violence and certain death. For as large as the wars appeared, their world was small. Filled with pitiful nights shivering with anxiety, momentary bursts of primal fear and a deep gnawing sorrow. A song of war stuck on repeat without the glory of any chorus or the stoic beating of drums. Sherman had seen it all up close and there was no glory in the madness, no sublime master plan in the cards. People endured. But the trees gave him hope, however fleeting, that others would choose a different path. That his world would fade.

Sherman knew better but was happy to still have the capacity to consider the thought. Then again, he wondered, what was this normal he longed for. It wasn't the surrounding crowd, full of drunks and criminals. White picket fences and a house in the burbs? Such niceties drove him to the army. No, not that. Somewhere in between?

He held that question while tossing an empty beer bottle in the fire like everyone else. Nodding to himself, he headed back to find Ruby. Through the open front door Gunnar was visibly pointing out back, gesturing a location to two men. Sherman glanced at them. Not the type to be lost.

CHAPTER SEVEN

The biker swung first. A fist motivated by the two yokels Sherman met at the first bar. Whether for money or drugs, it didn't matter. Gunnar had pointed out back, and that was that. Finding a willing participant wasn't difficult. Plenty of men inside relished a fight. The naked brutality of it. None of this came as a surprise to Sherman. The little warning bells in his head were clanging well before the man ever ducked under the door to step out.

The assumption is that giant men love to fight, something about their imposing size equates to violence or maybe it is just math. More wins against less. Seeing the biggest of the bikers come outside just made sense to Sherman.

The guys he had met in the Riverfront parking lot were inconspicuously sitting at the bar trying hard to act like they didn't care. Apparently trying to keep their noses clean. Sherman looked at them and then the guy closing on him like a runaway train. Big and mean with a face pockmarked by craters of youth. An imposing character.

"Ah fuck," he mumbled while backing up towards the crowd.

The biker had the height advantage, at least a head higher. Which also meant the reach advantage. A big deal in boxing, but not a factor in most brawls. People always ended up grappling with each over. Lots of grabbing and pulling, quick punches and kicks, maybe a head-butt or two. Based on the bikers' thick brows and scarred up forehead, Sherman guessed he had used it as a weapon more than once.

For reasons unknown, the tall guy went the boxing route. He walked up to Sherman as straight as a drunk man can. Booze makes you do stupid things, believing them to be clever. Maybe the man thought he was being inconspicuous, or maybe he didn't think it mattered.

Drunk, dumb or cocky, he reared back and tried to catch Sherman with a haymaker hook. An end it all now and let's get back to drinking punch. Sherman didn't take kindly to unwarranted aggression, even poorly timed and executed.

Ducking under the biker's punch, which soared an inch higher for every beer the guy had consumed, Sherman went to work with the clinical precision of a surgeon.

First came a stunning blow to the liver delivered with his left hand and a quick twist of his torso. The cost of missing too high. It slowed the bigger man down and made him stagger back in pain.

Next to go was mobility. While the biker was doubled over by an overpowering sensation to curl up in a ball, Sherman savaged his opponent's knee with a single kick. Two audible pops and an agonizing howl confirmed that both cruciate ligaments had torn. Reflexively the guy fell to the ground, a futile reaction to prevent further injury.

It ended with spite. There was no reason for anything else. The biker was out of commission and in need of reconstructive surgery. Sherman could have walked away, but didn't. Angry over Tillerman's death and the blatant attempt to cause him harm. His ire welled up inside from a never-ending spring and right then seemed like an excellent place to let it flow unchecked. Some broken bones might dissuade others from trying something similar. Better to make an example out of the guy. The people watching respected few things, but power was among them, so he savaged the man's temple with his army issue boot. The howling stopped.

A palpable energy, almost Romanesque in vulgarity, was building in the crowd after seeing the carnage. Cheers and jeers erupted from riled up drunks. More guys, some of them fellow bikers, were coming out of bar spurred by the sounds of violence. Sherman backed up a few steps, not sure of how the next few seconds would play out. More fighting or no fighting. Only two options existed.

One logger, a dense man with a thick, unkempt beard and piercing brown eyes, stepped forward. Sherman stood his ground while the man kept coming, showing no sign of his intentions. Finally, he bellowed a primal laugh and held out a beer in recognition.

Sherman took it and nodded.

Some fellow bikers crouched around their injured friend, weighing the options. Theirs was a tribe, and it had laws and customs clear only to its members. Sherman didn't know what to expect when two men stood up and stepped over the inert body.

Neither looked particularly intimidated nor cowed by their friend's injuries. Two on one wasn't ideal, but in Sherman's world the odds were often much longer. The guy to his left styled himself some modern Zapatista and wore a red bandana around his neck. His pal had ink climbing out his jacket and up his neck. A snake or some mythical creature. It was hard to tell in the dark.

Sherman stood his ground as they drew near, "No offense guys, but your friend swung first."

No response but smiles. Not the understanding type, more of the smirking I'm going to enjoy hurting you variety. A bit twisted, but not sadistic. Sherman knew the look well.

"Have it your way," said Sherman as the tattooed guy circled around behind him.

Zapatista came in swinging. A bit too early for his friend to exploit their tactical advantage. He was a bit out of reach and still moving sideways. Sherman stepped into the first couple of punches, closing the distance with one opponent while creating space with the other. It cost him a decent hook to the ribs, but the toll was worth it.

When the biker twisted back, aiming for another body shot, Sherman rocketed his fist straight up through the guy's chin. With a crackling pop, the uppercut landed cleanly and loudly. The lights went out and there was nothing left but the uncontrolled fall to the ground.

One on one. Sherman didn't have time to consider such marginal improvements. The tattooed guy charged hard on seeing the last punch land and caught Sherman squarely in the lower back with his shoulder. A fifteen-yard penalty in the NFL, but effective in a fight.

For a moment Sherman struggled to catch his breath. The hit and the weight of the biker overpowered his lungs. Switches buried deep in his brain flipped on, flooding his system with adrenaline. A flicker of panic skipped through his mind, but experience and training prevailed.

The biker tried to choke him out. Sherman felt the guy's arm wrapping around his neck and knew it would end badly. Should have kept punching, he thought while reaching over his head to grab the biker's jacket. With a groan he rolled forward, flipping his assailant onto his back. Neck tattoo held on, but not tight enough. Sherman landed an elbow to his ribs that loosened the grip further. Then he went to work.

Grabbing the biker's arm, Sherman rolled to his right, wrapped his legs around the guy's neck and pulled hard on the tendons that keep the arm intact. The move was classic judo, but he had never done it in a proper fight. Throwing someone over your shoulder or tripping with a leg, sure, that happened. An arm bar seemed too UFC to use in actual life, yet there he was slowly applying more pressure as the tattooed guy screamed. His voice went louder and louder as the arm slowly broke down. Tendons stretching to their breaking point, the soft tissue tearing. Right before it all came apart, Sherman let go. The guy passed out from the transition.

The bar was pretty much empty by then. Everyone, including Ruby, was outside watching. He saw her in the crowd, a conflicted expression on her face was somewhere between disgust and attraction. Sherman got another beer from the loggers for his effort.

Less pleased were the bikers who now faced a conundrum. If they let Sherman go without retribution, some would perceive weakness. However, they had already lost three dutiful soldiers for the cause. Broken men don't intimidate people, so the more that got hurt the worse their criminal racket became. Sherman could see the odds being calculated.

It was Ruby's newfound friend that finally stepped forward and extended his hand.

"Fucking hell. Let me buy you a beer."

Sherman shook his hand and the guy pulled him closer and growled, "If I ever see you again, I'll burn your corpse in the woods."

"I'm glad we agree on something," answered Sherman with complete sincerity. He inspected the faces attached to all those leather jackets just in case someone wanted a little retribution.

Ruby walked over while Sherman drank a beer, "What the fuck was that!"

"Someone didn't like me. Sent the big guy out."

She raised her hands in disgust, "You nearly killed him."

"Thanks for your concern."

"Fuck," she said and sat down on a chair. "I thought you were playing nice. Keeping a low profile or some shit."

"I'm not exactly blending," he replied.

Ruby nodded.

Sherman nodded towards the bar, "Listen, did you see the two guys talking with Gunnar?"

She gave nothing but a blank stare.

"Dirty flannel and the other had an old army jacket."

"Kinda scuzzy?" she asked.

"Yeah, I guess so."

She nodded, "Jimmy and Dean."

Sherman laughed at the names.

"Ashley's cousins."

He stopped laughing. "Really?"

"Yeah, why?"

"I think we got off on the wrong foot. They don't seem to like me all that much."

"I don't understand."

Sherman pointed to the still unconscious bikers, "The sausages started this."

"Well, if you called them that then I can see why."

"I said nothing. They already knew who I was."

"How? Those boys only know Ben Franklin as the guy on the hundred."

"Best guess, the cops told them."

Ruby shook her head with mild disbelief, "Okay Dan Brown, so now the cops are in cahoots. Did the Illuminati stage his death too?"

Sherman said nothing at first, realizing that he might have divulged too much already, "How long have you lived here?"

She raised an eyebrow. "A few years. Why?"

"Curiosity," he answered.

Ruby narrowed her eyes, "Frank, you're hiding something. I don't like secrets."

Sherman smiled, "We should be going."

She looked around at the crowd and the three men still lying on the ground and wrinkled her nose. "I suppose so, but you owe me a drink. I'm still sober."

The thought of a mildly intoxicated person driving down the road made Sherman cringe, let alone a completely wasted one.

"Bookers?"

Ruby grabbed his arm in hers and walked toward the parking lot, "Sounds like a date."

CHAPTER EIGHT

Old man or hipster? It was the eternal debate with Tillerman. The anachronistic life he led often made Sherman wonder if his friend had been born in the wrong decade. The woodworking tools out back dated from the early twenties. The pour over coffee filters came from Italy. His preferred choice of shirt was denim or wool. Truth be told, the man was just born that way. Lived his entire life slightly out of step with the rest of the world. Lagging a few paces or decades behind any trends was the norm.

The Lieutenant never cared that much about the opinions of others. Sherman appreciated that about his friend. Never did his loyalty waiver. Not to himself or those close to him. Standing in the kitchen made it feel like Tillerman was still there. A physical reminder of his friend in all his uniquely human qualities.

Sheets rustled and a bed spring twanged as Ruby got up from the couch. She padded into the kitchen wearing nothing but a full zip fleece only halfway closed, leaving a long valley of skin and cleavage exposed.

Looking at the coffee she said, "Oh, thank god. I can't handle awkward hookup hangovers without caffeine."

Sherman laughed and handed her a cup. "That bad?"

"The worst."

"Good to know."

She winked, "Ribs alright?"

A minor bruise from the fight had formed on his left side, reminding him of unfinished business. "Probably fatal," he replied.

"Oh, I'm sure," quipped Ruby in between sips of coffee.

Sherman slowly enjoyed his cup, absorbed in the memories of previous mornings.

Ruby stretched her arms up high. The fleece jacket followed, and Sherman could see she wasn't wearing any underwear. He stared for a moment before his modesty got the better of him.

"You can keep looking," she said with a smile.

"I didn't know if you had a morning after rule."

"Yeah, don't let it happen, so I guess I'm breaking that one right now."

"Maybe not so bad," he joked.

"Still trying to figure you out."

"There isn't much you haven't seen," he added.

She smirked, "Because the cover tells the complete story."

Sherman shrugged, "It's a short book."

Ruby laughed at his simplicity before going back to the questions. "So what happened last night?"

Sherman smiled, "Between us?"

"Okay, smartass. I'm familiar with those mechanics. I mean at the Crosscut."

"Probably exactly what you expected."

Ruby raised her hands in defense, "Hey now, I didn't think anyone would try to hurt you. Maybe some tough talk, but nothing more."

Sherman observed her reaction. The accusation was just part of the act. Cruel perhaps, but he wanted to see how it played. Something was nagging at the edges of his mind, like a string too small to grab but always within reach.

She genuinely looked appalled by the insinuation.

"I believe you," he finally replied.

"Well fuck you, I didn't know this was a test."

"I'd apologize, but it needed to happen. I don't know

this place or whose side you're on."

"This isn't war Frank, it's not all cloak and dagger."

"No, but my friend is dead just the same. I don't intend to let that lie. Do you understand what I'm saying?"

Ruby looked at his face and saw the intensity, the singularity of intent. She had seen such steadfastness before, but it was always coupled with cruelty. A father intent on discipline or a boyfriend not accepting no. This was different, though she knew those in his way would suffer.

"Yeah, I understand."

"Look, I'm not a good man. The good man is dead. I'm just the consequence."

She scoffed, "And what's the price? Eye for an Eye?"

"And blood for blood. There's nothing else."

Ruby turned to stare out the window and sip her coffee to avoid the questions she was afraid to ask. Deep down she had known, but this wasn't her world. It was a momentary joyride on the edge of society. A rebellion against the past that had left her stranded in this town, this job, and this life she led.

Now she was confronting the very real specter of substantial violence. Not the daily abuse she suffered as a child or grew into as an adult. Not the mundane verbal drivel she received at the bar. Looking at Sherman, at the visible scars and the wounds hiding beneath the surface, she saw something more. More than just the capacity or intent to hurt and maim. Plenty of men had passed through her life who had one or both. Cruel men, weak men and narrow-minded fools. All of them willing to use violence for personal gain or satisfaction. But the man standing before her was neither weak nor cruel, and Ruby felt a growing knot of fear at the unknown.

Sherman interrupted that thought, "Sorry if that came off a tad intense."

Ruby smiled weakly, "Yours is a different world."

"Trust me, it isn't worth visiting."

"Then why stay there? Why not leave?"

"Keep digging and you'll find out," answered Sherman.

"You telling me to stick around?"

Sherman laughed, "I don't pretend to believe that I can tell you what to do. The decision is yours alone."

"Damn right," she said laughingly.

"Alright then. Breakfast?"

"I thought you'd never ask."

Sherman asked where, but stopped mid-word. The sound of a car door snapped up his attention. First one, then a second muted thud. Two doors, two cars.

Ruby watched his face change, "What's wrong?"

"You might want to change. We have company."

"What? How?" she stammered.

Sherman ignored the questions. He was already putting on pants and a shirt.

Ruby was fumbling to find some underwear when there was a loud knocking at the door. The intensity was both aggressive and arrogant. Only overly entitled people knocked that way.

"Cops," said Sherman as he ambled over to the door.

"Good morning, Sheriff," he said. The words came out before the door had even swung open. From the close of the first car door, he knew who was on the other side. In his thinking they were late. If they really wanted to rattle his cage, they should have come at first light.

The Sheriff wanted to ratchet up the intensity. Gone was the western shirt and bolo tie, replaced by the block lettering of SHERIFF written across the bulletproof vest. He still wore the cowboy hat, but it sat lower on his head, not casually tilted back.

"Mr. Sherman. We need a word," said Reinhold. His hand never moved from the handle of his pistol as he spoke.

"Come on in Sheriff," Sherman motioned him inside, but took the precaution of walking first, lest the lawman get skittish.

The Sheriff followed but kept his hand in place.

"Ruby, I believe you know Sheriff Reinhold."

Ruby smiled. She had found some pants but was still only wearing a zipped-up fleece on top.

"Ruby," said Reinhold, tipping his hat in her direction. He looked unsurprised to see her in the house.

Sherman smiled, "You can invite your deputies inside. I unlocked the back door."

Reinhold scoffed, "Fair enough, Captain." He motioned towards the sliding glass door leading to the deck.

Barrios and Simpkins dutifully entered with an aggressive flair. With shotguns on their shoulders, and they showed no intention of diffusing the tension. Ruby recoiled back towards the wall a step but stopped from moving any further. Sherman had shot her a quick glance that instructed her to stay put. He didn't want any sudden movements. Not with all the guns out and ready.

"Heard there was a commotion last night at the Crosscut. You wouldn't know anything about that, Captain?"

"You already know the answer to that."

"Don't you fucking talk back," barked Barrios.

The Sheriff continued, "You sent a man to the ER."

"Ah, the big guy. He swung first."

"Witness said you sucker punched him," enjoined Simpkins.

Sherman didn't bother looking at the deputy when responding, "The trouble with eyewitnesses is that memory can be such a fickle thing."

The Sheriff flashed a toothy grin that had about as much good will as a junkyard dog. He was smiling alright, but it was more bite than benevolence. "You're right about memory. Things can get fuzzy. Maybe the order of events shifts slightly. But people don't forget those who sinned against their kin. Not in small towns. Not here."

Sherman nodded in understanding. Point made and driven home.

"They set the probate hearing for Monday. Stay out of my sight until then."

"Sure thing, Sheriff. Didn't mean to stir the pot."

Reinhold nodded for his deputies to leave. They obliged with shotguns raised, slowly backing out the way they entered. On the way out he winked at Ruby with a lasciviousness that sent a shudder down her spine.

Ruby held her breath until the engines burbled to life down the hill. Exhaling, she looked pale and shaken. In all the threats she had received over the years, never had one been at the barrel of a gun.

Sherman gave a squeeze of support after seeing the fear gripping her face. "First time being intimidated by the cops?"

"I've never had a gun pointed at me before."

Sherman nodded, "Scary shit."

"Kept looking down the barrel, sure that I could see the end coming." She looked up at him, "How are you so calm?"

"I've been in your shoes too many times to count. It gets less frightening."

"I'd prefer not to find out if you're right."

"I'll cross my fingers for you."

"Frank, what the hell is going on? No sugar coating."

Sherman took a breath and motioned for her to sit down, "Tillerman was murdered. The crash was staged. Someone grabbed him on the way to town, someone driving a dually."

Ruby's eyes narrowed as she thought of all the people she knew who owned one.

Sherman continued, "They took him into the mountains for a few hours then forced enough booze into him to black out. He was probably dead before they put him back in the truck."

"Jesus. I thought this was just some normal small town."

"It gets worse. The cops showed up the next morning and tried to plant some evidence."

"What?"

"Empty bottles of booze, I think."

"I was wondering why you weren't surprised to see them."

"Not the first time they've threatened me."

"Why not leave?" she asked. The question was half directed at Sherman and half at herself.

"I think you know the answer to that."

Deep down she understood his conviction but had been unmoored for so long that it almost hurt to see what got lost.

"How about that breakfast?" she asked.

"You still have an appetite?"

"I will by the time we get there."

"Okay, where to?" he asked.

"Georgette's."

"Never been."

"It's the only decent place in town," said Ruby.

"Sold."

Georgette was probably the only native French speaker for a hundred plus miles, but her pastries were so good that the locals now ordered *en francais*. Sherman and Ruby grabbed the only two-top left in the place, which wasn't over ten tables. The quintessential European cafe feeling made Sherman immediately reminisce about the past. He always landed on the Continent between stints in one sandbox or another.

Then there were the occasional assignments. A low-level Saudi Prince in Paris, two Chechens in Hamburg, the siblings in Baku. The list wasn't long, but far bigger than the US government would ever admit.

Years ago, a fellow operator started tattooing his body count, at least the confirmed ones, in small squares on his arm. It covered most of his bicep by the time a roadside bomb severed the limb and the practice. Sherman wondered how much of his own forearm Europe would consume. The cumulative total was enough squares to make a chessboard.

"What are you getting?" Ruby's question caught him still stumbling through erstwhile days.

"Croissant and a shot in the dark."

"Espresso and coffee. Under caffeinated, are we?"

Sherman shrugged, "I'm an addict."

Georgette walked up while Ruby was still chuckling to herself. No one knew what possessed the Frenchwoman to move to Byron Mills. Some said she was running from her past, which made her appearance in town almost commonplace. Either way, people had long since stopped searching for an answer. Questions beget more questions and were best avoided altogether.

"Ruby. *Bon jeur mademoiselle.*"

"And a good morning to you, Georgette. How are things?"

"*Tre bein,*" she answered with the sort of warm smile that somehow only comes with age. Sherman guessed late fifties. "Who is your friend?"

"Now where are my manners? Georgette this is Frank Sherman."

"*Monsieur Sherman, enchante.*"

"*Tout le plaisir est pour moi.*"

Ruby's eyebrows raised in surprise at the unexpected. Sherman ordered for them and bantered with Georgette in French for a few minutes before she excused herself to get back to work.

"Aren't you full of surprises?"

"I'm still working on it, but it is close enough to Spanish."

"You know Spanish too?"

"Barely. They called my high school Spanish teacher Coach, so there wasn't much structure to the class, let alone learning."

Ruby was shaking her head in disbelief, "Any other languages?"

"Arabic."

"Arabic?"

"And a little Farsi."

"Jesus."

"Oh, and a smidge of Pashtun."

"Okay, okay. You're making me feel bad."

"It's a survival thing. If you can't understand the language, you'll never know when to duck."

"Bleak view of the world."

"I know," said Sherman with a tone of seriousness that bordered on fatigue.

"You learned all that in the Army?"

"Sink or swim."

Ruby raised her finger and said, "Hold that thought." She pulled out her phone that was softly vibrating and looked at the screen. "Oh shit, it's Ashley. Do you think she knows?"

Sherman shrugged as she answered. From the audible sobbing, someone had told her. A tinge of guilt flashed through Sherman's mind for being happy that it was not his responsibility. That was a conversation he hoped to never have again. The knot in your stomach, that churn of guilt about surviving. You're alive and their loved one is not. Wondering how to show empathy when all you feel is relief that it's not your family on the other end of the knock on the door.

The conversation continued as Ruby tried to console her friend with genuine empathy. Not the false sentiments that Sherman had once spoken.

"Sure, sure," Ruby was saying, "we'll be over there later." She looked at Sherman with a soft smile, "Yeah, he is with me now. Okay, hang in there sugar."

She looked drained after hanging up, "We're gonna swing by her place in an hour."

"Sure. How's she doing?" he asked.

"Not good at all."

"She alone?"

Ruby shook her head. "Judging by the racket, I'd say her brothers were there."

"Plural?" Asked Sherman.

"Yeah, three of them. All older."

"She's got thick skin then."

"And a sharp tongue. Smarter than two of them by a mile," added Ruby.

"That leaves a smart one?"

Ruby bit her lip for a second in contemplation, "Tanner is something else. Should teach college or something."

"I take it he never left."

"Not everyone gets the chance to leave."

The thought would have been antithetical to Sherman's worldview twenty years ago when getting out from under his father's shadow was his only motivation in life. That all changed with the war. He watched inexperienced men swallow their wanderlust for family and tribe. Saw them take up a calling, a gun, an ideology, all in the name of bloodlines. Most of those men were dead, buried under the rubble of American military might. There was a certain strain of fanaticism with those who stayed.

They finished in silence, each caught up in their own moribund thoughts. Sherman paid and thanked Georgette, promising to return soon.

CHAPTER NINE

Cloud by cloud, a storm was building overhead as they pulled into a small parking lot that fronted Ashley's apartment building. It was a set of four adjoining units, two stories in height and painted with off-putting accents of sea foam green. Cars took up most of the parking spots, expected for two old Ford diesels of an indeterminable original color. In a land of single-family homes, it was the only apartment complex in town.

Ruby knocked on the door of the first apartment harder than Sherman thought was appropriate, but quickly changed his mind when he saw who opened it. A childish man, maybe early twenties with an eighth grader's mustache, opened the door with gruff reluctance. He was thin, wiry and a few inches taller than Sherman.

The man stared at Sherman and growled, "Who the fuck are you?"

"Good to see you too, Rhett," replied Ruby.

Rhett scowled at the intrusion of a stranger.

"Meet Frank Sherman. Sherman meet Rhett Thorne."

Sherman tried to extend his hand but all he saw was Rhett's back as he walked out back shouting, "Ashley. Company!"

Ruby frowned and Sherman shot her a wink, "Nice guy."

"Yeah, a real catch that one," she said.

They moved into the living room, and Sherman could

hear some argument going on upstairs. Not a shouting match, but something with quiet intensity. Ashley finally emerged shaken but smiled when she saw her friend.

"Hey Ruby, thanks for coming over."

"Of course darlin', anything for you."

They hugged for a long minute with Ruby whispering small comforts into Ashley's ear. An embrace not just of friendship but of some shared sacrifice. It had a sisterly quality to it.

"You must be Sherman," said Ashley, "I feel like I've known you for years and we haven't even met."

She bounded over and gave him a tight squeeze that Sherman imagined being like a little sister would have done. He immediately took a liking to her and could see why Tillerman had been so enamored. Brown hair, freckles and wickedly expressive smile.

"I'm really sorry to meet like this," said Sherman.

Ashley nodded solemnly, "Me too."

He could see the tears slowly forming in the corners of her eyes, "How are you doing?"

"I'm a complete fucking wreck," she sighed. "Oh my god, I didn't even ask how you are doing. I'm so selfish. You knew him for years. Ah, fuck."

Sherman smiled, "Don't worry. I'm only a little better than you, but I've had a few days to process."

"You've done this before, haven't you?"

"I'm afraid so."

"Does it get easier? Tell me it gets easier."

Sherman sighed and shook his head.

Ashley buried her face in her slender hands and sobbed for a few moments while Ruby softly rubbed her back in support.

With a deep breath she shook off the wave of grief and forced a hesitant smile, "Can I get you two a beer?"

Ruby nodded and Sherman agreed, but wondered why a woman who just lost her boyfriend to drunk driving would offer beer to break the tension of an untimely death.

The three of them sat on the couch, beer in hand, for an awkward moment of silence. No one quite knew what to say. Sherman had questions, Ruby had words of encouragement, and Ashley looked on the verge of melting into the couch.

Silence was golden when you didn't need answers but Sherman was approaching junkie status in his quest for knowledge.

He broke the ice, "How did you and Tillerman meet?"

Ashley's face lit up with the memory, momentarily transporting her out of the dreadful present. "I bought a coffee table from him. Nothing fancy, real basic birch, but I saved up for it. He was just so himself, completely and utterly at home in his skin. We got to talking and never stopped." She looked out the window into the distant gray clouds, "Until now I guess."

Ruby patted her knee in support, "You two had something special, that is for sure."

"Ashley, I apologize in advance, but can I ask you something personal?"

She was bent forward with her head between her knees but looked his direction and nodded.

"They told you what happened, right?"

She nodded again.

"The whole story? The drinking and the crash?"

Another nod.

"Okay, here is the question. Do you think he drank that night?"

Ashley's bolted upright and her face contorted with shock as if she had never questioned the story. "What do you mean by that?"

"Tillerman was an alcoholic, but he'd been sober for over ten years."

"He told me. On our first date, no less."

Sherman smiled, "The process is important in the program. Do you think he slipped?"

She pinched the bridge of her nose in concerted

consideration and was saying something when another brother walked down the stairs.

Interrupting their conversation, the man asked, "You okay sis?"

"I'm fine, Tanner. You remember Ruby and this is an old friend of Tillerman's."

Sherman extended a hand, "Frank Sherman."

"The Frank Sherman?"

"Afraid so."

"Well shit, I've heard some crazy stories about you."

It perplexed Sherman. His friend rarely told war stories to people that did not have his complete trust and this guy didn't strike him as fitting the mold.

"From Tillerman?" he asked.

"Who else? Anyway, what was that one from the other day?" Tanner looked at his sister who was shaking her head without recognition, "Oh right, some blue-on-green attack in Peshawar that nearly got you both killed."

Even at eight years old, the memory was still fresh in Sherman's mind. Spring had ended, and the mud had almost turned back to solid earth. Afghanistan, like an alien planet, had its own seasons, and the fighting season had just begun. Sherman and Tillerman were both on their third tour, which on the grand timeline of the country was just a blip on the radar. Even within the war on terror three tours felt like a brief but fucked up summer vacation, stuck in a land haunted by the ghosts of lost armies.

The entire country felt claustrophobic no matter if you were on the steppes or climbing up a nearly vertical walled valley. There was no escaping the war. It was everywhere. It had always been there and would always be there. It was Afghanistan's dirty little secret that everyone knew, but nobody dared say out loud. The war would be there, with or without the Americans.

Tillerman understood that unspoken truth, but back then Sherman saw it as defeatist. Only later did he see the entire thing was farcical. Wars of ideology aren't winnable, not in the Army's narrow focus of conquer and control. Hearts and minds aren't won by money or power. They shift gradually over time, like a glacier cuts a valley. Someday the Taliban and ISIS would vanish into the history books, but not because of foreign intervention. No. They would cease because the whims of the people changed. For fifteen years Sherman had fought, not because he thought it was a winnable war, but because they could lose it.

The Army's naïve mentality sent them to some valley to win over a few tribal elders who supposedly weren't the Taliban's biggest fans. Enemy of my enemy is my friend thought the brass and in went a JSOC team to see how much it would cost. Nobody in Afghanistan fights for free unless it was for freedom.

Security was tight for the meeting. Apaches sat fueled and ready. Warthogs were in the air. Sherman had every angle covered. The list of potential munitions was longer than his arm. On paper it looked good, on the ground it felt reasonable. The mistake they made that day wasn't one of oversight, it was one of hubris. They assumed the almighty Special Forces war machine had done its due diligence. That it had checked the local cops, vetted the guests, verified the intel.

Common courtesy saved their life. Thirty minutes into the meeting, Sherman and Tillerman stepped out. Intel had picked up some chatter in the area, and it didn't sound mundane. They excused themselves and went outside to get the Apaches in the air.

The local magistrate had hired his nephew to appease his sister. What good was a position of power if he didn't use it? Turns out the nephew had other allegiances that he neglected to share for obvious reasons. He used the uniform and bloodlines to the magistrate to sneak in enough explosives to vaporize the house and everyone in it.

Sherman couldn't understand why the nephew waited until they left or why he didn't wait for them to come back. It didn't matter. The explosives killed everyone, turned the entire place to golf ball sized bits of mud and bone.

Four Americans and a room full of reasonable men died. Then the ground attack started. Sherman had scarcely dusted the dirt off when the first mortars started falling. The infantry wasn't far behind. Forty guys swarming into the valley to finish whoever remained, which was just Sherman and Tillerman.

The Apaches were in gun range by the time the Taliban attacked. It was a complete massacre. Just little white blips on the infrared camera. A squeeze of the trigger. A burst of 20mm high explosive rounds and then nothing. They didn't even find bodies, just stringy bits of flesh.

Sherman learned a valuable lesson that day. Don't trust anyone, even relatives of someone you know. Turned out the nephew was running drugs with Taliban, got to be a powerful man before Sherman put a hole in him some months later.

What Sherman couldn't understand is why Tillerman told this story at all. There was nothing redeemable about their actions or the outcome. It was just war, just Afghanistan.

"I'm sorry to hear about what happened. He might have been fucking my sister, but he seemed alright," said Tanner.

Ruby raised her middle finger in his direction while Ashley quietly sobbed. Her eldest brother had a way of getting under her skin.

Undeterred, Tanner continued, "Well, the wood carving was a little weird. Cutting down trees. Now that's a job. Making rocking chairs is a shade queer."

"Fuck you Tanner," yelled Ashley as she ran off into her room with Ruby close on her heels.

Tanner shrugged towards Sherman. "Girls."

Sherman said nothing because there was nothing to say. The episode may have been callous and crass, but also calculated. Ashley was in tears and not answering any of his questions. That alone raised his suspicion.

Simultaneously cracking a beer and a smile, Tanner

motioned for Sherman to meet him outside. The other brothers were sitting on loungers, seeing who could spit farther.

"Ha!" Yelled Rhett, "I told you I'd win."

"Get fucked," replied the largest of the three. Sherman put the man a shade over two-fifty and maybe six foot two.

"Rhett, Grady," said Tanner, "meet Frank Sherman."

The brothers waved a hand without looking at him.

"He was a friend of Tillerman's."

"Huh," said Grady, sizing him up. "You don't look like some army bitch."

The guy had sixty pounds on him, but Sherman was already looking forward to hurting him in the future.

"Listen guys, I have a question for you," Sherman said.

"You waiting for an invitation?" sneered Rhett.

"Do you know why Tillerman was talking to your dad a few days ago?"

Grady turned his enormous head, "Where?"

"The bar."

Tanner scratched his beard, "Maybe he tired of the wood whittling and went looking for an actual job."

The brothers erupted in a spate of laughter, but all Sherman saw was an evasive answer from a clever man.

"I'll take that as a no."

The brothers were back to the spitting and ignored the comment altogether until Grady blurted out, "Hey, were you the one who sent John to the ER?"

"Was he the big one?"

"Yeah. That's some fucked up shit."

"He swung first," retorted Sherman.

"Doesn't sound like John," said Tanner.

Sherman smiled, "People are full of surprises."

"Ain't that the truth," added Rhett.

"I heard you broke out some real Kung Fu shit," said Grady.

"Something like that."

Rhett spoke up again, "You learn that in the army?"

"Among others."

"God damn boy, you are one cool cat," said Tanner.

"Why did he swing first? You disrespect the man?" Rhett asked.

"Got my first glimpse of the man when I saw his fist coming."

Grady scoffed dramatically, "That old boy may take offense easily but it ain't for nothing. What you do?"

"Park too close to his chopper?" offered Rhett.

Sherman shrugged. The bombardment of justifications was doing nothing to quiet his suspicions.

"Shit," added Tanner in a moment of respite, "probably got too drunk and forgot his glasses. Anyway, what brings you here?"

"To town or where I stand?"

Tanner pointed to the ground.

"Wanted to meet Ashley. Commiserate."

"You hadn't met before?"

"Work keeps me away."

Tanner tilted his head ever so slightly, "And what unit did you say you're in?"

"I didn't," said Sherman.

The response elicited a laugh from all three brothers.

"Army for sure. Special Forces?" Tanner asked.

"Still don't look like no army pussy to me," added Grady.

"Ignore him," said Tanner. "Spill the beans. What did Tillerman say about my sister?"

Sherman found the question odd, a bit too probing, and lied in response. "Oh, nothing untoward. Just the rough outlines."

"Huh, untoward?" asked Grady.

"It means inappropriate, raunchy in this context," answered Tanner.

"Why not just say that," mumbled Grady, "fucking fancy words."

A door closed inside, and Sherman could see Ruby in the living room with Ashley nowhere in sight.

Tanner looked. "Tequila," he surmised.

Sherman narrowed his gaze in response, not understanding the statement.

"She likes to drink away the problems. One of her better or worse qualities depending on your proclivities."

"Some vice, some virtue," added Sherman.

Tanner nodded, "Come to the bar sometime, beers are on me."

"I'm not a persona non grata there?"

With a laugh Tanner answered, "Those boys will un-bunch their panties in a few days. If you're in town that long."

His comment hung for a moment like an omnipresent cloud and Sherman wondered what the man knew.

"To be determined," he finally said.

"I like your style, no bullshit."

Sherman turned to the other brothers, "Boys, nice to meet you."

Rhett waved.

Grady muttered, "Bye-bye ghost man."

Momentarily confused by Grady's reply, Sherman crossed the room to Ruby. Anxiety danced across her face. "How's she doing?"

"Chased the worm and her demons."

"She out?"

Ruby nodded.

"This place isn't exactly restorative," said Sherman.

"I can barely hear myself think," added Ruby.

"Should we take her back to the house?"

Ruby frowned, "His house? I don't know if that would be any better,"

Sherman grimaced with doubt, "Fair point, but can it be any worse than this?"

Ruby shifted her stance and muttered, "Fuck. You're probably right."

"It doesn't matter at the moment, they'll never let us take her away."

"She'll be out for hours, maybe tonight?"

Sherman agreed, "Late. I don't want those assholes to know."

"Okay, let's go. This place drives me fucking crazy. Those two are constantly undressing me in their minds, I can feel it."

"That's probably the benign part."

She punched him in the arm, "Thanks, very comforting."

"Did Ashley say anything I should know?"

"Mostly sobs and the ghosts of the past. You learn anything from those idiots?"

"Ghosts."

"I'm too tired for riddles Frank."

"Grady said 'bye-bye ghost man' when I walked out."

"So. You're a bit spectral."

"No, it's not that. The Sheriff used the same word when they showed up at Tillerman's house. Said you can't kill a ghost."

"Coincidence?"

"*Shabh* is what the Taliban called us. Arabic for ghost."

"Alright, that is spooky."

Sherman couldn't help but feel he was missing something. A connection. A link. "Feel like a drive?" he asked.

Ruby raised her eyebrows.

"I have a hunch."

"Why not? This day is just getting stranger by the minute."

CHAPTER TEN

"This is morbid," voiced Ruby.

Sherman nodded in agreement. They had parked in a small turnout just down the road from where the crash occurred.

"What do you expect to find?" she asked.

"I'm not sure, but it's like porn," started Sherman.

Ruby finished the sentence, "You know it when you see it."

"Exactly."

She opened her door and climbed out, "Let's go find your smut."

Upper Mill Road was a thin ribbon of blacktop fighting with the river for space as it snaked out of the valley. Few people lived that far up, just a handful of families and old ranches handed down for generations. Several miles further the asphalt gave way to dirt, and the road ended abruptly near a rocky escarpment at the base of a granite massif. It felt like whoever had built the road kept going, driven by the insane idea that the geography would become more conducive with altitude.

They walked in the middle of the road, hugging the dotted yellow stripes, hedging their bets that two cars would not come at the same time. Blackberry bushes hemmed close enough that the shoulder had disappeared years ago.

"It's quiet up here," said Ruby.

Sherman grunted in acknowledgement. A fine mist was falling, having broken free of the cloud's clutches. It made for an exceedingly small world with damp gray walls. Even the distant baying of the sheep seemed muted.

From what Reinhold said, Tillerman hit the most obvious tree on the entire road. An old gnarled oak about four feet thick with a branch that spanned from across the road. Someone had climbed up and tied a flannel shirt roughly above the center yellow line. Some prank of yore.

"That always been there?" asked Sherman. The shirt looked tattered and old.

"As long as I have," answered Ruby.

Evidence of the impact lay strewn about the ground. Chunks of plastic, metal and glass, those building blocks of industrialization were everywhere. The cops had put little effort into cleaning up the place.

The sight of small red puddle made Ruby gasp.

"Brake fluid," said Sherman, knowing any blood would have long since washed away in the rain.

Running his hand across the U-shaped gash in the oak, it was hard to dispute the crash. Thinking back to what remained of Tillerman's truck, it all made sense. A body in considerable motion and an immovable object. The physics wasn't difficult, but the geometry was all wrong.

No matter the direction of travel, when Sherman looked at it, the marks made little sense. The impact was perpendicular to the road. Laughing at the obvious, he turned around towards the ranch entrance. A gate covered a small, nondescript dirt road opposite the tree. Passing through the small gap in the undergrowth, it surprised Sherman to see that the space opened up the further up you went. A small pasture, normally obscured from the road, created one of those hidden gems of natural beauty you rarely find without trying.

Having followed him Ruby asked, "What are you looking for?"

Sherman stopped at the first turn, some hundred and

fifty feet up the driveway. Looking back towards the road, it did not surprise him to see the tree dead center in the driveway like the uprights of a field goal post.

He pointed to the oak, "That."

Ruby looked, "You mean he drove down the hill from here? That makes no sense."

"I know, look at this." Sherman walked back and pointed to the bumper height scar. "The angle is all wrong for someone driving on the road. What are you going to do, make a perfect left turn into the tree at speed?"

"So, he came down the driveway. That proves nothing," countered Ruby.

"Maybe, but why was he up here and why didn't he brake?"

"Too drunk."

"But not drunk enough to crash before?"

"Fine then. What's your theory, Sherlock?"

"Someone took care to make it look like an accident. Tied the wheel and jammed the gas pedal. Downhill like this, you could easily top thirty or more by the time you hit the tree."

"That seems survivable," said Ruby.

Sherman had already considered this point, "He was dead already."

"How can you know that?"

"I can't for certain, but that's what I would have done. No point in risking it. Someone could have seen the crash and got help."

"You live a dark life Frank."

"If you only knew," mumbled Sherman.

"Can we go now? I've got that creepy, someone-is-watching-me feeling."

Sherman sniffed the damp air. The same feeling had triggered his own warning bells several minutes earlier. Someone was out there and not that far away.

"Sure, give me one more minute." Rooting around the nearby trees, it didn't take him long to find what he sought.

Holding up the cigarette butt, he proclaimed, "Lucky Strikes."

"You and half the town."

"Same as the ambush spot."

"This isn't Fallujah," countered Ruby.

"Tell that to Tillerman."

"Low blow," she added.

"Maybe, but these guys are using a similar playbook." Taking a moment to consider the craziness of their situation, he smiled at her. "Come on, let's go eat something hot."

With the rain and thoughts of some wartime ambush swirling in her head, Ruby missed it. Just a flash of green paint and a Chevy logo hidden off the road past where they had parked. A vehicle likely belonging to the two surly gentlemen who had accosted him at the Riverfront Bar and Grille. Jimmy or Dean, thought Sherman, maybe both. He needed to have a word with those boys soon, but getting Ashley out took top priority tonight.

They stopped at the Mill Cafe on their way back to Tillerman's house. He ordered a burger and fries. She got a patty melt with a side of soup. It wasn't exactly gourmet, but after the day they were having the comfort part of comfort food had top billing. Sherman picked a table in the corner facing the door. The place had enormous windows across the front. Lots of visual real estate to see if Jimmy and Dean had followed them back to town. There were a few explanations for the continued surveillance and Sherman didn't like any of them. Obviously, they wanted to know what he knew. At some point he would move beyond just a nuisance and graduate to a threat. Whenever that happened, he knew preparation was key. People may call those boys hicks, but there was nothing benign about their abilities.

When the tab came Sherman paid and told Ruby, "Let's get a little rest before tonight."

"I'm pretty fucking wired," replied Ruby as she fidgeted in her seat.

"Adrenaline and shock. Your body is all mixed up."

"I feel like the morning after a twelve-shot night."

"Believe me, it only gets worse if you don't rest."

"Take me to bed then," she said sarcastically.

It was dark by the time they got back. Not late, just not light. Somewhere around the prime-time television hours, not that Tillerman had one to watch. Out of an abundance of caution, Sherman did a quick sweep around the house. Nothing was out of place or unusual, but something made him do it. By the time he finished, Ruby had passed out on the couch. Sherman found a nearby leather recliner and set his phone alarm for a few hours later. His internal clock was never that good. The compass was spot on.

The crackle of gunfire woke him up, not the shrill ring of an alarm. Rifles to be exact, which is one of the first things his mind comprehended. Second was the distance, at around two hundred yards away. Last, was the knowledge that whoever was shooting wasn't aiming at the house. The impacts sounded metallic and the only object worth shooting at was the jeep parked out front.

Ruby was awake now and trying to sit up, still somewhat dazed by the current situation. With a quick jerk, Sherman pulled her to the floor.

"Don't move," he instructed.

She nodded with eyes wide as few more loud cracks echoed past them into the darkness.

"Good, I'll be back soon," said Sherman as he crawled towards the back door.

"No, no, no. You're not leaving me here," hissed Ruby.

"You'll be fine. Just keep your head down. If they're still shooting in fifteen minutes, call Brummet and then the cops."

Fifteen minutes sounded like an eternity. Ruby had experienced her fair share of violence but couldn't recall ever being shot at. "We could be dead by then."

"Hang in there. They haven't actually shot at the house."

Sliding open the door, he exited into the damp night

with several more shots ringing out as a greeting. Sherman's best guess put the shooter out on a slight ridge two turns down the road. It was visible through the trees from the front door if you looked hard enough. The shot wasn't difficult if you found the right line of sight, which they had.

Sherman ran hard for three hundred yards. Heading right at them was suicidal, so he picked a spot two hundred yards off to the shooter's side. Simple math meant he would have to run close to five hundred yards.

The shooting had stopped by the time he made the turn towards the flank, but his ear had already confirmed the caliber. NATO Standard 5.56mm. A Mini-14 or AR-15. Something semi-auto with a decent-sized magazine.

He slowed to a jog for the last hundred yards. Earthy forest smells mixed with pungent wafts of cordite. It was the spot. Fifty feet short, he stopped and listened. He could hear nothing but the empty night and a few cows. In the distance a door shut, and a throaty engine burbled to life. Not exactly a truck sound, but Sherman wasn't sure.

Finding the exact location was easy. Even with minimal light, the spent brass still glimmered. Kneeling, he could see Ruby's car between the trees. Not so much the house, but an easy shot on the car. He pocketed a few shells and headed back, knowing that Ruby was close to losing it by now.

Coming back in through the same door, Sherman hoped for a less surprised reaction. The plan failed. No sooner than he had stepped inside then a baseball bat nearly smashed in his teeth. Ruby had swung hard from a hiding spot, narrowly missing.

"It's me," he yelled while ducking under another swing.

Ruby dropped the bat, "Fuck. You scared the hell out of me!"

"I see that. Did you call the cops?"

"After this morning! Hell no."

"Fair point, Brummet?"

She shook her head, "Did you see who it was?"

"No, only heard the vehicle drive away. Something with

95

a big engine."

Ruby's eyes narrowed in thought, "Diesel?"

Sherman wasn't a car guy but had been around enough army trucks in his life, "No, but it rumbled pretty loudly."

"Did the tires screech?"

He thought for a moment, replaying those few seconds back, "Yeah, the rain muted it."

"It wasn't a truck," she said definitively.

"What else is there in this town?"

"A 1968 Camaro."

Unable to hide his surprise, Sherman asked, "How do you know that?"

"Deputy Simpkins drives one. Loves to rev that big-block. Thing is, he can't drive for shit. He always chirps the tires when taking off."

"I didn't take you for a car girl."

Ruby shrugged, "In another life."

The seriousness on her face only deepened his intrigue. There was more to her than a Southern lilt.

"Speaking of cars, I've got unwelcome news," added Sherman as he led her out front.

"Fuckers," grumbled Ruby with a deep sadness as she looked at the remains of her jeep.

Small slicks of oil puddling underneath and the exterior looked all too familiar. High velocity rounds do a number on cars, even those built like a tank. Chunks of safety glass crunched under their feet as they circled. Sherman didn't smell gas, so he tried the ignition. Nothing.

"I think the message is clear," said Ruby.

"If they were trying to get us to leave, shooting the only mode of transportation was a terrible idea."

"Mistakes were made," added Ruby. Although Sherman couldn't tell if she meant Simpkins or herself.

"Is there somewhere you can lie low?"

"I've been running long enough. Eventually you've got to stop."

Something about her eyes, the way they stared at an

unseen horizon gave Sherman pause. Tillerman had the same look, like he could see the demons trudging behind in his wake, knowing one day that the road would end. In that moment lay a decision, to stand or succumb. Ruby, he thought, was standing at that junction. It made him want to know, to ask all the questions she peppered him with the previous night. But the timing wasn't right. Maybe another time, another place or another life.

"I better call Brummet. We need a ride," said Sherman.

Brummet answered on the third ring, which seemed responsive considering the hour of the night. He didn't sound too sleepy or too drunk. Positive signs.

"Mr. Sherman, it's late."

"That it is."

"What can I do for you?"

"I have a personal and a professional question for you."

"No time like the present."

"First, are you available to drive now?"

"It's your dollar."

"Second, and this one is a bit prying; do you own a gun?"

There was a pause on the line before Brummet answered, "I'll be there in thirty minutes."

Sherman looked at Ruby and shrugged, "He'll be here soon."

"And the gun?"

He shrugged again and waited.

The old cabbie was punctual and when he heard the old Crown Vic rumble slowly up the road Sherman kicked himself for sleeping. Awake, he would have heard Simpkins and company on their approach. Mistakes.

Sherman didn't take any chances and waited for Brummet under the cover of a giant sycamore nestled at the edge of the road. Instinct told him the immediate threat was gone, but eventually the cops would stop underestimating his willingness and abilities. Simpkins and Barrios probably thought they had scared him out of town. The overt threat to Ruby seemed like a cheap shot, but maybe they saw her as a point of weakness. A fulcrum to push him out of town. Perhaps they were right.

Brummet cut his lights once he saw the driveway and turned up the hill in complete darkness. By the time he opened his door, Sherman was coming out of the woods, having made sure no one else was following.

"Sorry for the late hour," said Sherman.

The old man turned towards the unexpected voice but didn't seem all that surprised, "Sounds like you're in a bind."

Sherman pointed to the jeep, "You could say that."

The mangled vehicle was still dripping fluids and Brummet drew in a sharp breath, "Christ, Captain. What have you done?"

"I think we struck a nerve."

"You're not one for embellishment. Is Ruby okay?"

"Shaken but unhurt."

"That girl's already seen enough?"

"How so?" Sherman asked a bit too eagerly.

Brummet waved his finger, "That's her story to tell, not mine."

Sherman nodded, but thought it was worth a try.

"Normally I'd drive you to the airport now, but you don't strike me as the running type."

"It's only been four days and you already know me."

"It appears stubbornness is your only trait."

Sherman couldn't help but laugh at the truth, "That's one of two."

"And the other?"

"Good aim."

"God help them," replied Brummet with a sigh, "How can I help?"

"We need to kidnap Ashley."

"Say what?"

"She needs our help," interjected Ruby, who had wandered outside.

Despite the bewilderment in his eyes Brummet nodded, "Don't make me regret giving you my business card Mr.

Sherman."

"I'm surprised we're not past that point already."

Ruby was tired, frightened and cut to the point. "Do you have what Sherman asked for?"

The cabbie nodded and reached into the car. With reverence and shame, he handed Sherman a wooden cigar box that was in between old and ancient.

Sherman could read his expression, "You sure about this?"

"Yeah, it's just gathering dust in a storage shed."

They walked inside, and Sherman set the box on the kitchen table before opening it. It seemed too important to open like some common package. He wasn't sure what to expect, but the contents were both surprising and mundane. Neatly wrapped in an old oil cloth was Russian made Makarov pistol. There was an inscription on the side of the slide that Sherman couldn't read but looked Vietnamese. Although he didn't know Brummet very well, the cabbie didn't seem intent on remembering the war. Perhaps haunted, but not the type to keep trophies or souvenirs.

"North Vietnamese officer?" Asked Sherman.

Brummet nodded, "It's not my proudest moment, and I sacrificed a bit of myself by doing it."

"No judgment here. War has a way of twisting you into places you never thought possible."

"Indeed," replied the cabbie with a sigh. "All those years I could never bring myself to get rid of it, like that would whitewash my guilt. Somehow that was worse than just hiding it."

It was feeling Sherman knew well, and he often wondered who would stare back in the mirror when his war ended.

"And you're okay with Sherman taking it?" Asked Ruby.

"Yeah, I'm not ashamed of what we did there but how we did it. As for this," he pointed to the box, "the Captain has my confidence."

The pistol wasn't exactly pristine and showed a long

brush with the past, but as Sherman disassembled it he was certain it would still fire.

Ruby watched with a mixture of surprise and apprehension at the fluidity of his movements, "Have you ever seen one of those before?"

"On both sides of the barrel," Sherman answered.

When finished, he loaded eight rounds into the magazine, inserted it into the gun. The slide closed with an audible clack. One bullet remained on the table and Sherman deftly removed the mag and added the last bullet. Nine rounds. If a firefight came, he wouldn't last long.

There were other things to consider and Sherman turned to Ruby, "Can you see if Tillerman has a black jacket and balaclava?"

There was a bank robbery joke there, but Ruby's nerves were beyond humor. All she could do was nod and go searching. It took a few minutes, but she returned with a black rain jacket and a dark green mask.

"Will this work?"

"Perfect," said Sherman. "You two ready?"

Brummet and Ruby nodded.

"I've never said this pleasantly, but let's go kidnapping."

Brummet chuckled, and Ruby would have laughed, but her life was twisting out of control, again.

They piled into the old sedan and Brummet eased the car into gear, drifting around the first bend before turning on the headlights. All three sat in a pall of silence, each tending to the garden of their own fears.

Sherman hoped the brothers were not home. If he was on thin ice with Reinhold before, this would surely send the powers that be over the edge. When that happened Barrios would surely enjoy pulling the trigger. That conclusion rested on a yet unproven relationship between the cops and the brothers who were likely following them. He needed more information.

Sherman leaned forward from the back seat to ask, "Random question for the locals. Do Jimmy and Dean know any cops?"

"Those yokels from the bar?" asked Brummet.

"The same."

"Those boys ain't exactly on the right side of the law. You know them better, right Ruby?"

"Not really my crowd, but I'm sure they all went to high school together."

"Who?"

"Jimmy, Dean, Barrios, Simpkins, Tanner. All those boys grew up together."

"No shit," mumbled Sherman.

"On different sides of the tracks now," added Ruby.

"Maybe, maybe not," said Sherman as he leaned back into the old bench seat with a growing sense of unease. A detective he was not, but the threads of a conspiracy were starting the show. Where Tillerman fit into the web was unclear, but if anyone could cobble together some clarity it was Ashley. He only hoped she was sober when they arrived. On second thought, maybe it would be easier to carry her if she passed out. People who kick and scream rarely go quietly. People with a liter of tequila might be more amenable.

CHAPTER ELEVEN

Illuminated like small streaking comets in the old sedan headlights, the rain was back and slowly gaining intensity. The three of them sat parked about a mile away as the crow flies from Ashley's apartment. Only a small, wooded field separated them. The soft pitter-patter had grown into a violent din, and they huddled almost intimately close to hear.

"Keep the car running, I'll meet you back here in thirty minutes," instructed Sherman.

Ruby was still hesitant about the plan, "What happens if the boys are there?"

"If they're asleep, the plan still stands."

"And if they're not?"

"I'll still meet you in thirty."

Brummet couldn't help but interject the obvious, "And if they wake up?"

"I don't plan on killing anyone if that is your concern."

"It wasn't," Brummet replied.

With a look that signaled their apprehension Ruby said, "Well, I am."

"Good," replied Sherman. "I'm glad you're still redeemable."

She scoffed, "I'll leave that to St. Peter."

Such comments secretly drove Sherman mad. He wanted to know more, but it was never an appropriate time to ask. Settling for a sigh, he pulled on the balaclava. The action took him back in time to cool and dry desert nights. Back to when the knock at the door was a breaching charge and terror came in many forms. From Iraq to Afghanistan, the last thing many people ever saw was his masked face. *Shabh* they said—ghosts. Both the unseen figures haunting the night and the souls they left behind. Arabic had a knack for dual meanings.

Tillerman's jacket was decent but no match for the torrential waves cascading down. Sherman's pants had soaked through within a hundred yards of the car. Chilly water slowly worked through his socks and into his shoes. It made a squishy sloshing sound as he ran. All of it felt familiar, hidden under the mask and the night. The only thing out of place was the rain and the landscape. Gone was the sand, replaced by oaks and knee-high autumn grass.

A mile didn't take Sherman long, seven or eight minutes with the weather. Through the rain he could barely make out the darkened outline of the apartment building. A few lights glittered through the mist, mostly on the porches and from the glow of a lone TV, but nothing in Ashley's unit. Sherman followed the dark all the way back to her sliding door. With twenty minutes to go there was no need to rush and he physically couldn't get any wetter.

Any noise coming from the inside was well and thoroughly dampened by the rain. Sherman stood there and waited. Time could be an asset or a liability. Speed and power could overwhelm even those expecting trouble, but with only nine shots and no backup, a breach scenario wasn't in the cards. Besides, Sherman wasn't much for grand entrances. Most people never saw him, never knew he was even there. A slow and hidden burn is the most dangerous.

Sherman reached out and gave the door handle a gentle push. It slid a few inches begrudgingly. Unlocked, like most doors in most small towns. Was it trust or ignorance? He'd never know, but after tonight Ashley needed better security.

With a quick move he was inside, the rain nothing but a

muted splatter on the roof. The hood was useless, and he let it fall back to his shoulders, but he kept the mask. Something told him anonymity was still needed.

The house was quiet. A dead silence only amplified by the constant rain. The couches were empty with no sign of the brothers, but evidence of their earlier presence still littered the place. Empty bottles of whisky and beer crowded the top of an already small coffee table. An empty pack of Lucky Strikes lay crumpled and half-buried in the couch cushions. Sherman wondered who the smoker was, but at this point everyone in the damn town seemed to prefer the brand. His clue was quickly losing any value.

Cheap carpet covered the floors in a wall-to-wall beige. Ascending the stairs, step by step, a slow tension churned his stomach. This wasn't Iraq, but the bullets were the same caliber. Stopping after each footfall, he listened for anything. A creak, a pop, a cough. Any sign of human presence. He could hear only the dull patter of rain and his own breath. It was the silence of nothingness or ambush, with the latter trying to trick you into assuming it was the former. Nothing was ringing his warning bells. It felt almost casual, like coming home after a night out.

At the top of the stairs a flash of light unraveled his sense of calm. Yellow beams splashed against the hallway walls, announcing visitors. Given the hour, Sherman doubted it was anything but trouble. He picked an open room and went inside. Tall stacks of boxes leaned against one wall. It was bare everywhere else, as if someone was moving in or out. Judging by the closet, it must have been a second bedroom.

Sherman grimaced as the front door opened. Whoever it was had a key or knew that it was unlocked. There was no hesitation, no juggling the knob. They just came in like they owned the place. Footsteps on the stairwell meant it was time to draw his pistol, which he did with mechanical precision. From the sounds, it was two people. They reached the landing and conferred with whispers.

"Remember, she doesn't get hurt."

"Not yet."

"Not your kin. Not your call."

"I don't work for you."

"Fuck off."

More footsteps down the hall. Then came a loud knocking, followed by someone fiddling with a locked door.

"God dammit Ashley, open up!"

There was a pause, like someone looking at the clock, before she answered, "Fuck you Rhett, it's four in the damn morning."

"Pa wants to see you."

"He can wait until it's light like a normal person."

"This isn't a request," retorted Rhett.

"I pay my own bills. He ain't got no right to bully me around."

"Don't start with this shit again. Kin is kin. You're coming with us and that's final."

"Make me," yelled Ashley.

"Dammit," grunted Rhett. "Johnny kick that fucking door down."

Sherman had heard enough. He holstered the pistol and tiptoed down the carpeted hall before they could do any damage to Ashley.

Johnny didn't hear him coming but felt a searing pain in his kidney as Sherman landed a brutal strike designed to incapacitate. A kick to the back of the knee put Johnny kneeling on the floor, still gasping for breath. Sherman grabbed the right side of the man's head and with a grunt smashed the other side through the drywall. Rhett was still yelling at Ashley but turned toward the sound of his friend's head crashing through the wall.

"What the fuck," Rhett gasped while looking at Sherman's masked face a few feet away.

Rhett went for the Beretta tucked into his waistband and cleared belt leather before Sherman caught his wrist with a judo chop, sending the gun thumping somewhere onto the darkened ground. From there it was over, all but the details. Rhett stood there too stunned to fight back, and Sherman landed a quick punch to the gut that doubled over the younger man. A knee to the face knocked Rhett out altogether, but Sherman kicked him in the ribs for spite. Maybe he broke them or maybe not, but at that point he didn't care. He looked for the Beretta, but it had disappeared under some closet door. Not worth the time, so he knocked on the door.

"What the fuck is going on out there? You better not be fucking with my apartment. I told you I'm not going," yelled Ashley.

"Ashley, this is Frank Sherman. Do you mind if we talk?"

"Wait, what?" she stammered at the swiftly changing circumstances. "Why are you in my house and what happened to Rhett?"

"Rhett stepped out for a while."

Ashley opened the door. Trust, it seemed, was transmutable. She had trusted Tillerman, who had implicitly trusted Sherman. Rhett's limp body lay contorted on the floor.

"Jesus Sherman, what did you do?"

No longer hiding his face, Sherman smiled, "Probably sticking my nose where it doesn't belong."

"Fuck, you'll be lucky if they don't cut it off."

"Let's hope not. I'm fond of it."

Ashley's brain was still playing catch up when she glimpsed the guy with his head stuck in her hallway wall. "And who is that?"

Sherman turned to look back, "Johnny, I presume."

Her mood darkened with the name. She grabbed onto the door frame for support her knees buckling.

"You know him?"

She nodded slowly, "He works for my father."

"In what capacity?"

There was no answer, Ashley just grabbed at her mouth

and ran to the bathroom. Tequila and surprise had taken hold. Retching sounds echoed down the hall.

If a brother lying unconscious on the floor did not bother her, then who was Johnny and why was he different? With a light kick, he pushed the man out of the wall and onto the floor, before emptying his pockets. What Sherman found set his teeth on edge. Two pairs of police grade zip cuffs, a bottle of morphine, pliers, garden shears and a small bag of what he guessed was meth.

"That's for me, isn't it?" asked Ashley, back from emptying her guts down the septic system.

"It would appear so."

She slid to the ground against the doorjamb with her arms crossed, "Fuck me."

"Who is he?"

"Bad news."

Sherman understood, he had seen it before. "We need to talk, just not here."

Ashley looked confused.

"They'll send someone else," added Sherman.

There was no response. She couldn't stop staring at the pliers on the floor.

"Come with me. Ruby and Brummet are waiting nearby."

The sound of her friend's name brought Ashley back from whatever void she had been looking into. "Yeah, okay," she said.

"Great. You might want a jacket and some boots."

There was a quizzical look on her face that Sherman recognized. He answered the unasked question, "I think it best if we left out the back and walked to the road."

Her blank stare meant the message still wasn't getting through. He elaborated, "Someone will see us leave together. Maybe the same someone who redesigned Ruby's jeep with an assault rifle."

A look of genuine concern flashed across her face, "You got shot at?"

"The car got shot. All we got was the message."

"Christ. Tillerman told me you were persistent, but what are you still doing here?"

Sherman shrugged, "My leave isn't over yet."

"Fine, fine. Let's go before they wake up."

"Follow me," said Sherman.

Nine minutes remained of his original thirty when they left. One mile back to the car. They would be late, hopefully not too late. Sherman rushed, but Ashley was in no shape to run. Even in the rain he could smell the tequila washing slowly out of her pores.

The old cab was still there, still running, when they exited the field. Sherman never dried and his clothes were dripping. Ashley felt just as wet but looked worse for wear. Hung-over, wet, cold, and those were only physical issues. Her shock and confusion regarding the night's events creased her brow.

Sherman held the door open for her, as if the small act of chivalry would matter, before sliding across the seat. From Ruby's gasp, it was clear the pair had not seen them coming.

After she recovered her breath Ruby said, "Hey hon."

"You're late," added Brummet.

"I know," said Sherman.

"Trouble?"

"Something like that."

"Who?" asked Ruby.

"Rhett and Johnny," answered Sherman.

Ruby sort of squinted, "Johnny?"

Ashley bobbed her head in acknowledgement.

"Crazy Johnny?"

Ashley nodded again.

"Care to fill the rest of us in?" asked Brummet.

Sherman answered for them, "He does the wet work."

Brummet asked, "How do you know that?"

"His kit. The tools he had. They aren't for pleasant conversation." Sherman turned to Ashley, "What did you do?"

"Hey, don't point the finger at her," said Ruby, jumping to her friend's defense.

"Stop acting like children," said Brummet. "Ashley needs to tell us what happened. Why would crazy Johnny be knocking on your door at four in the morning?"

Sherman wanted to thank the old man for his clear thinking. This was no time to let emotions dictate the conversation. It was only a matter of hours, maybe minutes, before someone else came looking for Ashley and found Rhett. Someone always came. It was inevitable. Curiosity, ego or something in between, it was inevitable.

Sherman squeezed Brummet's shoulder, and the old man nodded with an unspoken understanding. He dropped the car into gear, and they rumbled off into the rain-streaked night.

"Where are we going?" asked Ashley.

"Brummet's house. It's the only place we have left," answered Sherman.

Ruby took her turn at second guessing, "What happens if they find us?"

"Run or fight, but I don't think they realize it involves him, unless he told them. Brummet, did you spill the beans?"

Brummet chuckled, "Not yet. Their offer seemed low."

"I appreciate the gallows humor, but this shit is no longer funny," retorted Ashley. "I've already lost the man of my fucking dreams and now my kin wants to cut off a finger or two."

"You're thinking straight and that's good. Leverage is all you have. Something you did or you know. Until they have that figured out, you're worth more alive than dead."

"What the hell do I know?" Ashley asked.

"I'm not sure, but we need to figure it out soon. "Brummet, how is your coffee supply?"

"Stocked," came the reply.

"Good. Coffee first then story time."

Everyone agreed as Brummet continued to drive towards his house. Sherman kept an eye out the back window. He didn't see any lights, but he couldn't suppress the sense that someone was watching; that the darkness had eyes.

CHAPTER TWELVE

The kitchen smelled of French roast and late-stage bachelorhood. Dirty dishes crowded the sink, but none looked all that used. A few discarded plastic tops from microwave dinners littered the countertop. Sherman wondered if it was a glimpse of his own future. Adrift after the war, unable or unwilling to find solace in others. Doing whatever came his way as the days passed into years. At least he would have survived it all, but for what?

"Sorry for the mess. I wasn't exactly expecting company," said Brummet a bit sheepishly.

Ruby smiled at him, "Thanks for taking us in Herr Schindler."

"I really appreciate the help," added Ashley.

Brummet was practically blushing from the kind words and pretty faces, "Well I had to give up my canasta night."

"Sure, old man," quipped Sherman.

"Just saying," retorted Brummet.

"Noted," said Sherman before turning to Ashley, "What do we need to know?"

With wide eyes she took a deep breath, "Where do I start?"

"You left a few days before the crash, right?"

"Yeah, but I had no idea he was falling off the wagon."

Her body language, the way those shoulders hung as if racked by their own crushing grief or eyes that screamed for solace, looked truthful to Sherman. Truth, at least, of one's own making.

He could sense Ruby glancing his way, wanting to say something, but Sherman wasn't ready to go there yet.

"I believe you, truly, I do," he reassured her. "Why did you leave? Where did you go?"

Ashley smiled meekly, happy to have some positive words directed towards her, especially after a day spent with her brothers.

"I went to visit my mom. I go once a month." Memories came flooding back, and she cried. "Tillerman and I got into a fight the night before. That never happened, we never fought."

"But that night was different," prodded Sherman.

"Yeah, Tillerman didn't want me to go. He never said why, but I took it personally, like he was trying to control me."

"How did you leave it?" Asked Ruby.

Ashley sobbed more heavily, "He dropped it. Apologized. He was good like that."

"And you drove out to your mom's place?"

She nodded, "Tillerman dropped me off at the Crosscut that morning."

"Why the bar?"

"Pa lets me borrow the Mustang. My truck is a proper piece of shit and likes to overheat."

"So, you drove to the coast?"

"Yup, drove to mama's."

"Everything went okay?"

"She got kinda agitated, but that's just mama."

"Stuck around for a while and then headed back. I knew it was bad when Tanner showed up at my apartment unannounced."

"He told you?"

Ashley scoffed at the thought, "Couldn't tell just how much he was faking the sympathy, but he and Tillerman never really got along."

The time seemed right to fill in some gaps, so Sherman dug further, "Any idea why Tillerman went to talk to your dad?"

"He did what?"

"Friday, after you left. He wanted to talk to the old man."

Ashley shook her head in disbelief, "I have no idea."

"What did your brothers want today?"

Ashley chuckled, "To be there in my time of need, if you can believe that. Typically, the only thing my brothers have ever been there for is to try to sleep with my friends."

Ruby snorted in agreement, and the two friends shared a knowing look of disgust.

"What did they ask?" interjected Brummet.

"Um, asked about my trip. How it went. Where I stopped. Then Tanner started picking at me. He's good at finding those emotional scabs and making them bleed anew."

"Why did he care?" Asked Sherman.

"Wanted to know about my plans with Tillerman. Former plans, I guess."

Sherman nodded. He could see the wild howl of pain welling up behind her eyes. It was a rare hurt and he felt a momentary pang of jealousy that she had such an amazing connection with someone. But none of it was the smoking gun he so desperately wanted. Guilt, he needed a guilty party. Only then could he justify the coming carnage.

"Do you always take the Mustang?" Brummet asked.

Ashley nodded, "Why?"

Sherman wasn't sure what Brummet was fishing for, but he went with the current. "Tell me about your dad?"

"It's complicated."

"When is it not?"

"He's a hard man. Grew up here. It's in his blood. He left once, for the war, vowed never to leave again."

"That apply to his children as well?"

Her voice teemed with sarcastic truth, "The nail hath

been struck."

"My father had similar thoughts about me," added Brummet.

"But your mom left," said Ruby to Ashley.

"Of course! Who could live with that asshole forever? Thing is, he loved her, loved the family too, but after Ma left it all went downhill. Pa took to the bottle often. The boys bore some beatings, but he kept a special hate for me. Must have reminded him of Ma."

"But you couldn't leave," said Sherman.

"Tried once. Met a boy from Spartanville. We were in love or whatever resembles it at eighteen. Told him, 'Pa, I'm moving to the city.' Well, he took it about as bad as I thought. Broke both of my boyfriend's legs. He ended it that night in the hospital."

Ruby looked on like she recognized the character in her own story.

"What about the bar?" Sherman asked because there was more to the story than just a terrible father, but there was no way to find it without looking.

"Been in the family for years. Practically grew up in the place. Slinging booze is about the only marketable skill I got."

"What about the drugs?" It was a shot in the dark, but Sherman thought it made sense.

Ashley looked up a bit surprised, either like she was getting to that point or hadn't planned on including it. Then she sighed and continued as if there was no point in a lie. "Mostly small-time stuff. Pa grew some weed like everybody else around here. Usually just sold it to the bikers and the loggers once Uncle Sam opened up the forest again."

"And now?"

"Honestly, I don't know. I steer clear of that place whenever I can. I moved into my place at twenty-one. Paid my own bills, lived my life."

"But you borrow his car?" asked Sherman.

"Yeah, a year ago the ice thawed a bit. Pa apologized for

being such a shitty father, even reconnected me with Ma. But my truck ain't but a mile from breaking down. Part of his penance, Pa said, was letting me take the Mustang."

"No strings attached?"

Ashley shrugged, "I mean I take it to the car wash down there, but that is about the only string."

"Every time?" asked Sherman.

"Sure. Pa still has a stick up his ass, just a little less mean now."

"Same place?" asked Brummet.

"There ain't but one in town," answered Ruby.

Brummet glanced at Sherman to make sure they agreed. Sherman nodded. He had seen enough of the Wire to recognize a drop.

Brummet continued, "The car wash, is it full service? Or a do-it-yourself place?"

Reality sank further in with the weight of each subsequent question. Ashley felt exhausted, but she wasn't stupid.

"You've got to be fucking kidding me. He's using me as some drug mule."

Sherman shrugged, "Yes and no. You're surely being used. For what is still a mystery."

"What do you mean?" asked Ruby.

"Well, we do not know if you are exporting or importing."

"Or both," suggested Brummet.

"But you think I'm just another pawn," bemoaned Ashley. She was crestfallen, having convinced herself that this time would be different, that he changed, that he cared.

Sherman knew it would hurt her, but it needed to come out, "Yes and I think Tillerman found out and they killed him for it."

The idea was too far beyond what Ashley could mentally accept. Her wires crossed, and she retreated to some far corner of her mind. She tilted dangerously starboard and Brummet had to prevent her from hitting the ground.

Ruby looked furious, "Why did you say that? You knew she'd blame herself."

"I did," he said frankly, "but I need her motivated. Anger is better than sorrow right now."

"She needs time to grieve. Not to have her emotions toyed with."

"Accept then act."

Exasperated, Ruby asked, "What does that even mean?"

"She needs to know the truth, accept it for what it is and then take action. Tillerman's murder involved her family, that much I am sure. There is no future where that is not true."

"That is some cold-hearted military logic," replied Ruby. She was cradling her friend's head in her lap while Ashley stared absently at the ceiling.

Sherman kneeled next to them and said, "Don't take the bait, don't swallow the guilt. You didn't kill him."

Ashley sighed forcefully, "Might as well have pulled the trigger myself. I should have kept him away from them."

"Your family?"

She bit her lip and nodded, "I showed him off like some trophy, like proof that I could have a decent man." Sitting up, she looked coldly in Sherman's eyes. "I want to be there at the end."

"What are you talking about?" asked Ruby.

Ashley looked at her friend for a moment and then back at Sherman, "Tillerman told me the stories. Not just the glossy or funny ones. I know who you are, or at least who you were. I want to see the ashes fall."

The words hit Sherman square in the gut, and he had to sit down like a winded boxer. Never did he think Tillerman would share that story. Their bond must have been immense. Ruby and Brummet exchanged glances of confusion and worry over the sudden change.

"Frank, what is she talking about? You're freaking us out," said Ruby.

"Some things are better left unsaid," remarked

Brummet. The look on Sherman's face was one he recognized. A mile-deep stare into the past, mired in the pain, the hate and the blood.

Sherman blinked away the heavy sin of memory, "No, it's okay. She's talking about Tillerman's last mission. The reason he left the Army."

Brummet offered him a beer which he gratefully accepted before continuing, "I don't like to tell these stories. Hell, I don't like to dredge up the past. He must have really trusted you, loved you."

Ashley nodded. Silent streams of tears rolled slowly down her face.

"It was late September, near the end of the fighting season in Afghanistan. The Taliban were proving far more capable than the brass ever thought possible. Apparently, no one had ever read a history book about the fucking country. Anyway, we weren't winning spectacularly, and Iraq was heating up, which pulled away our resources."

He took a swig of beer and a deep breath, "One day intel got a tip. A top Taliban commander would attend his son's wedding three valleys away. Command authorized a surgical strike on his car. One missile, one car. They estimated collateral at under five."

Ruby cut in, "Five is low?"

"No, but in the grand scheme of that war five was low. We kept the team small, only four operators. The Blackhawk dropped us off the night before and we hiked fifteen miles to arrive before dawn. The spot was an amazing, wooded valley filled with an ancient cedar grove. Reminds me of this place a bit. Beautiful as it was the trees blocked our view, and we had to get closer than was prudent. By the time guests started arriving we were less than five hundred yards away."

Brummet squirmed at the memory of something similar, something sinister in the recesses of his mind.

"Most people just lump the country in with Iraq. All desert and Arabs. The ignorance of the masses with a war out of sight and mind. That place couldn't have been further from the sand and heat. We posted up near this little pristine creek with crisp icy water, hoping that would provide a simple route out afterward. The commander arrived last. The world waits for important people. Halfway through the ceremony our plan went to shit, just like all well-laid plans. Security was tight but sparse and they only had a few guys patrolling the area. It didn't matter. Three of them walked over to the stream for a drink. We got two without a sound, but the third got off a burst of rifle fire before Tillerman put him down."

"Exfil?" Asked Brummet.

"The nearest spot was five miles," answered Sherman.

"So, you ran," said Ruby.

"For all of a hundred yards. A guy named Fox caught a round in the thigh, shattering his femur. I figured we were close to fucked. Dragging him five miles would be tough, but we didn't have another option. Roberts was pulling dead weight when he went down. Took a round to the neck. Bled out by the time I got to him. I looked at Tillerman. There wasn't anything left to say. He called in the fire mission."

"Danger close," said Brummet, half caught up in an ancient but very much alive memory.

"Two hundred feet, maybe less. The drones came first, then the Warthogs, finally the Apaches. The rules of engagement were clear. Everyone was a combatant. Man, woman and child. We dropped enough explosives to start a firestorm."

Ruby closed her eyes, "Everyone burned, didn't they?"

Sherman nodded, "We survived in the creek, but no one else walked out alive. Ash fell like snowflakes on the first day of winter. Hundreds died, some innocent, some less."

"So do I get to see it?" asked Ashley.

A pall fell over Ruby's face, all horrified and crushed, upon realizing what her friend was asking. "You can't mean it, Ashley? "

"I'm sorry Ruby, but kin is no excuse. They took him

away from me."

"And you'll be just like them."

"She's right," said Sherman. "You don't want to walk this path. It's full of the worst human ugliness."

Ashley started sobbing, slowly curling herself inward into a compact ball, hoping to keep the world at bay. There was a certain beautiful simplicity to her love and her hate that Sherman recognized in himself. A binary world of all or nothing. He understood it, even if the world was anything but ones and zeroes. Everything was a sliding scale of dissonance.

"Look, I feel your hurt, your hate. I promise nothing, but I'm not leaving until the scales hang clear," he said.

Ashley nodded.

"If you want to cross over that line, I won't stop you, but know that it comes with a price. One you cannot get back."

She nodded again.

"Okay. One more question before we get some sleep."

"What?"

"Where does Johnny live?"

CHAPTER THIRTEEN

The damp blanket of night had lifted, leaving the woods steaming under an ever-rising sun. Sherman wanted to leave earlier, under the cover of darkness, but sleep was more important. Lose too much and your edge goes with it. So, he had slept on Brummet's floor, the pistol within constant reach. When he left, the gun stayed with the old man. Better it than nothing.

Ashley had filled in some sordid details about Johnny, none of which Sherman found surprising. Over the years he had met men of the same mold. Some wore uniforms, some did not. They came in many shapes and faces. Americans, Germans, Iraqis, Afghans and Iranians. Their allegiances lay with the Army, CIA, Taliban or ISIS. None of it mattered. Who or why they fought was irrelevant, but they all shared a singularly sadistic streak. The contents of his pockets had told Sherman that Johnny belonged to that abhorrent group. Ashley confirmed what he already knew. What had surprised him was how close Johnny lived, at least as the crow flies.

Byron Mills, like many rural towns constrained by geography, grew outward where the terrain allowed. Brummet lived in one of the few contiguous neighborhoods. There were sidewalks, and the streets connected, even if there was only one way in and one way out.

Johnny, however, lived up the mountain off some half-paved scar they called a road. It was a fifteen mile drive, but only three miles as the crow flies. A slight ridge provided the only separation between the small valleys. Sherman marveled at the proximity.

By ten that morning he stood at the crest of that ridge looking down towards a small yellow single-wide that Johnny called home. The pad got hewn from the hill with no regard for aesthetics and it gave the place an off-putting appearance, like a zit you can't help but notice.

A newer Ford truck sat out front, but Sherman wasn't sure the man was inside. No one had come or gone since he first laid eyes on the place, but that didn't mean much. Without knowing the original state of things, Sherman's gut said Johnny was home and sleeping off a concussion.

Trees masked most of his approach, but Sherman still crouched in thigh high grass, slogging his way to the back door. Those last few yards always racked his nerves, wondering if someone was watching or waiting. Leaving the pistol suddenly felt like a mistake, but Sherman pushed back the thought. Fear wouldn't bring the gun back into his hands. War had taught him to overturn such counterproductive thinking. It was self-defeating, and Sherman wasn't in the habit of losing.

The property was littered with the results of careless or carefree ownership. No neighbors, no HOAs and no stigma or shame for how you left things. A pile of trash or unfinished projects? No one gave a shit. Privacy mattered, junk did not.

From what Ashley had told him a few hours earlier, the place was likely a rental. Johnny hadn't been in town for long. The ladies couldn't agree if it was nine months or a year. Brummet didn't know the man well, but his occasional interaction forged an impression of an out-of-towner working some well-paid job. The fancy truck pointed towards oil money, but those jobs had fizzled with the drop in crude prices. In fact, none of the three knew what the man did for employment. Ashley said he worked for her dad, but the details of that arrangement were murky. Ruby has assumed Johnny worked with the loggers, basing her theory on a few glances from a bar stool at the Crosscut.

Sherman didn't know who Johnny worked for, at least not yet, but he knew what he did. Having been in the business of violence for so long, Sherman could spot those of the same persuasion and inclination. From the moment he emptied Johnny's pockets, he had known all he needed to about the man. Every substantial organization has someone like Johnny on the payroll. They're interchangeably called goons, lawyers, soldiers, enforcers, sicarios or fixers. Invariably they arrive to correct a mess, or to ensure that one does not occur. They speak the language of threats and lawsuits or result to force when things get unruly. Sherman had seen the means to that mess in Iraq and it never ended pleasantly. Contractors dropping innocent civilians, innocent civilians stringing up contractors from bridges.

As Sherman gave the man more thought the similarities grew apace. There was something out of place about Johnny. Lots of people move to rural towns. Some come from cities and bring a certain impatient temperament with them, but they learn to moderate their expectations with time. People adjust, at least the ones that call the place home. Visitors chafed at the inconveniences, the limited selections and narrow attitudes. Brummet once saw Johnny arguing with the market owner over quinoa. Incensed that the storekeeper didn't carry the grain, let alone know what it was, Johnny nearly punched the poor man. Only someone riding a wave of impermanence would be so rash.

Cardboard or thick paint covered the windows. Poor man curtains for someone working late into the night. Duct Tape and a box worked better than any fancy blackout curtains. A cheap and easy solution, but it came with a price. No one could see out.

Visibility aside, entering the house was risky. If Johnny

was inside, which Sherman's gut said was true, opening the door and streaming in light would surely invite a nasty response. Going from light to dark would also wreck his vision and put Sherman on the defensive as it adjusted.

"Fuck that," thought Sherman aloud. He needed to get Johnny outside.

It only took a glance at the fancy, expensive truck sitting in the driveway. Sherman checked the front door just in case. It was unlocked, and he chuckled to himself that even the bad guys were complacent. The truck was pricey and strengthened his plan.

With a heave, Sherman kicked the driver side door hard enough to imprint his boot in the sheet metal. On cue the truck responded with a trill beeping but no alarm. He waited and listened for a minute but couldn't hear anyone stirring inside. On his second attempt, when foot met door, an ear-piercing wall of sound got triggered. Sherman hated it like every other alarm because they made his life more complicated, but this was an exception.

From inside, Sherman could hear a person scrambling to find the keys while knocking over everything else. The alarm beeped off. A minute passed, just enough time for Johnny to lay back down, then Sherman kicked the truck again. An obscenity laced tirade grew with intensity as the front door opened. It amplified the blaring alarm. Sherman ducked around the corner and waited.

"I'll fucking kill you kids," yelled Johnny as he came out of the single-wide. Wearing nothing but black silk boxers, he had a bag of frozen vegetables pressed against his head with one hand and Glock-19 in the other. A pair of dog tags rattled around his neck like some badge of honor. He clicked the button again, stopping the nausea inducing noise about the same time he saw boot prints on the truck door. A quizzical look passed across his face. One fleeting moment of disbelief that someone would mess with a man such as himself. That moment ended with fear filling the gap. A tingling climbing up his neck. Johnny tried to raise the pistol up in time, but it was too late. Sherman caught him square in the face with a rough cut 2x4 he found leaning against the house. The man went down with a hollow thud.

Grabbing him by the wrists, Sherman hauled Johnny back inside, and gratefully picked up the gun. With a roll of duct tape he found much too easily, Sherman adhered Johnny to a kitchen chair. Blood from his broken nose slowly pooled in his lap, the black silk boxers glistening more with each drop.

CHAPTER FOURTEEN

"Captain, we found something," said the Major with monotone rigidity. No mention of the passing days. He had the intel now and was relaying nothing more.

"Major, your timing is impeccable."

A well-rehearsed chin scratching was audible on the other end before the major replied, "Out with it."

Sherman held up Johnny's dog tags, slowly turning them over again and again, "I've recently become acquainted with someone I'd like to know more about."

The Major grunted, "Name and rank?"

"Johnny Schanker, Specialist Third Class."

"Wait one," answered the Major. His usual gruffness was still very much intact, but he was also breaking the law and that said more about the man's loyalty that any tone of voice.

Sherman rifled through drawers as he waited for the Major. There wasn't much for furniture in the house, a fact which did not surprise him in the least. The place was a dump. Some cheap rental for those living a hard-edged life. A no frills existence where stainless steel and marble were not words used to describe a kitchen, but a rock yard. Despite his carelessness in walking out of the house earlier, Johnny left nothing lying around, at least nothing incriminating.

The porn collection strewn about the TV stand said

enough for Sherman to understand the man's tastes veered towards the edge of acceptability. Young, incredibly young, women being humiliated and subjugated was the choice du jour. Nothing illegal, but extreme.

Johnny's wardrobe also edged towards some stereotype. Black leather jacket, fancy shirts and gold chains. Sherman shook his head in dismay.

"Tony fucking Soprano."

Despite searching through what minimal storage existed, the proof he sought was still missing, but he knew it was close. A man like Johnny couldn't stand to have it far away. Johnny needed to feel it and the fear it could generate. That got him off and brought out that trembling adolescent joy.

The Major still hadn't confirmed when Sherman started looking beyond the obvious. His favorite place was vents, but the single-wide didn't have any, just a window AC unit and some space heaters. The bedroom, with its silk sheets and king-sized bed, seemed like the place to start. It just had one of those cringe inducing feelings about it. Ashley had relayed some rather salacious accusations about Johnny a few hours earlier and the more time Sherman spent in the house the stronger the bell of truth rang.

Normally the details didn't bother him too much. Facts describing the past held little meaning, and he had seen plenty of gruesome acts of human ingenuity, but Sherman couldn't help but feel his indignation rise with Ashley's words. He had committed nothing to memory, but the salient details involved Johnny, a thirteen-year-old girl and what any other police force in the country would classify as rape. Lucky for Johnny the Sheriff was as crooked as the river. No charges got filed, and the family left town after their car mysteriously burned to the frame in their front yard. Ashley was unclear on the culpability for the intimidation, but the original sin was enough to warrant a rough-cut timber to the face.

As Sherman recalled the sound of Johnny's nose breaking with unconcerned mirth, the image of the pine two-by-four led him into the closet. The type of wood covered the room, and as he pressed against one wall; it gave an audible pop.

"Figures," he said aloud.

Removing the panel revealed those secrets Johnny took pains to keep in the dark. Neatly rolled up was an antique leather surgical kit. It served the darker purpose of organizing the tools of a brutal trade. A modern-day Torquemada.

"Captain," interrupted the Major.

Sherman was still looking at the shimmering stainless steel blades and heavy-duty pliers, "Go ahead, sir."

"Specialist Schanker did two tours with the 327th MP battalion in Iraq. Dishonorable discharge for conduct unbecoming. Apparently, the guy had a penchant for cruelty."

"I'm getting that feeling," interjected Sherman,

The Major grunted in understanding, "Did a spell contracting in Afghanistan a few years back. After that it looks like he only worked stateside."

"Thanks Major. What did you find out about the LT?

There was a pause and a rustle of paper, "Tillerman sent a text the night he died."

"To whom?" asked Sherman with a measure of surprise.

"Undeliverable number."

Sherman squinted and rubbed the bridge of his nose, "What number?"

The Major related all ten digits while Sherman organized them like Scrabble tiles in his mind.

"That's one off from my number."

The Major said nothing as he already knew.

"What did it say?"

"Spruce," answered the Major.

Sherman was bewildered, "Spruce?"

"Confirmed."

"Never straightforward with him was it," reminisced Sherman.

"Do you know what he meant?"

"Not yet," answered Sherman.

"Good hunting then Captain."

"Thanks again, Major."

"Don't thank me yet. I will need you back soon. There is a situation brewing in West Africa."

"How long do I have?"

"Three, maybe four days," came the Major's reply.

"Understood. I'll tie up my loose ends by then."

The Major ended the call without replying.

From the moment Barrios and Simpkins stepped through the front door, time was not on his side. Reinhold's probate ultimatum played back in Sherman's mind. That was twenty-four hours away, which meant he might have to deal with Byron Mills' finest before too long. With duty calling in the form of some shit storm on another continent, Sherman could feel things constricting. At least the Major had given him some time, which was better than no time. Three days was enough to create some closure, even if it was only a row of shallow graves.

Sherman fished out the rest of Johnny's dirty secrets. There was a collection of snuff porn, some adolescent looking jewelry and a brick of cash. The porn didn't raise an eyebrow even if it raised the stakes, but the jewelry made him sigh.

Holding the small collection of lockets and bracelets made him queasy, "Trophies. You twisted bastard."

The glinting gold was a reminder of Johnny's violent conquests over girls with no power to fight back. He would enjoy hurting the man. Letting Johnny leave a whole person never crossed his mind. As for the cash, well that answer came as a byproduct of everything else.

Dousing Johnny with a bucket of ice water brought him out of his blissful unconsciousness and back into a world of pain and shrinking horizons. Johnny looked down at his hands and feet, at the duct tape adhering his skin to the kitchen chair, and knew genuine fear for the first time. A heart sinking feeling of despair. That was before he saw the instruments neatly displayed on the table or fully realized there was a man standing behind him.

"What do you want?" yelled Johnny, his voice overloaded with fear.

"Nothing," said Sherman.

"Fuck off."

Johnny wasn't a weak man, but none of that mattered. He knew it. Sherman knew it. No one beats the system or outlasts the pain. Eventually those who suffer concede. It may be the truth or a convenient lie. What they give up doesn't matter to the tortured, it is only a means to stop the pain. That's the dirty little secret about torture. It always works but rarely succeeds.

Sherman pulled up a chair and looked closely at the man, bound and bloody. "Look Specialist, let's cut the crap. You have information, and I have power. This isn't your first rodeo. You know how this can go."

Johnny smiled. The thought of pain for no end had rattled his cage. This was different, just the common banality of suffering for information.

"You stink of authority. Captain or Major?"

Sherman nodded at the observations, "Not bad. I'm Captain Sherman."

"MP?"

"They looking for you? Or should they be?"

Johnny's eyes narrowed, "Just some Captain then. Who you with?"

"JSOC. Task Force Orange."

His pupils contracted and Johnny lost what little color he still had. "A fucking ghost."

Sherman nodded, "Now, let's get back to our question and answer routine. I ask, you answer."

"You gonna leave me breathing afterwards?"

"No guarantees," answered Sherman, "but I didn't come here to kill you."

"Just torture," sneered Johnny.

"Something like that."

Johnny spat out a wad of congealed blood on the floor, "And if I refuse?"

The thick industrial pliers were already in Sherman's hand and Johnny barely saw a flash before a searing pain ate up his vision and sent his ears ringing. Without bragging or rubbing it in, Sherman held up the fingernail as the factual answer to the question just asked. Tears streamed down Johnny's face and snot was trying to escape the bloody mess inside his nose. With short, shallow breaths he managed a weak nod.

"Good. Let's start with an easy one. Who do you work for?"

The look on the Specialist's face suggested that he too was contemplating the very question. "The old man."

Ambiguity shaded the answer and there was a moment of internal debate before Sherman slammed a ball-peen hammer onto Johnny's knuckles. The handle was painted a cheery blue and the entire thing felt heavy. With his wrists taped to the chair there was nowhere to hide, nothing to do but watch in expectant horror at the pain to come.

Fighting to get out a word through the haze, Johnny muttered, "I'm telling the truth." It was a plaintive plea, like that of a child.

"I don't doubt the age or the gender but you're obscuring the facts. Which old man do you mean? And weigh your words carefully."

Johnny shook his head and sobbed. He was afraid of them, but Sherman didn't give a damn about him or them.

"Last chance to clarify, Specialist," said Sherman as he raised the hammer again.

"Wait, wait, I'll tell you. Jesus Christ, just hold on," Johnny pleaded.

Lowering the hammer, Sherman looked the man in his eyes, "No more fucking about."

"Clarence Stockwood, I work for Clarence Stockwood." Johnny exhaled deeply after he spoke, like somehow getting that off his chest would stop the pain.

The name meant nothing to Sherman, and he held up his hands in mock confusion, "Care to elaborate?"

"The biggest meth distributor in Northern California," clarified Johnny with exasperation.

"Now we're getting somewhere," Sherman smiled, "What business does Clarence have in Byron Mills?"

Johnny snorted bloody snot bubbles at the obvious answer but was soon screaming again as Sherman broke a thumb with the hammer.

"Don't be a smart ass. I want specifics," said Sherman with a menacing clarity.

Tears were still streaming down the Specialist's face as he answered, "They're cooking here. Clarence partnered up with old man Thorne. Clarence does the cooking, Dell provides the land, security, and transportation."

"Transportation? How?"

"I don't know, I swear. I just watch the cooks," said Johnny.

"Make sure the poison is pure?" Mocked Sherman.

"Exactly. Look, I have nothing to do with them," Johnny added.

The comment piqued Sherman's interest, "Them?"

"Dell's family," replied Johnny.

"Why do you think I care about them?"

Johnny shifted about, "You were at Ashley's house, right?"

Maybe he didn't realize it or he was just stupid, but Johnny was talking himself towards a dark hole. "Specialist, I'm going to give you one chance to come clean. You know why I'm here. You tell. You live."

"Look man," said Johnny emphatically, "I had nothing to do with it. Nobody told me shit ahead of time."

Sherman couldn't help but believe him, "What about after?"

"Simpkins called me the next day, joking about almost fucking up one of the LT's friends."

The thought of that half-wit coming close to landing a punch made Sherman laugh with anger, "I'm sure he did. And you heard nothing else? No bragging?"

Johnny shook his head slowly but emphatically.

Some kernel of truth sparkled in his eyes, and Sherman thought better of inducing more harm. "Fine, but what were you doing at Ashley's house?"

"Dell asked me to go. Wanted to scare her, shake her up a bit I guess."

"Why?"

Johnny shrugged, "Didn't say, and I didn't ask."

Whatever truth was told, the sum felt light. The brick of cash spoke volumes about Johnny's relative position of power in this twisted tale. Sherman could feel the Specialist was selling himself short but didn't think he pulled serious weight. Fancy clothes and a fancy truck were the trappings of power, but not the genuine thing. Where did that leave Johnny on Sherman's shit list? Not remarkably high, but well within reach, and he just had two more questions to ask.

"Specialist, hypothetical question, since you weren't involved," said Sherman. "Who killed my friend?"

With a pathetic and beaten shrug Johnny answered, "I don't know, that's not my cup of tea."

Sherman let the lie percolate. The jewelry shone a blazingly bright light of Johnny's true nature. No one could hide from that past and those proclivities. But he wanted Johnny to think, just perhaps, he had beaten the system. It didn't last long.

Without looking away, Sherman grabbed a pair of garden shears sitting on the table. Nice German steel, ergo-friendly grip. Only the best for Johnny.

The Specialist saw the metallic gleam and instantly tried to talk his way out. "I swear, swear to God, I ain't got no idea who killed him. Please. Please."

His protests fell on deaf ears, Sherman had stopped listening. With a vice like grip he grabbed Johnny's right pinkie finger and slid it into the cruelly smiling shears. Johnny was screaming, sobbing, shaking; anything to stop what was unfolding. A runaway train in the Rockies would have been easier to stop.

The bone crunched with a dry crack reminiscent of a chicken wing and far easier than Sherman had expected. Blood came profusely at first but slowed, as did Johnny's moans. The pain was too much and his head lolled unconsciously to the side.

Sherman slapped him awake once the initial shock had worn off. Muttering and sputtering, the once cocky man could barely speak. His mind reeled against the damage; the flood of pain triggered neurons.

Pinching his cheeks, Sherman asked Johnny once more, "Who killed my friend?"

"I don't know, I don't know," Johnny whimpered.

Sherman grabbed the shears again.

"Barrios," sobbed the broken man.

Sherman knew it wasn't the truth. He knew that Johnny would have said any name, even his own mother's. Despite that, he found a strange satisfaction in hearing the deputy's name. A justification for that to come.

"One last question, Johnny. How old were those girls?"

With a heavy sigh Johnny responded, "What girls?"

This time Sherman didn't hesitate or wait for contrition. He pulled the trigger on the Glock and, with a damp clattering, sent bits of Johnny's skull ricocheting off the wall. For a small caliber, the 9mm made an awfully large noise in the acoustically cramped single wide.

It was a scene worthy of some B-rated horror movie, but very much real. Pulling the trigger didn't bother Sherman. That solemn bit of humanity was long gone, even if the torture was a bitter pill to swallow. He wasn't proud of anything he had done, but there was something especially disappointing about how things had gone down, even if it felt inevitable. Sherman felt a little less whole because of it. Even though he lived in a giant gray area of society,

Sherman was acutely aware when he crossed a personal line,

Cordite and blood overwhelmed the stench of stale beer that had previously filled the house. There was such a finality to those smells. It was an all too familiar reminder of actions and outcomes that unleashed the past. He had spent so much time enveloped by those odors he wondered if they would ever wash off.

Covering his tracks didn't seem all that important. Anyone who knew the score would surely point a finger at him, but Sherman knew the value of plausible deniability. The recently deceased Specialist had an extensive list of enemies, many of whom were family members of those poor girls unlucky enough to have crossed his path.

In the closet Sherman found two pre-cut pieces of black plastic sheeting just big enough for a body. Part of Johnny's sadistic tool kit. He wrapped up the corpse, placing the jewelry in his pockets as evidence, before sealing the ungodly package with duct tape. Unceremoniously, Sherman deposited the body in the back of the truck, grabbed the cash and a box of 9mm ammo he found next to the cereal boxes. He locked the door on his way out and, almost as an afterthought, threw the bloody 2x4 down the hill.

CHAPTER FIFTEEN

As a valley town built upon the perpendicular 'T', there was only one four-way stop in Byron Mills. The junction occurred on the drive to Upper Mill Road close to town. It so happened that there were two ways to get there. One traveled a relatively flat path, the other traversed more vertically and directly from the main road. Where Sherman came to a stop, on the direct approach, he would make a right to head up the road, following the same direction of travel Tillerman had supposedly made on that night. Straight was an option, it being a four-way stop, but that ended not far away at the town cemetery. Sherman idled for a moment in the dead man's truck and considered if his friend would want to be buried there in some small plot beneath an oak tree. Such a thought or consideration had not previously crossed his mind. Consumed as he was by a rather self-centered path of vengeance. Maybe Tillerman had a will, or perhaps probate would decide.

Considering the potential last wishes of his only genuine friend, it took Sherman a moment to notice the giant red truck approaching from his left.

"Just my luck," muttered Sherman, thinking of the corpse rolling around the truck bed as he watched the dually roll to a stop.

Barrios turned right and pulled his pompously oversized truck next to Johnny's recently confiscated Ford of similar size and self-importance. Rolling down the window, the deputy leaned out and brought his hand up to his face, mimicking a phone. Johnny's tinted windows prevented him from seeing the identity of the driver, let alone the Glock pointed squarely at his head.

The encounter was momentary. Sherman gunned the Ford into the turn, and Barrios continued on his way to town. Only after they parted did Sherman regret not pulling the trigger. A missed opportunity to cross off a name while blaming it on Johnny with his conspicuous truck. Ultimately, such an outcome would have been too easy for Barrios. Sherman wanted the deputy to suffer and reveal the next link in the chain.

There was a certain animal satisfaction in driving past the now infamous tree in Johnny's truck with the lifeless scumbag wrapped in plastic sheeting. Karma still existed amongst the barren patches of violence.

As the road rose into the surrounding mountains, so too did the drop. Sherman drove until his dust obscured all the houses and the road seemed to challenge gravity itself. At a small cut-out he turned the truck around and backed up to the cliff's edge where the tailgate would hang into the space below. With a heave he rolled Johnny out of the truck and for a moment the body seemed to float in the air before careening down the embankment, end over bloody end. Sherman knew better than to call it a truism, but brutality begets brutality. Such actions continue well past the tipping point of no return where the fires you ignited burn the brightest.

Johnny saw it at the end. At least that was Sherman's hope. What he would see at the end remained a mystery, but he doubted it would come much differently than Johnny or Tillerman. A life spent on the coattails of death doesn't end any other way.

The twists and turns of the drive back brought Sherman a certain bit of clarity that interminable stretches of open road do not. The mind wanders across the yellow lines of straight nothingness into a petty world of thoughtless slumber. Sharp turns jerk the mind screaming into the present. Sherman existed in that world. The moment, the now.

Johnny had been useful in pointing out an alliance, but Sherman knew drugs were involved. There was no surprise in learning the drug of choice was meth. Northern California was awash in the poison, the 'Meth-Frontier' they called it.

Before catching a bullet, Johnny had mentioned that the land leased for cooking was up near the logging operation. With nowhere else to start, it seemed like the obvious next step. It tied into his nagging suspicion about the fire road. Sherman felt convinced they took Tillerman up into those mountains. The thought of sneaking around in the woods brought a smile to his soul. After all that unfolded that morning, the only question left for Sherman was how he would visit Barrios. Sooner felt better, but he had a feeling the opportunity would lag.

Parking the truck out front of Brummett's house was out of the question and well past suicidal. Operational discipline was what the army drilled into him until it was his primary mode of thought. Mistakes will get you killed; stupid mistakes will get everyone killed. Sherman drove around the neighborhood until he found a 'For Sale' sign. The house was a single level ranch with a rear facing garage that hid the truck from prying eyes on the street. Stationary assets made for easy ambushes.

Looping back was easy enough and Sherman soon hopped over the fence into Brummett's backyard. He approached the sliding glass door slowly and knocked loudly. The blinds behind were drawn, and he took a step back to be more visible. Sounds of friendly banter suddenly stopped, and Sherman could sense the barrel of a gun pointed his direction. A window blind to his left cracked open momentarily before Ruby stepped out with a steaming cup of coffee in hand. It had only been two hours since he left, but the air felt different.

"Did you find him?" asked Ruby as she sipped her coffee.

Sherman motioned towards the door, and they stepped inside. Brummet and Ashley smiled, but the tension bent their faces.

"Well?" inquired Ruby, her face was pensive with his silence.

Sherman placed the Glock on the kitchen table, "Yeah, I found him."

Brummet glanced down at the pistol, "How did you leave him?"

Ashley, who was studying his eyes, responded first, "I think we all know how it ended."

He nodded and the four of them stood in reflective silence as they each processed the knowledge that Sherman had murdered a man. Three of them also grappled with the realization that Johnny would not be the last to die. Sherman had long ago shed any such doubts. From the moment Barrios walked through that door dripping swagger, Sherman knew that Tillerman was only the first of many.

"Good riddance," said Brummet, finally breaking their collective silence.

Even Ruby seemed to agree. Despite her flirtations with hard-edged men, she had a soft heart that seemed out of place.

"What did he say?" Ashley asked.

Ruby looked perplexed, "Why would he say anything?"

Ashley turned to her friend with a cold stare that Ruby shrank from as she connected the dots.

Sherman let things sink in before replying, "Your dad is working with Clarence Stockwood. Does that name mean anything to you?"

Ashley shrugged, but Brummet knew the name and spoke up, "Meth king of the north."

Ruby cast him a sideways glance, "How do you know that?"

"I hear things," came his cryptic reply.

Ruby glared at him with mock intensity.

"Johnny oversaw the cook. Your dad arranged transportation," added Sherman.

Ashley looked worried, "The Mustang?"

Sherman shook his head. "I doubt it had drugs. Best guess is money." He tossed the brick of cash onto the table.

Ruby gasped, "Jesus, how much is in there? Wait, did that come from Johnny?"

"Yup. Ten grand. Newly minted."

Brummet thought out loud, saying what everyone else was thinking, "We should check that car."

They had no lawful authority. Burden of proof and innocent until proven guilty were foreign concepts. Under the rules of war, actions defined an enemy. Picking up a gun or posing a threat justified lethal action. From what Sherman could tell, just about everyone he ran into met those criteria.

Rife with hesitancy, Ashley asked, "What did he say about Tillerman?"

"Denied any involvement but pointed the finger at Deputy Barrios."

Ruby shook her head with rigorous seriousness, "Why did you kill him then? If he wasn't involved, why do it?"

He elaborated, "Johnny's dead not for any grievance I had, but for the very sins you suspected." They locked eyes for a moment and Sherman thought he saw a flash of understanding for his defense of seemingly indefensible.

A deep sigh leaped from Ashley's chest, "So the rumors were true."

"I found things that no man should rightfully have." The image of the jewelry, the cruel mementos, were fresh in his mind.

"Good riddance," added Brummet.

"I agree," voiced Ashley, "but why was he in my house?"

"Your dad sent him over to rattle your cage," Sherman answered.

"Thanks pops, mission fucking accomplished. Did he say why my cage needed rattling?"

Sherman shook his head.

Ashley looked distraught, "What the…" she stammered. "Why? I don't even know what the hell is going on."

"Your family disagrees," added Brummet.

Ruby chimed in, "Those boys know something. Tanner quizzing you like that, it ain't normal."

Ashley spoke after a brief pause, "You think they did it, right Frank?"

"I can't say for certain, but my gut says yes."

"And you trust that enough to act?" she replied.

The question was fair enough. Their world was not contingent on instinct alone. Life didn't hinge on a misplaced rock or the sounds of silence. Sherman roamed the inhospitable path and his brain was fine-tuned, not to the niceties of social cues, but the tiniest details of that which did not belong. Broken branches, upturned dirt and unknown shadows imbued his surroundings with a menace that had kept him alive far longer than statistics allowed. Those well-worn mental pathways were working to unravel an answer for a different ball of yarn, and it kept flashing back to the text.

"We have one more thing to go on," said Sherman after weighing whether to share. "A source in the army tracked down Tillerman's last text."

Ashley said nothing but looked hopeful and he felt bad it came to him and not her.

"Cut the suspense," said Brummet.

"He tried to send it to me but got the numbers wrong. It just said 'Spruce'."

"That mean something to you?" asked Ruby.

"Not particularly," answered Sherman.

"Shit," said Ashley shaking her head. "There's a blue spruce grove on my daddy's land, the only one in town. I told Tillerman about it not too long ago." She scoffed a bit and added, "Some LA types wanted some rustic looking chairs. Probably thought the wood would be blue."

"Means nothing," said Ruby.

"Not yet," snorted Ashley.

"Can you point to it on the map?" Asked Sherman.

"No, but I can take you there," she answered.

Involving Ashley any further was a terrible idea, despite her commitments to the contrary. Sherman knew it but couldn't tell her so. She wanted and deserved closure as much as he did, but it wasn't the only reason he was considering her offer. Unlike neatly demarcated cities, rural America rambles. Property lines get hazy and topology is merely a fancy word. Sherman didn't doubt his ability to find the grove, but time was limited and rural towns contained sizeable spaces.

"Alright," said Sherman to everyone's surprise.

Brummet interjected but stopped short, knowing the futility of his intent. Instead he merely asked, "Do you need the car?"

"No, we're good," replied Sherman before turning back to Ashley, "How far once we park?"

"Thirty minutes, maybe more."

The old clock hanging over the stove pointed towards early afternoon and Sherman stared contemplatively at its slowly turning hands. "Ruby," he finally asked, "you working tonight?"

"Uh," she stammered, "I guess I'm on the schedule but..."

Sherman cut her off, "Keep up appearances. Don't let them know anything has changed."

"Not a chance," she replied.

"They're looking for Ashley. You don't show up at the bar, well, it doesn't take a detective to make that leap."

Ruby shook her head, "Fine, I can just drink away the night."

"Brummet will keep a stool warm too."

"Will I?" replied the old man.

Sherman peeled off a hundred from Johnny's stack of

cash and handed it over, "Order something expensive."

Brummet raised his jacket pocket containing the Russian pistol with a questioning look on his face.

"Your call," said Sherman.

The old man sighed with a shrug and wandered off to help Ashley, who was rummaging through the kitchen.

"Frank, I don't like where this is heading," said Ruby in a gloomy voice. It was the first time they had talked alone since the previous night. "I'm worried for her. Shit, I'm worried for all of us."

"Me too," he replied.

"Then why not help her run? That stack of cash would start a fresh life."

A grin creased the corners of his mouth, "Forgive my ignorance, but she doesn't seem like the running type."

Ruby sighed, "We're not all cut out for that life."

The quip raised his eyebrows with intrigue and he looked at her wanting more. Nothing came. "Look," he finally said, "I'll talk to her on the ride up. There are always choices, I just get the sense she has already made hers."

"Thanks Frank. Death already had its fill with my life. I don't care to see more."

Whatever ghosts rattled around her past seemed closer to the surface than he had yet seen, "You want to talk about it?"

A tired smile crept across her face, "Maybe another time. Look, I know it ain't over, just take care."

Sherman slid the cash her way, "There are always choices."

Ruby tapped her fingers nervously against the table in a concerted effort, "Like I said, I've done enough running for now."

He nodded and pulled the stack of bills back, "Let me know if there is something else you need."

For a woman grown unaccustomed to such civility, it was a tender offer, and it almost made her blush.

Done rummaging in the kitchen, Ashley asked, "We

going?"

"Grab your jacket. Brummet, you have a flashlight?"

The old man already had it in his hand, "Took some looking."

Sherman smiled as he tucked the old Maglite into his pocket, "Alright then." He motioned toward the back door, but Ashley looked confused.

"It's too far to walk," she said.

"I know."

Her eyes narrowed, "You took Johnny's truck?"

"No one will think twice about seeing his truck if he worked up there," said Sherman.

"Until they come knocking on the door. How you gonna explain that one?"

Sherman shrugged, "Politely."

Ashley followed him over the fence, still shaking her head at the plan, but carrying an abiding feeling that she couldn't turn back.

CHAPTER SIXTEEN

"I told Ruby I'd offer you a way out," Sherman said after they'd been driving for a few minutes.

He turned out of the small suburb Brummet called home and onto the central road. An old, dilapidated building on the corner announced itself as a general store. The forty-year-old Camel ad out front reinforced its age. Despite the crumbling asphalt, weathered red paint and long since removed gas pumps, the place was buzzing with customers. Chain link fencing cordoned off a portion of the parking lot and a hand-painted sign advertised secure storage. As if that was a concern.

"I figured she would say something," Ashley said as she stared absently at the passing store like it was any other scenery made redundant with time. Turning her gaze back to Sherman, she added, "What do you think?"

"Same as I told her. There are always choices."

"You and Tillerman continually trumpeted choice. Don't you ever feel trapped, like there is only one path?"

He nodded, "Sure, but that just means all your options suck. Variety still exists even in the deepest of shit."

"Do I detect a hint of optimism, Frank?"

"Just pragmatism."

Ashley laughed a little. It was self-assured and sweetly full of life. Unabashed, just like Tillerman. Watching her exuberance filled Sherman with a touch of apologetic envy for the life his friend had made.

"Is that a no on the escape plan?" he added.

She scoffed and let out a lengthy sigh, "No. Everybody here is running from something, even the ones that never left."

Long shadows of the past haunt rural towns. Something about all that space left room for harsh comparisons. The lines were so crisply defined. Cities offered no such spotlight, just blotchy patches muddled with overlapping shades of gray. Byron Mill had plenty of sun, but most people kept their eyes off the ground for fear of glimpsing their own darkness.

He couldn't help but ask, "Ruby too?"

"Not my story to tell," answered Ashley like Brummet before her.

"Worth a shot," he mused.

They headed back towards the bar, but Sherman's knowledge ended there. She had said to head up but clarified nothing else. Up was enough to get them started. Upstream, uphill; it was all the same.

Silence filled the truck like a calm river, free of anger or awkwardness, like an old friend it hummed to itself. The town passed by in waves. First the general store in its eclectic glory, then came the mill looming large with its stone edifice and venerable timbers. A smattering of businesses clumped together on the west side of a tiny hill that divided the commercial strip in two. The town wasn't big enough for competition save for two movie rental stores clinging to life on the back of slow rural internet speeds.

"Who lives on the hill?" Sherman asked while glancing up. A large white columned portico loomed over the circular driveway in some vain attempt at self-importance.

"New old money," answered Ashley rather cryptically.

He raised his eyebrows with intrigue.

"Daddy left the son his company. Construction. The boy likes fancy things."

"Money doesn't buy taste," added Sherman after seeing

the oversized Corinthian columns.

"Sure don't. They make a show of getting a new car every few months."

"Too much work," snorted Sherman. Simplicity anchored his view of the world and the excess made no sense.

"No wonder you and Tillerman got along so well. Two peas in an outdated, grumpy pod."

"Maybe when I wore a younger man's clothes," quipped Sherman.

"I just assumed you were born this way," added Ashley with a smile. "Besides, you're not that old."

A somber mood took hold of him. "Sometimes you glimpse yourself in the mirror and there is no age, just some youthful apparition staring back. Other days I wonder who that can be with all those scars, that slowly retreating hairline and vacant eyes."

Ashley sat with the thought for a few seconds and considered her own scars, visible and otherwise. Eventually she said, "I don't see any gray."

Sherman winked, "It's on the inside."

Rolling eastward, they descended into what constituted the rest of the town. Gas pumps, coffee shop, they all came and went, but Sherman could hear Ashley hold her breath as they passed the Sheriff's station.

"They don't know," he said.

"How can you be certain?" She asked.

"We'd be dead in a ditch if they knew," he answered.

"You're not reassuring me at all," added Ashley.

"Not trying to sugarcoat it," acknowledged Sherman.

"Sounds like you're trying to scare me."

"Pretty sure that's already been done," he added solemnly.

"More like gutted," she quipped.

Sherman answered with as much tenderness as his voice could convey, "I know the feeling."

Ashley gave him a sad smile, half drooping in the

corners, as if drawn down towards her grief.

By the time Johnny's truck rumbled past the small elementary school, they were out of town. A few businesses lived ahead, but most were motels catering to adventure seekers and migrant loggers. Sherman eased the truck off the central road, ready for an even steeper climb towards the bar. The road, sensing some slackening in density, became more sinuous and aggressively vertical. It rose, twisted, and then fell back down to the river. Finally, it surpassed some escape velocity and separated from the earthly water below, gaining elevation with each subsequent mile.

"About halfway up, turn right onto Skylark," instructed Ashley.

Sherman nodded as his brain mentally constructed the road ahead. He had a knack for space and instinctively knew things like exits, lines of sights, pinch points. Nothing savant like, nor did he have a photographic memory, but it was just something he did well.

Trees passed slowly by as they took one sharp turn after another. Oaks came first, their ashen branches anchored in the air. The banks of the river and the hidden drainages glowed a lively orange from the sycamores clinging to fall. The occasional pine poked sharply through, looking upset it wasn't higher up the mountain.

Sherman scratched the scruff slowly reconstructing itself back into a beard. Watching with a memory in her eyes, Ashley smiled. "You know Tillerman started growing his back over the last month. Never saw him not clean shaven," she laughed a little. "He had the same damn itch you got."

A bitter metallic taste flooded his taste buds as the image of his best friend lying dead on a stainless-steel gurney looped continuously. Sherman was so focused on the wounds, the depth, the angles, all the details of an untimely death that he missed one important fact. From the first moment with the unit to the day he tore off the uniform, Tillerman wore a beard thicker than Saint Nick. All those years since, not once had Sherman seen the faintest shadow of stubble. The past, with its blood and murderous steps, always got washed down the drain with some cheap aftershave. Yet there he was, dead on the slab, wearing a full month of growth and Sherman hadn't even noticed. It never registered, there but unseen.

He turned back to Ashley, eyes curdling with remorse, "I didn't know."

"Why would you?" Her question carried a tinge of incomprehension.

"It's a long story," answered Sherman.

"It's a long drive."

"We wore the beard as a mask, a badge of courage for some distant war. For all that we were told was wrong."

"It's just a beard," replied Ashley.

"Yes, and no. To most it means nothing but a choice. A few moments at the start or end of the day."

"So, what then?"

"Truth, I guess," was all that made sense in reply.

Ashley's voice quickened, "Tillerman didn't speak of it that way. Truth sounds positive and noble. Nothing noble came from those stories."

Sherman sniffed the damp air, "The truth is born naked and free. We're the ones who dress it up and chain it down."

"So, we are just murderous animals at heart? Fucking bleak Frank."

"Sorry, I haven't seen the sunny side of man in quite some time," replied Sherman.

"Maybe you're just looking in the wrong spot."

"No shit," answered Sherman.

"Maybe Fiji."

He laughed and for a moment imagined a slow life on the beach. Maybe, just maybe, he thought. Buy a small bar on the beach, somewhere sort of touristy but not ritzy. Adventure seekers or backpackers would do. He could watch the waves, work and grow old over a cold beer. Why? Some peace and quiet?

"You think I could do it?" he asked.

"Retire? Shit Frank, I barely know you, but I doubt you'd do well in retirement."

Sherman nodded along with her assessment, having long ago accepted the probability he would die unnaturally. Growing old wasn't ever a guarantee, but it sure felt like a long shot. He harbored no death wish, but it was war. Someone had to die.

Ashley interrupted, "Can I ask you a personal question?"

"Of course," he replied.

"Did you ever hold it against Tillerman?"

"Leaving?"

"Yeah, it sounds terrible, but I can't help being pissed, like really fucking pissed, that he's gone. That somehow it is his fault."

The stages of grief, everyone goes through them and Sherman had experienced his share of cycles. Rinse and repeat. The process never changed, only the names.

"No, I knew he was done when we got back to base. Something about his eyes screamed out."

Ashley sighed, searching for words that meant something to her in that moment, but found none.

Sherman continued, "Own that anger, it is part of your grief and no one can take it away."

"You don't think I'm a terrible person for thinking it? For giving it a voice?"

"Not at all. I take years to move beyond the anger. Getting even won't help that, but..." he trailed off.

Ashley finished the thought, "You can't stop."

"It's genetic," replied Sherman.

She raised her eyebrows with suspicion.

"Or that is what I tell myself," he retorted.

Ashley shifted back and forth like she couldn't decide whether to say something.

"Go ahead," he said, reading her body language.

"How many friends have you lost?"

Sherman squinted into the past and she could see the

harsh lines of life forming in the corners of his eyes. The list was extensive. Fifteen years under the rubble of the Twin Towers. Loss was an unavoidable fact of life, but never an easy one.

He thought for another moment, "A baker's dozen."

"Jesus," muttered Ashley.

He nodded but said nothing more on the subject. A small wooden sign with a painted bird, arrow and cloud caught his attention.

"This it?"

"Yeah," she laughed. "Never realized it didn't have any words."

Most of the developing world used symbols to represent everything from soda brands to political parties on ballots, and it didn't surprise Sherman to see it in Byron Mills.

A faded yellow sign showed the pavement ended up ahead, which contradicted the fact that the asphalt was long gone, eroded over time and replaced by undulating washboards.

"How far from here?"

Ashley shrugged, "How close do you want to get?"

"You're a step ahead," said Sherman with a smile. "Close but out of sight."

She furrowed her brow and sunk into thought for a few moments, "Bartlet's have an old cabin not too far away. They're old now. Doubt they'd be up here."

Sherman liked that she knew the owners. It made explanations easier, but tactically he had to ask, "Is it close enough that you could run back?"

"Maybe a mile, but we'd be going downhill."

"Alright, you call the turn."

They rattled about, dust pluming behind, for a few more minutes before she pointed to a small, rutted cut in the surrounding trees. Sherman made the turn and squeezed the sizeable truck through before parking next to the cabin.

He cut the engine and smiled, "You ready?"

"Always ready for a hike," said Ashley as her voice

trailed into doubt.

Elongated shadows fell under the low-slung sun and gave the afternoon an undeserved chill. Ashley pointed off towards the north and Sherman took the lead. They followed a small gulley further up into the hills, snaking past green ferns and the occasional outcropping of poison oak. As the cool mountain air filled his lungs, Sherman couldn't help but feel conflicted. Never had a place felt reassuringly like home while also raising his blood pressure. Clashing feelings of safety and danger, joy and remorse, as if the war had come home to roost in his inner sanctuary. Such an invasion felt excruciatingly personal and threatening in unexpected ways. There had always been a fear of losing himself to the violence. Sherman had come to the brink ever so recently, leaning on Byron Mills like a crutch, yearning for some solace or perspective. Maybe he had found it, but his quiet place felt loud.

As with all places unknown, Sherman took his time. No reason to rush. They walked quietly and Ashley did her best to stay out of his way, knowing that it was anything but a normal hike. Suddenly her childhood backyard seemed frightening. Noises, normal forest sounds, took on a harsh hue. All the trees lost part of their majesty when someone could hide behind them. It felt constricting, like being trapped in a giant box of her own making. Sure, there was room to run, but it all felt hostile now.

Sherman had paused by a buckeye and she said in hushed tones, "How do you do this all the time? Everything seems dangerous, like the wonder got sucked out of it."

"Eventually the shadows get a little less ghostly and the sounds regain some life, but you're right, it fucks with your mind."

"Twisted," she added.

He nodded while looking around, "Just below that ridge?"

"Yeah, how did you know?"

Sherman shrugged and left Ashley with a bemused look

caught between humor and concern. He had glanced at his phone before they left the truck, taking a quick peek at the satellite and topo maps. Years of practice had sharpened that part of his mind. A minute or two was all that he needed to memorize a rough sketch of the place. The faint tones of a blue spruce grove just below a slight ridge connecting to a rocky point. Sherman threw in two escape routes as common practice, even though he expected nothing more than some enjoyable scenery. The clue felt farfetched, like he was missing something, but knocking on doors wasn't a strategy either.

The smell found Sherman before he saw the grove, wafting downhill like an old friend. Blue-gray branches reached toward the sky as they approached, and the resinous fruity aroma was enveloping.

Ashley was smiling but shrugged when Sherman looked her way. She hadn't known what to expect, but the experience was bringing up a childhood long since abandoned.

The two of them wandered a bit aimlessly uphill, reliving once discarded pieces of history. Near the grove's uppermost edge, Sherman stopped and sniffed again. The look on his face made Ashley follow suit.

Her nose wrinkled, "Cat piss?"

"Sulfur?" he wondered.

With widening eyes Ashley answered what Sherman could only assume, "Meth."

"Shit Lieutenant," muttered Sherman.

"Is this what he meant? Oh, god no, I told him to come here," cried Ashley.

"We know nothing yet," replied Sherman.

Ashley was standing with her arms crossed, awaiting some inevitably precarious outcome, "Now what?"

The only obvious answer was up, so he motioned towards the ridge and small rocky outcrop that would provide a modicum of cover. The stench intensified along with his anxiousness. The Glock was in hand by the time they reached the top.

Rising from the valley below, almost amber in the fading light, were the fumes and smoke from four trailer homes. Scattered in the pines, each one far enough away from the next not to cause a chain reaction of exploding chemicals should one go up in flames. An organized operation with a well laid out footprint. Such thought and planning didn't bode well, and Sherman knew it. Planning meant management, someone capable of making things run smoothly and safely. Someone with intelligence. Johnny was surely not that man. Another open question, another suspect, another threat.

"Jesus fucking Christ," muttered Ashley as she stared at the operation below.

"Whose land is that?"

Ashley didn't answer, not at first. There were too many pieces falling into place. Things her dad said or her brothers had done. "My father. Everything up to the fire road," she pointed off a quarter mile away from the buildings.

"Same road that connects into town?" Sherman asked.

"The one and only," she answered, shaking her head. "We used to go camping down there when I was a kid. Now it's what, some giant fucking meth lab. Pa's probably been planning this shit for years."

"Feeling used?"

Ashley scoffed, "You would think a grown-ass woman wouldn't fall for the same shit repeatedly, but here we are and there is my family's meth empire!" She was on the verge of tears, "You think Tillerman found this?"

"Maybe," mused Sherman.

His friend wasn't stupid. Even if he had found this place mere knowledge meant nothing. Tillerman only acted when he had leverage, an advantage of some type. This didn't feel like enough. Only one half of the equation: drugs and money. He could see the former but only guess at the latter.

Somewhere in the distance a car door slammed, echoing their direction, and Sherman spotted a dust trail rising close to the fire road.

Ashley felt shaken by the sight. "We should go."

"Agreed, but I want to see who showed up," said Sherman.

"Frank, this is the part of the movie where the bad guys sneak up and ambush the oblivious duo."

He couldn't help but grin, "There is no one up here but us."

"How can you be so sure?"

"Sound travels too well up in these hills." It was a fact he had noticed on their way up.

"What does that mean? You'd hear them coming? Shit, I haven't even seen you take your eyes off those buildings since we got here."

Sherman sighed with a hint of frustration, "Anybody coming from behind us would have to navigate the same terrain we did. Now I'm quiet, but I know we made a racket on our way up. That leaves the threats in front of us. Organized or not, these boys don't fear discovery. You get my drift?"

Ashley hadn't considered the obvious, but then again, she had never wanted such a life. "So, what if they don't fear the law? It ain't uncommon around here."

He nodded toward the road below, "And now we know why."

Even with the distance Ashley knew the man crossing through a clearing in the pines, "Skinhead Barrios! I should have known. That dumbass Simpkins must be close behind."

"Skinhead?"

Ashley nodded, "Dude went through a neo-Nazi phase in high school. A real prick."

"Nothing like a fascist with a badge," added Sherman.

"All the more reason to leave," pleaded Ashley.

"Agreed, let's go."

The pair worked down the ridge and back into the spruce grove where the fumes finally faded. Somewhere between the blue trees and the truck, Sherman stopped and stepped behind an oak. He wasn't sure why, but he had stopped double guessing his intuition a long time ago. The sudden move dumbfounded Ashley but she followed suit. Hidden by the tree's gray hide, Sherman waited and listened for the faint rustle that set his instincts into action. It didn't take long for his ears to pick up the vague wake of movement through the woods.

Glancing over at Ashley's fear etched face, he knew they agreed. All she saw staring back was concentration. No fear or apprehension, just the face of someone working to solve a puzzle. For Sherman, fear was a luxury he could not afford. 'Respect but never fear your enemy' was an oft-repeated phrase of his father's. At that moment he was respecting two people moving his direction about three hundred yards downhill. They were moving deliberately and quickly, not the plodding march of carefree hikers.

Doing his best to keep elbows and arms hidden, Sherman pointed towards the approaching pair who still hadn't come into view. Ashley nodded and pressed her thin frame against the tree like a toddler trying to hide between a parent's legs.

Two hundred yards and closing. It wasn't exactly pistol range, so Sherman had but two choices. Stay or move. With no visibility, moving wasn't worth the risk. He was behind decent cover with the advantage of slope and surprise. He knew they were coming and, judging by the sounds below, the interlocutors did not.

One hundred yards and closing. Whoever was now within pistol range, but it wasn't worth the risk of being outgunned in a prolonged fight. His team always tried to hit hard and fast. Overwhelm even if you can't outgun. Alone with eighteen rounds wasn't in that category.

Fifty yards closer and Sherman could make out two men approaching. The gold stars on their chests barely glinting in the now fading light. Another quick peek and he could make out Simpkins and his terrible bowl haircut. He didn't recognize the other man, but that mattered little. Both were threats and nothing more.

The lawmen weren't expecting company and chatted away, oblivious to the world around.

"This is bullshit, we're not some rent-a-cops," said the deputy whose voice Sherman did not recognize.

"You took the money, man," chided Simpkins.

"Not like I had much choice. You know I hate being the last one to a party."

"Then stop your bitching. It's only for a couple of days, until that fucking jarhead leaves," said Simpkins.

"Or dies," added the other deputy.

Both men shared a brief laugh over the remark at about thirty-five yards away from the oak tree. It was well within Sherman's range with that pistol model, but he waited.

"Maybe this one will be less involved," offered Simpkins.

"Ah fuck off, you enjoyed beating on that townie just the same."

Simpkins laughed, "Dude had it coming."

"Ain't that the truth? You don't fuck with the money."

"What you doing with your cut?" asked Simpkins.

"Shit, Arlene is already making plans to use it all up. Wants a pool and some other nonsense."

"Just get one of those inflatable ones from Sam's Club," offered Simpkins.

"Nah, she wants a legit one. Concrete, diving board, the whole nine yards. Wants the neighbors to be jealous."

Simpkins laughed and the other deputy continued, "I told her we live in a fucking trailer, ain't nobody gonna be jealous of us."

The laughing continued when they were only fifteen yards away from Sherman.

He glanced at Ashley, nodding that something was about to happen. She looked so frightened, so young, and Sherman wondered what contorted shape his face took when the first bullet with malice had spun his direction. No doubt there were similarities.

Using the tree for partial cover, he leaned out to the left with the Glock raised, staring down the barrel at the deputy's own expression of shock and confusion.

Over the front sight, Sherman could make out Coe on the deputy's name badge before he pulled the trigger. Even left-handed he caught the man square in the forehead, just below the green brim of his department issue hat. High velocity blood splatter sailed into evening air, settling almost invisibly on the dark green grass below. A brief scream leaped from Ashley's throat before she stifled the rest. Simpkins had barely reacted, just sort of fidgeted towards his gun, when the second round Sherman fired hit him dead center in the vest. The force was enough to put him on his knees, sucking air, hoping to catch his breath. By the time Simpkins looked up all he saw was the bottom of Sherman's boot knocking him down the rain-soaked hill. A half-dead manzanita stopped his tumble, but not without a few serious lacerations.

Sherman chased the deputy down while Ashley slowly regained what little composure she had left. Simpkins was already bleeding badly from his temple when Sherman caught up. He grabbed the deputy's service weapon, which had stayed in the holster, and motioned for Ashley to grab the rifle some yards back.

"Deputy," said Sherman with a sigh, "we have little time, but you have a simple choice. Talk and I'll leave you breathing. Don't and you'll join him." He pointed to the lifeless corpse a dozen yards away.

Dazed, Simpkins wiped away the blood streaming down his face and tried to focus on the figure crouching in front of him, "What do you want?"

"Names. Who organized the attack on Tillerman? Who did the beating?"

"Fuck you, jarhead," spat Simpkins.

"God damn it, Matt," pleaded Ashley. "This isn't one of your games. People are dying." She pointed to Sherman,

"You fucked with the wrong guy."

Tears started mixing with blood as Simpkins cried, "I didn't want to hurt him, but Barrios told me we had to."

The contrition looked genuine, but Sherman didn't care if the deputy felt remorse. He wanted information, not contrition. "Who else?"

"Just the four of us, uh, uh, Barrios, Cole and Reider."

Sherman looked to Ashley for confirmation on the last name. She nodded, "Another deputy."

"Quickly, what happened that night," urged Sherman, aware time was slipping away.

"Really, I didn't want to do it," whimpered Simpkins.

Sherman tapped the Glock against the other man's knees, "Details deputy,"

"We met Barrios at the bridge, pulled the Lieutenant out of the truck and beat him good, but he was still breathing when Barrios left again."

"Where did they go?" asked Sherman.

"Don't know."

"The Sheriff, was he there?"

"No," whimpered Simpkins.

"Did he know?"

The deputy shrugged, "How would he not?"

"You may have left him breathing, but he was dead when you staged the accident."

Simpkins looked up with surprise, "How did you know that?"

"I told you Matt, wrong fucking guy," said Ashley cutting in and growing angrier with each admission.

"Fine," said Sherman, "who paid you?"

"Johnny," came the inevitable reply.

"Was he there?"

"Nah, just us boys."

Sherman's frustration grew. This guy was proving of little intelligence value and he knew someone had heard the shots. That someone would be closing in.

"Last question. Who did you shoot up Ruby's car with?"

Sherman's question was met with another face of disbelief, but it faded quicker this time. Simpkins hesitated, then looked at Ashley, "Rhett."

Her heart sank in that moment of betrayal. Sherman could see it but didn't have time to say anything, not yet.

"If I see you again, I will bury you and your family. Clear?"

Simpkins nodded.

"Good," continued Sherman before he shot the deputy in the abdomen just below the Kevlar vest. The bullet hit with a strained thud, passing clean through and into the soft earth.

"Jesus Frank, you said you'd let him live," yelled Ashley.

"No. I told him he'd be breathing when I left. He'll live if someone finds him in the next forty minutes, which is a lot more time than we have."

"What?" asked Ashley, showing her confusion.

"Someone heard those shots, no doubt they'll be coming over that ridge any minute."

She turned to look back up the hill, "Really?"

Simpkins was groaning but alive when they left. Sherman couldn't be sure of it, but not killing the deputy felt like a giant oversight. If it had been Iraq or Syria, the man would have been dead and rotting, but he was stateside or so the Major kept telling him. Although, the longer he was in town, the more he doubted there was any difference.

CHAPTER SEVENTEEN

"We need a new car," said Sherman as he leaned into the corner with the truck tires screeching in protest.

One road in, one road out. Haste was needed if they were to beat what seemed like an easy ambush. The drive in had taken them thirty minutes. Sherman knew he needed to cut that in half if they wanted to avoid the worst.

Ashley looked ill as she bounced around the tight turns, "Uh, I don't know anyone that has one we can borrow."

"Who said anything about borrowing?" asked Sherman.

She shrugged, "I guess Grand Theft Auto isn't a concern at this point."

"They broke the social contract first. Now they're trying to tie up loose ends. Repercussions will follow."

"Loose ends meaning us?" asked Ashley.

He nodded, "And I mean to burn the rope up."

Northern California was no Fallujah or Raqqa. Sherman knew a life of solitary confinement awaited him if arrested by real police. If Reinhold caught him, well, he didn't want to consider the outcome, but ISIS or the Taliban wouldn't be much worse.

"If they catch us," said Ashley, trailing off into a similar line of thought.

"You think Simpkins will talk?"

"If he survives. You fucking shot him, remember!" Ashley admonished.

"He'll live," Sherman said.

She rubbed her temples, "Matt's dumb, but he ain't stupid."

Sherman liked the description, "Let's hope so."

"You weren't serious about, you know, killing his entire family?" she asked with a touch of actual concern.

It was a question people instinctively answered in the negative, but the more Sherman considered such a horrific act the more he questioned how far down the rabbit hole of horrors he would go. Moral standards, the rules of war, these things had weight and meaning over there. Back home, where law supposedly pervaded, Sherman felt the rising tides of violence. Like the frog in the slowly heated pot, unwilling to jump out because the heat comes on so incrementally that it hardly notices. He didn't know if he would realize when to get out before being scalded or worse.

"No," he finally said after a pregnant pause that Ashley filled with seeds of her own doubt.

"That wasn't very reassuring Frank."

He gave her a half-shrug, half-nod, before asking, "What about that car?"

She waited a beat with his deflection, "Maybe one of the motels?"

"Good for dumping the truck, but a tourist would notice their car missing. You know of anyone out of town? Maybe something you overheard at the bar."

With a wrinkle of her nose to show serious thought, Ashley waded into the morass of the previous week. With so much ugliness, it took some effort to think only of work. "Yeah," she eventually said, "Mrs. Swanson is on one of her cruises all month."

"Does she drive something noticeable?" he asked.

"A white Ford Taurus," offered Ashley.

"Perfect. Where does she live?" asked Sherman

"Oh, uh, I'm not sure. Near Brummet. I think," she answered with a bit of embarrassment.

Sherman grabbed his phone and dialed the recent

number. On the second ring Brummet answered, "Captain?"

There was a tinge of doubt at the end of his greeting, as if he had inadvertently answered his own death sentence.

"Still kicking," Sherman assured.

Brummet sighed with relief, "Good to hear. What's up?"

"You know a Mrs. Swanson?"

"Yeah, sure. Why?"

"We are borrowing her car," replied Sherman.

"Ah. Third house from the end of the cul-de-sac. The green door," he explained.

"Thanks. Any excitement on your end?" wondered Sherman.

"Nothing inside besides the usual sexually insensitive commentary, but there are two burly bikers parked out front. Been that way for some time now and they don't seem like the teetotaling type."

"Ruby recognize them?" asked Sherman.

"It ranged from vaguely yes to vaguely no," came the reply.

"So outside of her circle then," remarked Sherman knowing that the bartender had a large radius of rather dubious friends.

"It would appear so," was Brummet's gruff reply. He knew strangers in the night were not there for friendly banter.

"Alright, hang tight and I'll take care of them," informed Sherman.

Curious as he was, Brummet said something but reeled his question back in to a simple, "And then?"

"Leave normally, make it look like you're dropping her off then head home. If you spot anyone, call me and keep driving."

"What could go wrong," mumbled the old man, wondering if he had bitten off far more than he could chew, but more than enough to choke on.

Sherman tossed the phone into a cup holder and tried to

think where the bikers fit into an ever-widening web of criminal activity. They were coming out of a series of tight turns. Back and forth, left then right. On the last corner, he glimpsed a smudge of white that triggered all his training and instincts.

"Get down," he yelled at Ashley while mashing the accelerator to the floor. The big V8 roared to life and drowned out Ashley's meek reply.

Blocking the road ahead was a white late nineties model Crown Victoria Sheriff's sedan. Most departments were phasing the venerable cars out, but not Cumbre County. Reinhold had other things to spend his budget on and a updated car for a recently hired deputy was not high on the list. His was an old school brand of leadership where the lowest on the totem pole was unworthy until proven otherwise. Deputy Reider had yet to uncheck either box.

The boyish man had picked a decent spot to block the road. After the slow back-and-forth turns, where the speed bled away, but with enough space that he could still react. Being new and from a department with interests outside of law enforcement, Reider never received the level of training consistent with standards. Not to say he was incompetent, in another place he would have made a fine deputy in time, but he was encountering a situation few veteran officers would have overcome.

If there was a tactical checkbox, Reider had an appreciable amount of ink on the page. Decent location? Check. Decent cover? Check. He was hiding behind the sedan's engine block, which was the best spot to stop any incoming rounds. Clear line of sight? Check. Element of surprise? Check. Firepower? Not so much. Just a department-issued pistol of the 9mm variety and one 12-gauge shotgun without slugs. Backup? None to speak of. But the biggest unchecked box happened, as it usually does, in the moment. That split second when it all goes south. Sherman did something that Reider didn't expect. Reacting without hesitation, Sherman floored the truck, erasing all that carefully constructed space in a matter of seconds. Reider blinked when he should have been shooting.

With the Ford in a full-throated growl and the space between them almost gone, Sherman aimed directly for the front panel of the sedan. Though it had taken some time, Reider had gotten the Crown Vic nearly perpendicular on the narrow road. This was no small feat and the front bumper only had a few feet of clearance to the dirt mountainside from which they cut the road. The back wheels were almost on the meager shoulder. A precarious stripe of dirt separating the asphalt from a two-hundred-foot drop in the valley below.

Still shocked, the deputy fired a few rounds from his pistol before the massive truck plowed into his car. Sherman ducked at the last second, but Reider's aim failed and nothing came close to the windshield. The impact was tremendous, and, like a well-timed pinball paddle, it sent Reider flying into the air. Geometry, unfortunately, worked against the deputy and Sherman watched as a body flew up and over the cliff's edge and into the void.

Sherman blinked for a second as he slammed on the brakes, waiting for the airbags to deploy. Nothing happened. Johnny's giant aftermarket grille guard had done its job. Once past the sedan he stopped to a collective sigh.

"What the hell just happened?" asked Ashley. Her head was still buried in the center console.

"Nothing good for him," muttered Sherman. "Stay here," he added before running towards the sedan.

The shotgun was lying in the road, scuffed but in one piece. That went in the truck before Sherman opened the Crown Vic's driver side door. The keys were still in the ignition and he jammed the old column shifter into neutral before turning the wheel hard right. From there it didn't take much effort to push the old car over the edge. No guardrails or berms impeded his progress. A minute later the back wheels cleared level ground, and gravity took over. Sherman didn't even bother to watch. The sounds echoing up from the valley below painted a clear enough picture. Destruction was destruction no matter the locale.

"Why bother?" asked Ashley as they drove off.

"Never leave them anything that can be used against you," he answered.

"What is that? Some Sun-Tzu proverb?"

Sherman laughed, "The Major isn't that clever, but they're cut from the same merciless cloth."

"Shit Frank, where do you fit on that spectrum?"

"Somewhere on the grim side of right," acknowledged Sherman.

"I'd wager farther down than you think," added Ashley without considering her own descent. She thought about her words from the previous night, "Sorry, I shouldn't judge."

"Go ahead, it won't hurt me, but don't lie to yourself."

She sighed, "I'm overcome with this raw anger at him, at them, at the world. But I don't understand what it means."

"That's grief, deep and unfettered. There is no meaning. It's a process," he mumbled.

"What's your process?" she asked.

Sherman couldn't deny she had a point. His path was already strewn with bodies. Whatever ghosts he had come here to escape were no longer hiding in the shadows. If he had hoped for a restart, it wasn't in sight. Only more of what was over there. It all made his sprouting stubble itch.

"Touché. We're probably in the same place, I just whittle it down to a pointy end."

"Men and their sharp objects," she quipped.

They were closing in on the bar and the pair of bikers.

"In all seriousness, thanks for being here," said Ashley.

Sherman smiled and nodded, "He was a wonderful man. A great friend."

"That he was."

With the bar around the next bend, Sherman flashed a mischievous smile.

"What's that for?" she asked.

"Hold on. I saw this once at the destruction derby in Redding."

Ashley clutched at the handle overhead like a passenger in rough seas. The parking lot was ahead of them and Sherman could see the duo parked out front, casually leaning against their Harleys while watching the exits. Judging by their stance, they cared little about the periphery. With a flick of the wrist, Sherman sent the giant truck careening into the small gravel parking lot. The bikes were close to the street with nothing but a few dilapidated railway ties to separate them from traffic, not that it affected the Ford. Sherman had switched off the headlights, so it was no surprise that the two refrigerator sized men took a moment to react. Just dim running lights and the rumbling V8 cued them into the nearly five-thousand-pound truck barreling closer.

With a screeching crunch reminiscent of fingernails on a chalkboard, but with more bass, they crashed into the bikes. Ashley cringed at the sound and the impact. The truck's massive steel bumper sent the Harleys spinning like shiny tops, twinkling glints of chrome below the lone streetlight. Sherman slowed enough to make sure the motorcycles were out of commission, watching in the mirror long enough to see two dazed men roll about in the gravel. He gave Brummet a call when they had rounded the first corner back towards town.

The old man was laughing when he answered, "You put the fear of god in those two. Oh man, better than pay-per-view."

"Take that Gravedigger," said Sherman feeling a childish rush of adrenaline. "They out of commission?"

"Shit, the bigger one pissed his pants and they are both covered in cuts."

"Alright," said Sherman in a renewed tone of seriousness, "time to get the check."

"No problem, I've already spent every dime on surf and

turf."

"And scotch?"

"Quality over quantity tonight," Brummet assured.

Sherman wanted to keep Ruby safe and away from the growing firestorm, but doubted that it was possible anymore. The bikers had seen them together, and he had put at least two of them in the emergency room. At least he knew they weren't an innocent party to the mischief.

"Swing by and have her grab some supplies from her place then head back. If you're followed or something ain't right, you call me but keep driving," instructed Sherman.

"You got it, Captain."

"Alright, time to steal some old lady's car," he said with a chuckle before hanging up.

"They okay?" asked Ashley.

"Yeah, all good. Time to deprive Mrs. Swanson of her transportation."

"You know she used to be my piano teacher," remarked Ashley. "Oh my, she'll be pissed."

"A real knuckle buster?"

"Used to pace with a wooden Westcott ruler, you know the ones with the metal edge, just waiting to pounce on some missed key."

"The good old days," mused Sherman.

Ashley laughed gently, "Back when you could get away with corporal punishment." She gazed out the window for a minute, lost in those childhood textures, before adding, "She was a real Nazi."

Sherman couldn't help but chuckle, "Piano in the Teutonic tradition. Beaten until perfect."

"I'm looking forward to this," she admitted.

"A little payback after all?"

"We tried to tee-pee her house one Halloween. Crazy bitch came out with a BB gun. Tanner still has one lodged in his shoulder." She shook her head in disbelief at such a childhood, "What a bunch of hoodlums we were."

Sherman laughed along with the picture she had painted.

"The funniest part was the next morning. Reinhold was driving around the neighborhood pulling down rolls of toilet paper, but he was too lazy to get out of his truck. So, he ends up tearing apart all these lawns in pursuit of the 'Great Vandalism Spree of '98'."

"Classic," said Sherman. He wondered if the Sheriff would get out to dirty his hands after the night's violence.

They were over the hill splitting the town in two, heading towards the little suburb Brummet called home. Passing by the empty Sheriff station reminded Sherman that they needed to ditch the truck sooner than later. If the cops weren't on to it, the bikers would be.

"Isn't there a motel near Brummet's?" he asked.

"Yeah, there's an old Best Western on the main road, maybe a quarter mile further."

"I think we need to ditch the truck now and then liberate Mrs. Swanson's car," Sherman added.

"You sound worried."

"Call it an abundance of caution," replied Sherman. "Those bikers weren't amateurs, and they have the manpower to mount a search. It's best to get rid of it now and risk the walk."

"I trust your judgment and god knows Tillerman did," she added sadly.

"Thanks. Not to question your resolve, but I want to make sure you haven't reconsidered."

Seeing what Ashley had suffered changes people. No one comes out the other side unscarred, even if there are no physical wounds. Violence, cruel and personal, messes with the mind, upends the neurons and remaps a personality. Spend too much time, too close, and another person emerges. Sherman knew the process, the unintended consequences, all too well. He wasn't the same person who swaggered into the recruiter's office fifteen years earlier. That kid was long gone, those beliefs flattened under the cruel weight of three wars, like the goodness was just scooped out.

"Life is messy, god knows mine has been, and I expected nothing less from you. You're a hurricane Frank, but right now this place needs some decimation."

Being compared to a natural disaster was new for Sherman, but he had left behind trails of destruction and his anger was swelling with intensity. Each new stone turned over brought him closer to the edge over which all compassion and emotion fell away. Disconnects like that were usually demarcated by deployment in far-flung corners of conflict scattered lands, not Northern California. Yet there he was stepping, sometimes willingly and sometimes not, closer to his own personal precipice.

A knot grew in his stomach at the thought and he unconsciously scratched his beard, "I'll keep that in mind."

Ashley gestured towards the slowly straightening road, "Motel is about a mile ahead."

Sherman nodded, "I think there is a gym bag back there. Can you see if the guns fit?"

Sliding over the center console, Ashley dug around on the floor until she found a smallish black bag.

"Maybe if you had a hacksaw."

The rifle and shotgun were much too long, but some concealment was better than none.

"Do what you can," said Sherman as he turned into the motel parking lot, passing by the front office like some normal guest already booked for the night.

The lot was big, dimly lit, and stood as a divider between two buildings. Judging by the relative age of the paint, Sherman guessed the two-story lodge was a more recent addition, maybe within the last thirty years. How demand warranted extra rooms was a question he could not answer. Parked near the back were two 28-foot Class C RVs and Sherman used their drab tan exteriors to shield the truck from any prying eyes in the motel office.

"Let's go," he said.

Ashley nodded and handed him the bag. She had wrapped a dark green hoodie around the exposed stocks.

Sherman smiled at her foresight. With barrels facing in, it made using them in a pinch much easier.

The swirling edge of a storm was sweeping across the horizon, intent on precipitation, and whatever residual warmth remained washed away with the winds. They walked casually towards the detached lodge like any other couple heading in for the night with luggage in tow. At the end unit they detoured into the darkness of an adjacent field. From the relative safety of knee-high grass, Sherman and Ashley worked back towards the main road, angling towards Brummet's neighborhood.

At the road's edge, Sherman stopped in the shadows to listen for oncoming cars. Nothing but the wind caught his attention, and they slipped across unseen save for a nearby owl hooting into the night. The flat land Brummet lived in was separated from the central road by a tiny hill which lent an exclusive quality to the homes hidden behind its height.

"You ever sneak in or out of here when you were younger?"

"Once or twice," answered Ashley a bit sheepishly.

Sherman knew Barrios lived there, and that was an encounter he wanted on his own terms. "Any tips?" he asked.

"The gulch," she replied.

"Do tell."

"There's a little stream running between the houses and the hill. It has a dirt path next to it. All the kids called it The Gulch. We'd go there to drink and smoke or fuck if you were lucky," elaborated Ashley.

"Right up my alley. Where does it end?" asked Sherman, trying as he was to assemble a mental map of the area.

"Shit, it's been years," muttered Ashley. She thought for a few moments in the inky stillness. "By the Pearlman's place, so, uh, three-ish blocks from Brummet's house."

"That's east?"

"Yeah."

The picture came together in Sherman's mind like a

detailed topo map. All the minor pieces of where and how fell into place and he motioned for Ashley to follow. They walked silently in the chilly darkness with only the wind and crickets as company.

Finding the gulch was easy enough, even without light Sherman knew enough to keep tacking towards the small creek. Once there, he handed the bag back to Ashley and unholstered the Glock. A heavy duffle bag slung across his back would not help his reaction speed if things went badly and Ashley took the bag without a second thought. She wasn't a tremendous fan of the dark, let alone the myriad dangers, real or imagined, which lurked in shadowy recesses. Besides, the weight of the rifles, their gleaming metal parts, gave her a sense of comfort.

The creek hummed with life. Crickets, frogs, cicadas and bats all fed into a cascade of noise and smell. Sherman could see his shoes and a few feet of trail, but anything more faded into an oily apparition. Having seen worse paths in far more hostile corners of the world, Sherman moved with a level of speed and confidence that Ashley struggled to match. The duffle kept snagging on branches, only making thing worse.

A hundred yards later, Sherman pushed her back into the bushes with a modified mom stop; the universal safety push away from danger. Ashley almost screamed but caught her voice moments before it rushed into the open. She watched breathlessly, her heart pounding, as a young couple stumbled past, hands clasped in furtive lust.

Sherman felt Ashley's apprehension, the sudden rise and fall of her breath, and squeezed her arm in reassurance. Wandering through a tar black night wreaked havoc when violence was a probable outcome. The teenagers knew no such threat, so their passage was drunk and gleeful, while Sherman and Ashley strained at each new and unexpected sound.

As the nascent lovers receded into the enveloping darkness Ashley let out a sigh of relief, "I think we're getting close."

Two hundred yards away, maybe a shade less, was Sherman's internal calculation, and he murmured his agreement. A dogleg right, then an exit onto the street. If he were a city planner, there would be a streetlight illuminating the gap. The lonesome yellow glow of a sodium-vapor lamp. From what limited knowledge he had, Cumbre County did not subscribe to planning, zoning codes or otherwise.

By the time their feet hit pavement in the chilly air, Sherman knew he was right. The only light came from a few stray porches lit in the early evening. They walked in the shadows, eyes prowling for any flashes of light or the hum of engines.

The last few blocks unfolded without incident. Mrs. Swanson lived a modest but tidy ranch style set back from the street. A pair of ancient sycamores stood sentinel on either edge of her property. Old lumbering giants in a relatively young part of town. They followed one of those massive shadows around to the rear of the house, but all the doors were locked.

"She used to keep a key under the statue," said Ashley as an old scrap of memory unfolded from the recesses of her mind.

Sherman followed her outstretched finger to a three-foot-tall replica of the Venus de Milo, "Classic taste I see."

"It's concrete," remarked Ashley.

"Not everyone can have marble," grunted Sherman as he lifted the statue revealing an old rusty key long since forgotten.

Muscle memory took over and she opened the door with well-oiled pop. Once inside, they headed left down an overgrown hallway padded with thick shag carpet. Sherman glanced at the seemingly endless line of Disney cruise pictures stretching back decades.

Glancing back at his expression, Ashley qualified, "She has an unhealthy relationship with Mickey Mouse."

Sherman smiled back while hiding the Glock behind his back. He drew it when they entered but wanted to keep it out of view. Shooting an old lady was not part of the plan, but stranger things had happened and that was a story he didn't want to retell.

Ashley found the garage and light switch with minor effort. Under the dull fluorescence the interior was orderly; tools hung on peg boards with thin chalk outlines ensuring they got returned to their correct location. An older model Ford Taurus sat in the center, looking almost pristine despite fifteen years' worth of use. The perfect used car, driven rarely and slowly.

The keys were handing on a hook near the door with a personalized label made from one of those machines advertised on late night television.

He tossed them over to Ashley, "Get it started but don't open the door yet."

Sherman loaded the duffel into the back seat while she started the sedan. Purring to life, he waited for the engine to warm up before turning off the overhead light.

"I'm gonna open it up manually. Kill the lights when I lift and then pull past."

Ashley nodded, and he grabbed the red handle hanging down from the motor. It took a hard yank, but the door disengaged from the chain. The lever stuck with a mechanical clank, and Sherman lifted the doors while Ashley killed the headlights. Garage doors always felt heavier than they should, and it took some grunting for Sherman to lift it high enough for the Taurus to exit. They could only hope no nosey neighbor had seen their actions.

The block was dark, but Ashley drove a good half-mile before switching anything on. Having the car was one thing, but Sherman wasn't sure how they would keep it hidden, at least not yet. Out of sight was the key, especially given that they were close to the scene of the crime.

"Keep driving, I'm going to find out where they are."

"Uphill?" asked Ashley.

"For now."

The intersection was clear as she turned past the general

store and gently opened the throttle on the white sedan. A strangled moon struggled to break through the cloud cover, leaving only a residual glow on the earth below.

Sherman dialed and let it ring. A speck of doubt grew as he waited, only to be erased when Brummet answered.

"Captain," said the old man, his voice heavy with tension.

"Problem?"

"Three bikes just pulled onto the road behind us," answered Brummet. His rising blood pressure was almost audible.

Sherman grabbed Ashley's arm and pointed towards the turn for Upper Mill road, telling Brummet, "Keep it steady and head for the crash site."

The sedan's tires squealed in protest as Ashley yanked the wheel hard right, treating the aging Taurus like some Formula One race car. Sherman grabbed the handle as the Ford raced up the hill and through the stop sign, not bothering to obey any traffic laws as they tried to get further ahead of the taxi. Back and forth they went for another quarter mile. The soft suspension swayed like a boat between the swells before Sherman pointed to a darkened driveway with room for a car to pull off the road.

"Drop me off here then go hide down there," he pointed off into the darkness. "I'm going to switch with Ruby."

Ashley understood and nodded, "Should we wait here?"

"You know who lives here?"

She shook her head no.

"Wait for the bikers to pass then follow us up. Call if you see more coming."

"Be careful," she added.

Sherman smiled as he grabbed the duffel bag out of the back seat. Carefully he placed Simpkins' Sig Sauer service pistol on the passenger seat. Ashley glanced at it for a second and tried to say something, but she looked up to find nothing but darkness.

The taillights disappeared down the driveway in what

Sherman knew was a short but frightfully long way. From the cover of a small juniper tree, he dialed Brummet. It had only been a few minutes, but they often felt like lifetimes when the menace stalked so close.

The old man must have had the phone in his hand and it barely rang, "Yeah."

"I'm at the first driveway past the orange tree. Just below the down slope," explained Sherman.

"What's the play?"

"Pullover and I'll switch with Ruby. Ashley is waiting nearby."

Brummet sounded worried, "These guys aren't discrete and they might see it."

"Take it slow until the last corner then make some space, but remember to kill that dome light," said Sherman.

"Don't worry, I smashed it earlier. See you in two or three minutes."

The hour was getting late and clouds still clung to the treetops like a swarm of swirling mosquitoes, hovering but not yet biting. Sherman glanced around, unable to see his own feet. Great for sneaking around, not so good for a gunfight. If you can't see the sight, aiming becomes guesswork. A fact he would have to deal with shortly, assuming the bikers were not just on some very coincidental late-night ride.

The Harleys were audible first, mechanical bagpipes howling in the distance, then came headlights and the muffled cough of the old Crown Vic. Sherman slid closer to the road and kneeled behind a small boulder, waiting for his moment.

It came with the thumping clank of anti-lock brakes as Brummet brought the car to as sudden a stop as physics would allow. Out jumped Ruby, not much more than a shadow thrust into the night. He should have said something and almost did but thought better of it. She suppressed a yelp as he whisked by her and into the car. Nothing but a faint flash and his lingering smell told Ruby what occurred.

"End of the driveway," yelled Sherman as he closed the door. Brummet already had the Ford moving and Sherman hoped she had heard him correctly.

"I told her," assured the cabbie, but leaving things unsaid was not something Sherman ascribed to.

Brummet was staring at the stocks protruding from a duffel bag sandwiched between his passenger's legs, "So what now, Captain?"

"Slow it down. I want them to catch back up."

"And then?"

"What would the Vietcong have done?" asked Sherman.

Brummet slowly shook his head up then down as if reliving the answer, "Draw you away from base, then shoot the shit out of you."

It was Sherman's turn to nod, "Exactly."

"Where?"

"Not too far from here, just before the tree," answered Sherman.

"The straightaway?"

Sherman patted the black polymer rifle stock protruding from the bag, "Yes, I acquired some firepower on our excursion."

Brummet's face was tense, "What happened up there?"

"The largest cook operation in California, I'd wager," replied Sherman matter-of-factly.

"A Thorne clan operation?"

"Speculation, but I would guess so. Thing is, that place was organized, not some redneck bullshit," added Sherman.

"Don't underestimate them. Some talented men found an untimely end doing just that," said Brummet.

"I won't, but the layout seemed methodical," Sherman said as similar layouts passed through his mind. "Not just that, it looked military."

Brummet raised his eyebrows, "You think it involves someone else?"

"Johnny was a boot, if they got one working for them,

why not two?" asked Sherman thinking through the problem aloud. "Someone organized and precise, maybe logistics or army corp."

Byron Mills wasn't that big, but a steady stream of arrivals and departures made it difficult for Brummet to pinpoint any one newcomer.

"Shit," said the cabbie, "lots of industry folks in and out recently. Maybe the girls would know."

Looking over his shoulder Sherman could see two lights holding back in the distance, "Yeah, maybe so."

"And the guns?" asked Brummet.

"Cumbre County Sheriff's Department," replied Sherman.

"Reinhold's gonna be on a warpath," muttered the old man.

"All the more reason to get you hid."

Brummet looked surprised, "You think Ashley will take to that? Boy, you really don't know her."

"If not all three, then you and Ruby," added Sherman, wanting to limit their further involvement.

Brummet said nothing in reply. He just stared ahead into the thinly lit night. Sherman knew the old man had run from something. Whether that was the past or the future, he wasn't sure. Men who run too much or too long take a stand at some point. Exhaustion kicks in and they come to the edge of losing what little they've gained; when running doesn't take you any further away and the ghosts nip at your heels.

"No disrespect," continued Sherman, "but this won't end well. Someone will come knocking on this moldering door and when they do, well, wearing orange might be the best outcome."

The old man shrugged wearily, "Can't win every hand."

"Your dollar," said Sherman, "but at least get Ruby out of this mess."

Brummet laughed at his line turned against him, "I'll do what I can."

"Thanks. Now gun it. We need more space."

Like a cantankerous old drunk, the Crown Vic slowly revved to life and wobbled forward at an ever-increasing clip. By the last turn it was skidding along the asphalt with Brummet struggling to keep the back end aligned with the front.

"Take the driveway across from the tree, then turn it around," Sherman instructed.

Brummet nodded and the anti-lock brakes thudded again as he mashed the pedal to the floor. At the last moment, he cranked the wheel right. The car groaned in protest but slid the front end onto the dirt drive. Pulling the shifter hard into reverse, he did his best police style three-point turn. Sherman hopped out into the puffy dust cloud, rifle in hand, while the sedan sat sputtering from the effort.

"Wait for my signal then hit the high beams," instructed Sherman as he lay down next to the car. A ribbon of cold grass was underneath as he unfolded the legs on the attached bipod.

Simpkins had put an 8x scope on the gun. While not exactly a sniper rifle, it was decent enough at range. Not award winning, but Sherman pegged the straightaway at only a quarter mile, maybe four hundred yards. The high beams wouldn't reach that far, not even half that distance with any measure of effectiveness. He was betting the bikers would keep their lights on low. That meant waiting until they were hundred yards away. When it comes to ballistics, a football field is almost nothing. Bullets of almost all calibers are lethal at that distance, assuming the user can keep them on target.

Two headlights appeared well after the rumble of their engines echoed through the small valley. Three hundred yards away, just smudges of unfocused light in the scope. The men were closing fast, fearing the loss of their target.

At a hundred- and fifty-yards Sherman yelled, "Hit it."

Brummet flipped on the high beams and the bikers reflexively pulled hard on the brakes, coming to a stop about

110 yards from Sherman and the rifle. They were not exactly lit up in glorious illumination, but that didn't matter. He could see them through the scope with their leather jackets and drawn pistols. Three hundred and thirty feet. Not far for Sherman. Not far at all.

Steadily but evenly, he squeezed the trigger while keeping the center cross over the biker's heart. The unlucky one. The closest one.

Squeeze, fire, repeat.

Two shots echoed into the night. Fifty-five grains of lead, copper and steel propelled at over two thousand miles per hour. From muzzle to chest, it took a tenth of a second. About the same time for the average person to blink.

Unlucky biker number one was to Sherman's left. He never saw it coming. Not the threat, not even the muzzle flash. That fact fizzled out somewhere on the optic nerve.

The second biker got a little more time. Danger exploded in his hippocampus, releasing a cocktail of adrenaline. Having seen a fair share of gunfire in his lifetime, the night got a little colder upon recognizing the star-shaped flash. Despite his weight and size, the biker was a nimble man and almost dismounted his bike when Sherman found his silhouette. Like a baseball bat to the chest, the second bullet unseated its target, sending the man tumbling to the ground. The unmanned bike landed on top.

Sherman inhaled and popped to his feet like shortstop after diving for a ground ball. His first shot had been slightly off center, but the range was too close to matter. Center mass was all it took. The second shot had him worried. It was all reaction and no timing. There was no planning, no waiting for the moment. A shape filled the scope, and he fired. Now his target lay behind a bike, not moving, but potentially still breathing. An unconfirmed kill by army standards.

Taking the first hundred yards at a jog, Sherman covered the last ten cautiously. Silhouetted by the high beams, his shadow loomed over the fallen motorcycle and he sidestepped to see clearly. By the time he peered over the bike, the gun in his hand was redundant. Visible in the dim light was a leg pinned under the bike and an expanding pool of blood. A pistol was laying out of reach despite desperately outstretched arms. The guy was out of the fight, and from the gurgling sound Sherman knew his time was short. By angle alone he guessed it punctured both lungs, which meant seconds left, not minutes. Sherman had seen a lot of death, but a bald middle-aged white man was new. The American soldiers, his friends, had been young, as were most of the men burdened with dying for cause or country. The others were army statistics on one of two categories: combatant or civilian. No gender, no age, just numbers. For Sherman there were faces, stories and lives, but no futures. Some stuck with him over the years, bubbling to the surface over coffee or a passing stranger on the street. Looking down at the biker, he was certain this image was already in the past.

Sherman searched the men and relieved them of wallets, phones and guns. Then he went about the morbid task of clean-up. First came the bikes. Keys went over the blackberry bushes in one direction while he pushed the bikes off the road and down the hill on the other. They didn't stay upright for long, but the underbrush seemed to swallow them just the same. The process for the riders was remarkably similar, as were the results. Only the blood remained to tell tales, and even that story was at the mercy of the rain.

Brummet killed the high beams as Sherman walked back. He could have helped, but it was better that way. Less exposure, although a district attorney would have no trouble in making a case with or without such direct involvement. Sherman tossed the rifle and pistols in back while the old man searched for words. Brummet had seen nothing like that since Vietnam and even then, he couldn't remember coming across someone as proficiently cold-blooded. Two shots, one second, both bikers dead. Then the methodical covering of tracks.

"Who the fuck are you?" he asked, mostly rhetorically, as Sherman got back in the car.

"You've met my kind before. All wars have them," answered Sherman. His father was the original Captain Sherman of the Marine variety. That his son joined the Army was something he could never live down.

Brummet thought back to his own war. The dusty wash of chopper blades, the rows of body bags swelling in the sun, the stifling heat of rice paddies and his uncontrollable fear in the grim jungle night. One tour, one year, was more than enough to fill a lifetime with anxiety. Not everyone lived it as a nightmare. The Captain was right, he had met men like him before. Brooding, concentrated men with a seriousness in their eyes and an easy fluidity to their movement. Men who walked in the jungle like a second skin. They came and went unencumbered by any prevailing political winds or cultural chasms. Conscripts, such as himself, eyed them with a mix of awe and lunacy. Who would volunteer, they wondered? Yet those men came back from the field when Brummet's friends did not. Yes, he had seen men like Sherman before.

"What now?" he asked.

"Now we hide," answered Sherman. Between the two bikers in the hospital and the two destined for the morgue, the number of groups gunning for them was too high. They needed a place off the beaten path in a town built on the sentiment.

"Spartanville?"

"No, best keep this in a single jurisdiction," said Sherman.

"I'm sure Ashley knows a place."

Sherman paused at the faint arcs of oncoming headlights, "As long as it's not familial knowledge."

The car slowed in the distance and Brummet flashed his lights to let Ashley and Ruby know it was okay. He got a reply and shifted into drive as his passenger shifted the guns around the backseat.

Sherman glanced at his phone, no service, then up at the car again. He wasn't a car guy, choosing to pay for the oil change rather than doing it himself, but the geometry coming his way was all wrong.

"Brummet, do those look like Ford Taurus headlights to you?"

"Shit," muttered the cabbie.

"Reverse," yelled Sherman.

The Crown Vic squealed to a stop and then again as Brummet mashed the accelerator, launching the car backward. He was too focused looking over his shoulder at the road behind them to see the shooting start.

CHAPTER EIGHTEEN

The night reverberated with staccato cracks and metallic pings. Sparks flew as bullets struck steel and bits of glass twinkled in the halogen light as the windshield shattered. Sherman could feel the air pressure spike as rounds passed through the car. He had yanked the recline-lever on his seat hard enough to break the plastic handle and watched his miniature world come apart.

Brummet sped backwards down a tiny hill just past the tree. It wasn't much of an elevation change, but it came quickly enough to throw off the shooters in the truck giving chase. Struggling with a locked seat belt, Sherman slid all the way into the back. Broken chunks of safety glass covered the guns and they slid across the seat with each successive turn. The pistols seemed the most manageable weapon given the situation, and he grabbed them before climbing back into the front seat in time for another straight stretch of road.

The truck closed the gap and everything became a much more kinetic space. Nearly blinded by the high beams, Sherman knew their luck teetered on the edge of oblivion. They needed space, so he stuck the biker's Beretta out what used to be the front windshield and emptied the magazine into the brightness.

"Turn us around," he yelled as the truck slowed and weaved to avoid Sherman's wild barrage.

Brummet yanked the wheel hard, and the sedan spun around with a squealing hiss. More shots rang out and Sherman's headrest exploded in a cloud of synthetic padding.

"Fuck," screamed the old man.

"Floor it," implored Sherman.

With the chase on, their odds were slim. The road had no exit, just an end. Outnumbered and outgunned, Sherman's mind switched into pure survival mode.

"We need out of this car," he told Brummet. The old man nodded. His eyes were wild with fear.

"Take the next driveway," Sherman instructed, "I'll buy us some space."

Grabbing the second pistol, he fired another magazine at the truck who was closing in again. Like someone unaccustomed to real violence and winning at all costs, the driver slowed, making room for Brummet to take a hard-left turn.

The driveway was narrow and flanked by an old twisted cedar fence with rust-colored boards and nails half-way back to their natural state. Sparse sections of pea gravel still clung to what was once a well-kept entrance. Time and circumstance had taken that wealthy sheen off the road, nothing outlasts those twin pillars of eventuality.

Brummet tried valiantly, but the car couldn't cope with the pace he built up. They fish tailed into a small oak close to a long-forgotten house still boarded up after the owners had died. Their children never returned but could not let go. So, the house sat slowly decaying away on the edges of memory.

Light from the truck was streaking through trees around the bend as Sherman threw open the driver's door and pulled Brummet out. Grabbing the old man's shoulder his hand met the familiar warm viscosity of blood. A lot. Brummet had taken at least one, maybe two rounds but kept on driving.

"You tough bastard," grunted Sherman as he shuffled

off into the underbrush with the cabbie over one shoulder and the guns dangling from the other.

The timing in those moments was key and Sherman knew they had a fighting chance when they cleared the first clump of buckbrush without getting aerated by the AR-15 wielding shooters. Despite his stubbornness, Brummet was fading fast and Sherman cursed himself for not noticing the wounds earlier, as if that would have changed anything. That the old man hadn't passed out already gave him hope, but the odds of getting medical treatment were poor. Their fate rested on the next few minutes. They couldn't afford a night in the woods. The best outcome for that was only one corpse in the morning.

Shouting behind them told Sherman it was time to make a stand. He put Brummet down in a slight depression surrounded by thick grass, not deep but enough to keep him from getting prematurely killed by a stray bullet. It was a stark equation. If Sherman lived, they might have a chance. Faint slivers of moonlight cut through the patchwork of clouds. Even under the ghostly light, the wounded man's face was pale. Blood loss was taking hold, bit by bit, minute by minute, he was ebbing away.

"Hang in there, old man," said Sherman as he placed the shotgun down. It wouldn't do Brummet any good in his condition, but it would be Sherman's personal Alamo. The stand of last resort.

Taking stock of the deteriorating situation, Sherman knew his chances weren't great, but that had never stopped him in the past. The rifle still had thirteen rounds, but the scope was useless in such poor lighting and Simpkins had removed the iron sights. He still had an almost full mag in the Glock and two more pilfered from the deputies. It seemed the color of your intentions didn't change what gun you used. Cop or criminal, they all shot the same weapon. Sixty-two bullets, give or take, against a mostly unknown force. He had seen two muzzle flashes plus the driver, so at least three, maybe more.

Deep in his pocket the cell phone gently vibrated, signaling an incoming text. With service he could call Ashley and get Brummet help, assuming he lived through the next few minutes. Out of habit or curiosity, he glanced down at the screen, keeping the light hidden behind a tree. It was from Ashley with one word: Barrios. Sherman sighed, not with anxiety, but almost relief. Now he knew who was out there and it revealed a wry smile.

"Here we go," he said to himself and the bitter night.

Three flashlight arcs sawed through the brush in a staggered search line. Sherman could hear a muted voice giving gruff instructions. The man in charge, he thought. Moving off to the side, he hoped to gain the flank but realized the men were heading directly toward Brummet. Forty yards and closing.

Visibility came and went with the clouds. A minute here or there, sometimes only seconds. As Barrios and his crew moved further in, the terrain opened as the thick undergrowth gave way to more grass and trees. Sherman watched the flashlights creep closer. As shafts of moonlight illuminated the area, Sherman picked some cover twenty yards to his right, further up the flank, and took a mental picture of all the steps required. He memorized the rocks, the trees, the route with its low dips and pockets of wet grass. Shouldering the rifle like he had thousands of times before, he took aim at the nearest light. With a useless scope, his muscle memory took over. In the dark blue of night, a rifle was a rifle. He distilled all those years of practice into a near blind shot in Northern California. Braced against the tree, he let off a string of five rounds in under a second, not caring much about the grouping.

The sharp cracks cleaved the silence, leaving chaos rippling in the darkened gloom. Sherman was already running towards his pre-picked spot while a cacophony of screams and shouts echoed off the trees. He had hit flesh, and not just superficially. The voice was intense and soaked with fear. More bullets and shouts followed. Panicked bursts that tainted the live oaks with the bright orange hue of an unnatural fall.

The two remaining men moved to their left, toward the truck, the screams and Sherman. All the shooting had given him time and light to plan another move up the flank in a giant hook that would prevent the men from escaping. Sherman decided not to leave anyone alive. The men might have been tough, even cruel, but he was merciless and vindictive.

"Turn it off," shouted one man.

Flashlights clicked off, but not before Sherman zeroed in on another target. This time he emptied the magazine in an eight-shot string that left another man gurgling in the midnight air. He was close enough to see the guy fall, to see the impact and know it struck lung. Dropping the useless rifle, he sprinted towards a buckeye that promised the best cover. Bullets snapped around him, hissing and popping as they went. The remaining shooter emptied one magazine, then another, spraying a wide arc of fire through the area.

As Sherman slid into the tree through a field of leaves, there was another burst and he felt sharp tendrils of pain explode from his left bicep.

"Fuck," he mouthed to himself.

With a deep breath, Sherman forced his arm to move. To his surprise, it still flexed, still rotated. Ripping off the shirt sleeve, he took a quick look before wrapping the wound in fabric. There was a decent amount of blood, but it stemmed from nothing more than torn flesh.

Random or well-aimed was the question racing through his mind. The woods had fallen into an eerily bleak silence with only the crickets brazen enough to make a sound. Searching through the thick blanket of leaves, Sherman found a softball sized rock which he heaved about a dozen yards to his left and into a bush. The cracking branches caused a burst of bullets. They made the mistake he wanted.

Before the last shell hissed in the damp grass Sherman sprinted away from his tree. There was a small window to move while the man recovered from the sensory onslaught of shooting in the dark. A few seconds before ringing ears and dilated pupils returned to normal.

Short, hard, adrenaline filled breaths filled the air nearby after Sherman stopped. Fear and anxiety exhaled into the cool night. Cordite clung to the humidity like glue. Sherman raised his pistol at the nervously crouched figure, the barrel mere inches away, and pulled the trigger. The shadow of a man was oblivious. The single pop felt muted compared to the chaotic minutes that had preceded. As the gunshot faded into the night, Sherman heard the truck engine roar to life.

Four men, not three. The realization hit hard. He should have known better. As the rumbling diesel faded around the corner, he found Brummet still breathing, but unconscious in the shallow pit. Using the truck to get the old man out wasn't an option anymore, and the cab was mostly scrap metal. Seeing no other option, he dialed Ashley and hoped that AT&T wouldn't decide their fate.

One bar hovered ominously in the corner as he waited, mumbling curse words.

Call failed, read the plain looking alert.

"Fucker."

He took a breath and tried again. All the worst-case scenarios circulated in his mind. The odds of keeping a sixty something year old man suffering from a gunshot wound alive without proper medical attention. Only one scenario ended with Brummet alive.

The lone bar flickered on and off as the second call failed. He put the phone on the ground while he dialed once more. Sherman ran his hand over the cabbie's shoulder, smearing the slowly congealing blood as he checked the damage. There was a dime-sized entry wound just under his clavicle and Sherman rolled Brummet over looking for the exit, hoping for a clean shot. He found it a few inches from the shoulder blade.

"Lucky bastard."

"What? Sherman, is that you?" came a thin voice from the phone still on the ground.

"Ashley, we need help now," he pleaded.

"Where?" she asked with dread in her voice.

"Half-mile past the oak tree, Ruby knows the one. First driveway on the left. I think the sign on the road said Krantz."

There was a pause, "I know the place. Five minutes."

"Watch out for Barrios," Sherman added for good measure.

"He just passed. We were out looking for you."

"Okay, hurry. Brummet's been shot."

"Jesus," was her only reply before the call failed for the last time.

Five minutes wasn't long, but time equaled life and he needed to get the old man to the road. Grabbing Brummet under his arms, Sherman started the laborious process of dragging him out of the woods and onto the driveway.

"Stay with me," he murmured, hoping that the wound was not any worse than experience suggested.

They had reached the buck brush when lights careened down the road, bouncing with speed. Sherman looked hard at the shapes and felt confident enough to step into sight as the car approached. The sedan skidded to a stop, and the two women leaped out to help him.

Ruby was first to reach them. Sherman glanced at her face expecting panic, but saw the calm and clinical look of someone who had seen it all before.

"Back seat, now!" she ordered.

Sherman moved while Ashley stood at a distance, looking pained but not distraught. As he slid Brummet into the back seat of the car Ruby hopped in through the other door. She was all business and immediately began cutting away the old man's shirt with scissors from a small black bag. They locked eyes for a moment and Sherman saw a shared spark of professionalism and camaraderie. He instinctively moved out of her way.

"Frank is driving. Ashley is helping me. Let's go."

Byron Mills, like any small town, had a doctor but Brummet was in no condition for someone accustomed to house calls, flu shots and sports physicals. He needed a hospital; the only question was which one. Reinhold held Cumbre County with an iron fist, but Sherman didn't know what sway the Sheriff had one county over. Ruby was still too busy assessing the situation to give him a timeline, but the Army's rule of thumb was sixty minutes. The golden hour. Half of that had elapsed and the drive to the nearest hospital would eat up the rest.

The piano teacher's Ford drove like a brand new car and Sherman kept the fastest pace he could without sending Ruby or Brummet careening around the back seat. Quick on the straightaways and even through the turns. Glancing over his shoulder didn't give him much more information. Ruby had the old man stripped to his waist and was methodically searching for other wounds while keeping pressure on the obvious one.

Minutes passed as they exited Upper Mill Road and onto the major drag out of town. Ruby was busy instructing Ashley on how to help stabilize their unconscious patient. Her directions were crisp and concise but not overly authoritarian. Nurse or doctor? Sherman barely considered the question.

"Prognosis?" he finally asked once they had passed the small regional airport on the outskirts of town.

"One GSW, through and through. Broke the second rib but came out clean. He's on the verge of shock but stable for now," rattled off Ruby in a clinical voice.

"Will he make it past Spartanville to the next hospital?"

Ruby looked to Ashley for a location, "Ebenville is another thirty minutes," she replied.

Ruby nodded, "Not ideal, but I think he'll make it."

"Why?" asked Ashley.

"Spartanville is the first place Reinhold or Barrios will check," said Ruby, reading Sherman's train of thought.

"Of course," mumbled Ashley.

Sherman turned north onto some country road he knew went on for days, hoping to avoid the highway, which felt like an undue risk.

"RN or MD?" he asked Ruby.

She had Brummet's feet in her lap, pushing what blood remained back toward his vital organs. "Doctor," she finally said.

"Baltimore or Chicago?"

Ruby sighed with exhaustive mirth, "Chicago."

"How did you know?" interjected Ashley.

"You're too good with that to be from somewhere boring. Had to be a big city with lots of gun violence. Maybe Savannah, but I don't think the southern bit is true either."

"Damn Frank, you're good," said Ruby with a laugh. The drawl had fallen away, replaced with crisp New England enunciation.

Genuine shock flared across Ashley's face, "I thought you were running from an abusive ex. Shit girl, you've got more skeletons than Brummet."

"We're all running from something," replied Ruby.

He wanted to press her, to ask her why, from who, but it didn't really matter. She was right, everyone was running from their past like it was a hungry tiger come to devour them whole. The truth was somewhere in between. Hidden by the flotsam of guilt and shame it drifted through life unidentified because it was easier to keep it nameless, to keep running.

Miles passed as Sherman kept the Taurus about four over the speed limit, milking what he could while avoiding some awkward police stop. Everyone was silently lost in their own world of shock, and exhaustion as the adrenaline faded to memory.

Ashley's head randomly snapped to attention, and she turned to Sherman to ask, "What happened up there?"

"Mistakes," he replied.

She waited, demanding more.

"We thought it was you, it wasn't. Brummet got shot as we drove away. They followed us into the woods once we ditched the car," added Sherman.

"And that was their mistake?"

Sherman nodded.

"What price did they pay for that mistake?"

Something was off in her voice, something unsaid.

"This is about who, not what, right? Did you see who was in the truck?" asked Sherman.

Ashley's chest heaved, "I'm almost sure Grady was in the back. Didn't see who was inside, but Barrios ain't the kinda guy to let another man drive his truck."

"I could barely see my hands out there," Sherman demurred. "Three guys got out to give chase. At least one stayed with the truck."

"And the ones who got out?" she asked.

"They're fucking dead, Ashley," interjected Ruby. "Frank isn't trying to win hearts and minds here. No offense, but men like you fight whatever war is in sight and right now Ashley your family is the enemy. Shit, you even labeled them as much."

Ruby was brisk but not wrong, and Sherman's beard itched as he listened.

Ashley folded herself into the seat, a momentary physical retreat from reality, "I guess I was hoping it wasn't them."

"Don't take this the wrong way sweetie, but Grady was a racist, sexist, asshole. He was kin, and you didn't even like him," added Ruby.

Having no siblings, Sherman couldn't compare. He had lost friends he considered brothers, but not a brother he didn't consider a friend.

"Nobody likes my family," retorted Ashley, "doesn't mean it don't sting."

"He could have driven away," offered Sherman in a moment of consolation, although he didn't know why. Given a second chance, no one in that truck would still be breathing.

Ashley smiled sadly, "Grady was too dumb to run. If he got out, it was to hurt you."

"They tried," said Sherman as he raised his arm.

"Badly?" asked Ruby, suddenly involved in the conversation again.

"Maybe ten stitches," he replied.

"Pullover and switch with Ashley. Cops are going to ask questions if you walk in there too."

Ruby had a point and Sherman knew better than to argue with a doctor. He pulled off onto a small dirt patch and switched into the passenger seat. She had a needle and thread out by the time he buckled up.

"This will hurt, but I've seen your scars and you already knew that," she said with a small twisted smile.

More truth and more pain. Sherman grimaced, drifting off somewhere deep in his mind as she cleaned the wound. A memory surfaced as he pushed against the discomfort.

It started with the suffocating smell of diesel fumes and the whine of a tank engine. Heat, but no sun. Darkness without stars. A desert night in what felt like Iraq. Sherman struggled to place the event, but there was nothing to it. Just the sounds and smells of action. His stomach churned with anxiety and there was a searing sense of pain, but he still couldn't remember why. Then, for an agonizing moment, the horizon flashed a dazzling orange, and it all came tumbling back.

Ramadi. After the surge started. He was operating in support of the Marines tasked with securing a section of the old city. Grunt work. It was dirty and brutish fighting the likes of which American troops hadn't seen since the Tet offensive in Vietnam. The boys were young and green. This was to be their moment, their Khe San. A baptism by fire to prove their might, courage and strength. Sherman recalled that the commander's speech before the battle had been rousing. Something about standing on the brink of Marine Corps lore and destiny and some other bullshit people who don't fight tell people who do. Charlatan, he thought, which is why JSOC had embedded a few Delta teams in support.

The Marines came into contact almost from the outset of the operation. Mostly small arms fire and RPGs from the outlying buildings. Sherman watched a tank split apart an old squat apartment complex like a concrete watermelon. Chunks of cinder block seemed to float like puffs of cottonwood through the air. Watching tank shells flatten the neighborhood, he knew the operation would be brutal and utterly useless. It wasn't about winning hearts and minds. It was just dead Iraqis, the more, the better. Body count was the only statistic to matter that night.

The fight continued apace as they advanced. A window would open, some kid would fire a few rounds from an AK and the Marines would blow up the room with a rocket. So went the cycle. They met harassing fire with overwhelming force. Then it all went sideways. Some repurposed artillery shell shredded the tank from beneath and what had been a few random shots turned into an unending staccato of dissonance. Frantic calls for evac dominated the radio waves. Sherman grabbed his team and headed out.

Dead dark is what they called those starless nights. Only the flashes of rifle fire and random explosions provided any light. Using the roof for access, Sherman's team attacked a building full of insurgents firing on the Marines. He took point as they descended a small stone staircase filled with acrid smoke and cordite. The memory of those rooms had a surreal quality, like walking into some circle of hell. The militiamen were too busy trying to knock down the wall that they didn't see the Americans enter. It all happened so close, so personal and visceral, yet Sherman experienced nothing but the cold calculation of trigger pulls and reloads. Blood, screams, shouting and gunshots filled the rooms as they moved down each floor.

As Ruby tied the last stitch a twang of pain sent him back to the two bullets that went through his armor. In all that chaos he couldn't say who pulled the trigger and it didn't matter. There was no vendetta or grudges. His men were the only ones to exit alive. It all started and ended that night.

They carried Sherman out, shielding him behind a still running tank. The fight continued, on and off, as the Marines counterattacked. When the Blackhawk roared overhead, blood loss and morphine had taken the sheen off his conscious mind and all he could do was stare into the darkness above.

"All done," said Ruby as she finished wrapping his arm in gauze. The work was tidy and clean. Not a hack job.

"Thanks Doc," he replied with an exhausted smile.

"I shed that name years ago."

"Maybe, but the talent never left," he replied.

Ruby dropped her veil of seriousness for a moment, "Thanks, now where did you go? Most people would have screamed."

"Oddly enough, to the first night I ever got shot."

Ashley looked over at him, "How many..." she asked before trailing off.

"A few," answered Sherman, eyes planted on the road.

"I don't know if that was modest or macho," quipped Ruby. "From what I saw the other night there were several."

"Some bullets, some shrapnel, it's all metal."

"Doesn't that just scare the crap out of you?" asked Ashley.

Sherman squinted at the question and looked down at his hands, "Sometimes, sure, but not in the moment."

"And what about after?" continued Ashley.

"Or before?" added Ruby.

"I'm not a machine. Of course, I get scared, get worried and jittery. I used to make promises I'll never keep. It's the human condition. What I don't make room for is doubt."

"Like the cause of all this chaos?" interjected Ashley, "Because there is some fundamental shit we've done that I don't agree with."

"No. Myself. I don't doubt myself."

"So, you're cocky," she chided.

"Confidence," said Ruby, "isn't cockiness."

"There are plenty of things worth second guessing, but the man I've become is not one of them," concluded Sherman.

"Fair enough, I wish I could be so sure," said Ashley. "Tillerman had that, he seemed so comfortable in his own skin."

"He too was still running," gently reminded Ruby.

"Only from the past," Sherman added, "He seemed to have found a future."

Ashley wiped away the tears that were trickling down her cheek. All those intangible pieces that come to form a persona, a life, were unraveling around her in the space of a few days. A deer in headlights would have looked more self-assured. A dead love, a dead brother and the realization her family wanted her dead left behind a numbingly thick mental haze.

The car was drifting, edging closer to the center yellow lines. Sherman could see the look in her eyes. A searching, yearning gaze into the past, into the future, wondering what happened. It was easy to get lost in that. He gently squeezed her leg. She blinked it away for a moment and straightened out the Taurus.

Ebenville glowed in the distance. A pale-yellow aspect amongst endless rows of almond trees. The city wasn't any bigger than Spartanville and had it not been for the railroads it would have remained a tiny hamlet. A blip on the agricultural map. As it was the Union Pacific didn't like Spartanville, the result of some lingering family feud, and built their tracks some twenty miles away. Spite bestowed prosperity, but that was a bygone era when railroads dominated the economic landscape. The city before them was a shell of rusting industry and infrastructure, vestiges of a once promising future. Cows and nuts kept the small main street alive, but it was only a matter of time. Kids left never to return, and those who stayed struggled to find work or meaning. Prosperity now looked like a shitty truck and a decent pair of boots.

As they turned into a mostly empty parking lot near the hospital Sherman asked, "You think they can handle Brummet?"

"Trust me," said Ashley, "these guys see their fair share of valley calamity. Farmer's losing arms, drunken antics and hunting accidents."

"I'll make sure they don't ruin all my hard work," added Ruby.

Sherman had hoped she would volunteer to stay, "Thanks. You got a story of for the cops?"

"Oh Officer," crooned Ruby in her southern drawl, "we was just stopped for a smoke when 'dem boys over on county road started shootin' cans."

"Alright then," he chuckled, "I'll call to check in a few hours." Motioning for Ashley to get out, he added, "Good luck."

Ruby smiled and Sherman tossed her what remained of Johnny's ten grand. "In case Brummet doesn't have insurance," he joked.

She scoffed and said something, to challenge the gesture, but stopped short.

"Good luck, sugar," said Ashley as the pair drove across the street and up to the emergency room entrance.

From the poorly lit pavement, Sherman and Ashley watched the ensuing chaos slowly unfold as the medical staff rushed to get Brummet inside. Ruby was close on their heels, watching every decision like a hawk.

Once everyone had entered the hospital Ashley asked, "Did you know her story before today?"

"No," he admitted.

"What or who do you think she is hiding from?"

"Beats me, but I'll be damned if I don't want to know. You can ask her when this is over with."

"If I ever see her again. You just gave her ten large worth of escape money," chided Ashley.

He shrugged at the truth, "I know."

The wind picked up and blew a steady stream of leaves and trash across the desolate lot. Sherman looked at his watch and the small luminescent dots pointing to one o'clock in the morning. Time was short. Probate hearings and Reinhold's threats didn't matter anymore. Now he was up against Uncle Sam's demands and could not ignore them. One way or another, the army would come to get him, be it for a mission or the brig. The Major could only stall for so long. When it all went bad, as it always did, their friendship would take a back seat to the mission. Two days and not much more.

"Let's find a ride," he said.

Ashley looked around the almost empty lot and put her hands up in the air, "So many to choose from."

"Come on." Sherman motioned toward a beat-up old Chevy pickup. He had spotted the battered blue exterior on the way in and pegged it as the best candidate for being unlocked. He wasn't wrong.

"Why does this not surprise me," said Ashley as he hotwired the truck.

"Your tax dollars hard at work," grunted Sherman while pushing the wires back into place.

"Finally doing me some good," she scoffed.

The old truck stuttered to life with a determined effort and Sherman pulled out onto the empty street. Statisticians say car theft is only the first step to violent crime and Sherman thought they couldn't be more correct. Having left most of the guns behind in the dark, he needed to restock. None of the piddly ad hoc crap he had been doing. No, he wanted a proper kit and knew just where to look.

"Are we heading back?" Ashley asked wearily.

Sherman nodded, but his crooked smile gave her pause. It harbored no humor, no warmth, just the resigned menace of those fully committed to a cause. The smile of a fanatic.

CHAPTER NINETEEN

"You can't be serious," exclaimed Ashley.

They had parked behind one of several old antique shops in Byron Mills and the dusty gravel lot swarmed with riparian sounds and the earthy aroma of decay. Sherman had picked it not for some unseen beauty but for its geographic proximity to the Sheriff's station. It made an ideal staging ground. Only three buildings away, but completely out of sight.

"Afraid so," he said. "We need what they have."

"Why not rob a gun store?" she asked.

"You have one in town?"

"Well, no, but we could have found one in Spartanville."

Sherman stayed silent.

"Fine, fine," she continued, "but what if someone is inside?"

"I'll improvise," he answered.

"You mean shoot them?"

Sherman shrugged at the obvious truth.

Ashley sighed, "What do you want me to do?"

"Keep the truck running and stay out of sight. I should be back in ten minutes," he instructed.

"You know how terrifying ten minutes alone in the dark are, right?"

"I do," he said sympathetically. The raw edge of terror, of the unknown, was nothing new. He had felt its terrible power in the mountains of Afghanistan and the haunted streets of Syria. He saw men buckle under the inner voices of fear and run for their lives.

"Ten minutes," she repeated.

He nodded and slipped over a small rock wall separating the parking lot from the vegetation below. The clouds responsible for the dead dark earlier in the night had departed, leaving a soft lunar glow on the sand below. Sliding through the softly swaying cattails, Sherman quickly emerged behind the station in mud smelling of tadpoles. There he waited, but not for long, just a minute. With crickets and frogs as the only witnesses, he hopped over the wall next to a yard enclosed by chain-link.

Cumbre County under Reinhold didn't have much prosecutable crime and the impound lot was empty save for a few automotive remnants of drunk driving. Strung across the fence top were a few compulsory strands of barbed wire. Enough to deter teenage vandals, but otherwise ineffective. Starting at the corner, Sherman scaled the fence in a few swift moves, careful not to snag anything during the transition over. The Glock was already in his hand and he picked his way to the back door. Seven minutes remained.

They locked the door. Surprising or not, he couldn't decide, so he moved onto the windows. Whatever previous life the building had, the priority was not security. A few bars covered the larger windows, but the bolts attaching it to the wall were on cheap and it sagged at the corners. Sherman yanked on one, and it rattled. He was certain it would come off given time, but Ashley was waiting, alone, exposed and in the dark. The third window was frosted and reeked of cigarette smoke. The restroom, he mused. Sherman gave the cheap white vinyl edge a push and the entire thing slid up with a well-oiled pop.

"Too lazy to smoke outside," he said to himself before easing through the tight space.

Except for a lone bulb near the front door, the station was inky. An HVAC system hummed overhead and there was the occasional squelch from the radio room, but Sherman didn't hear any life. During his brief chat with Reinhold he had got a decent look at the layout of the station, not that it took much deduction. The armory had the word stenciled over the door in drab army font.

The United States government had been generous to the Cumbre County Sheriff Department. Through the 1033 Program and its largess, Reinhold acquired enough military hardware to start an African coup. M-4 rifles sat next to MP-5 submachine guns and shotguns from various manufacturers.

"Fuck me," he muttered in astonishment.

Rural cops didn't need half of what existed in that room, and Sherman set about liberating what he deemed necessary. From a hanger he grabbed a tactical vest, inserted the hardened steel plates and threw it on. One more went into a backpack that was sitting on a corner bench. On top of that went magazine upon magazine of NATO standard 5.56mm ammunition. About three hundred rounds in all. For sanity's sake, Sherman added another Glock and ten more magazines. Then he slung two rifles over his shoulder. One with a short-range sight and one with a longer 6x scope. Skipping the night vision and fancy thermal cameras, he grabbed a radio, extra batteries and a flare on the way to the back door. Everything in the room was prepped, and he knew the Sheriff was gearing up for a fight.

No point in leaving them anything, he thought, before lighting the flare and tossing it into Reinhold's office. The cheap vinyl curtains and brownish carpet went up faster than a stack of kerosene-soaked briquettes.

Smoke was visibly rising in the distance by the time Sherman got back to the truck. He was one minute late. A reddish-orange glow lent a certain hellishness to the scene as they drove out.

Ashley hadn't said a word as he got in the truck, but shook her head at the flames, "You just couldn't help yourself."

"They are prepared for a war," he retorted.

"And now they have one," she added, speeding away into the fading night. "Now what? Hide?"

Sherman looked at his watch. It was almost 3:30 in the morning and they needed to rest soon, but he had one more visit in mind. "Not yet. Barrios owes me an answer."

"For what? He's scum, guilty as sin, you know that already."

"It's not about what I already know," he said.

"You going to beat it out of him like Johnny?" she wondered.

"No need, that man has no spine. He'd point the finger at Jesus if it got him off."

"And you think he'll just crack like that?"

Sherman's face shone with indifference. It didn't matter if Barrios came clean at first sight, he was still going to hurt the man. Either circumstance would not lead to him still breathing.

"Fine," she resigned to say, "Where am I dropping you?"

"Close to his house."

"Then more waiting?" she asked.

"Afraid so."

"Fuck that, I'm coming with you," she exclaimed.

As a leader of well-disciplined men, Sherman didn't hear no often, but he didn't lead zombies either. His team trusted him to make the right decision, and if they thought otherwise their objections were manifest. Ashley still had her individual spunk intact; it hadn't been hammered out in basic training. Her expression was solid and unyielding, with the strength of a warrior and the stubbornness of grief.

"Fine. Park around the block. We'll go over the neighbor's fence," he agreed.

"I thought you'd fight me on that."

"Would it have changed your mind?" he asked.

"No."

"Then I saved us some time."

The plan was asinine, and he knew that outright, but she

could just as easily catch a bullet in the truck while waiting. This way he could keep her close, even if that came with its own set of consequences.

The volunteer fire department was wailing its way to the blaze as they turned into Brummet's neighborhood. Noise seemed to consume the entire town. Sirens blared in the distance and the roar of motorcycles racing up and down the central drag had turned the night into a small-scale Sturgis. They had passed a group of four bikes parked by the general store. Ashley grimaced as she saw them but managed not to hit the brakes and arouse any alarm. The men eyed them as they went by, but nothing else. Just another beat up truck, which even at that hour wasn't uncommon.

As instructed, Ashley parked the Chevy down a darkened cul-de-sac one street over from the deputy's house. Sherman stashed the bag under the gnarled brambles of a blackberry bush near the truck, but not before giving Ashley the extra vest and pistol. The body armor was comically large and fit like a Kevlar moo-moo, but something would always beat nothing in a gunfight.

It was a quarter to four in the morning as they wordlessly crossed over the street and through the well-manicured yard of some family. Sherman didn't care whose property he trespassed through, but a small wooden sign caught his eye. *The Krenshaw Family*, it read. Years ago, he had served with a Sergeant of the same name. Jamaican by way of Puerto Rico, with the waist of a tree trunk. The M249 he had carried look positively small in comparison. Yet another contact lost over the previous decade.

The family had a dog, something big and loud judging by the height of the fence and the size of the toys stalking about in the fescue. Sherman motioned for Ashley to climb over it when she pointed to a gate. How friendly, thought Sherman, but still pointed up. She shrugged and swung herself over with remarkable ease despite the ill-fitting vest. Sherman slung the rifle and followed her over, landing in some infrequently cut grass.

A sliding glass door led into the rear of the house. Ashley looked on apprehensively as he slowly pushed the handle. The door did a little hop over a poorly sunk screw before easily sliding open. A small town after all.

The place was a bachelor pad from top to bottom and lacked furniture or amenities. The only framed picture Sherman could see was a bunch of painted albeit naked women from a Pink Floyd album cover. Boots and jackets lay haphazardly in the foyer and stacks of empty Busch cans covered the dining room table. There were a few dirty dishes in the sink, but he guessed the deputy did most of his cooking on the grill out back. The only other thing of value besides an oversized television was a massive gun safe on the far side of the living room.

From down the hall they heard the distinctive ringing of a phone.

"Shit," said Ashley before covering her mouth.

Sherman moved past the reclining couch and against the wall. Peeking around the corner he could see down the hall towards the bedrooms and the noise.

"What!" came a yell, "For fuck's sake. Yeah, I'll be there," followed by the sounds of someone stumbling about in search of clothes.

The hallway light came on and Ashley froze before ducking under the oak table. Sherman was out of view around the corner, roughly halfway between Barrios on one end of the house and the front door on the other. He leaned the rifle against a sparsely used bookshelf and waited.

Muttering obscenities, Barrios flipped on the living room light and walked right by Sherman. Lost in his own nightmare, the deputy didn't notice the figure in the corner as he went to retrieve his service weapon from the safe.

"Good morning, deputy," boomed Sherman.

Startled and bewildered, Barrios leaped back with a shocked look of despair, like when a nagging fear comes to pass. The cocky smile of a few days earlier disappeared, replaced by the fresh memory of zipping his friends into body bags. Waxy, blood covered skin and empty eyes, those were the images he couldn't shake, and they had cracked his thin shell like an egg. No level of machismo overcomes the smell of blood and piss and fear.

Barrios looked at Sherman and then at Ashley, who was slowly rising from her hiding spot. From the vests they wore and the call he had just received, the connection clicked and with it grew his anger.

"You fucking bitches," he spat, before closing the gap with Sherman. Being scared and being cornered create two unique reactions and right then rage fueled his aggressive stance.

Watching the deputy, who loomed over Sherman by a heavy four inches, begin to advance made Ashley instinctively want to raise her gun, but she didn't. There was something so calm and unworried in Sherman's stance, so self-assured. Tillerman had that confidence, and she ate it up like an antidote to her own confidence issues. So, the gun just hung there, and she watched in some strange out-of-body experience.

Sherman stepped forward to meet Barrios. The rifle was against the wall, the pistol in his holster. He had no plan to shoot but every intention to harm. Their body language escalated into physical momentum and Barrios went in swinging.

For years he had done just that. A switch flipped by rage sent his fists flying at anyone willing to stand in front of him. His knuckles had broken many noses and they kept a certain calloused feel, but Barrios always hid behind his badge and he swung without knowing loss, without knowing pain.

Aggressively talentless, the deputy dropped his shoulder and threw a cascade of punches like some third-rate UFC fighter. Sherman watched it come with the patience of a surfer waiting for the wave. He ducked twice, let a left hook glance across his shoulder, then hit Barrios in the solar plexus with enough force to crack a sheet of plywood.

Ashley chuckled as Barrios sank to his knees, retching bile and half-digested leftovers onto the carpet. Sherman stepped in again and smashed knee to nose. Blood spurted everywhere, and the deputy curled into a ball on the floor looking like another drunk passed out in his own bodily fluids. He whimpered softly.

"Two questions for you deputy," said Sherman. "Did you do it and who ordered it?"

Barrios just glared back and Sherman broke the deputy's clavicle with a single boot strike. The resulting howl of pain was loud enough to wake his neighbors had they given a damn.

"Did you do it?" repeated Sherman.

All the snot and blood made it hard for Barrios to breathe and he rolled around in pain unsuccessfully trying to clear his nose. The cheap beige carpet under him was slowly staining with splatters and smears of blood. Whatever shield of arrogance he had built over the years vanished and he felt crushed by its loss.

"Answer the question, John," instructed Ashley. Her tone was flat and matter of fact. The compassion she had shown for Simpkins didn't exist for Barrios.

"I didn't fucking kill your boy toy," replied Barrios between labored breaths.

"Who did?" she yelled.

"You did! You stupid bitch!" spat the deputy.

Ashley looked perplexed and hurt. The gun wavered at her side as if her hand was deciding separately from her brain. Sherman watched her face contort with grief and shades of understanding.

Barrios tried to laugh at her discomfort, but Sherman kicked his ribs, sending him in search of air. Finally, the deputy added, "You took their money Ashley, and they took him. Eye for an Eye."

"Who?" Sherman demanded.

"I don't fucking know," Barrios laughed painfully. "Whoever Reinhold and Thorne sold out to. I'm only the delivery man."

"Where did you take him?" barked Sherman.

"Into the arms of her loving family," he sneered.

Sherman kneeled down and placed the barrel of his pistol over the deputy's kneecap, but said nothing.

"Wait, wait," pleaded Barrios. He was under no illusion of what Sherman was capable of, but still hoped to see the sunrise mostly intact. "You know the spot."

Sherman didn't quite know what to make of the claim. The deputy could have been bluffing or stalling for time. The mind will say anything to survive, which is why torture only works to extract words, not truths. Yet watching Barrios broken and bloody on the floor, Sherman didn't see deception, just a fading glimmer of hope only those too far gone can see.

"What the fuck does that mean?" Ashley asked when the low rumble of motorcycles reached their ears.

A block or two away, thought Sherman. He grabbed Ashley and pointed out the back door. "Time to go," he hissed.

Ashley moved back, almost unwillingly at first. She wanted more. Something was unfinished, unknown, and it gnawed at her stomach. She tried to implore Sherman to stay, but his eyes said otherwise. They screamed run.

Bullets came crashing in by the time he grabbed the rifle and they squeezed through the backdoor. Not the sporty crack 5.56mm, but something Sherman instantly recognized as the dry thud of AK-47 rounds. They tumbled through plywood and drywall, shredding everything inside, including Barrios. The deputy caught three through the back and abdomen as blood oozed onto the carpet. The guy was dead, Sherman knew as much, but he stopped near the fence line to fire a single shot. Was it pity or spite? He didn't know, and it didn't matter. The round hit Barrios squarely in the temple. In and out and all over. One less problem, one less complication. Just another body in a number too big to count.

Ashley was already climbing over the fence when he pointed one yard over. Experience told Sherman not to retreat the same way he entered. That and he couldn't shake an uneasy sense someone had seen them and tipped off the bikers. How else would they have known? The question bounced around his mind front and center.

They jumped, catty corner, into someone else's plain grass filled yard. Sherman expected contact and landed rifle at the ready, but nothing came. The bikers had stopped firing and their engines roared back toward town. Lights were hesitantly popping on throughout the neighborhood. Byron Mills was not your typical sleepy town, but bursts of automatic rifle fire had woken no one up before. Curtains parted uneasily and Sherman assumed most of the street was armed behind locked doors.

Something still nagged him about the Krenshaw house and he kept the M4 aimed where he would have shot from, which was the second story corner bedroom. It overlooked Barrios' living room and the yard they were using as an exit. In the briefest of flashes Sherman saw the blinds quiver, followed by an almost indistinct orange glow. Just a smidge of movement and light. Given the same circumstances in Iraq or Syria, he would have fired a magazine into the building, but some residual civic duty checked the impulse. The moment only heightened his internal warning system. The lights were blinking, the alarms blaring.

"Start the truck," he hissed while sliding over to the blackberry bush concealing the bag.

Looking shaken, Ashley nodded and raced across the street and up the cul-de-sac when a single hyper-sonic crack knocked her face down on the ground.

Time slowed.

Every bell in Sherman's mind was ringing full tilt. The snapping hiss, the direction of the shot made it plain where to fire. With methodical precision he shot through each window in the Krenshaw house, starting with where he'd seen the brief glimmer of a figure. The compulsion to avoid collateral damage fell away into the abyss of survival. If Sherman was wrong, this wouldn't be the first civilian killed under his watch and given the conflict it sadly would not be the last.

Inserting a fresh magazine, he racked the bolt before moving to Ashley. The bullet that struck her was from something big and fast, that much Sherman knew. Only one question raced through his mind. Had he inserted the metal plates into her vest as well? He cursed himself for not remembering. Her survival depended on that decision. Caliber alone does not defeat armor. Speed is the killer.

When he reached her Sherman didn't bother to check for a pulse or triage her wound. He grabbed the collar of her vest and dragged her around to the front of the truck. Sitting behind that small-block V8 was the best armor they could have at the moment. Judging by the dry asphalt, it looked like wonderful news. No blood trail or sticky streak of black shone in the pale light. Sherman could see the exposed plate and white spalding from the impact site. He sighed with relief even though Ashley was still out cold. A bloody contusion on her temple said the culprit was ground not lead.

With an abundance of caution, he got the passenger door open and lifted her into the cab without ever taking his eyes off the house. The sounds of screen doors squeaking open and thudding shut meant the mostly retired suburb was up early. Sherman knew they didn't have much time before Reinhold, or the bikers found them. That or the neighbors came out with Mossbergs and Maglites. The modern equivalent of pitchforks and torches.

With a twist, the Chevy grumbled to life, and Sherman dropped it into reverse. The tires squealed as he raced to the T-junction, turning hard away from the threat. It was a precarious move. Contained within a thin steel coffin that might sputter to a standstill at any moment, they were easy targets. Although he couldn't be sure, Sherman thought he saw the same orange glow from a small attic window, just a speck of light between slotted boards. In the space of a deep breath there passed a moment of tension and apprehension as he waited for the shots to ring out. Nothing came. No crack, no shattered glass or metallic ping. They cleared the corner and sped out of the small neighborhood.

The general store's lights were on, although the neon open sign remained dormant. Sherman monitored the rearview mirror for unwelcome travelers, but the roads were vacant. It was almost four in the morning. Ashley stirred and moaned on the bench seat, the blood on her head crusting over.

"Ah, fuck me," she said drowsily, "What, what, happened?"

"You got shot."

"I did what?"

"You got shot in the back," repeated Sherman.

She tried to sit up but the combination of back and head pain was too much. "Oh," she said while massaging the massive lump forming above her left eye.

"Someone at the Krenshaw house shot you. The bump is from the fall."

"Who are the Krenshaw's?" she asked incredulously.

"The family behind Barrios," he responded in mock explanation.

"Ugh," she gasped, "that place is a rental. Wait," she wiggled her toes and moved her legs, "oh, thank god."

"You'll be fine," replied Sherman matter-of-factly.

"Well excuse me," she muttered, "Someone just shot me." Ashley paused as it sank in, "Holy shit Frank, someone tried to kill me." The adrenaline and shock wore off, and she sobbed with fear then anger then regret. She cried through most of town, with the rumble of the truck matching her shuddering shoulders.

The night was old and fading with the first tendrils of morning. Sherman could feel the town waking. Lights were blinking on and coffee being brewed for those early risers. With daybreak imminent, they needed a place to lie low and rest. Recent events had Sherman grasping for answers but finding only questions.

He squeezed Ashley's calf, "Got a decent place to lie low?"

She unburied her face from the seat, "I don't know Frank. Everything seems so small, so hopeless."

"Not even close. Believe me, you'll know real hopelessness when it beckons."

"You suck at reassurances," she chided softly.

He chuckled, "Never my strength."

Ashley sighed with thought, "There are some cabins in the mountains. We'd hike past them as kids."

"Silo your life. Think of a place your brothers won't know about," suggested Sherman.

"Uh, oh man, this town ain't that big."

"You would be surprised," he added.

"Ah-ha," she exclaimed moments later. "Tillerman had a camp on North River Road. Used it to mill wood."

This was the first Sherman had heard of the place, but his friendship was never built on full disclosure. Secrets weren't dishonorable and everyone needed those hidden corners and unlit spaces. Like a cord of wood, his own past had many. Some bore recent cuts and still oozed sap, while others were dry as bones.

"Anyone else know about it?" he asked warily.

"Don't think so. I only ever heard him describe it."

Tillerman wasn't boastful, so Sherman had no reason to doubt its existence, however there were always shades of truth.

"Can we find it?" he asked.

"I think so. He told me where it was. Just never had a reason to go up there," she replied.

Sherman nodded, "Works for now."

Crickets still chirped as he turned left over the largest bridge in town. Decades earlier, a sudden warm storm had reduced a predecessor to hulking concrete pylons. The skeleton of that much lower bridge was still a visible reminder of engineering hubris. Winding along the relatively flat road, Sherman couldn't help but think how little he knew about Byron Mills. Tillerman had cared little for politics, nor was he city council material. Anonymity just wasn't possible anymore, so he had picked a town content with obscurity. Hiding was easier when no one looked. He realized he knew more about tribal Waziristan or rural Syria than the politics of Cumbre County.

"Tell me about Reinhold," said Sherman.

"Fucking asshole," responded Ashley.

"Besides the obvious. You said he's been Sheriff since you were a kid. What's his reputation?"

"A fucking asshole," she repeated sarcastically.

Sherman looked over but said nothing.

"It's a small county and a smaller town, so mostly petty shit. The kids hate him because he doesn't tolerate youthful indiscretions. The adults like him because he keeps the kids in line," she answered.

"What about gossip or rumors?" he asked.

"People don't really take to that around here," replied Ashley.

"Everybody whispers," said Sherman. "What of his past?"

"Old family. Been here since the gold rush, they say. His daddy was Sheriff, so some think it was just a given he'd wear the silver star too. I honestly can't think of anyone who has run against him in an election."

"He always been dirty?"

Ashley laughed, "Entrepreneurial is what they call it around here. I can't say for certain, but probably. Most folks want to be left well enough alone, and Reinhold does a fair job of keeping crime amongst the criminals."

"Like your dad?"

"Yup," she confided, "like my dear old dad."

"They ever mix it up?" asked Sherman.

"Sure, here and there, but nothing major. From what my mom said, they went off to Vietnam together," she replied.

It surprised Sherman, "Wait, Reinhold and your dad both fought in Vietnam?"

"Yeah, got drafted in the early seventies, I think."

"Same unit?" he asked.

"Don't know. Pa never really talked about the war much. Not that he was embarrassed, but it always seemed like some inconvenience on his path to something bigger."

"Did Reinhold ever hassle him about the pot?" asked Sherman.

She took a thoughtful breath, "I remember him stopping by the bar years ago, almost regular like, but it never seemed antagonistic. Mostly small-time grief over the liquor license or some other nonsense.

Sherman looked ahead, lost in thought.

"Trying to put the puzzle together?" she asked.

"Something like that," he mused.

"And?"

"Still missing the center, but I think I have the borders."

"Turn after the apple orchard," she said, pointing ahead. Sherman nodded.

"What's missing?" she asked. "You've got Pa and Reinhold running drugs for that Stockwood character."

"With bikers as extra muscle," he added.

"And me as the money launderer," she said with a sigh.

"We are missing someone."

"The only other organized group is the loggers," she added.

Sherman gave the idea some thought as he turned up a narrow gravel road sandwiched between apple and walnut trees. It made sense. Logging came with transportation, with distribution. No cops checked the cargo. It was always in plain view. The theory fit into his expanding understanding of the operation, but it didn't feel complete. No, there was someone else. Whoever had put that camp together, maybe the same person who shot Ashley. That one orange glow in the window.

"Shit," he muttered excitedly.

"What?"

"It's the same person," he said absently.

She shrugged, unable to follow his train of thought.

"As we left Barrios, I thought there was an orange glow in the Krenshaw house, something small and faint. Then you got shot and I'm sure I saw it again when we left."

"Like a cigarette?"

"A Lucky Strike," he said.

"That's oddly specific and ridiculously common."

"I found a few stubs from where they took Tillerman," he elaborated.

The road further narrowed and Sherman kept his senses open for trouble.

"Your suspect list is long. This ain't a blue part of California and most people here don't give a damn about the Surgeon General."

"Anyone you know smoke them?" he asked.

Ashley inhaled then spoke, "Pa, Tanner, all the bartenders at the Crosscut, most of the loggers, shit I used to smoke them not that long ago."

Tanner, the smart brother. Sherman focused on the man. Intelligent, manipulative and over-confident was his initial impression from their brief encounter. Cold-blooded murderer? It didn't seem to stick, but his retelling of Tillerman's story was strange. The insider attack, the family connection. Maybe his friend had felt the same way. Why else share it with a man he knew would use it as some boast?

"Your brother never served, right?"

"Tanner? No, Pa wouldn't let him. He always said family first, country last."

"But he wanted to?"

"Sure, the Army wanted him bad. Scored real high on the ASVAB."

The Armed Services Vocational Aptitude Battery, Sherman knew the test well. It was the military version of the SAT, except useful. Army recruiters used it to find kids smart enough for skilled positions. Funny thing about the test; it didn't matter what you scored they would still let you get shot on the front lines.

"I think we need to find out what he knows," said Sherman.

Ashley didn't reply. There was no point. They both knew her family was neck deep into things they had no right to do and the fallout was nearly upon them.

The orchard was long gone in their faint spiral of dust, replaced by ancient oaks and clumps of burgundy manzanita. It took them a good ten minutes to wind back into some hidden flat on the ever-increasing slope surrounding the valley. Driveways peeled off occasionally sending tentacles of dirt over the hills.

"That's it," said Ashley, pointing to a small ramshackle affair scarcely visible from the road.

Sherman killed the lights and drove past the turn. The road contoured onward but wasn't much more than a rutted jeep track. People came up there, but Tillerman had the last scrap of flat land.

Sherman hopped out and waited for his eyes to adjust. He could have just driven right up, but the habits of precaution were too strong. If someone was waiting, they already knew he was coming. He had no element of surprise, but Sherman didn't like making it easy.

Satisfied his pupils had expanded, Sherman edged closer. Crisp night air hovered above the wet grass, seeping through his pants as he kneeled. Birds were chirping as the first strands of dawn edged over the mountains. A beautiful, empty spot. Sherman whistled for Ashley to bring the truck around.

She parked the old Chevy behind a small work shed that had served as Tillerman's mill. Sherman walked over to a plywood shack nearby that reminded him of the bare bones construction common at Special Forces bases in Afghanistan. Small and almost windowless, save for two overlooking the road and the mountains. Corrugated metal served as the roof, with a small metal flute poking out indicating a wood stove. The simplicity, the location, it all epitomized Tillerman's persona. It was a distillation of his beliefs.

If Ashley had hoped to find some hidden part of Tillerman inside, she only found disappointment. The interior was feverishly spartan. A stack of history books lay in one corner and twin-bed in the other. An old wood stove stood by the door, beckoning warmth and smoke they could not risk.

"Take the bed," offered Sherman, "I'll take the shed." He grabbed an extra sleeping bag from a pile of gear in the corner and headed out.

"You sure?" she asked.

"I'll feel better out there."

"Suit yourself," she replied.

Dead was dead. He didn't worry about hurting Tillerman's feelings anymore. Yet sleeping in the same room as his girlfriend, under the roof he built no less, felt like a betrayal. The mill was fine and Sherman found a spot near some half-cut spruce log. It offered an excellent view of the road and the slight rise Sherman would have used to attack the place. He slid into the bag, zipped up and fell asleep as the sun crested over the mountains, spilling into the valley below.

CHAPTER TWENTY

A shrill beeping woke Sherman up. The sun was overhead, and no clouds bothered to stop the rays. He looked at the screen: Unknown Number. Only one person who knew his number came up like that and only five people had it. Sherman hit the green button.

"Major," he answered.

"Captain," said the familiar baritone, "Our problem in West Africa is getting worse. You have eighteen hours."

"Understood. Where is pickup?" asked Sherman.

"We'll come to you. Regional airport tomorrow at zero-five-hundred hours."

"Copy that."

"You better be walking under your own power, Captain. I don't stop for invalids or pine boxes."

"Yes sir," replied Sherman with a smile. That was more encouragement than he usually got from the man.

"Out," added the Major as he hung up.

Things must have been getting worse for the personal taxi service. Eighteen hours didn't give him much time, but things were snowballing. Sherman knew it would get much worse in the unfolding day, but he was past a tipping point. Seeing it through to the end was the only option left. Shallow graves, hewn in haste, beckoned.

The smell of coffee wafted from the small cabin on the late morning air and the aroma pulled him out of the sleeping bag. He didn't have to, but he knocked on the door just the same.

Ashley opened it with her brows furrowed, "Are we being modest now?"

Sherman shrugged, "Manners, I guess."

She motioned for him to come in and grab a cup, "I think we are well past pleasantries, Frank."

"Thanks. You get some rest?"

"Didn't think I would at first. It all smells like him. But yeah, I slept better than I have in days. How was the shed?"

"Just what the doctor ordered."

She shook her head jokingly, "So we're rested, now what?"

Sherman scratched his beard. The base was back and rooted, but he couldn't help but confirm it was there. Shaving it had been a necessary shock, but growing it back felt strangely premature. He had craved time with his friend, away from the blood, but found only more death. Its orbit felt inescapable and familiar.

"We need to talk to Tanner," he finally said.

Ashley inhaled deeply, holding the thought for a few seconds before releasing. "I figured as much."

The possibility should have sent Sherman right to her father's doorstep, but something told him that fight would be different. Violence and cruelty belong to the young, but real venom builds with age. Thorne and Reinhold had been at it a long time. Sherman respected that experience and understood they had the most to lose and the furthest to fall.

"Did Ruby call?" asked Ashley.

She hadn't, and Sherman shook his head. The only call had been from the Major and he didn't see the need to divulge his timetable, at least not yet.

"I hope Brummet is okay," she added.

The old man was sturdier than he looked. Sherman didn't have any doubts about his fate. The bigger question in his mind was whether Ruby had pulled up stakes and left forever. She had run from someone or something, but that didn't mean she was flighty. Few people willingly face their demons, internal or external, and Sherman would not judge her for the past.

"Call her," he suggested.

Ashley nodded and dialed. Sherman could hear the ringing, one after another, and knew it would end with a voicemail.

"Hey sweetie," she started, "just checking in on you two. Call me when you get this. Bye."

After hanging up, Ashley just stared at her phone for another minute, her wheels turning. She and Ruby had been friends for years, co-workers for a little longer, but that felt frayed.

A muted buzz emanated from the idle device, gently shaking the table. They glanced down at the awaiting text message, but Sherman turned away to give her some privacy with the impending news.

"Brummet is stable," Ashley read. "Full recovery likely. I wish I was the same. At the beach, back to running. Can't handle more of this darkness. Sorry."

Despite their differences, the news came as no surprise. Ashley and Sherman had been thinking along the same tangent of possibility. They exchanged a glance soaked with reservations but let drop their own thoughts on Ruby. Instead, they sipped on Tillerman's strong coffee in silence, worrying their own worries.

Sherman's thoughts drifted across the ocean to the emerging problem in West Africa and then further back, to the other missions he and Tillerman executed. The thought of his friend brought him back the present and the next door he needed to knock on.

"Tanner?"

She nodded, "Are you asking where he is?"

"Or how do we find him?"

"Probably the clubhouse," she answered.

Sherman raised his eyebrows and waited for something

he didn't know.

"Right," she began, "Uh, it's an old golf course. The boys took it over a few years ago thinking it was funny or ironic."

"People still play there?"

"They made it a private club, basically a bar for their buddies. A bunch of permanently adolescent men drinking Busch Lite and hitting golf balls at a pond. Think redneck Peter Pan."

"Why there and not the Crosscut?"

"Avoiding Pa's wrath, I would assume," she answered.

"Alright, where is it?" asked Sherman, unable to recall ever seeing something resembling a golf course.

"Out by the ponds off Linley Drive."

"Wait, isn't that just down the road?"

Ashley slowly nodded, "Yeah, just beyond the catfish farm."

Ponds and fish hatcheries. There was a lot that Sherman didn't know about the town. A troubling deficiency in his opinion.

"Finish your coffee and let's go."

She shrugged.

Sherman rooted around the shack, grabbing what he knew would be at least the basics. He found water, granola bars and beef jerky. Exactly what he left behind for emergencies. After downing his coffee in a giant gulp, he crammed some jerky in his mouth and went out to the mill to prepare.

Ashley followed shortly after, "In a hurry?"

The answer was yes, but Sherman still wasn't sure he wanted to share that crucial piece of information. He had been going back and forth on the issue since the Major had hung up. Who was he protecting? Ashley? Himself? Or was it some vestigial form of politeness? No, he realized, it was better to tear that Band-Aid off now.

"Yeah, I got a call a few minutes ago. My flight leaves in a little less than eighteen hours," he said, waiting for a howl.

Having lost someone deeply important, Ashley was more than distressed. But she was not myopic or deluded enough to think Sherman would stay. Nor was she comfortable with the world he represented. Tillerman had still carried that edge with him, but it seemed well hidden or perhaps dulled. Sherman was different. He was the embodiment of everything Tillerman had left behind. Unapologetically so. That is what she found comfort in, the surety of his actions, not the means or ends.

"I wish you would have told me earlier," she finally said.

"Transparency isn't exactly encouraged in my line of work, but I'll play it straight with you."

"Thanks, feel like starting now?" she asked.

"Go ahead," he said.

"Do you think Tanner killed him?"

"Probably not, but I figure he knows who did," answered Sherman.

"Is it my fault?"

Sherman shook his head, "Not unless you took the money."

"I wish I had. We could have gotten the fuck out of here."

Sherman put on his vest and checked the rifle, "Do you remember anything out of the ordinary? Did you stop anywhere besides the carwash?"

She squinted at the past, "I got the car from the bar, grabbed a coffee at Georgette's and then drove to Ma's place."

"So, the carwash was later?"

"Yeah, at the end of the trip, before I came back."

"Do you always wait?"

"No, Pa wants to make sure the car looks nice. It's his passive aggressive way of showing my mom how well he is doing."

"So, anyone in the neighborhood had access," added Sherman, "having that much cash sitting around explains your mother's anxiousness."

Ashley nodded with shame. It looked like her entire family was in on some criminal enterprise and she never saw it coming.

Money is power goes the adage and Sherman could only guess what it meant to the Thorne clan. Was it their money or someone else's? The question had occurred to him earlier, but it made sense to ask it again. Such violence and brutality usually indicated high stakes or twisted individuals. While Ashley's family was on the far side of deranged, they didn't strike Sherman as spiteful. Killing your daughter's boyfriend had a certain venom to it. Maybe Thorne's 'family first' motto came at a price when crossed. Yet more unanswered questions. Sherman hoped Tanner held the answers, even if it meant spilling some blood to find them.

"Hop in," he said while tossing her the vest.

Ashley stared at the hole and the damage done the prior night. The memory was hazy but haunting, and it drove a freight train over her confidence. She looked over at Sherman and thought about what he must have seen and done, both he and Tillerman. The latter had come back broken; she had seen as much. Time would tell, she thought, what would happen to the other.

Sherman started the trunk and headed back down the gravel road. A minor armory lay on the bench seat between them. Both rifles, including the one with a six-power scope Sherman had specifically grabbed for such a scenario. Along with two pistols, one of which he had tucked under his leg for easy access, meant they were armed.

"How far is the clubhouse from the road?" asked Sherman.

"Maybe a quarter mile. It's kinda set back there," answered Ashley.

Golf courses have few trees, and Sherman pondered over the best approach. The satellite image from his phone was several years old but gave a rough sketch of the place.

Wanting a disguise of sorts, Sherman found a baseball hat emblazoned with a local lumber yard that Tillerman had left in the shed. Combined with a pair of cheap imitation aviators in the truck's glove box, he almost passed for a local. Ashley stuffed her hair into a beanie and called it good. They exchanged a look somewhere between apprehension and commitment before Sherman turned onto the thin asphalt ribbon of North River Road.

"Do you have a plan?" she asked.

"I have a goal and the means," he answered.

"So... no."

Sherman shook his head at the specifics. Those were malleable and changed with time and circumstance. It was the first part of his statement that begged a question. He sighed with relief that she did not ask. The goal, his singular focus, was putting both her brothers in the ground.

Describing it as a golf course gave the shabby grass too much credit. From the trees near where they parked, Sherman saw it as a lazily designed executive par three that had never hosted a CEO type. The holes circled around a putrid pond whose water feature and pump had long ago broken. As for the clubhouse, it wasn't much more than a double-wide trailer with a patio haphazardly attached. Through the scope he could make out four people milling about inside. The cars out front numbered five so there was someone else there he couldn't see. Two battered old Honda Civics, Tanner's truck, a Jeep and one familiar green Chevy filled up the small parking lot.

"Jimmy and Dean," muttered Sherman as he looked at the latter.

Ashley strained to see around their cover, "Who else?"

"Tanner. Two Civics and a navy-blue Jeep Cherokee."

"The Jeep is Rhett. The Civics are sisters. Anabelle and Corrine."

"Girlfriend or groupie?" wondered Sherman.

"Who knows these days," said Ashley. "They've been in bed with one of my brothers since eighth grade."

Sherman eyed some willows growing along a catfish pond. It gave enough cover to move them within thirty or forty yards of the clubhouse.

He pointed, "I think that is our best route for getting close."

"You want to know what Tanner knows, right?" Ashley asked.

He nodded without knowing where she was going with the line of questioning.

"And you're an expert shot?"

Sherman squinted at her with one eye, "I don't like the sound of this."

"Tough shit, Frank. I'm sick of this sneaking around. I'm gonna go ask them straight up. If they want me dead, then they better have the balls to do it themselves."

With that she got up, threw off the vest and started walking towards the back door. Sherman watched her go but said nothing. Finally, he dialed her number.

"You're not talking me out of this," she said, answering the call.

"Just keep the call going and put the phone in your back pocket. I'll be on mute but listening," he instructed. "Try to stay on the deck or near a window. I'm good, but not perfect."

"Now you tell me," she joked mordantly before placing the phone in her pocket slow enough to ensure he saw it.

The day was warming up, and the wind was mild. Decent shooting weather, but Sherman couldn't stop fidgeting. His cover behind the rock was fine, not great, but workable. It just didn't feel right. Ever since Ashley got up, he had a giant arrow over his head.

Dragging the bag behind, he crawled fifteen yards away into a small clump of buckbrush. Some animals had called it home recently and there was a decent-sized opening through the dense branches. Sherman angled himself so he was looking squarely at the back patio and watched as Ashley walked right up to the sliding glass door.

No one moved at first, and Ashley just stood there, arms crossed, leaning against the glass. Sherman watched Tanner turn his head away from the beer in his hand and stare with disbelief.

"You gonna get me a cold one or what?" she chided.

Sherman had to admit Ashley was playing it cool. Maybe she still trusted them at some level, or maybe the plan was a colossal mistake. Either way, the ball was rolling and not to be stopped.

"Where the hell have you been?" asked Tanner.

"Hiding from you assholes," she retorted.

"You fucking bitch," yelled Rhett. "How dare you come waltzing in here. Your new army boy killed Grady."

"She didn't pull the trigger, did you sis," said Tanner, playing some angle.

"Actually, I did," she replied to everyone's surprise.

Silence filled the air long enough to make Sherman ensure the call was still connected.

Ashley walked over to the cooler and grabbed a beer. It put her smack in the middle of the room, allowing a clear line of sight for Sherman. She cracked open the can and took a long swig like she owned the place.

"So who stole the fucking money?" she asked between drinks.

"You did," responded Tanner with only a thin layer of earnestness.

"Listen shitheads," said Ashley annoyed with the continuing ruse, "you killed the only person who ever really gave a damn about me, so pardon me for not putting up with your crap."

Tanner started laughing while everyone looked around for a clue what was going down. "Is this some joke?" he asked with half-seriousness. "The money was in your car. Then it wasn't. Draw your own conclusion."

"Oh, I have and it was one you," she pointed around the room.

The insinuation quickly gathered momentum as they exchanged sideways glances. Sherman could see everyone was edgy, but no one said anything.

Jimmy broke the silence and jumped into the conversation, "You're fucking crazy. Your boyfriend admitted as much."

The crosshairs hovered center mass over the man's dirty flannel shirt as Sherman watched his body language. Jimmy was nervous but trying to hide it. His brother, who was standing nearby and watching, slowly raised the back of his army jacket. Sherman knew the move well. It made getting the pistol out easier. One less thing to clear when drawing. Was it guilt or preparation? Sherman couldn't decide, but it didn't bode well for the rest of the conversation.

Smelling tension in the air, Tanner went to cut Ashley off, "Jimmy is right, your boyfriend gave it all up. So say what you want. It don't matter to me. Pa tried to talk them out of teaching you a lesson. Said one body was good enough, but business is business. Ain't no coming back now. Not without that money."

"That's right, Ash," added Rhett, "Your soldier man confessed to it all. He said you didn't know, but there ain't a shred of truth in that. We know it. You know it."

"You were there," Ashley hissed. It was more a confirmation than a question.

Two hundred yards away, Sherman knew it too. Whatever anger had driven him this far stayed under control. Behind the scope, behind the gun, the moment buried it.

"More," he whispered into the muted phone, "keep digging."

"He cracked like a rotten walnut," added Dean with a cruel smile.

Ashley's hands were trembling, and she set the can down, but didn't let up. "You can't hold a candle to that man. Look at you. Just fucking look at you! Holed up like a bunch of tweens in a goddamn fort! Doing what, huh, somebody else's dirty work? You're a sellout, a two-bit Judas."

Tanner snarled at the insult, "You broke the code.

Family first, Ashley, above all else."

"Sounds like Pa broke his own damn code and sold out to who? Some valley dope peddler?"

Rhett lost it and started yelling, "You insolent bitch. You always thought you were better than us. Better than Pa. Well, I got news for you. He never liked you. A fucking regret is what he said."

"He's nothing but a city stooge," she shot back.

"It's business," added Tanner, "and it was going fine until you two love birds mucked it all up."

"Now Stockwood's crew wants blood," said Rhett.

As Sherman heard the name, the same as Johnny's employer, he gritted his teeth. The man had actual power, with enough pull to convince Thorne to give up a daughter and make Reinhold nothing but hired security.

"You should have seen Krenshaw work him over," continued Rhett before Tanner cut him off with an angry glance.

"No," muttered Sherman, knowing that he had missed something, someone. The house, the orange glow, the single shot. What seemed like a coincidence, a common surname, no longer felt so easily explained away. His mind raced back in time, looking for the only man he knew by that name. A smirking Sergeant, cigarette dangling from his lips, stared back at Sherman. That was ten years gone, before they had lost touch and shipped off to different wars.

"Who the fuck is Krenshaw?" asked Ashley, picking up on her brother's apprehension.

Scrunching up his face, Tanner said with a sigh, "The man you owe some answers and about $2.3 million."

The sum was princely, but it didn't surprise Sherman. Based on the size of the operation, millions in profit seemed reasonable.

"I told you already, I didn't take the damn money," retorted Ashley.

"That's unfortunate. They're pretty convinced it's you or the money," replied Tanner with a remorseful tone.

It incensed Ashley. "So you're just gonna serve up your own kin to some city fucks?"

"Like I said, you picked him over family."

"God damn right I did," she yelled. "You ain't nothing but a bunch of sheep. Can't think for yourselves."

"Like you're any better sis. That fucking monster your man called a friend is on a warpath. Grady's dead and that is on you."

"Crazy bastard killed Coe and Barrios. Put Simpkins in a comma," added Rhett with a shrill tone. "Shit, all we found of Johnny was a pool of blood."

"Afraid you are next?" she asked with a monotone jab.

Tanner's eyes narrowed at her statement. The undercurrent of malice implied knowledge. His world was burning. The blaze started slow. A biker brawl, then Johnny went missing. He saw the smoke curling up, smelled its acrid scent, but it was always one ridge away. Now Grady was dead, along with most of his friends from high school. Suddenly it was his house and his life on the line and the spark was standing in front of him.

"And here I thought army boy was sending a message by kicking Rhett's ass at your apartment. But he wasn't, he was there looking for you," said Tanner.

Rhett watched as the wheels turned his brother's expression from mournful acceptance to outright rage.

"You didn't come here alone," Tanner continued with a yell, "he's fucking here. You brought him here."

Like the unexpected arrival of a rattlesnake, the tension in the room skyrocketed, and they cast glances out the window looking for the unseen specter.

"Oh shit," mumbled Sherman. The plan had worked insomuch as they had the next thread to pull, but the possibility of talking her way out, if such a thing ever existed, was gone. The center of his scope jumped rhythmically from one target to the next, pausing only long enough for a potential trigger pull.

"Ain't too bright of you to walk in here," said Dean as

he removed the pistol tucked into his pants.

"Not at all," echoed Jimmy, retrieving some off-brand handgun.

Ashley was shaking bad enough to drop her beer as she backed up toward the door.

"Shit just got real, cousin," snarled Jimmy.

Like a pair of bad cops, Dean chimed in, "Krenshaw said her or the money. He didn't say alive."

"Knock it off," ordered Tanner. "This ain't your call."

"You're not my boss," sneered Dean.

"But you'll answer to him if you hurt her now," Tanner growled.

"Better him than some fucking ghost," said Jimmy. Raising the pistol that had been twitching tentatively at his side, he pointed it squarely at Ashley.

Tanner yelled no, but it didn't matter. Scarcely had Jimmy's front sight passed over her frame when the window shattered and his chest splattered against a framed photo of John Daly hanging on the wall. Sherman had aimed center mass and hit a few inches high, a fact his mind recorded almost subconsciously.

The two sisters were already screaming and covered in wine-dark splatter as the rifle crack echoed around the clubhouse. Chaos sprang forth like swiftly churning water, sending bodies in motion across the room. Tanner wisely dove for cover while Rhett reached for the Smith and Wesson revolver hanging from a holster under his jacket. Upon seeing his brother hit, Dean took off running towards the front door firing his pistol towards Ashley. All he hit was Annabelle, who crumpled to the ground.

At two hundred yards away it took only a quarter of a second for Sherman to move lead from him to them. He flicked the scope towards Tanner after the first shot, hoping to land a follow-up, but the man was too quick. Then Dean flashed across the glass and he snapped off a reaction shot. The round struck shoulder, shredding the connective tissue and bone, spinning the callow man to the ground in a howl of pain. The pistol clattered harmlessly across the ground.

Having ducked with the shattering of glass, Ashley lay on the ground staring at Anabelle's lifeless body. She hesitated in a moment of sheer terror.

"Run," boomed Sherman's unmuted voice.

She locked eyes with Tanner for a brief second. There was so much fear and remorse in his expression that it could have oozed from his pores. Ashley's eyes narrowed. He'd always been the one who knew her best, and they had been very close once. Her face softened, then she ran.

Rhett has cleared leather and was firing out the window like Wild Bill Hickok when Ashley bolted for the open back door. Lots of siblings don't get along, but he always harbored a special enmity towards his sister. In a moment full of madness and chaos, fear and misplaced heroism, he turned the shiny snub nose at her back.

Unconcerned by Rhett's ineffectual shooting, Sherman was carefully covering Ashley's exit. A cruel spasm of rage spread across her brother's face and he saw the heavy revolver turn to follow her escape. He squeezed the trigger and Rhett dropped quicker than a house of cards on a windy day.

Over her shoulder Ashley saw his body fall on to the beer-stained carpet. She watched him struggle to breathe with a hole through his chest. The revolver lay nearby, still pointing in her direction, inert but menacing.

Behind relative safety, Tanner watched the demise of a second brother in as many days. Past mistakes aside, he wasn't foolish enough to think he could hit Sherman. His brothers subscribed to the nobility of a cause, to a heroic death. He was much too pragmatic for such nonsense. The only priority in his mind was an exit.

"Corrine! Come here," he shouted.

Shock had frozen her legs and turned her feet to stone. No matter how badly she wanted to run, her body wouldn't move. She just stared at her sister lying on the floor. Tears streamed down her blood splattered face.

"God damn it Corrine," screamed Tanner, "get over here."

The familiar but abusive tone momentarily snapped her free, and she ran over to the bar. No sooner had she reached the wooden railing then Tanner grabbed her around the neck with his arm. He pulled her close and pressed the muzzle of his pistol against her temple. A human shield.

They rose slowly together, Tanner hidden behind with only an old Colt .45 visible in Sherman's scope.

"Back up slowly," snarled Tanner.

Corrine wept silent tears as she glanced sideways at the steel barrel painfully pressing into her temple. She took small hesitant steps, wondering how far Tanner would take it, how it would end.

Watching through the small round portal of magnified glass, Sherman considered his options. Tanner could have just run, risked it, but the man decided that a hostage was a better bet. He assumed Sherman wouldn't shoot an innocent woman because he had morals. Some of that was true, but Sherman had shot innocent people before. Had it been some Al Qaeda leader hiding behind such a fearful youth, he would not have hesitated in pulling the trigger. However, that was there not back here. Circumstances were different, at least Sherman thought they should be, even if those shades of differentiation were turning gray.

His crosshairs hovered over her stomach, just below the last rib. The path of least resistance for putting lead through her and into him. No bones besides the spine, just soft tissue and organs. The smallest chance of bullet deviation.

Step by step the macabre couple made their way towards the front door in the center of the room. As they cleared the bar Sherman could see a tangle of legs shuffling back. Her skin, his jeans. A brief but significant debate raged in Sherman's mind before he pulled the trigger. The round hissed between her legs.

"What the fuck!" yelled a surprised Tanner as loud as he could. "I'll kill her, I swear."

Go ahead, thought Sherman.

The police radio, which had been a silent chunk of plastic, crackled to life with Reinhold's voice. "Dean just called. That Captain is at the old golf course. We can corner him if we hurry."

"You'll owe me," said a voice that Sherman found familiar.

"Just hurry. Take the east, I'll take the west," replied Reinhold.

Ashley was crouching nearby, having made her escape back to the bush. Sherman never took his eye off Tanner and Corrine who were a few steps from the door. It was time to go. Even if Reinhold was bluffing, every minute they stayed increased the danger.

"Sorry lady," he muttered before squeezing the trigger again and putting a bullet through them both.

Even at two football fields away, the screams from the clubhouse pulled on the heartstrings. Unfiltered, visceral, human pain reverberated in the air.

"What did you do?" exclaimed Ashley, having watched the pair fall to the ground.

Sherman gathered the gear, "Let's go."

"Did you kill her?"

"No, but they won't be walking out of there," came his terse reply.

As they hurried away Ashley was shaking with rage, grief and the overwhelming flood of adrenaline. Her hands slapped rhythmically against her things and her breath came in short gasps. If there was something to say, Sherman couldn't find the words. They needed to get out before the exits were blocked and the only option was a fight. So, he said nothing, and they kept running.

The Chevy was old and stolen, so Sherman winced as it started. Coming to the clubhouse had been risky, but they had a name and not just any name. The puzzle no longer felt blank in the middle. Pieces were still missing, like who stole the money in the first place, but he had what mattered, what he had wanted from the beginning. He had a neck for the noose. All the rage roiling just below the surface had thinned his calm veneer.

"Who is Krenshaw?" asked Ashley with a quivering voice. "Why were they talking about him?"

"He killed Tillerman," Sherman said.

She looked confused. The name held no meaning, no weight of history, no context. "How can you be sure?"

"I know him or knew him years ago. We all served together."

"Tillerman too?"

"Yeah," he answered.

Her face went pale, and she struggled to find the next question. "What... who is this guy? And how do we find him?"

Sherman answered but motioned for her to hide. The red and blue lights of law enforcement were racing towards them. He pulled the truck off onto the dirt shoulder before putting his hat back on. They were far enough away from the clubhouse for Reinhold not to shoot immediately, but not beyond suspicion. Sherman waived at the passing Sheriff. A friendly small-town gesture. Just two fingers, not the entire hand. A sign of respect he was sure Reinhold expected but didn't deserve.

With the crackle of gravel underneath, he eased the truck back out onto the pavement. The SUV had disappeared into the rearview and Ashley sighed with a deeply haggard breath. The corners of her mouth curled inward and dull eyes gazed out back. She was beyond weary. Sherman could see it scrawled across her face, etched into thin lines of fear fanning out across her forehead.

"There's only one place he'll be," answered Sherman.

She swallowed hard, "Is there another way to get to him?"

"We could just walk away."

"Don't tempt me," she said with a wince.

"Krenshaw is up there. Leaving the lab unguarded now

is too risky," concluded Sherman.

"Are we just waltzing in there? It's the middle of the day and half the fucking town is looking for us."

He looked at his watch. One o'clock in the afternoon. Sixteen hours left. Deep down, Sherman was hiding from the coming finality. Once he got on that plane he would never return. Leaving hinged on him being alive and them being dead. Which left Ashley's question hanging there like a sharp hook. Daytime was not the right time to go after Krenshaw or Thorne.

The radio hissed, "He's gone Reinhold. Ain't nobody here but corpses."

Ashley glanced up at Sherman, her face full of recognition.

"Fuck," replied Reinhold tersely. "Have your boys meet me at the Crosscut in an hour. We need to kill this dog."

"Killing him won't come cheap. You got the scratch for this?"

"Keep your nose out of our shit. You'll get paid."

The other man laughed, "Suit yourself, Sheriff." The radio fell silent again.

"That's Jensen," exclaimed Ashley. "He runs the local chapter."

"The biker gang?"

She nodded.

"I met the man at the Crosscut. We came to an agreement. One that he will not be keeping."

"I don't follow," she said.

"Told me he'd shoot me on the spot if he saw me again."

"Sounds like him."

"Well, I don't plan on being seen."

She shook her head and sighed, "Is this going to be over soon? Shit, can this ever be over?"

"Tonight, it has to be tonight."

Ashley massaged her forehead with shaky fingers, struggling to cope and understand her unfamiliar world. A salted land bereft of family or friends. There was nothing left for her, only a bitter past of deceit, and when the sun rose again, she would be equally complicit in its destruction.

"I need an out," she finally said.

Looking her in the eyes, Sherman saw the same hollowing he had seen in Tillerman all those years before. What little she had to call home no longer existed. Like a burned log, the only thing remaining were charcoal and ash.

"First flight out is at six in the morning. You'll be on it," he assured.

"To where?" she asked sadly.

Sherman pulled over on a small red dirt patch just before the bridge, "That's up to you."

"Why are we stopping?"

"You're right. We can't waltz in there, but Reinhold can." A slow, spreading smile twisted the corners of his mouth as he spoke.

CHAPTER TWENTY-ONE

The green and white Tahoe slowed as it approached the bridge. Sherman watched through the jagged edges of jimson weed as the door opened and Reinhold thumped out. The Sheriff surveyed the situation with the confidence of a conqueror, not the conscious pessimism of the oppressed. It was his domain, his law to administer, and his gait carried with it a certain surety. Mettle tinged his gravelly voice, and he wore a cowboy hat, low and tight. His hand hovered over the Sig Sauer P220 pistol sitting in a quick draw holster, waiting for a reason to use it.

"Everything alright miss," yelled Reinhold, maintaining a healthy distance from the truck.

Ashley kept her head under the hood of the old Chevy, just like Sherman had instructed.

"Miss," repeated Reinhold, drawing his weapon. The safety was already off and the stainless-steel receiver glinted in the fall afternoon sun.

Subterfuge was the key to the plan. Ashley hadn't agreed to all the terms, but Sherman had convinced her it would work if she didn't show her face. She gave a brief wave over her shoulder and continued to tinker with the engine. Anything else would have been a dead giveaway in the fullest of meanings.

From Sherman's vantage across the road, it was obvious the Sheriff found the situation too suspicious. An unfamiliar truck broken down on a stretch of road he passed by only ten minutes before. A truck that was also facing towards town and must have been traveling away from the clubhouse. There were more coincidences than explanations.

Sherman knew that a seasoned professional like Reinhold understood it was the innocuous details that would get you killed. Broken taillights, expired plates or nervous glances could be nothing or everything. Context was king. Standing on that road with everything that occurred in the previous forty-eight hours, Reinhold would have to act.

"Sheriff's department, hands above your head, now!" yelled Reinhold, with a boom of authority.

"Fuck," whispered Ashley under her breath as she slowly raised her hands.

"Take two steps backward toward my voice," instructed Reinhold. He stayed on the far side of the SUV, the engine between him and her. The pistol was aimed at her back.

Again, Ashley complied.

"Now turn around slowly, keep your hands in the air."

It occurred to Ashley that she might catch a bullet in the chest as the Sheriff saw her face, but non-compliance would surely lead to one in her back.

"Shit," muttered Reinhold as he saw her face. Jolts of panic screamed through his mind at his colossal mistake of not recognizing Ashley or the captain he knew was lurking nearby. In thirty years on the job and thirteen months in Vietnam, he had never been so wrong. Instinctual fear took over, not because Ashley was a threat, but because that was all he could manage. Taking one of them with him seemed better than to leave the corporeal world empty-handed.

Reinhold was quick, but Sherman was quicker. He didn't have to draw his weapon, didn't have to aim. That was all a forgone conclusion. By the time the Sheriff barked at Ashley to turn around he was out of his hiding spot and bounding towards the SUV with the Glock leveled at the sizeable man's back.

The pain, the sound and the force all came at the same time. The angle was oblique enough that Sherman easily avoided the armor plates in the Sheriff's vest. He fired three rounds straight into the Kevlar sides protecting the ribs. Ashley closed her eyes and grimaced at the staccato roar.

Protection, in the manufacturer's definition, had a very narrow scope. The vest stopped rounds, but not the kinetic energy. That still had to go somewhere and, in that moment, it fractured two of the Sheriff's ribs, almost puncturing his lung. Reinhold toppled over like a one-sided seesaw and tried to break his fall by sticking his left arm out in some half-cocked stiff-arm. A sharp crack reiterated the laws of physics, as the equal and opposite reaction of his fall snapped the Sheriff's wrist.

Gasping for breath between shrieks of pain, Reinhold didn't even try to reach for his pistol that had tumbled under the front tire. Ashley picked up the gun and his cowboy hat from the pavement. As she stood over him, barrel casually hanging above his head, Reinhold felt smaller than his frame allowed. From the depths of that fear he rolled over, hoping to grab the backup revolver strapped to his ankle.

"That's enough, Sheriff," commanded Sherman as his army boot fell squarely over the gun and Reinhold's hand.

With his knuckles slowly being crushed and two guns angling toward his skull, Reinhold agreed, "Fine, have it your way, Captain."

Sherman took the gun and the knife from the Sheriff's front pocket. He stripped off the vest and, after grabbing a pair of thick zip-tie cuffs, threw it on the front seat.

As the dense plastic closed around his broken wrist Reinhold winced equal parts physical and emotional pain. Over the course of a week, the comfy fiefdom created by his father had crumbled. A destruction of his own making.

"Get up," instructed Sherman.

The Sheriff demurred, his eyes burning with disdain for the younger man and fear of what he represented.

"Get in the back or I'll drag you behind," said Sherman coldly.

With a few grunts of pain, Reinhold moved his bruised and broken girth into the Tahoe's back seat.

Sherman smiled before slamming the door in his face. Taking her cue, Ashley hopped up front. She could have smirked at Reinhold's pain, at his obvious discomfort and fear, but she didn't have the energy. Each passing minute brought with it more danger and stress. It was taking a dreadful toll on her nervous system.

Seeing the Sheriff locked up in the small Plexiglas prison of his own car brought Sherman some small perverse pleasure, but he would still have preferred to put the three rounds in the old man's head. Luckily for Reinhold, his role in Tillerman's death was still unclear. He still had answers to give and a purpose to serve.

"I thought you were a better shot Captain," sneered Reinhold, hoping to rattle his captor's cage.

Sherman shrugged with indifference, "Grouping was a little loose, but close enough to scatter your corrupt skull across the road."

The sheriff swallowed hard and watched as the Tahoe turned right at the bridge, "Where are you taking me?"

"Let's set some ground rules here," answered Sherman. "This isn't some P.O.W. situation nor should those cuffs confuse you into thinking there are rights. Currently, you have value to me. If that stops being true or you get on my nerves, I will put a bullet through your head. Clear?"

"Crystal," grunted Reinhold.

"Good. We have a bit of a drive and I'm sure Ashley has some questions."

She nodded as they passed through town cloaked by the fear of law. No one looked too hard at the green and white Tahoe speeding downhill. Rumors were swiftly circulating at the coffee shop, but no one thought to ask questions.

"Well Sheriff, I think you know what I am about to ask," said Ashley in measured tones.

Reinhold bored down on her with all the menacing authority his eyes could muster, but she didn't blink at his dented power. The bond to civil society that had kept her unquestioning cracked and its repair felt dubious.

"I guess we're playing hardball," she said to Sherman.

Sherman rapped his knuckles against the Plexiglas divider separating the front and back seats, "It's not bulletproof."

Ashley held up the Sig Sauer in view of Reinhold and checked to see if a round was chambered. "Let's test your hypothesis," she said, satisfied the pistol was ready to fire.

"Girl, you best put that down," commanded Reinhold.

The crack was deafening in the confined space and it surprised Sherman. Although he was a long way from flinching, he hadn't thought Ashley would pull the trigger. A quick glance in the mirror confirmed Reinhold did not have any fresh holes. The cheap plastic seat was smoking from a small crater between the Sheriff's legs.

"Jesus Christ," yelled Reinhold as the bullet hissed mere inches from his manhood.

"Invoking his name won't help you," growled Ashley. She raised the pistol a few inches and waited.

"Alright, alright. What the fuck do you want to know?"

"What happened to Tillerman?" she answered bluntly.

Reinhold leaned back into the seat and sighed loudly, "All this for one guy."

Silence filled the void, but the barrel didn't move.

"I'll tell you what I know, but if you want it firsthand, go ask your father," continued Reinhold. Looking at Sherman's eyes, he knew that was their next stop.

"That's a given," replied Ashley.

"Your boyfriend came poking around the Crosscut. Wanted to talk with your dad. Said he had a proposition."

"What did he offer?" asked Sherman.

"Like I said, this is all secondhand, but Thorne told me the kid knew about the operation and the money."

"The money I was unknowingly driving around," said

Ashley.

Reinhold snorted, "If you say so."

"Stick to the story and hold your opinion," instructed Sherman.

"At any rate, the Lieutenant offered to help on the condition Thorne didn't involve you anymore."

"Bullshit," yelled Ashley.

The insinuation surprised Sherman. Tillerman was pragmatic but principled, to where he felt compelled to leave the unit over their actions. Helping drug dealers was a line too far out to consider, but if Reinhold held some truth, then his friend had remade himself. They say love changes people, not that Sherman had any context to compare.

"God's honest truth," preached Reinhold. "Ask dear old dad for the details. He only gave me the outline of their conversation."

"You can shoot him and see if his story changes," offered Sherman.

Ashley tilted her head in consideration and then looked at Reinhold.

"Truth's a bitch," he said. "Shooting me ain't gonna change it."

Sherman shrugged. He believed the Sheriff the first time, but wanted to see his jaw twitch in trepidation. "Why did you kill him then?"

"Now I wasn't involved with that," insisted Reinhold.

"Just the cover up then," Sherman concluded. "I think you call that accessory after the fact."

"Guilt is guilt," Ashley echoed.

"We staged the accident, that much is true, but I never hurt the man."

"Why did Dell do it then?" asked Sherman.

"Ask her," Reinhold scoffed. "The money went missing from her car."

"You mean my daddy's car," she corrected.

"No need to split hairs. You drove off with it a few days after your boyfriend stops by to tell your dad not to involve you in the money drops. It don't take much to make that connection."

"So, you thought he stole it," said Sherman.

Reinhold grunted, "Him or her."

"What did Dell say that night?" Sherman asked.

"That Tillerman admitted as much. Took full responsibility."

"And they thought he was protecting her," added Sherman.

"So it seemed," replied the Sheriff.

"And the money?" asked Ashley.

"I presume you didn't take it then," said Reinhold.

Ashley shook her head slowly.

"Well, this has been a colossal fucking mistake," he groaned.

"Did you take it?" asked Sherman, turning the tables.

"You think I'd still be here if I did?" exclaimed the Sheriff.

Sherman's eyes narrowed, but he said nothing.

"You don't believe anything I say. Got it," Reinhold added.

Truth comes in shades like anything else, but Sherman felt the Sheriff was painting it straight. "Take a guess at what happened," he finally added.

Reinhold shrugged his shoulders, the movement of which made him wince as tendrils of pain rocketed up his wrist. "Does it matter? Maybe they're already dead. Maybe it was some random kid who got lucky. My point being it ain't gonna change the outcome of this pig-shit misadventure."

All his cynicism aside, the Sheriff was right. Who pushed the boulder down the hill doesn't matter to the rock itself. Maybe to the survivors below, but once it is in motion, the instigator ceases to have meaning, only the momentum carries importance. Sherman understood what Reinhold meant. It was far too late to care about the start when only the end was in sight.

"I suppose you're right," conceded Sherman. "What I really care about is who killed him. I'm guessing you have that name."

"And if I don't?" asked Reinhold.

"Say so and you'll find out," responded Sherman coldly.

"Are you telling me there is a way where I don't end up in a pine box? From where I sit there is only one conclusion and me helping you ain't gonna change it."

"Then save your breath, Sheriff," concluded Sherman.

He kept the Tahoe straight past the airport and away from the river, heading toward the county line. Oaks gave way to walnut and pecan trees. Mountains ceded to hills. The Central Valley beckoned. About five miles from the border Sherman made a sharp right onto a chalky gravel road bounded by metal signs showing the owners of the land beyond. They stenciled Braxton Mining Corporation in foot high blue letters.

The Sheriff squinted in the afternoon light streaming through the window as Sherman watched the old man's mind process his situation. He knew Reinhold would catch on quickly. Thirty years of thinking from the gut had sharpened his wits, not dulled them. The flash of understanding came with a widening of his eyes despite the sun.

"You're not gonna find anything here," said Reinhold.

Sherman smiled, "You sound too sure to be a truthful Sheriff."

A dense metal gate blocked the road, and Sherman decelerated quickly as they approached. Chunks of gravel shuddered along with the tires, and Reinhold almost smashed his forehead against the Plexiglas partition. Just over a slight rise, invisible from the road, Braxton's former glory days lay like an open gash upon the land.

Strip mining came to Cumbre County during the former Sheriff's tenure, back when Reinhold was just a boy admiring his father. Braxton had gone looking for gold in the alluvial plain left by the river's descent and found enough to keep the doors open for fifty years. It all ended when the environmental cost surpassed the profits and Braxton shut down the operation.

"I told you," Reinhold said, "the place is closed."

Without responding, Sherman retrieved a pair of bolt cutters from the trunk. The gate was old and rusting in parts where the blue paint chipped off. Someone had repainted it many times, but not recently. The padlock, however, was brand new. It took a concerted grunt from Sherman, but the lock sheared open and fell to the ground with a dull thud.

With the creaky gate behind them, he drove across the disfigured expanse towards a small set of beige metal buildings. Ashley had known of the plan but that assuredness was quickly fading. Sherman needed something from the mine. That is all that he had said before Reinhold came rolling around the corner. Now she was left wondering what the Sheriff knew that she did not.

Having given it some thought and with daylight to burn, Sherman put the odds of it still being there at six in ten. Adding in Reinhold's over eager statement about not finding anything, it was closer to seven in ten. They drove past the buildings at a crawl until he saw the appropriate hazardous material sticker on the door. It wasn't so much a building as a reused shipping container half buried with sand.

This time there were three different locks to cut, each one was new and the stainless steel reflected the slowly fading sun. Sherman set to work while Ashley, and Reinhold watched from the Tahoe. The word explosives, written large across the door, explained everything they needed to know about the reason for their visit.

As the last lock clanged against the others on the ground and the door opened, Sherman said, "Funny thing about California. It's cheaper to just store hazardous materials than to move them."

Two minutes later he returned with a crate of modern dynamite, blasting caps and a spool of detonator cord.

Alfred Nobel would have been proud of his company's advances over the years since his invention of dynamite, but not of what Sherman had planned.

Reinhold swallowed hard as he watched the back of his SUV filled with high explosives. The window through which he survived the night was shrinking.

"What's your plan, Captain? Level the town? That's not gonna bring your friend back," said Reinhold once Sherman was back in the driver's seat.

"You're right, but the town isn't my target."

"The labs," added Ashley, her tone flat and matter of fact.

From the moment the stench revealed those carefully arranged trailers, he knew they needed to burn. Like the poppy fields of Afghanistan, the drugs would return somewhere else, but that was not his concern. Taking his friend had been their first mistake. Not shooting him on the spot would be their last. Dell Thorne, Krenshaw and Reinhold all tried to be clever. Hiding one crime amongst a man's past when they were so overt with everything else. They should have known better, known that even in Byron Mills the well-hidden eventually floats to the surface. He was just throwing dynamite into the pond.

From the back-seat Reinhold snorted in personal disgust, "From day one I knew that would bite us all."

"Didn't seem to stop you," Ashley retorted.

"No, neither did your kin. This was your father's grand plan."

Sherman started the car and headed back out, not bothering to hide their trespasses. The dirt swirled up in large plumes as they raced down the road. His watch read a few minutes past four. Two and a half hours to sunset, maybe three until dark.

"Question for you, Sheriff," replied Sherman.

"Captive audience," quipped Reinhold.

"From one criminal to another: How did this arrangement with Stockwood work?"

The Sheriff squirmed at the insinuation; however true it had become. "Thorne provided the land and distribution."

"Through the loggers?"

Reinhold grunted, "Stockwood provided the equipment, raw materials and know-how."

"So, the $2.3 million was his cut?" Sherman asked.

"It wasn't stock dividends."

"And your lackeys? Just hired guns?"

"Spare me your fucking judgment, Captain. I've heard some stories about you. Don't pretend you're some saint in this story. You murdered my men!" Reinhold almost spat as he spoke.

Sherman couldn't help but chuckle, "Jesus Christ. Sheriff, this isn't about right or wrong. I don't know if you've noticed, but we're standing on the same plank. I just happen to be doing the pushing right now."

"You killed his only friend," added Ashley.

It took a moment, but Reinhold grasped the simmering rage behind Sherman's cold eyes. As an unencumbered man himself, the Sheriff understood what good friendships meant. Too many years wearing the star had left him with only a few staunch friends in the world. He could empathize with such a loss.

"You know I used to be good at this job," he said after a few minutes of silence.

"Is that supposed to make us like you?" asked Ashley.

Reinhold ignored the question, "Spent many years walking on the right side of the law."

"You miss it?" asked Sherman.

"Most days, yes."

"What changed?"

It took a deep look inside, but he answered, "Age, I guess. Your vision fades with time. What had been black and white in my youth became gray in middle age. By your sixties it is all the same shade."

After fifteen years in the army, Sherman sympathized with Reinhold's lack of clarity. Out of duty and patriotism he had joined up to avenge those who perished only to find a deepening spiral of violence. Many of the men he served with had enlisted to kill those responsible only to discover the actual culprits had died with their victims. Constant conflict sustains itself and Sherman never could escape its pull, like the brutality itself had settled somewhere deep in his soul.

"Strange how it all slumps together, the right and wrong," he added.

Reinhold nodded, but the comment elicited a strange look from Ashley.

"You getting soft for him now?" she asked. "An hour ago he called you a dog that needed to be put down."

"We share a similar pathos, that's all," responded Sherman.

"What the fuck does that mean," she exclaimed.

"It means," answered Reinhold, "the Captain, and I have been driving on the same road for so long we've stopped seeing the dividing line."

Ashley glared at the comparison, but Reinhold sat unfazed, his chin carved from some stoic rock. Back on the road the Tahoe picked up speed as they headed upwards and back into town.

"Feel like setting the record straight now?" Sherman asked.

Reinhold looked up, "You gonna shoot me either way?"

"Can't say I've decided."

"Well I have," muttered Ashley, but Reinhold didn't seem to hear her.

"It isn't a flattering story," he continued.

Sherman shrugged, "They never are."

The Sheriff paused for a minute before continuing, "Dell and I go way back. We grew up together and fought side by side in the Ia Drang valley. Got to be good friends over there. Back here, well, things were different. I took my daddy's star and Thorne took whatever he could carry. But I owed him a debt from the war, so I kept things off the record."

"You kept him out of jail," said Ashley.

"I turned a blind eye to his pot business and all the other rackets your family got into. Told myself I was being a sympathetic friend."

"Not to us kids," Ashley groaned.

"I imagine not," he replied, "but I owed him. A few years back he walked into my office with a proposition. He'd found someone with an excellent product who needed space and transportation."

"Clarence Stockwood?" asked Sherman.

"I didn't know the name at the time, but yes."

"You should have told Pa to fuck off," added Ashley.

"I did. Nearly arrested him on the spot," confided Reinhold.

"Why didn't you?" wondered Sherman.

The Sheriff sighed down to his bones. "Weakness, loyalty, vanity, greed. Take your pick. Something was missing in my life. A void of sorts and I filled it with money."

"And drugs," Ashley reminded him.

"Hey now, I didn't let any of that poison loose on this county. That was my one stipulation. Keep it out of Cumbre," rallied Reinhold to his own defense. It was a weak one, but he clung to it like a life raft on the vast, empty ocean of his own future.

Ashley laughed loudly at the justification, "What utter bullshit."

"Sometimes you cling to whatever you can," suggested Sherman.

"Don't tell me you think he made the right choice," she snorted.

"Not at all, but even poor decisions have a context."

Snarling her upper lip, Ashley shot back, "Fucking excuses. He's as guilty as the rest of them."

Her point was valid and Sherman knew it, but Tillerman made many such choices and held on to whatever didn't pull him under. He wondered how Ashley would have judged him with that knowledge. Maybe she never had to because he left it behind, to look forward. Or maybe it was just the grief cutting to the core of her beliefs, providing the clarity she needed to see herself through.

"Sorry," she breathed. "I'm casting stones in my glass house, but he's still culpable."

Sherman glanced back at the Sheriff and the hard, cold, corners of his eyes. Guilt hid in those recesses. It lingered behind the clenched jaw and gritted teeth. Remorse and regret had bubbled to the surface not by choice but by circumstance. Was the Sheriff an honorable man? The question crossed his mind, but the answer was just a passing ray of sun on an otherwise bleak day. He had killed good men before and lingering doubts would not stop him from doing it again.

Climbing back towards town, the actual threat shimmered in the nooks of Sherman's memory. "Tell me about Krenshaw," he demanded.

From the back seat came a long, low whistle as Reinhold considered the question. "Well, I attached one string to the agreement and Stockwood added two more. That dipshit Johnny and your Mr. Krenshaw. I can assume I have you to thank for the former's disappearance."

Sherman scratched his beard and remained silent.

"Doesn't matter. Guy was a predator, not in the honorable sense, and I imagine his end was brutal. As for Krenshaw, the man is a beast."

"Describe him," instructed Sherman, not wanting to taint Reinhold's impartiality.

"Spanish accent. Puerto Rican, I think, but dark as night. Maybe from some other island out there. What else? Uh, tall as a redwood and thick as a sequoia."

"That him?" Ashley asked.

Sherman nodded.

"You know the man? Why is that not surprising?" said Reinhold.

"Knew the man," Sherman corrected. "I haven't laid eyes on him for almost a decade."

"Was he a mean son-of-a-bitch back then?"

Years prior Sherman had seen Krenshaw dismantle an Al Qaeda fighter by hand, snapping bones like twigs as he worked upward from toes to head. "Yeah, he was sadistic back then."

"Well, he must have aged like a fine wine because he's only gotten more complex in his viciousness."

"What's his role?" asked Sherman.

"He's in charge of operations. Stockwood insisted it was someone he could trust."

"And Johnny?" wondered Ashley.

"Quality control."

They passed the airport, and the Sheriff looked wistfully at an obvious avenue of escape. So did Ashley.

"That night," continued Sherman. "Who killed Tillerman?"

"I don't know," answered Reinhold casually.

The response didn't sit right with Sherman. Too generic, too blasé. He slammed on the brakes, launching Reinhold's head against the Plexiglas with enough force to break his nose. The popping sound made Ashley shiver.

"Who?" demanded Sherman.

"I wasn't there," pleaded Reinhold. "We picked up a corpse. I don't know who did it."

"Thorne or Krenshaw must have said something," responded Sherman.

Reinhold looked at Ashley, "Your daddy looked almost forlorn, like he had lost something irreplaceable. Krenshaw was plain smug. Ordered us to clean it up and then walked away. God's honest truth."

Placing the blame on someone specific gave Sherman a sense of closure. The very act itself was cathartic. It had a cleansing power, washing away all the grime leaving only those responsible. Culpability focused his rage but the more he dug, the thicker the grime became.

"It doesn't matter, Frank. They were both there," said Ashley.

"Along with your brothers," added Reinhold between mouthfuls of blood he was spitting on the floor.

"Was Pa upset over Tillerman or the money?" Ashley asked reluctantly. Her father never expressed emotions outside of anger. Deep down there still flickered some tiny spark of hope for her family.

"What do you think?" snorted Reinhold.

Ashley nodded in understanding. Her father worried about the money. His personal greed was greater than any parental bond. As far as she was concerned, the motto he imparted was all wrong. Family would always pale to his own self-interests. What little hope she carried fizzled away with the dull hiss of air escaping from a punctured tire. Had she any more optimism for their relationship Ashley would have felt deflated. Instead, it conjured a finality. A closure of one-way reciprocity. She had no father, not anymore.

Sherman watched her face slacken and eyes go blank. It was a look of loss but not pain. The absence of hope brought out determination and clarity.

"Barrios drove him up there that night, but who stopped him on the road?"

Reinhold raised his eyebrows, "For a ghost you make a fine detective."

It was the second time the Sheriff had used the word to describe him and the third instance since he had arrived. Once was a coincidence but three was insider knowledge. He silently kicked himself for not noticing it earlier. Krenshaw had warned them, told them who they were up against. They had heard but not listened or Krenshaw was cocky and thought Sherman wouldn't figure it out.

"How did you know about me?"

"I've noticed you around over the years, but it was Tanner who told me your past," said Reinhold looking off into the distance. "I should have listened. He was the one who took your friend."

At the sound of her brother's name Ashley snapped around to face the Sheriff, "Don't screw with me."

"I ain't. Tillerman knew too much. Who did you think took him?"

She turned to Sherman, "You should have killed him by the bridge."

"When you're behind the trigger you can make the call," he replied.

Ashley sighed, "I know."

The choice was simple to verbalize, even easy to make in a rage-filled moment. It was the consequences that could crush one's spirit slowly. Thinking about the remarkably simple action of squeezing that ribbon of metal filled her with dread. Stress induced pressure bore down on her chest and despite her bluster Ashley doubted that she could ever go through with it.

Reinhold considered a cynical reply but the slowly clotting blood clogging up his nose held his tongue. He wasn't dead yet and didn't want to hasten any changes to his corporeal form.

Daylight clung to its last hours as they passed by the general store, the flagpole clanging in the evening breeze. Despite the workday ending it was empty with jittery residents heading straight home. The local news came on a weekly broadsheet and wouldn't go to press for another three days. Breaking news came by phone call or word of mouth. It was a town of whispers, not chat rooms.

Sherman slowed down as he approached O'Toole's service station. Like a ghost of some former past, the gas pumps had no hoses or gas. It was past closing time but the door to the office was still open when he slid out of the Tahoe.

"Shoot him if he tries anything," instructed Sherman before closing the door.

Reinhold took the statement as fact not a threat and Ashley kept the pistol in sight.

Knocking on the glass door as he entered, Sherman

found Tom sitting in the corner behind an old desk and even older stacks of paper. The room had the pleasant clutteredness of someone who long ago had given up on rational organization. Customer invoices made but never sent mingled with grease-stained tools and dirty rags. A pair of well-worn overalls lay over a chair whose seat had long ago disappeared under boxes and mail.

"Mr. Sherman, to what do I owe the pleasure?" asked O'Toole upon seeing him enter. Despite the Sheriff's department tactical vest and Glock strapped to his chest, Tom was unfazed by his appearance.

"I'm looking to buy a few propane tanks of the five-gallon variety," answered Sherman with a smile.

"I keep a few spares around the side," responded Tom with a jerk of his thumb. "Follow me."

O'Toole glanced at the white and green Tahoe parked next to one of the empty gas pumps and cast a wry smile, "I could have loaned you a car Mr. Sherman."

"The color suits me," he replied.

The old mechanic grunted and pointed toward a large propane tank mounted on white metal brackets at the base of the hill. An old tow truck lay nearby wheel-less and slowly rusting. Green grass was infiltrating its way through the body, reclaiming what had once been stripped from the earth. The metal carcass was older than the rest of the discarded cars in the lot. A personal reminder of the past.

"My son says I'm a hoarder," said O'Toole after catching Sherman's sideways glance.

"Is he right?"

"I call it nostalgic."

"Generational differences then," replied Sherman.

"Exactly. Now how many tanks did you need? You could probably fit six in the back, assuming you don't have any other, uh, cargo."

"Five would be great."

Tom nodded, and started gathering up the tanks dispersed about the place. "You don't mind if they're past due for an inspection, right?"

"I won't be needing them for long," answered Sherman.

"Mm-hmm," said O'Toole as he finished one tank and started another. "Looks like we'll have a wet one tonight."

A near cloudless sky hung above them with only a hint of wind in the air. The old man didn't seem like the type to watch the weather channel, let alone own a smartphone.

"If you say so," replied Sherman.

O'Toole licked a greasy finder and held it up into the air, "Yes sir, pressure is dropping."

Something else was in the air and it had nothing to do with a barometer reading. A throaty rumble was rising in volume, growling closer by the second. With his back to the road, Sherman heard them coming from the left, heading downhill. No doubt looking for the Sheriff. He was overdue by an hour for the rendezvous and the bikers were searching. The racket grew louder as they spotted the Tahoe and pulled into the station.

O'Toole looked up with disdain and shook his head, "Friends of yours?"

"No, but I think we're about to get acquainted," replied Sherman.

At several stones lighter and a hand shorter, Sherman's outline looked nothing like that of the Sheriff's, but the white letters on his vest were enough to convince the bikers. They saw it as official and didn't question the incongruity in size.

"Hey Reinhold, where the fuck have you been?" shouted one man.

Sherman pretended not to hear over the sound of the compressor and crouched down next to O'Toole. The snub only provoked anger as the two men advanced.

"They armed?" asked Sherman quietly.

"Not visibly, but they don't travel empty-handed."

"Hey Sheriff," came another shout.

"You deaf?" enjoined the other man.

Tom squinted and waved as the men advanced. They

pointed to Sherman and tried to convey their frustration to the mechanic who put his hand up to his ear like he couldn't hear.

The space next to the shop wasn't over fifteen feet wide, with most of that being occupied by the defunct truck. The bikers had started thirty feet away and had covered two-thirds of that distance before Sherman stood up and turned around.

Closest to Sherman was a skinny kid only five years out of high school, if he had graduated at all, with a beard patchier than cell service in the mountains. The guy didn't look important. His jacket lacked in badges and his hands in scars. It looked like he had drawn the short straw for a wild goose chase. The name Scooter scrawled across a blue patch on his chest. The name was not intimidating, and neither was his size.

As he saw Sherman's face for the first time Scooter blinked. The gap between expectations and actuality caused him to pause, freeze in his step even though inertia carried him forward. He stumbled for words at the stranger glaring back.

Complacency and inexperience cost Scooter reaction time as Sherman swung an empty propane tank at his head. Thirteen pounds of steel connected with enough force to fracture the kid's skull and send him bouncing unconsciously off the brown cinder block wall.

Standing a few steps further back, the second biker was older and crueler. With a shaved head and handlebar mustache he reminded Sherman of a circus strongman a few years past his prime. Aged and slower, but no less dangerous. The scars on his head and cluttered jacket testified to that fact. On his chest was a patch of the old soviet hammer and sickle with the word Baba. An unveiled reference to the boogeyman of Russian folklore.

As Scooter's head still resonated off the propane tank, Baba went for a long knife sheathed on his waist. Sherman recognized the type. An old Russian infantry model that proliferated in Afghanistan. A relic of the war. Unlike most knives, the guard faced inward to facilitate throat cutting. The biker knew how to use it and held the blade with grim confidence.

"Dead man," bellowed Baba with a thick accent straight from the Urals. Then he lunged forward.

Going for his gun was Sherman's natural reaction, but the biker was fast and he almost lost a finger to the first viscous slash. Baba's bald head turned a light shade of red like an under ripe strawberry. Veins popped out of his temples. Rage welled up in his eyes.

"You kill my brother. Now I kill you."

The comment barely registered in Sherman's mind. He had killed a lot of brothers, husbands and sons. There were the two bikers on Upper Mill Road who had followed Brummet for too long. He didn't even recall their faces. Too many already haunted his past. Besides, he didn't talk during a fight. It was a distraction, and it fed emotions, and emotions created mistakes.

Baba missed again as Sherman weaved out of the blade's path. Failure was only adding fuel to his rage. Spittle formed in the corners of his mouth. Two more swings without flesh and his bald head was a bright red, but Sherman was running out of room to retreat.

The biker saw the situation and went to swing again, extending his arm further out, hoping to draw blood in the diminished space. Sherman read it like batter sitting on a 3-0 fastball. The twisted torso, an elbow cocked to the side. When Baba unloaded with all his anger, Sherman caught his wrist with the steel toe of his boot.

An audible snap made the biker's eyes bulge and the knife clatter to the concrete. Still raging despite the pain, Baba charged at Sherman with the power of a cornered bull. He launched himself headfirst at full speed only to be met with a freshly filled cylinder of propane. A traumatic brain injury was the outcome.

Ashley peeked around the corner and exhaled with relief

when she saw the two bloodied men sprawled on the ground. "You alright," she asked.

Sherman surveyed the damage. Survival looked shaky, but nothing looked immediately fatal. Although, from a triage perspective he couldn't decide who he would treat first.

There was a long slash across his vest that he hadn't noticed during the fight. "Yeah, I'm alright," he said while casually ripping a chunk of fabric off and tossing it on the ground.

"You alright Tom?" asked Ashley.

The old mechanic peered out from behind the big tank, "Never found those boys to be very amenable, but they must harbor some real hate for you Mr. Sherman."

"Just a misunderstanding," he replied while searching through their pockets.

Sherman slid the guns over to Ashley and took two wads of cash from the jackets. Each stack of twenties was thicker than his thumb. It looked like Thorne still had enough capital to pay off the hired muscle.

Sherman offered O'Toole the cash, "Hope that covers it."

"It's on the house. I don't want their drug money."

"So, it's an open secret," replied Sherman.

"Nothing secret about those bikes rumbling all over town. The guy you got stuffed in the back seat kept it mostly out of the county."

"Didn't think you saw him," said Sherman.

"None of my business, besides, I haven't voted for him in years."

"Who do you vote for?"

"I usually write in Matt Dillon," answered O'Toole.

Sherman laughed, "My dad was a Gunsmoke fan."

Tom gave a lighthearted shrug.

Sherman continued, "Thanks again for your help. Oh, I'd call an ambulance for those two, unless you want to wait for the coroner."

O'Toole pulled down his knit cap, "It wouldn't be neighborly to leave 'em, but it sure is tempting."

"You're a decent man Tom. Can't say I've met many before."

"I'd say good luck to you Mr. Sherman, but I get the sense that luck has nothing to do with it."

Sherman nodded and loaded up the propane. O'Toole had dialed 911 on an old rotary phone and was patiently explaining that two bikers had got into a fight on his property. Sherman gave him a wave through the window.

Back in the Tahoe he asked Ashley, "Did he give you any trouble?"

"Oh, he wanted to, but I dissuaded him," she replied.

Sherman glanced back at the Sheriff, "She threaten to shoot you first?"

He nodded.

"Figured you'd draw if I started," she added.

"You're right," he said tossing her the two-grand.

"What's this for?"

"Your plane ticket," he answered.

Ashley flashed a weak smile, "Let's hope I get to use it."

The small digital clock on the dashboard read half-past five. One hour to sunset. Twelve hours to an exit. In the distance a wide layer of ominous clouds appeared over the horizon. A storm was brewing.

Sherman scratched his beard, "What time does the Crosscut open?"

She glanced over at the dash, "Thirty minutes ago."

"Busy?"

"Maybe," asked Ashley uneasily.

"I think it's time to pay your father a visit."

"No way Frank. There are a dozen bikers at the bar. It's suicide."

"Past tense," he said. "I put at least four in the hospital and two more in the dirt. That leaves six at most."

"Long odds," chimed in Reinhold hoping in vain to influence the outcome.

"You're right Sheriff," said Sherman. "Ashley, hand me his phone."

Cumbre County received more than just secondhand weapons from Uncle Sam, and she passed over an older model Blackberry no longer used by other government agencies. Sherman searched through the contacts until he found a Jensen listed. He held up the phone for Reinhold to see.

"That him?"

The Sheriff nodded.

He tapped in a text message: *Found our rabid dog. Meet me at the place in thirty.*

The phone beeped almost immediately with a one-word response. *Ok.*

Sherman turned to Ashley, "Buckle up."

CHAPTER TWENTY-TWO

The burgeoning winter sun sank fast in the mountainous valley. Sunset felt like an enclosing wool blanket as storm clouds loomed overhead. Any residual moonlight reflected up only for the passing airplanes to see. For everyone else a hood of darkness cinched tightly on the dirt below.

A dozen minutes had passed since the last motorcycles had turned toward the meth labs. Hidden by a taco truck, Sherman had parked the Tahoe off the road as they waited for the gang to depart the Crosscut. Bikes roared around the bend as he mentally tallied their strength. Five Harleys, five men. One short of his prediction, but close enough. It was an educated guess, but still only a guess.

Ashley looked on expectantly as he wedged the Glock between the seat and the console.

"You ready?" he asked.

"Ain't gonna get any easier," she answered.

"Still time to run," suggested Reinhold.

"Don't worry Sheriff," said Sherman. "You'll still have a way out."

Reinhold swallowed a mouthful of bile and nodded. The only end he could imagine started with a barrel. Everything else was a trick. A cruel joke on himself.

Three more minutes passed in silence before Sherman started up the engine and headed into the mountains. He figured they had an hour, maybe more before the bikers second-guessed themselves. Eventually they would come looking again. Time is a curse, and humans suck at waiting.

"Tell me about the labs," said Sherman as they passed Ashley's place of former employment.

"They make meth," offered Reinhold, resentful of the question.

"Sarcasm aside, who set them up?"

"Krenshaw and some loggers."

"Anything special I should know about?"

"Like what?" asked Reinhold a bit exasperated.

"Blast-proof walls. Bullet resistant windows. You get the drift," explained Sherman.

"This ain't a war zone, son," replied Reinhold offhandedly before considering the past few days. "Well, fuck, it didn't use to be."

Sherman did not reply, and the Sheriff took a hard look at him for the first time. In all those decades wearing the star Reinhold had seen his fair share of criminals and a handful of dangerous guys. Murders, rapists and sociopaths had crossed his path, but Sherman was different. Something about his pale green and orange eyes didn't even seem human. More reptile than man. Reinhold suddenly felt cold despite the heater.

"They bought the trailers second or third hand," he offered. "From wherever was cheap, took cash and didn't ask questions."

"So pretty much anyone in town," said Ashley.

Reinhold shrugged off the comment as just the nature of Byron Mills. "Krenshaw mapped it all out. Gave the boys security rotations. Doled out discipline when needed. They called him the overseer."

"At least we know who was really in charge," chided Ashley.

The Sheriff glared at her with rising anger over his own impotence. He had failed himself, the badge he wore and his father's legacy. Easy money and an eroded sense of duty led to his dubious choices. Sitting in the back of his own vehicle swept away any protestations of his innocence. A prisoner of his own making with no idea of the sentence.

"Thorne will be ready for you," said Reinhold after weighing his dwindling options. Helping Sherman floated to the top in the brackish waters of his own future.

"There is a back door of sorts," offered Ashley.

Getting in wasn't Sherman's worry. He needed to keep Ashley safe and Reinhold out of view. He still had a plan for the Sheriff and didn't want to burn that card preemptively.

"What about a back road or trail?" he asked. "I want to keep us out of sight."

"There's an old logging road maybe half a mile before the parking lot," suggested Reinhold.

Sherman looked to Ashley for confirmation. She nodded, but her distrust was palpable. For good reason too. He doubted the Sheriff could have known his plans or communicated it, but that wasn't a given.

"Fine," he said, "what's through the back door?"

"Pa's office."

"Certainly direct," he mused. "Does he use it?"

"When he wants some privacy."

"Well, that's not in the cards tonight," said Sherman.

Ashley looked his direction, "I'm not going, am I?"

Sherman shook his head, "I know it's your dad, but…"

She didn't let him finish the thought, "He stopped being my father years ago. I just didn't know it yet."

"Anything I should convey?" he asked.

"A bullet," she quipped before hearing the callousness creeping into her voice. It was almost unrecognizable, and Ashley recoiled at the cold, hard, words falling from her lips.

She took some ragged breaths to calm herself down before adding, "No, tell him his family died with Tillerman."

Pain and betrayal shimmered from a well deep below her words. Ashley had always been on the outside. The only girl once her mom left. The only Thorne to walk her own line. All of that put her at odds with her father, but hidden behind all the garbage of her childhood she believed in family. Sherman had seen her reluctance before with Tanner, even the fading hope with her dad. He wondered if anything was left.

"I'll pass along your condolences."

Ashley nodded, rubbing her temples hard enough to dig out the past.

They were winding uphill on a road that now seemed familiar to Sherman. Zigzagging into the mountains one sharp turn at a time. Darkness had settled into the creases of the valley before he started driving but he kept the headlights off. Thunder rumbled to the west as they navigated by the residual light trapped under the clouds.

"Tell me about Krenshaw," said Ashley. "Did Tillerman know him?"

Sherman furrowed his brow. The question made his beard itch. "We were in the same unit together in Afghanistan, just a few years into the war. Back when it had meaning."

More thunder echoed up the valley as the first splices of lightening broke free and plunged to the ground.

"He was a Sergeant back then, maybe a few years younger than me, but hungry. In San Juan he was nothing, some poor kid nobody gave two shits about. Those mountains changed all that. Back home the only respect Krenshaw ever earned was through his fists. The Army loves guys like that. Someone with a chip on their shoulder and something to prove."

"Let me guess, the power went to his head," said Reinhold.

"I'm sure you saw it in Vietnam. War zones can be miniature worlds. Firebases become city-states fighting for survival."

"I don't get it," said Ashley, "was he acting like some king?"

"We had absolute power, so long as we had a monopoly over destruction. Krenshaw took advantage or maybe it took over."

"Did he kill innocent people?" she asked.

"We all did. People who were unlucky enough to still be there when we showed up. It was just part of the job, but he found pleasure in it."

"I knew he was a vile guy," reiterated Reinhold.

"Our mission was to sow terror. To hunt and kill. Krenshaw was excellent at all three. He reveled in the blood and death."

"Sounds like a sociopath," added Ashley.

Reinhold chuckled to himself, "Sounds like the Army got just what it needed."

"If killing won wars," said Sherman.

"Did you know what happened to him after Afghanistan?" wondered Ashley.

"No. We rotated to Iraq, and I made sure he wasn't there when Tillerman and I came back."

"Why is he here of all fucking places?" Ashley asked.

Sherman shrugged. He did not understand what drove the Sergeant. Money, power or maybe plain cruelty. Was he running like so many others in town? From the front seat of some SUV speeding through an unlit night, none of it mattered. One or both would be dead by morning. Only the past would remain.

"Why not?" offered Reinhold. "People have been disappearing into the valley for a hundred plus years."

Ashley didn't mince her words, "And how many of those did you disappear?"

"None that didn't deserve it," grunted the Sheriff.

Something cold about the way he said it made Sherman doubt that was true. The Sheriff's closet may not have any literal skeletons, but somewhere in the hills were a few makeshift graves. Sherman was not the first to dump a body down a deep ravine in Cumbre County.

Reinhold stopped defending himself and added, "I respected the past. Never asked too many questions or overturned old stones. Hell, I even turned a blind eye for your cab driver."

"What about Brummet?" demanded Ashley.

"I could have turned him over to the feds, but I didn't. No. I respected the man. He kept his nose clean, didn't make no trouble."

Sherman and Ashley exchanged a glance, but she asked, "What did he do?"

"Not mine to share."

"He's in the hospital with a hole through his shoulder courtesy of your men," added Sherman. "I don't think you're able to keep secrets."

The Sheriff was enjoying his moment of leverage, "So he was the one helping you."

"Not your concern. Not now. Never," said Sherman.

It was a bone that Reinhold didn't miss. Any chance to avoid a grisly fate was worth taking. He nodded, "Understood. Like I said, he's a fine guy. Sorry to hear he got hurt." His show of sympathy went nowhere, so he forged on. "Anyway, I turned away those army boys who came looking for him."

"AWOL?" asked Sherman, trying to connect the sparse dots he knew about the man.

"No. He did his time," answered Reinhold, "but that didn't stop him from running."

Only two reasons exist for the army to come looking for a soldier. Since his first guess was wrong that left Sherman with only one option. "They would court-martial him. For what?"

"You know government types play it close to the vest. All they said was war-crimes."

"That's broad," said Sherman.

"The entire damn thing was a war-crime. Brummet ain't a cruel man so I told them to fuck off."

Sherman studied the Sheriff's face through the rearview mirror. Reinhold was pleased with retelling the story, but not boastful. Rewinding the past few days, he remembered Brummet's vacant stares over his past and resurfaced grief that came with the pistol.

War forces hard choices for every generation, but Vietnam was special. It followed the halcyon days of Fascism's defeat under the boot of American greatness. When the U.S. could do no wrong and Kennedy inspired a generation to further spread his vision. That edifice of magnanimity crumbled in the jungle. Trust rotted away. Sherman joined without that sense of possibility. He was driven by indignation and rage. There was no grand redemption or adventure to be had. Only pain for pain, death for death. Revenge, plain and simple.

Ashley wanted to lash out against Reinhold. To say one good deed did not undo the damage or assuage her anger and grief, but she swallowed the vitriol. They sat without words, enveloped by the night and the engine's hum.

A distant rumble ended the moment of solitude. Sherman heard it first, his posture straightened with the acoustic anomaly. Ashley noticed the change, but not the source.

"What is it?"

"Listen," he said.

She cracked her window, and the sound grew with intensity. "Thunder?" she wondered.

"Motorcycle."

Even Reinhold had caught on and painfully managed to buckle up despite his hand.

The sound reached them first, but a lone light cutting through the night arrived in quick succession. It came at the start of a wide right turn as the road circled back around, a ripple in the mountain's vertical face. Sherman held the center of the single lane road. The high-beams cut the night, out over the empty space and the valley below. From a distance it would have looked like a lone flashlight against the great expanse, but up close everything came with such kinetic brightness.

In a moment of adrenaline pumping panic, the biker swerved towards the hill, somehow sensing the threat hurtling through the dark. Sherman closed the gap. All the sounds and lights collided in a screeching crash as he clipped the back end of the Harley. The forced twisted the bike perpendicular to the road and launched the rider on the mountainside, his body rolling to the pavement.

Seconds later Sherman brought the SUV to a shuddering stop and bolted out the door, pistol in hand. He headed downhill towards the sputtering motorcycle. A deep gouge in the loamy earth testified to the force of impact. Cracked but operational, the headlight cast out over the road's edge. Swirls of exhaust mixed with dirt gave off a ghostly pall.

A few yards past he found the rider struggling to stand. Even in the pale light Sherman recognized the skulls emblazoned across the jacket. The same skulls sat on the stool next to Ruby at the Crosscut. The owner had threatened to kill him later that night and worked for Krenshaw as extra muscle.

Jensen heard footsteps approaching. Although disoriented from the crash, he recognized Sherman's face. A kernel of understanding amongst the fog of chaos. Fear almost overcame his limp and he hobbled away with renewed vigor.

Six steps later Sherman used his Glock to end the escape attempt with a single shot. Jensen's knee exploded as the bullet tore through bone and tendon. He spun to the ground with a howl of pain. The biker was lying on his back breathing heavily from the traumas of bullet and crash.

"Fuck you," he spat as Sherman squatted next to him.

"Glad you remember me."

"You ain't making it out of this valley alive," Jensen hissed.

"I guess we have something in common," Sherman said flatly.

Jensen never went for his gun; it had fallen out during the crash. Nor did he flinch, but Sherman shot him again just the same. There was no howl of pain, only the distant hum of the SUV. He dragged the man by the boots across the road, a thin black streak of blood trailing behind, before pushing the body off the cliff. The motorcycle followed a minute later. Trees were briefly silhouetted by the tumbling light before it too died.

Ashley and Reinhold had sat in the Tahoe, transfixed by the mechanics of what had just unfolded. The Sheriff understood Sherman was a dangerous man, but that knowledge was indirect. He had not seen the fight at O'Toole's, only the result. Callousness was nothing new in his world. He saw it in Vietnam, in the drug-addled homes of negligent parents and the poverty of choices in a forgotten America. But those moments were infrequent. They came as a stark reminder of the baser nature and cruel twists of human fallibility. Happenstance had brought not one, but two men capable of the most egregious acts of violence into his county.

Deep down Reinhold knew he owned the blame of what happened that night. He was not a religious man but muttered the lord's name regardless.

Ashley overheard the quiet utterance, "I told you he won't help you here."

"Can't hurt to hope," replied the Sheriff.

"That's dead too."

Sherman got back into the car and closed the door with a grunt. He took no pleasure in killing the biker, nor anyone else. The army teaches detachment and trains away the direct emotional ties to other human life. Over the years he had gotten exceptionally good at operating in a box far removed from any moral or emotional influence. However, it did not come without a toll. With time his capacity for detachment grew but everything else shrank proportionally. Sherman relied on his visits to Byron Mills and Tillerman to reset. That opportunity was gone and so was any chance of leniency.

Cracks of thunder rolled up the road as Sherman moved the shifter into drive. The Tahoe was warm, but the storm crept into the cabin. Ashley shifted in the passenger seat, aware of the enveloping distance. The three remained silent for several minutes as the next confrontation loomed up in the mountains.

Reinhold looked out over the valley like he was seeing it anew. It held no stark beauty, no geographic wonders, but it still felt like home. That much was the same. Acres of oaks and sycamores held soft memories accumulated like leaves on the dirt.

Reinhold spoke up, "Your exit is about two turns ahead."

Sherman nodded and refocused his attention on the surrounding area. He slowed the SUV before making the turn, not wanting to overcommit. The road was old and overgrown. Foxtails guarded the cutout entrance and their still standing stalks suggested no one else had driven down it in quite some time. It wasn't a great spot and had no easy exit, but it was better than driving right up.

Satisfied, he yanked the wheel, guiding the Tahoe about thirty yards down the road. Far enough to keep it out of view of any passing cars but within range of a quick escape.

He turned to Ashley, "I think you know what comes next."

"Which part? Me waiting alone with Reinhold or you shooting Pa."

The temp was steadily falling. Sherman slipped off the vest over his head and added Tillerman's jacket as a layer against the coming cold. He took a long look at her flat expression and the way she fervently gripped the pistol. Ready was not the word that came to mind, but her eyes held a level of acceptance that Sherman took as readiness. He grabbed the non-scoped rifle and smiled, choosing not to answer her question.

"How long should I wait?" she asked, knowing that was the only answer he would give.

"An hour. If I'm not back by eight shoot him and leave town."

The Sheriff's upper lip quivered somewhere between fear and rage, but he kept quiet. Staying alive was his sole priority, and it put him in the odd position of wishing Sherman good luck.

Ashley felt the weight of the gun in her hand. Somehow that awareness made it feel heavier. Like the bullets themselves, each possibility had a mass.

"Okay," she said with a slow nod of her head.

Pulling back the bolt, Sherman press checked the M4 to confirm a round was in the chamber. The golden hue of brass peaked out, confirming the weapon was ready to fire. He repeated the process with the Glock. It was a ritual performed thousands of times for an over a decade until Sherman was barely conscious of the action. He checked the magazines before placing them in pouches on the vest. His mind memorized each feature, each mag and piece of equipment until it was just second nature. Then he ripped off the white stenciled letters announcing a blatant lie. He was not a SHERIFF and no chance existed where Thorne bought into that subterfuge. They were just a bright spot in the otherwise black night. A risk. He slipped it back on over the jacket. Finally, he flexed the knees and arms, popping any joints that obliged. The popping was a minor detail, but even the tiniest detail was deadly.

Watching him go through all the motions, Ashley couldn't help but see it as some morbid pre-game ritual. The practiced, almost OCD, moves looked no different from a batter stepping up to the plate. Tanner had played outfield in high school, not well, but Sherman's focus reminded her of him. He liked the mental aspects, the statistics, the odds, and the data behind it all. She saw it as one man throwing a rock at another wielding a club. Nothing more than a crude fight repeated over millennia.

"You'd be a decent baseball player," she joked.

"I was," replied Sherman as he slung the rifle and walked away.

Ashley wanted to take back the remark, to say something like good luck, but the darkness had already swallowed him up.

Driven by the storm, harsh air swirled through the trees. Leaves rustled off from their branches and scattered across the old dirt road. Whatever its purpose in the past, no one had driven down the rutted path in ages. A relic of a timber boom long since bust.

Soft earth sank beneath Sherman's boots. Most of the leaves were too saturated from previous storms to offer much crunch. He liked the conditions. Chilly rain kept people inside. Thunder masked his approach. The lightning discouraged modern conveniences like night-vision. Of all the times he had walked into the darkness, few had such advantages. Some had been hotter, some colder, but all of them fell under the shadow of the stars and stripes. The moment felt both new and old.

Whispers of activity drifted down the hill, but it was the smell of cigarettes and stale beer that confirmed the bar was nearby. Sherman tacked back uphill towards the tree line near the back door. He walked carefully, taking deliberate steps in the dewy grass. A gnarled pine provided cover, and he kneeled on a bed of brown needles. Then came the waiting.

On the far side of the building a bonfire crackled, sending embers up above the roofline. Specks of orange floated up to meet the coming storm only to fizzle and fall away as ash. Someone was drinking. The clink of bottles carried with their indistinct banter.

Sherman watched the back door for a good ten minutes. Staring any harder, he would have seen through it. Nothing looked out of place, nothing was amiss and that had him worried. Going in blind was bad enough, but this was Thorne's backyard. That came with serious advantages. Brute force might get him in the door, but it wouldn't lead him out. Not in one piece. Rigging the door was too easy. Lots of options. Bombs, guns, even a high voltage current to the doorknob were all easy to arrange.

Looking around at the piles of discarded scraps of wood and metal strewn around gave Sherman an idea. He grabbed an old twisted length of two-by-six, the longest one available, and gently placed one end under the doorknob. It took a little muscle, but he wedged the other end against a pine tree. A stopgap measure to prevent anyone from running out the back door.

More thunder rumbled in the distance. It was growing noticeably closer. Rain would follow. Sherman stepped back into the trees and circled around the building towards the gravel parking lot. He weaved between soft-skinned redwoods while catching glimpses of the fire beyond. Only a few days ago he considered the trees an escape route from the bar fight. He admired their soaring height and the monolithic chunks of time for which they stood. Memories of his past seeped through their branches. Snippets of boyhood. Now the redwoods were something else altogether. Like a path, they carried him to the parking lot, to the edge of a choice.

Shrouded by the night, Sherman counted the trucks. Nine pickups of varying degrees of decay staggered around the gravel semi-circle. It wasn't the closest one, but he spotted Tanner's truck almost immediately. The kid was incredibly lucky, or cursed, to be alive. Sherman couldn't decide which one.

A battered Ram truck from the eighties was nearest to the tree he was hiding behind. The red paint looked more orange than cherry, but appearances meant less than money in Cumbre County. If it ran was the only thing that counted.

Sherman didn't care either way. He only wanted two items. Peeking through the window, he was in luck. Empty packs of cigarettes littered the floor. Like every vehicle in the lot, it was unlocked. The door creaked when opened, but no one who heard cared enough to investigate. He grabbed the half-full pack on the bench seat and flipped open the lid. The owner wedged a cheap green Bic lighter in there. He took the lighter and a dirty rag soaked with oil from a two-stroke engine.

The door popped as it closed, but still no one cared.

Tanner's truck was in the middle of the lot, having not been the first to arrive that evening. Sherman took notice of the fact. Recently shot men park as close as possible to the door and the awkward angle suggested he stopped in a hurry. Three vehicles to the left meant early arrivals. Early arrivals meant planning. Planning meant nothing good for his future.

"Shit," he muttered to himself, feeling like a wolf circling a staked animal. The bar was a trap. It was the only sensible answer. The question became who the bait was. Tanner? Dell? Both?

Two burly Scandinavian guys were standing around the bonfire sipping long-necks. Their beards gave Sherman a tinge of jealousy, and he scratched his own growing scruff. The conversation seemed mundane enough. Typical work complaints. A dig about their boss, money problems. Nothing about him.

Sherman moved closer over the hard-packed gravel, truck by truck, until he reached Tanner's. The gas cap had no lock, and he flipped it open. He stuffed most of the oil-soaked rag into the tank, leaving only a small tuft of fabric to light. Turning the Bic slowly in hand, end over end, he debated when to spark up.

The loggers were still nursing their beers, but otherwise acting nonchalant. Sherman took a quick peek from his fresh angle and something that had been obscured became clear. Both had coats on, but the taller of the two needed a new tailor. His torso was longer than his jacket and the barrel of a pistol poked out into the elements. Despite the distance, Sherman felt sure it was a Czech made CZ-75. Chambered for a 9mm round, it was common, accurate and reliable. He assumed both were armed. No leap involved with that conclusion.

Nine trucks did not indicate how many men were in the bar. Given Reinhold's warning, he assumed the upper end of possibility. Twenty was reasonable, which left eighteen unaccounted. The number was probably lower, but even with only seven inside, a shootout would be disastrous.

The wind had picked up as the storm bore down on the valley. A lone growl rode the air currents up the hill. The loggers heard it as well and set their beers down. The guns came out with the unexpected visitor.

A pair of dull square lights swayed in the distance. Another truck. The two men edged closer to the road, straining to get a look at the intruder. There was a distinct clank to the engine, one they recognized. They swapped the guns for beers and the men started joking about the driver.

Sherman removed the rag and moved out of view to wait. The crappy old green Chevy surprised him. The truck was all too familiar.

"What the fuck are you doing here, Dean?" he wondered to himself. The guy should have been in a hospital nursing a bullet hole in the shoulder. Tough or dumb, the decision was a toss-up.

The truck shuddered to a stop in the grass close to the front door. Dean slid out with more whiskey than Kentucky in him and staggered inside.

"Jesus, Dean," yelled the shorter man, "what the fuck are you doing here?"

With one arm in a sling and a bottle of sour mash in the other, Ashley's cousin looked downright haggard. A bad man in a bad way.

He raised the bottle impotently, "You say he's a coming, well I... I..., want my fair cut from the man."

The unscheduled arrival did not sit well with the taller man. "You drunk idiot. Reinhold called and said he got that boot stomper already."

Dean whirled around but was beyond drunk and ended up dropping his bottle while attempting not to fall on his face. "What you'd say?" he yelled.

"For fuck's sake," replied the man. "Karl would you help this degenerate find more whiskey. Maybe he'll pass out and spare us the running of his mouth."

"You always were a little bitch Sven. What kinda name

is that, anyway? Sven! Fucking Eur-o-peans."

Karl gave Dean a whack on the head as he herded the drunk into the Crosscut. "Shut up before someone shoots you in the other arm."

As the door opened Sherman caught sight of at least five more men sitting around a few tables. There were guns and beers out, but they seemed relaxed. The ruse had worked. How long would it hold?

Sven chugged his beer and muttered, "God damn dimwit." His blonde beard glowed orange in the firelight. A Celtic warrior two thousand years earlier would have mistaken the man for one of his own.

At six and a half feet tall, the logger cut an imposing figure. Sherman sized the man up from behind Tanner's truck. Instinct told him to take the man out, but then no one would be around to see the blaze.

The lighter was already in his hand when he stuffed the rag back into the gas tank. Thumbing the flint wheel always felt rewarding. Although he was never a smoker, Sherman could still see how those sparks were part of the ritual. Holding the red button down hard, he waived the flame briefly over the rag. The oil-soaked fabric went up in a flash. He disappeared just as quickly.

Had Tanner filled his tank, the fire might have failed to ignite the fumes, but adrenaline and blood loss from taking a bullet meant he headed straight back. Trivial thoughts have a way of sinking into the mud when survival is on the line.

Sven was too busy cracking open another beer to see the initial burst of flames in the dark parking lot. The brief flash of reddish-orange lasted only a second. It took a few more for the primary explosion to kick off.

When the flames finally reached the fume filled tank, Tanner's precious truck exploded like a can of hairspray in a campfire. It wasn't an enormous boom, but it was a bright one. Gasoline makes for good pyrotechnics and that was what Sherman wanted. A big show.

The beer bottle Sven had been holding shattered as it hit the ground. He stood frozen by the flames rising into the clouds above. Fear followed shock and the gigantic man ran hard for the front door, crashing through it like a bull out of the gate.

At the sound of the explosion and Sven's dramatic entrance, men spilled out of the Crosscut and into the chilled night air. The fireball had long since dissipated, but the fire remained, slowly reducing the truck to a charred frame. Noxious smoke, pushed by the wind, made their eyes water. Some coughed. Most tried pitifully to fan the fumes away.

Standing on crutches that did nothing but confuse his center of gravity, Tanner could scarcely believe his eyes. Jumbled questions bounced around his Vicodin numbed mind. Had he left a lit cigarette in the truck? Was he even smoking on the drive up? His memory came up empty.

Some men laughed; others shook their head in mock disbelief. Such was their world that a truck engulfed in flames resonated normality. While they gawked, Sherman circled back through the trees. Hiding prone between a chunk of quartz and the thick hide of a redwood. He was on their flank. The selector switch was on single-fire, and his finger rested confidently on the trigger. Through the holographic sight, only a faint red circle surrounded the closest man.

"Get your goddamn guns," boomed a voice from the doorway. "He's here!"

A thin, wiry man stepped out with hands gesticulating towards the trees. Sherman couldn't see much, but knew it was Dell Thorne. No one else could have held that kind of authority. From muzzle to bar it wasn't much more than the California mandated fire break distance. A hundred feet, no more. Even the gusty wind held little sway over the bullet's trajectory.

Seven men were within view. As the motley crew went to grab their weapons Sherman opened fire. The stillness ruptured under a continuous crackle. Shell casings flashed in the momentary bursts of orange before disappearing into the night.

Having shot enough rounds from an M4 to make a Fort Bragg instructor green with envy, Sherman didn't waste bullets. He went center mass down the line.

Four of the seven fell on the dusty gravel parking lot, their wounds incongruent with survival. Panic scattered the other men. Dell dove back into the bar while Tanner just crawled to safety. That left Sven cowering behind a generic looking blue GMC.

There wasn't much for the logger to do. The options, as they existed, were simple: fight or hide. Sherman centered the sight between Sven and the bar. Keeping that angle allowed him to see both. The man poked his head out hesitantly.

"Not worth it," muttered Sherman.

He hoped the man wouldn't be an issue, but then someone in the bar started making gestures. The two were planning something. Considering what he would do, Sherman aimed at the door frame and waited.

With the faintest word, Sven popped up and fired the pistol blindly in Sherman's direction. Ineffective fire that he ignored. A heartbeat later a man leaned out of the bar with some imitation SKS intent on ending the standoff. In that briefest of moments, Sherman recognized the man who had given him a conciliatory beer days earlier. An act of kindness or enmity? When the moment came to decide it did not matter. The door got splattered with his past.

Enraged by the death of his friend, Sven did something stupid. He should have ducked down and stayed hidden. Instead, he reloaded. Sherman caught him in the act and put a round close enough to his heart as not to matter. Ballistic damage rarely quibbled over millimeters.

The ground was soft with the bark of decaying trees and it felt like running on a pillow top mattress. A thin veil of mist had descended as the storm clouds collided into the mountains. For the first time since Barrios barged into Tillerman's house, he felt a sense of freedom. There was no turning back, no way out except through them. All those switches he had to flip back on when he returned home were reset. To abide by societal rules, laws, or morals required energy. Running in the woods, Sherman knew it was just him and them. No nuance. Nothing else. The simplicity was liberating.

He checked the rear of the bar first. The lumber was still holding as men smashed against the door trying to break free. The wood barely flexed and stuck further with each attempt. Fire codes didn't really apply to a place like the Crosscut. There were only two doors and no working windows. He hurried back to the front.

None of the men out front survived. A bloody patchwork covered the small wooden deck in front of the bar. The oily surface was undisturbed. No footprints or evidence of anyone leaving. Sherman switched the rifle to his left shoulder and waited at the corner facing the only unblocked exit.

With the windows covered by plywood, there was only one unobstructed view into the primary room. By his count, there were at least four men inside. Two with the last name Thorne, cousin Dean, and Karl were not among the dead. Assuming Dean was too drunk and injured to shoot straight, that left three guns aiming at the front door. Sherman added up the odds. They were not in his favor.

In the process of moving closer to the entrance Sherman stopped at the first sheet of plywood serving as a window. A small rectangular cutout near the top housed a neon Pabst sign. It was too high for him to peek through without climbing on the ledge. He laughed at the thought of them seeing his neon blue face spying inward. A bullet would surely follow, leaving him with more holes than biologically necessary.

Shadows danced at the base of the sheet. They caught his eye. Through time or shoddy work, the bottom of the plywood had separated from the window frame. A quarter inch gap had formed. Big enough for him to see the dirty floor inside. A pair of steel toe work boots and jeans were standing on the other side of inch-thick laminated wood.

With a flip of his thumb, Sherman changed the fire mode to full auto. One step back for safety, then he emptied what remained of the magazine. Splinters and blood filled the bar as bullets shredded wood and flesh. When the gun went dry, he dove around the corner.

From the ground Sherman watched as they added fifty more holes to the front wall. Chunks of siding spiraled in the air. The air trembled with shock waves as the gunshots echoed around. He counted at least four different guns amongst the roar. Caught by the mist, narrow arcs of light streamed out in the night. There was a cruel but functional beauty to it. He swapped for a fresh magazine without taking his sight off the door.

Another blast of gunfire sent more pieces of wood tumbling by his prone figure. The moment of pause that followed quickly shattered. Dozens of rounds punctured the flimsy walls. He was losing his advantage of visibility and fire superiority.

"Fuck," grumbled Sherman as he crawled closer to the bar. If someone peeked out, he didn't want to be just lying in the dirt.

"Turn off the damn lights," yelled Thorne from somewhere inside.

"Got it," responded Tanner.

The woods plunged into darkness. Only the embers of the burning truck and bonfire remained. Their soft glow worked to silhouette anyone standing out front.

Sherman lay there unmoving. He trained his gun on the door. The options were few. Leave or stay. Fight or flee. Everything else downstream was just a tributary of that decision.

How badly did he want the Thorne clan dead? Was it worth the cost? Rarely did he consider such questions.

Orders were orders, and he trusted the Major not to send him on some suicide mission. That was over there. Back here, things were different. He had made it personal. Suddenly the strength of his conviction was in the spotlight.

Tanner and Dean needed killing, but not if the price was dying. With Dell it felt different. However, Sherman didn't know the man, not yet. He was a mean bastard, but his true grit remained unspoken.

"Too late, too far," he said to himself.

He would not cut and run. If they wanted to hide like rats, he'd treat them as such.

Sherman grunted and ran towards the parking lot. The commotion brought a barrage of bullets. A few came close enough to pop and hiss by his head, but only the ground took a direct hit.

As the last few sporadic muzzle flashes faded Sherman slid behind the wheel of the old Dodge Ram. The search for keys took him a few seconds before he realized they were still in the ignition. The truck rumbled to life, and he jammed the shifter down into reverse, cranking the wheel hard right.

Taking a deep breath, he centered himself before mashing the gas pedal. The truck roared back. Plumes of gravel and dust sprayed into the air. Sherman ducked below the dashboard. He was in clear view of the bar now.

The windshield shattered under a violent fusillade. Chunks of safety glass lodged in his hair and body armor. Bullets snapped overhead.

With a quick twist of the lever, Sherman turned on the lights and then flipped on the brights. The time for hiding was over. He dropped the truck into drive, gave it enough gas to get going and then jumped back out. Like a steamroller, the Dodge crunched slowly forward. Sharp arcs of illumination penetrated the darkened bar.

The truck was mobile cover, and Sherman walked behind it like a Humvee in Fallujah. Every time a burst of gunfire shattered the mountain stillness, he fired back.

Bullets for bullets. The zip and pop of rifle fire echoed off the gigantic trees.

Gerhardt, the bouncer, was the first to fall. He had knocked over a two-top table and was trying to fit his gigantic frame behind the thick wood. As Sherman switched from right to left, he spotted the thick man hunkering down. He put three rounds over the top of the table, and into the bouncer's shoulder. It splattered the bar stool behind Gerhardt with crimson as he spun to the floor.

Four guns went down to three. Thorne, Dean, and Tanner remained. Two bodies dove into the office after the bouncer went down. Sherman saw the flash of legs seeking safety.

The empty metal magazine clanged on the gravel as Sherman reloaded. Without someone pressing on the gas pedal, the truck had stopped against the front wall of the bar. No inertia remained. Steam hissed from several holes in the radiator, and they shot out one of the lights.

Sherman reached through the front door, his fingers searching for the rectangular plastic plate of a light switch. When he clicked it on there was a flicker of time when he half expected to be missing an arm.

In the modest light of sixty-watt bulbs, the aftermath was apparent. Shell casings littered the floor. Wood chunks and slivers lay across tables and chairs. The corner by Karl's body was dripping with blood. Bright red trails snaked down the wall as gravity battled with viscosity.

Clearing his corners first, Sherman worked his way towards the office door. He could see Gerhardt's chest still rising. Somehow the pale faced doorman was drawing ragged breaths. Sherman kicked a nearby shotgun further away and kept on moving. The man had a chance of living and he had no intention of changing that.

Over all those years of active duty, Sherman had developed an intuition for situations like those brief steps across the open bar. Working unseen to his conscious mind, an overdeveloped part of his brain processed information that most people glossed over. Noises, smells and even rocks out of place were suspicious. All those neurons moved his focus towards the bar.

A bottle clanked, and Dean stood up, pistol in hand, roaring with rage. The man was still blackout drunk. He was too numb and dumb to think it through. Like those spaghetti westerns he and Jimmy enjoyed, the idiot thought he could get the best of a ghost. The only thing he shot was the wall before Sherman put four holes in his chest and a shelf full of bourbon behind him. Only the booze was worth mourning.

Out of instinct, Sherman snapped back to the office door and added a patchwork of new craters. While the brass was still bouncing off the floor, someone on the other side howled in pain.

"Jesus fucking Christ," yelled Tanner.

Out of sight, Sherman hugged the wall next to the door, "Did I get your other leg?"

"Fuck you."

"Shut up boy," Dell Thorne instructed his son.

As Tanner whimpered Sherman emptied the mag in the sound's direction. The callow man had crashed to the ground in a sobbing, piss-soaked mess.

"How about now?" Sherman asked, finding some joy in the suffering. It wasn't his finest moment, but neither were the preceding days.

"What do you want, Captain?" shouted Thorne.

"Ah, glad to hear you know who I am," replied Sherman as he racked in a round from the fresh magazine. "But don't be obtuse. You know damn well why we're all here."

"He stole from us. You expect me to just roll over."

"I'm not here to judge," said Sherman, "but to remind you those choices come with a price."

"Losing two sons ain't enough?" yelled Thorne.

"Don't forget about the daughter you tried to kill."

"She ain't no child of mine. Not after helping the likes of you," snorted the old man.

"Don't kid yourself. You threw her to the wolves long before I showed up," Sherman reminded him.

"Family first. I didn't raise no runners. But she couldn't help herself. The gall to get mixed up with some out-of-towner. The girl moved out as soon as she could."

"And that justifies a bullet?"

"Like you said Captain, choices come with a price. Taking that money was hers," Thorne said solemnly.

"And Tillerman?"

"Happenstance. He come looking in the wrong places and had the gumption to tell me to leave my kin out of it. My kin! Not his."

"He loved your daughter, you know that," said Sherman.

"Love ain't got nothing to do with family," retorted Thorne.

"You're a brutal bastard, Mr. Thorne."

The old man laughed, "I pale compared to your kind. That man Krenshaw broke Tillerman down like a butcher with a prized hog. Had him singing like a canary to protect her."

"Forgive my sense of utter fucking doubt on that account," said Sherman.

"That was the consensus amongst those present," replied Thorne.

"Since you're stalling for time Mr. Thorne, will you indulge my curiosity?"

"It gonna change the ending to this?"

"Nothing's written yet," answered Sherman.

"Go ahead," replied Thorne as he motioned Tanner to get behind the same desk he was using as cover.

"How did Tillerman suss it out?" Sherman asked.

"The drugs or the money?"

"The former."

"I ain't rightfully sure, but he'd been buying extra wood off some loggers."

It wasn't the answer Sherman had been expecting, and it didn't explain the text from his friend. It left him wondering.

He changed the subject, "Did you think you could just sweep it under the rug?"

Thorne grunted, "Like I said, happenstance. Didn't know someone like you was gonna show up."

A bottle of Everclear 190 proof caught his eye. He circled back around the bar to grab it and a dry rag. "Well, Mr. Thorne where does that leave us?" he asked while assembling the Molotov cocktail.

"An impasse I'd say, unless you plan on getting the fuck off my property."

"I'm afraid we've come too far for that."

"What are you waiting for?" taunted Thorne.

Sherman gave a half-shrug. He could have gone in earlier, but his curiosity ran too deep. The question of who took the money nagged at the fringes of his mind. Like a dog with a bone, he couldn't let go. Gnawing on it, bloody gums and all.

He set the bottle down and aimed at the door handle. Tanner yelled in fear as the cheap white wood disappeared into a haze of splinters. In a show of discipline Dell held his fire, waiting like a continental soldier for the whites of Sherman's eyes.

With no lock, the door creaked open under its own inertia. Everyone was holding their breath. Time limped forward. Last chance, he thought before sparking the lighter. The towel lit quickly, and he tossed it as casually as a wadded up fast-food wrapper goes into the trash.

Thorne saw the object come flying in and instinctively pulled the trigger on the 12-gauge he held against his shoulder. By the time he racked another shell into the chamber, flames erupted against a narrow row of shelving. The blaze quickly consumed extra bar rags, and cleaning supplies. The dingy room glowed red, orange, blue and green. Chemical fumes mixed with smoke and pooled against the ceiling.

A tipping point loomed. Thorne had two options, both unbearable. Stay and burn or run for it. The first was a certain and painful death. The second was an almost certain and painful death. Sherman took a few steps back and crouched behind an overturned table. He was sure the patriarch would pick the latter. Laying down without a fight didn't suit the man's temperament.

He flipped the selector switch. Full-auto.

Dark gray smoke was billowing out. The room was compact. It wouldn't be long before there was no air left. Flames licked around the top door jamb.

Out came Tanner, tumbling and tripping over his injured leg like someone had pushed him from behind. Sherman fired twice but didn't follow him to the ground. The kid was just a decoy.

From within the smoke came the shotgun's thundering blast. Dozens of pellets cratered into the table. A few hit his vest. Sherman shifted low right as Thorne came out firing from the hip. The old man was downright surgical with the gun and put two more rounds on top of the first. Heavily lacquered shards of table ricocheted around the floor.

As Thorne stepped out of the smoke, eyes red, and raging, Sherman emptied his rifle. Some twenty plus bullets hit center mass. Brass casings seemed to bounce around the bar for a five second eternity. Cordite wafted from the barrel as he stood up and inserted another magazine.

The shotgun was on the floor, its walnut stock speckled with red. Thorne slumped against the wall next to the bar. Overhead, crisp night air leaked through the fresh holes in the siding. Everything below was a bloody, tangled mess.

Though fading, Tanner was still alive.

Sherman stood over him, "You got grit kid."

"All for what?"

"Nothing, I'm afraid."

Tanner coughed. It made him wince with pain. The bullets had ruptured his spleen, and his blood pressure was plummeting.

"I hope you fucking die," he spat.

"You'll get your wish one of these days. Don't you

worry," replied Sherman.

"Your friend knew we were coming. Will you?"

Sherman shook his head and placed the muzzle of the Glock against Tanner's forehead. "No, I doubt it," he answered before pulling the trigger.

The short crack of the pistol sounded small compared to the preceding racket. Two generations of the Thorne family were gone. Only Ashley remained.

The bouncer looked on. His pale face followed Sherman as he walked towards the door.

"Keep pressure on the wound," he said while tossing the injured man a towel. "And start crawling." Then Sherman pointed towards the flames spilling into the bar, "I don't think the rain is coming soon enough."

The truck was still hissing steam as he exited past the bodies. Men with pasts not unlike his own. Fathers, brothers and sons. Hard edged men doing what they could to survive. He stepped over them and felt nothing. Not fear or anger, guilt or shame. He was not calm or excited. Flames jumped into the night as the building crackled towards its end. The war, his war, was back.

CHAPTER TWENTY-THREE

Reinhold saw him first. A lone figure emerging from the thick fabric of night like someone stepping out from behind black theater curtains. In a blink, Sherman was there. Ashley was too busy pointing the pistol at the Sheriff and staring at the road behind her to notice. They had seen the faint glow of fire almost ten minutes before and it frayed her nerves.

"Jesus," mumbled Reinhold.

She turned and let out a lengthy sigh. It was a conflicted feeling. Relief and sadness, but not in equal parts. If he was standing it meant everyone else was dead. Many have wished their parents ill, some were even deserving of harm, but very few saw it come to pass. Ashley didn't know if she wanted to be in such company.

The dome light went on as Sherman opened the door. In the sudden burst of illumination, they saw a wild looking man. Blood splatter added a dreadful color to Tillerman's jacket. Several shotgun pellets were visible as small orbs of silver embedded in the black nylon. Then there was the smell. A pungent combination of wood smoke and chemicals. It twisted Ashley's fond memories of childhood campfires into something else.

Sherman smashed the light before they could look harder. The shattered plastic startled Ashley for a moment. Reinhold said nothing.

After regaining her composure, she asked, "Are you

okay?"

He rubbed his beard. It no longer bothered him. "I'm not bleeding."

"And the rest of them?" asked Reinhold, sizing up his captor's state.

"Not anymore" replied Sherman.

"Everyone?" asked Ashley in a quiet voice.

"The bouncer was still breathing when I left."

Ashley sat with that news as Sherman backed out to the pavement. It wasn't unexpected or unwanted, but there was a totality to the knowledge. She felt it in her chest. Not like the crushing weight of Tillerman's death, but it brought no sense of relief. Just a dampening or deadening of time, history and memory. An ending of sorts.

They were heading downhill, the faint glow of fire fading, when she asked, "Did he say anything?"

"Oh, he said many things."

"Any repentance?" asked Reinhold, mostly joking.

Ashley snapped, "Will you when the end comes?"

Reinhold hung his head.

"No apologies were forthcoming," said Sherman, "but he said something that I can't quite get out of my head."

"What?" she asked.

"He called this whole mess a happenstance."

"Does it matter how we got here?" asked Ashley.

"No, it doesn't, but I assumed Tillerman's text was a clue for what we found."

"What changed?"

"Apparently he found out about the drugs from some loggers. Maybe they sold him the wrong log."

"He mentioned running into Sven a few months back," added Ashley.

"Sven's dead," said Sherman as a matter of fact.

"Jesus," muttered Reinhold.

Ashley shook her head at the Sheriff's constant invocation of a higher power but said nothing. It was the timeline that had her mind churning through the past. "So, he knew for months?"

"At least the drugs. I'm not sure about the money."

"Why didn't he tell me?"

Sherman shrugged, "Maybe he wasn't sure. The man liked to have things nice and tidy before acting. He always read the intelligence files cover to cover for every mission." It was a polite assertion. Deep down he guessed Tillerman didn't trust Ashley, not completely. Maybe he even suspected her involvement or complicity.

Reinhold had come to the same conclusion but thought better of voicing it. The pistol still pointed in his direction. It did nothing to loosen his tongue.

"I guess," said Ashley, hesitant with the response.

"Does his text mean anything else to you?" asked Sherman.

She shook her head with self-evident dissatisfaction.

"What was the text?" asked Reinhold. He knew that being helpful was his only way out alive.

"Spruce."

The Sheriff gestured towards the trees, "That's vague."

"Anything specific?"

Reinhold considered the word. For him it was only a tree. It meant nothing else. Not a code or euphemism. Just timber.

"It's mostly lumber in these parts," he said.

The transformed product jump-started Sherman's mind. He had accepted that the text referred to something in its natural state. The grove of trees made sense, but that wasn't everything. Thinking back over the years since Tillerman landed in Byron Mills. One specific memory stood out from the jumbled fragments. Not long after Tillerman sobered up, Sherman stopped by unannounced. He had caught a bullet near the Pakistan border, and for his sins got a month of rehab. His friend barely looked up when Sherman walked into the shop. On the sawdust-covered table Tillerman was sanding the last few pieces of a new chair design. A pleasant look of joy beamed from his eyes. One that Sherman wished he knew. The chair became a bestseller. The wood was spruce.

Sherman got lost in the memory, staring off towards some distant flicker.

"You okay?" asked Ashley.

"Yeah. Just considering something unpalatable."

"Care to share?"

"Soon enough," he answered.

Ashley thought about pressing him, after all they had agreed to transparency, but she refrained. There was a pall to his face that urged silence.

"Which way would those assholes take?" asked Sherman. He knew there could be more than one entrance to the fire road.

"Upper Mill is the most Harley friendly way," answered Reinhold.

Everything seemed to spin off that road like thread leading to his friend's death. If the bikers went up that way, they could easily stop someone else from doing the same.

"Other options?"

"Some 4x4 trails."

"South River Road," suggested Ashley.

"A little out of the way, but that works too," agreed Reinhold.

There was a symmetry to the route that appealed to Sherman's desire for retribution. They took his friend up the road to die. Through some perverse logic of karma, he would come for them the same way. Nothing felt right about the town anymore. Not like it used to. The walls were tumbling down, and Sherman was ready to give them one last shove.

"That sounds like a plan," he said.

Ashley agreed with a nervous nod. She was along for the ride as much as the man handcuffed in the back seat. Even though she wanted to be in control, that rock had rolled well downhill. There was no stopping it. No turning back.

Her life was over. Dead. The man she loved was on a

slab in the morgue and so was at least one of her brothers. As for the rest, she could only guess. A shallow grave? The fish pond? Charred in the rubble? The answer did not matter. The outcome was all the same. Her chest tightened, and she struggled to take a deep breath.

"Focus on the road," suggested Sherman.

The comment startled her. "What?" she asked.

"Keep your attention on the road. Act like you've never seen it before."

"Why?"

"It will help slow your mind down. Let you take that breath trapped in your chest. The one you can't seem to get out."

Following his advice, Ashley visualized the drive anew. Hundreds, even thousands of times she had gone up and down. From town to bar and back. As the light veered back and forth, she noticed the unseen. In those bright cones of clarity were pieces of the past long forgotten. The creek they hiked up some summer. A sign her brothers threw buckeyes at during the spring. She started weeping, grieving for her losses. Then came the breath.

Sitting in silence, Reinhold watched Ashley try to cope and understand a tiny piece of her new world. He felt a roiling sea filled with waves of empathy and antipathy. Conflicting emotions swelled, then crested, finally breaking across his chest. There was genuine sadness in his world, and he wondered if he would see another fall afternoon. The venom was still inside, but his fate and their fate were bound tighter than the plastic around his wrists.

As lightning flashed overhead Sherman wound the Tahoe down the mountain. Having grown fond of the drive, it was a shame he would never see the road again. Nor the town. Although, those thoughts were far from his mind. A distant knocking on the fringes of consciousness. The next few hours were far more important.

The town was empty save for a few brave or ignorant residents. Whispers had turned to shouts, and most folks knew something wicked was unfolding. The body count was too high. Reinhold sensed the unease seeping into his county. It pained him not to answer the calls and feel that level of importance and respectability.

"Haven't seen it this quiet in years," he said as they passed shuttered shops and unlit neon signs.

"Bracing for the storm," Ashley suggested.

Reinhold almost quipped back about the rugged nature of Cumbre County, but her storm did not involve the weather. He took a slow breath, "They ain't wrong to hide."

"You think someone called the authorities?" asked Sherman.

Reinhold laughed and replied, "You have the authorities handcuffed in the back seat."

"He's right," said Ashley. "It's not like they're gonna call the feds."

It was the nature of tiny rural towns to look the other way or sweep things under a very thick rug. Sherman was starting to feel otherwise. Someone would come snooping and he didn't want his name attached to anything, even if he existed outside of conventional life. Bodies beget questions, and that number was only increasing.

Staying left, he angled the Tahoe up South River Road. The smell of decay mixed with bay trees near the river's edge. He smiled at the memories.

"Where's this fire road entrance?"

"Just past the pomegranate orchard," said Ashley. "Keep heading past the Bailey place and through the cow gate."

"Won't that raise some suspicion?" he asked.

"Old man Bailey is too old and too drunk to notice," added Reinhold.

"We did it in high school," said Ashley. "While his drinking couldn't get any worse, his hearing has surely suffered."

Sherman couldn't argue with the ravages of booze and time. He hoped the old man didn't intervene. Shooting an innocent man was something he wanted to avoid, but not at all costs. One more stat would not stop him. Not anymore.

Whipped by the winds, wet leaves tumbled across the road only to stick on whatever they hit first. Against the overhead flashes Sherman could see the old sycamores swaying. Many things would fall in the coming hours, but only a handful would be trees.

Crimson red hues glistened in the mist off to his left. Sherman slowed as they approached the dirt driveway. Unsettled by the lightning, horses in nearby stalls brayed against the night. A few dogs barked at noises real and imagined. They drove without lights, trying not to wake up the cantankerous drunk who lived nearby.

The air was electric. It made for strange nights full of the unexpected. Sherman wondered, "Is Bailey armed?"

"Who ain't," answered the Sheriff.

"He pulled an ancient double barrel on us once," said Ashley. "Said his pappy had put men in the very same ground we stood on. Threatened to do the same with us if we came around again."

"Mr. Bailey always had a flair for the dramatic," added Reinhold.

"Did it stop you?" Sherman asked.

"No," said Ashley with a laugh. "We were too young to contemplate our own death. He was just some crazy old man getting in the way of drinking."

Such a rebellious streak amused Sherman. It wasn't part of his personal story. The drinking he had, but not the disobedience. His actual act of rebellion had been going to college and not enlisting the day after high school graduation. Even that only lasted a month. The second tower had barely fallen when he burst into the recruiter's office and put pen to paper.

"Frank were you a square back in the day?" she asked.

"Unremarkably boring," he answered.

"How…" she said but decided against it. "Never mind."

"The army attracts all types," suggested Reinhold.

Sherman understood what Ashley was trying to ask. "It

doesn't take broken homes to make a man like me," he said.

"I meant nothing by it."

"I don't offend easily," he assured. "You figured Tillerman, and I had that in common."

She nodded.

"Fair assumption, but I had a stable enough childhood. We moved around and my dad was an asshole but not an abusive one."

"He serve?" asked Reinhold.

"The original Captain Sherman. Retired a full bird."

"Army?"

"Marines," said Sherman.

"So, you're the disappointment," joked Reinhold.

"The worst."

"Was he a real leather neck or some pencil pusher?" asked the Sheriff, already knowing the answer.

Sherman's father wasn't a braggart, and he made sure his son wasn't one either. There is no place for false modesty on the battlefield. It was an axiom he exemplified. At least that is what he wanted everyone to think. Truth was, he bragged a lot, but only in select company. When the boys would gather around the grill, beers in hand, they would live out the glory days.

"Certainly didn't push any pencils," he said as they stopped at the gate. It only took him a few seconds to unclip the chain and swing the old creaky metal hinges open.

As the fence receded from view Reinhold spoke up again, "Wait, was your old man in Vietnam?"

Sherman grunted in acknowledgement.

"We heard about a Marine sniper back then. Captain S. was all they ever called him. That right?"

Again, he nodded but said nothing.

"Jesus, boy," added Reinhold, "you didn't fall far from the tree. Shit, you're like an aspen popping up from the same roots."

"What are you jabbering about?" asked Ashley.

"He ain't gonna say anything," suggested Reinhold, "but

his family probably killed more people than Pol Pot."

"I don't pretend to know who that is," she scoffed.

The Sheriff hung his head, "His dad shot a lot of folks in that war."

"He was equal parts asshole and shooter," admitted Sherman.

Ashley was unfazed. She didn't want to believe that she was like her father. The idea comforted her, even if it was complete fiction. "Can't think of a father who ain't an asshole," she added.

"I guess that's the nature of being a dad," said Reinhold. He felt a loss at missing out on that reckoning. His only marriage was to the badge.

The dirt road had turned into a rutted cow path. "I guess the kids don't sneak around no more," observed Ashley.

"Generational," offered Sherman with a shrug.

"Each one gets a little worse," Reinhold grumbled. His crotchety nature was getting the better of him.

"We'll see about that," Sherman said. His generation had yet to start a war. They'd only died in them.

As they neared the bridge, he slowed to a stop next to a patch of miner's lettuce. The river sloshed around just over the berm as the storm clouds swirled above. The air felt charged, like the molecules themselves were on edge.

"One of those nights," said Reinhold as he gazed out at the flashes of lightning.

Sherman nodded as he listened for engines in the night air. "Can you hand me three magazines from the floor?" he asked Ashley.

He slid them into the empty pouches of his vest one by one. The Sheriff was right. It would be one of those crazy nights.

"Keep an eye out while I rig something up," he told Ashley.

The dome light came on when he opened the tailgate, but he left it intact. Sherman needed the light to assemble things.

Demolitions was never his strong suit, but he'd seen enough IEDs to know the basics. Starting with the propane, he arranged the cylinders into a diamond shape with one in the middle. Using duct tape, he stuck the sticks of dynamite around the center tank. Sherman figured if the middle one went, so would the rest.

Next came the blasting caps. Those created the larger explosion. Dynamite needs a trigger. It's too stable for plain old heat. Throw it in a fire and it will burn away without exploding.

After inserting the caps, he ran the attached cord in each stick back to a single strand. The spool he grabbed from the mine had about two hundred feet of cord. Given the burn rates and length, he reckoned there would only be a three second delay, maybe less. Sherman had hoped he could create a longer timer but knew someone would have to spool it out. Two hundred feet suddenly looked small.

Reinhold watched him fill the back of the Tahoe with a giant incendiary device. When Sherman got back inside the Sheriff looked unsettled. "You're gonna drive us up the hill with a bomb in the back?"

Sherman looked at Ashley, "If you have to shoot him, aim high."

Her expression was not one of amusement, but neither was the statement. It was a fact. One that Sherman felt he needed to remind her about. Minor details are the most dangerous.

Rain started a gentle pitter-patter on the windshield. The softness of the sounds belied the power swirling outside. As the storm crashed into the mountains it gained force, readying itself for quite a night.

"It's gonna be a wet one," Reinhold noted.

Sherman was more concerned about the lightning and was glad the detonation system was not electric. Although, the comment reminded him of one of the first commanders he'd served under in JSOC. The man was old school. A Vietnam vet. Five tours as a SEAL. More metal on his chest than the tin man. He used to say the same thing before a brutish mission. His generation referred to it as wet work. The reference, Sherman learned all too quickly, related to the blood spilled. It stuck to their clothes, soaked through shirts and seeped into boots. Bloody footprints leading to the showers were an unsettling but common occurrence.

The further they drove, the more Ashley and Reinhold fidgeted. Edging towards the brink frayed their nerves, and they were both showing signs of unraveling.

Ashley was twirling her hair while Reinhold couldn't stop tapping his foot. Neither of them asked what came next, but they looked terrified.

Yet only Reinhold felt his life hanging on so delicate a balance. Nudge it one way or the other and it would be fatal. If Sherman didn't kill him, and Krenshaw caught even a whiff of suspicion, he'd be dead. The more he thought about it, the crueler his fate became.

Having built up the courage, Ashley asked, "Frank. What is the fucking plan here? Right now, I feel like a suicide bomber in this damn truck."

Reinhold leaned forward to hear the response despite the added pain.

"You're not far off," answered Sherman.

Ashley waited for more with her eyebrows raised.

"The Sheriff here will drive into the compound and park between two buildings."

"And then what?" asked Reinhold nervously.

"Then Ashley detonates."

The Sheriff couldn't believe what he was hearing. "You gonna give me time to get clear?"

Ashley watched Sherman's face for a clue to his answer. She had seen enough to know that he had no compunction about killing. Not even her father showed such a capacity for violence. Yet the Sheriff was still alive, and she had been wondering why for some time.

"That's up to you, Sheriff," informed Sherman. "Your survival is conditional."

Reinhold snapped, "On what? Your good graces."

"I would have shot you on the street were that the case."

No one in the truck doubted the veracity of his statement. "Right," said Reinhold woefully, "What are the terms?"

"When this is over, assuming the best, you will call the feds and tell them you just stopped a serious meth operation, but you need their help."

"You're not seriously going to let him off the hook for this," growled Ashley.

He ignored the comment, "You'll give whatever evidence you have that implicates Stockwood."

"What if I have nothing?"

"At least part of you is still a lawman. I'm sure you saved something as insurance."

"It might implicate me," said Reinhold.

"Not my problem. Besides everyone you colluded with will be dead by morning."

The Sheriff sighed, "Anything else?"

"Leave us out of your story, now and forever. If I hear anything about me or them, I will come for you and everyone you know," answered Sherman. His voice was a calm lake devoid of any emotional ripples.

Reinhold took it all as fact. Elation and dread commingled in his mind. He nodded in agreement, "I can do that."

The thought of him living sat like rancid meat in Ashley's gut. She figured the Sheriff was as guilty as the rest.

"I don't like this, Frank," she hissed.

"I heard you the first time, but it doesn't change our need."

"What fucking need?"

"If you want to get out, to lead some semblance of a life, then someone needs to own this mess."

Ashley shook her head in disgust, "It don't feel right. It ain't just."

Looking in the mirror at the Sheriff, Sherman couldn't

have agreed more. Reinhold was a corrupt piece of shit, but the federal law would descend on Cumbre County soon enough. The bastard might get some commendation for all of it, but that was the nature of politics. The bad guy would end up looking good and they would be long gone.

"You're right," he said, "but nothing here is right. What they did, what I did, it justified none of it."

"I don't get you, Frank. They killed your best friend," she said, implying that was all she needed to know.

Sherman didn't expect her to understand what he knew. What he'd seen over there. The three of them didn't have enough fingers to count all the best friends he buried from either side of the trigger. He didn't feel sorry for resorting to violence, but there was no pride either.

"They did and they're dead. That's the sum of it. Can't get any more closure than that. You'd be a fool to believe there is something more, but everyone may dream," he added.

Rage welled in Ashley's eyes. Her heart was pounding with anger and sadness. It thumped so hard she thought it might break a rib. Only her mom had said forgive and forget. Even that only lasted until the divorce from her dad. All her experience said be vindictive. Restraint was a pill almost too large to swallow, but she choked it down.

"What do you need from me?" she finally asked.

"Light the fuse."

Upon hearing that, Reinhold's pupils dilated with fear. Minutes earlier he had the odds of Ashley shooting him at fifty-fifty.

"You're gonna leave me with that choice?"

"I am. Blow him up or not. It's your call."

Despite the anger and grief, the color on her face vanished with the thought of obliterating another person with her own hands. The thought churned up bile. She was not alone in feeling queasy. Reinhold couldn't even look at the woman thirty years younger in the eyes.

"How long should I wait?" asked Ashley.

"It's a three second delay and the Sheriff here isn't in sprinting shape." He looked over his shoulder, "So head for a tree."

"How big is this boom?" asked Reinhold.

"Not sure."

"How much wire is there?" Ashley asked.

"Two hundred feet."

"So, we both better run," she concluded.

"I can park between the first two buildings, closer to the road," Reinhold suggested.

Sherman nodded, "Then find cover."

"An old bladder will be my excuse. Assuming they don't shoot me on sight."

"Ashley, you'll light the fuse when he gets to cover," instructed Sherman.

"Or gets shot," she added.

"And when this plan goes to shit?" asked the Sheriff. For soldiers, it was the obvious question.

"Run. Then she lights the fuse."

"Fuck," muttered Reinhold.

"Indeed," enjoined Ashley.

"Glad we agree," said Sherman.

The gentle drops turned to thumping as they drove further up into the mountains. Sherman kept the lights on, knowing anything else would raise suspicion.

Even without the rain, no teenagers were out partying. The town was on edge with rumors spreading faster than a prescribed burn. What was said in confidence now took on a life of its own.

"We used to drink over there," said Ashley as they passed a small dirt clearing next to the road. "It seems like a lifetime ago."

She remembered those blurry nights, "God, how young and dumb we were. Rhett and Grady used to throw .22 longs into the fire. They called it hillbilly roulette."

"Sounds like a well misspent youth," Sherman said.

"Even back then I knew I didn't belong. Not with those

assholes."

"You got stuck with the family first bullshit, didn't you?" asked Reinhold.

She turned towards him a bit surprised, "How did you know about that?"

"Dell was spouting on about that back in Vietnam. We'd be humping through some sweltering elephant grass and all he talked about was family first. He didn't even have a fucking family yet."

"Family of one," she grumbled.

"Those jungles changed him, changed us all. No one came back quite right in the head," said Reinhold.

Ashley looked over at Sherman and realized that he had never come back. Tillerman had left. Brummet had run away. Even her father walked out of the steaming jungle. Yet the man driving them into the mountains remained in his war.

"Why are you still doing this, Frank?" she asked.

"The soldiering?"

"Yeah. Why not get out?"

He rubbed his chin, "It just is."

"And what happens when it isn't?"

"Then I'll be dead," he answered.

"So, there's nothing in between."

Sherman had come close to quitting before. He had even contemplated it on the flight to San Francisco a few days earlier. There was life outside of the army and the war. He just wasn't sure if he wanted it. What would he do? Wander across the country? Maybe, but he was not fond of motels. The only thing he'd ever considered was a beachside bar somewhere warm. Southeast Asia or Fiji.

"Not yet," he replied.

She wrinkled up her nose in disbelief but softened her stance. Unwilling to leave, she had stayed in Byron Mills too long. Then Tillerman came around and staying didn't seem so bad. They had talked about leaving over a heaping plate of fried chicken, but the topic fell away with the seasons.

The meal stood out in her mind more than the conversation. Tillerman would have remembered.

The road, which had been steadily climbing, leveled out and Reinhold leaned forward. "We're getting close," he said.

"How far?"

"Maybe a mile."

Sherman eased the Tahoe onto the thin layer of pine needles skirting the dirt road. They cracked like bowl of Rice Krispies. He grabbed the pistol and circled around back. The plan forming in his head didn't leave much room for error. If they spotted him, it would get ugly quick, so he smashed all the rear lights. Chunks of plastic and slivers of glass littered the forest floor. He doubted anyone would notice until much later.

No one said anything as he climbed back into the truck. Ashley had accepted there were certain things that he knew, and she did not. Having lived through a few battles, Reinhold understood the calculus. Being seen often meant being dead. The Captain's attention to detail impressed him.

"When will they see us?" Sherman asked.

"It's almost straight for the last quarter mile, but they've likely heard us already."

"I know."

"There's gonna be someone by the road," said Reinhold.

"I know."

"They'll notice the wire."

"I know."

The sheriff shook his head, "And an empty back seat."

"It won't be empty."

Reinhold narrowed his eyes, "That's a serious risk."

Sherman didn't have to say anything. It was obvious from his look that he understood the risk and the consequence.

"And where am I?" asked Ashley.

"You're in the back," answered Sherman.

"Like hell."

"You can still shoot him if something happens,"

reassured Sherman.

"What if the bikers shoot me on sight? I don't exactly look like you."

Sherman nodded at the possibility. She was still wearing the tactical vest and beanie, but that didn't disguise the difference in size. "It's a risk," he acknowledged.

"A risk is buying expired fish," she groaned. "This is stupid."

"Lay on the floor, face down. If they look too hard, I'll make sure they stop."

"Fuck," she muttered.

"Slow down before you get to them," he said to Reinhold.

"How far out?"

"Fifty yards. I'll need time to slip out."

"Then what?"

"If you're right about the distance, then stop by the guard. Otherwise stop at the entrance. Either way, I'm letting her out," replied Sherman.

"And then?" Ashley wondered.

"Hold on to the spool. Light it when he's clear."

She nodded meekly.

They drove the last remaining minutes in silence before Sherman stopped one final time. He slid out and stood by the door as Reinhold climbed in. He leaned in and returned the cowboy hat. "Sheriff, if I see you again tonight consider yourself a dead man."

The older man nodded. He understood that Sherman still saw him as a threat. One not worth underestimating. "Don't worry, I'm headed for the hills after the first shot."

"Oh, I'm not concerned. Think of this as an undeserved gift," replied Sherman.

Reinhold held up his still bound wrists. Sherman cut them with Tillerman's knife before closing the door.

The gun in her hand was shaking as Ashley climbed in the back seat. Sherman gave her an unreciprocated smile and closed the door, before rolling the front passenger window down.

"Slow before the last turn," he instructed.

With his broken wrist resting limply on his leg, Reinhold didn't look imposing.

Standing on the running board, Sherman reached for the handle inside. With the rain coming down, he accepted the ride would be wet. He kept the Glock pointed at Reinhold.

"Keep it under twenty-five. Knocking me off won't stop what's in the chamber."

"My life is riding on your success," replied the Sheriff.

"We'll see how you feel about that in the morning."

"If we see the sun."

Rain angled through the open window and splattered against the Plexiglas divider. Ashley kept her face buried against the dirty floor. She wondered if Reinhold had ever cleaned it. A trivial thought given it might be the last thing her eyes would see, but she couldn't help it.

Sherman kept the pistol leveled at the Sheriff's head until the last moment when Reinhold slowed before the last turn. He jumped off at a running pace and headed straight into the scrub brush next to the road.

The undergrowth was thicker than expected and it took him several seconds to push past and into the pine beyond. Reinhold was coming to a stop some fifty yards ahead and Sherman ran in a low crouch to catch-up. By the time he got close it was clear there were at least two men guarding the entrance.

"You're fucking late, Sheriff," yelled the biker who had emerged from the trees to flag down the Tahoe.

"Traffic," Reinhold snarled.

Another man stepped out on the passenger side. He switched on a flashlight and flooded the interior with a harsh white light. Reinhold preferred the older incandescent models. There were a lot of advances he found uncomfortable; technology was at the top of his list.

The second biker looked through the back window, "He still breathing?"

"Last time I checked," answered Reinhold.

"He ain't too big," said the man.

"He's quick," responded the Sheriff.

A radio crackled to life. "Hagan, is that him?" boomed a commanding voice.

The back of Sherman's head tingled with recognition. He knew the voice. It had been many years, but it was all coming back.

Hagan was leaning on Reinhold's door. He fished out the device. "Yeah. The Sheriff and his plus one."

"Search the damn truck before you send him up," instructed Krenshaw.

"Alright," replied the biker over the radio before turning back to Reinhold. "Open 'er up."

"It's unlocked."

"Humor me," said Hagan while motioning for the other man to join him.

Reinhold sighed and tried not to wince as he got out of the SUV. He kept his fingers crossed as they moved towards the back.

The man with the flashlight kept staring at the crumpled figure on the floor. The scene before him didn't look right. He swore his girlfriend had the same hiking boots with the strip of pink across the heel. Something felt off.

Not one to speak up under normal circumstances, he opened his mouth to say something, but Sherman got there first. He caught the burly man by his wrist, making sure the flashlight didn't drop. Using the Glock as a hammer, he landed a savage blow at the base of the skull. The biker went limp and fell on the muddy road below.

Hagan was impatient and wanted to get the search over with. The rain kept rolling down the back of his neck. It left him agitated.

"Hurry," he shouted towards his friend. Standing behind the truck was darker than usual. His mind recognized that fact but not the cause.

The light swung into his face as Reinhold opened the

rear gate. "The back, you fucking idiot," he yelled.

As the Sheriff stepped away the harsh light revealed a surreal scene of explosives and wires. The Sheriff held his breath, waiting for the inevitable bullet.

"What the…" exclaimed Hagan as he looked up at his compatriot, only to see the stock of a rifle surging at his face.

The faint sound of cracking bone and splattered blood surprised Reinhold. He hadn't heard or seen anyone. Then he knew.

"Take the flashlight," instructed Sherman. "Pretend like you're doing a half-ass search."

Still a bit bewildered, Reinhold grabbed the light and looked under the Tahoe. Sherman had both bikers in zip ties and duct tape muzzles before the Sheriff stood back up.

"These two are your responsibility," he told Reinhold.

There was no room for disagreement. The Sheriff nodded and got back in the driver's seat as Sherman went to get Ashley out.

"Time to go," he said.

The pattern of the floor mat was etched into her forehead. Dark bags clung around her bloodshot eyes. The gun was still shaking in her hand.

"Doing great," said Sherman as he pulled her up.

She exhaled what felt like an eternity of air.

He handed her the spool, "Hold on to this."

"Then what?"

Sherman handed over the lighter, "Blow this place up."

Ashley inhaled the damp, stormy air.

"I'll meet you back here afterwards," he instructed.

"If there is an after."

He shrugged, "Run if anyone is still talking."

She didn't know what to say, "Good luck, I guess."

Sherman tapped on the roof before disappearing once more into the night. As Reinhold pulled away Ashley found herself alone again. Lightning crackled overhead like the knell of some last judgement.

CHAPTER TWENTY-FOUR

The world according to Krenshaw boiled down to one lesson he learned at a young age. Violence and coercion weren't just the tools of powerful men, they were the hallmarks of the truly important. Genghis Khan, Alexander the Great, they spoke the true language of force. The ex-sergeant mulled that over as he balled his giant hands into a fist and cracked all the knuckles in a single string of pops. He started doing it to intimidate others but found it focused his energy. It kept his wits sharp and the cold at bay.

Hagan or the other man whose name left no mark couldn't be trusted. They were weak and dumb. No point in wasting talented men down there. If Reinhold was telling the truth, the guards were redundant. If not, then they were already dead.

There was little to see through the rain, even with the night vision assist. Headlights shimmered in the distance and the arc of a flashlight bounced around. He picked up the radio to say something demeaning, but the door slammed, and the SUV lurched forward. Tapping his finger against the Romanian-made PSL gave him a level of reassurance. It could take a man's arm off at five hundred yards. The distance was beneficial when needed, but Krenshaw preferred to smell the blood.

The radio hissed to life again. "They're coming up boss," observed one of his men.

"I can fucking see that."

"You want me to bring them up to you?"

"No," answered Krenshaw. "I'm coming down."

The thought of Captain Frank Sherman in distress brought out a satisfied smile. Years had passed since they last saw each other, but Krenshaw still harbored a special rage for the man. The captain was a right piece of shit in his opinion. Too business like. No savagery, no spirit for the job. He resented that but hated Sherman for something else altogether.

Reinhold parked the Tahoe between the two closest buildings. It wasn't a usual parking spot, so he hurried away.

"Pull it up here," shouted one man.

The Sheriff recognized the face but didn't know the name. Another valley asshole with an attitude.

"I got to piss," he yelled back. "Your boot stomper is in the back."

They passed each other as Reinhold headed for a nearby tree. The biker was holding up his hands in frustration.

"What a dick," he muttered. "Can't even park the goddamn truck right."

Upon seeing the exchange, Krenshaw's blood pressure rose. The Sheriff was bought and paid for cheaply. Such vanity and lack of conviction brought out his vindictive streak. Weakness was the greatest sin, and he despised Reinhold for his shortcomings.

Krenshaw yelled to the biker headed towards the Tahoe, "He's mine Charles."

Charles stopped and turned towards the booming voice. A knot twisted in his stomach. Until then, he had feared no one in life besides his father. Some boys, the ones with screws loose upstairs, liked their new boss. They enjoyed his sociopathic tendencies and brutality. Charles found the entire thing claustrophobic. He rode for the freedom. The gang work just paid the bills.

"All yours," he replied, hoping it would be a quick murder. The rain was gaining momentum, and he didn't care if the guy in the car lived or died.

"Prostate problems old man," sneered Krenshaw as he passed the Sheriff.

Reinhold had run behind the tree thinking he would pretend to urinate. As the adrenaline kicked in, he had a quasi-religious moment of relief. Knowing what was coming, he hoped the redwood would deflect the blast. The last thing he wanted was for the feds to find him dead with a dick in hand.

Two hundred feet away, Ashley lit the fuse and ran across the road. She found a temporary home underneath a fallen pine and vowed not to move until it was all over. The next flight out felt like a distant dream. An almost quaint outcome to the nightmare unfolding around her.

The explosion didn't register as pain for Krenshaw. It felt more like scorching air against his face. A blast from a blow dryer on high. The concussive wave knocked him to the ground. As he was falling the Tahoe's lack of taillights sprung to mind. His brain had latched onto the missing detail earlier, but the detonation warped his thought process.

Buried deep down in his hippocampus the urge to fight metastasized. He flexed his fingers and toes. All bent. The sky was almost white and Krenshaw blinked into the rain above. Cornea shock, he thought, just temporary. As the world above faded to black once more, he sat up.

Across the compound, the fireball's size surprised Sherman. A bright orange blast thirty feet up and fifty feet out. Had it not been for the weather, he was sure they'd all been running from a forest fire. Nothing substantial of the Tahoe remained. Bits of the frame and the engine block survived, but everything else got ejected or burned. It reminded him of an overheated tin can. Everything popped, leaving the metal twisted and disfigured.

Although the army would have called it an improvised explosive device, Sherman's bomb bore none of the hallmarks of those high explosives. It was all fire and little boom, but he wasn't trying to punch a hole through a tank or blow up a marketplace full of people.

Mobile homes, however, aren't known for their sturdiness. Nor are the chemicals used for making meth. The volatile nature of the process was well known to Krenshaw. He had spaced the second-hand trailers accordingly. Each was far enough from the others to contain the explosion to one unit. For all his planning, a propane fueled IED did not cross his mind.

As the blast shattered the windows, those poor men working inside had only a few milliseconds left to live. Fire surged through the broken glass, igniting the unstable fumes created during the cooking process.

Reinhold had barely zipped up when the surrounding forest went from night to day and back again. Not one, but three times in quick succession. He hugged the tree tighter than any woman. Four hundred years of growth saved his life. Charles was not so lucky. His charred corpse landed a few feet past Reinhold. It was still sizzling. The Sheriff ran away, retching into the night.

Chaos came swiftly to those still alive. Men were shouting at each other. Some stood rooted in the ground. Others paced back and forth; their attention consumed by the blaze. The cooks from the remaining trailers sprinted out, old school gas masks still covering their faces. A veteran of the Somme would have found a savage familiarity in the scene.

Under the cover of confusion, Sherman moved out from the trees and towards the nearest lab. There wasn't much within the compound to use as cover. A byproduct of fireproofing. The buildings themselves were time bombs, and he paused in their shadows for only a moment. Some bikers had parked on a flat grassy spot some twenty feet further. Sherman used the metal frames to hide his movement closer.

Keeping count of who remained was difficult without an accurate starting point. Six bikes sat in plain view. Two owners were unconscious, and one was barbeque. That left three plus the normal operating crew, of which Sherman was sure a few had gone up with the trailers.

He counted five men milling about the burning buildings. Two wore leather jackets. Two had gas masks. One looked like a Cape Cod fisherman stereotype. But there was no burly Puerto Rican. Krenshaw was still missing.

Sherman braced the M4 against the seat of a chrome encased Harley. He put an extra mag out. The men weren't much more than silhouettes against the blaze, but it defined them. Six rounds per target. Not much more than a long squeeze on full auto.

The Ahab impersonator took the first burst. It was nothing personal for Sherman. The man was the furthest from the group. The lot of them turned to look at the result. The bikers knew the score and bolted. Having used too much of their own product, the cooks stayed put. Sherman dropped them both before they considered their mistake.

Hitting a target on the run is hard. Putting three rounds center mass on a dark, rainy night was a skill. One of the few Sherman possessed. One he never thought he'd use back home.

As the first man fell. his eardrums filled with metallic pings and snaps. He was taking fire from his right side. Two guns. A pistol and something that sounded like an AK but without the rate of fire. His brain said SKS.

Suppressed, Sherman ducked behind the two-cylinder engine. A round shattered one of the tiny mirrors. Little slivers of glass embedded in his hair and beard.

If the remaining biker realized he was no longer a target Sherman knew he would find himself in a crossfire. Moving was the only option. He stuck the barrel of the rifle through one wheel and fired what remained in the mag. Grabbing the extra one still on the seat, he retreated behind the trailer. With a flick of his thumb, he ejected the spent mag and inserted the other. There was nothing conscious about the action. It happened without thought. Nor did he lose a step.

As his sight came back, Krenshaw blinked away the involuntary tears watering down his vision. He stood in a hurry. Gunfire echoed around the compound. He knew the pistol was Kowalski's. The polak fancied himself a modern gunslinger. The kid watched too much TV.

The barking was Bobby and his SKS. The guy was an ignorant backwater racist, but Krenshaw didn't judge. Political beliefs aside, he liked the man's intemperate attitude and proclivity towards violence.

It was the sharp cracks that made him move. Burst after burst of 5.56mm ammunition. After Afghanistan, the noise was impossible to forget, but no one on his crew used that caliber.

"You fucker," he shouted before sprinting towards the firefight.

After breaking contact, Sherman swung back into the pine trees on his right. The trailer was catching rounds from the overzealous shooters. Acrid smells drifted out. A few more sparks and the entire thing would blow. He took his chances in the forest.

Small streams of water were forming as the storm bore down. They snaked around the giant trees, forming a saturated patchwork. It soaked Sherman from the waist down, but his core was still dry. Visibility was a dozen yards. He stayed on the mounds of pine needles to avoid the splashing sounds his boots made.

It was coming down in droves, as his father used to say. Sherman never quite got the cattle reference, but the storm almost sounded like a stampede. Faint fragments of shouting passed through the deluge. Telling how far away it came from was impossible, but he pressed forward.

A sloshing sound came from his left, closer to the compound. Whoever it was, they were not far away. Sherman shouldered the rifle and waited. The quiet roar of the rain enveloped him as he stayed motionless in the dark. Slight noises stood out.

A muffled curse. The splash of feet in shallow water.

Grunts from someone losing their footing. Each subsequent sound growing louder with proximity.

The SKS came into view first. The pressed steel receiver was almost invisible between the light oak stock and fore grip. Then came Bobby. Sherman reckoned his proportions made him more square than rectangle. Almost equal parts height and width. Short, fat and clumsy. Add in racist and that was Bobby in a nutshell.

He was moving through the trees like a bowling ball. Knocking over bushes and trampling saplings as he went. Bobby kept wiping away the water from his eyes. His shaved head did nothing to stop the rain drops from rolling down into his face.

Sherman watched the bumbling figure approach and then stop less than ten yards away. He stood there blinded by the water like a deer in headlights. With a bullet in the chamber, Bobby was already dead. The details were just a formality, yet unknown. An unformed future.

For all his confidence, Bobby didn't see it coming. He could pontificate about the superiority of the Aryan race but couldn't recall the color of his shoelaces. Clueless was how his mother described his observational tendencies. He was too focused on killing a man that he didn't see Sherman draw the knife. Nor did he notice a shadow approach.

The pain was profound. It was quick and overwhelming. Sherman stuck his thumb behind the trigger moments before the blade hit flesh. He didn't want the rifle going off and alerting the others. When it was over Bobby didn't have a continuous main artery left. Sherman was still holding the SKS as the local boy left a dent in the saturated soil.

Krenshaw was on edge. There were no gunshots. He had watched a ghostly figure disappear around the trailer, but didn't have time to pull the trigger. There was no doubt in his mind it was the Captain. The bodies sprawled about in their own slowly fading blood were proof enough. The local cops were in his pocket, and the feds weren't that good. Only one man was that capable.

Running after Sherman would do no good. Krenshaw wasn't egotistical enough to give chase. The sergeant had an above average sense of his own capabilities, but he knew there were limits. "Don't play their game" his drill instructor once said, misquoting Sun Tzu. Krenshaw liked the sentiment. It spoke to his own internal desire not to give an inch. A go fuck yourself attitude.

If following Sherman wouldn't work, he'd have to cut him off. Krenshaw knew he had range and a night vision scope. Those were winning advantages.

"Let's go," he shouted towards the remaining biker.

"Fuck you," responded the man.

Insubordination was not something that Krenshaw took lightly. Challenging his authority was tantamount to treason, and that was a death sentence.

The man, whose name Krenshaw couldn't even recall, knew he'd made a mistake almost immediately. The sergeant raised the PSL to his shoulder and knocked a fist-sized hole through biker's chest.

"No, fuck you," he spat before running off towards the far side of the compound.

Mike Kowalski was no more Polish than the sausage. His kin had moved to Cumbre County some hundred years prior, and they'd been scraping with the law ever since. For all its cosmopolitan nature, the settlers of Byron Mills didn't fancy the Poles. Too many Germans lived there for any integration to work well.

Because of those grievances, the Kowalski family was very protective of their national inheritance. Mike was no different, but with a twist. A child of the East and the West, he idolized both the Russian mafia and the Wild West outlaw. Gold chains and track suits came from one end, a quick draw holster and cowboy hat came from the other.

While Bobby was getting cut to pieces in the blinding rain, Kowalski waited near the farthest building. His gut told him that Sherman would try to flank around. He leaned against the trailer and waited. The low-slung hat kept the rain away.

With the square man bleeding out in the rain, Sherman worked his way around the perimeter of the compound. He moved quickly and quietly from the tree to tree until the faint fiery glow was well over his shoulder. Then he turned left and swung back towards the trailers.

Four men were alive when he entered the forest, and now only two remained. The man with the pistol and Krenshaw. As Sherman pushed out of the trees on the backside of the lab, he saw the strangest of outlines against the still burning buildings. With one heel against the siding and a cowboy hat pulled low against his eyes, Kowalski cut an anachronistic figure.

The small puddles around his boots were merging, but didn't come close to Kowalski's own volume of confidence. An internal clock struck high noon. He stood up and headed into the trees. There was a methodical slowness to his step as those dark brown eyes of his devoured the surrounding view. The Pole's hand hovered over the holster, stiller than any helicopter.

Sherman took one look at the sheer amount of arrogance walking towards him and mentally scoffed. He couldn't imagine what kind of game the cowboy thought was afoot, but it brimmed with a shameful level of naiveté. What a waste, he thought.

The center of the rifle sight hovered over Kowalski's chest. He kept walking. The pistol was still in his holster when Sherman pulled the trigger.

Staggered by the impact, the cowboy managed one more step before falling face first into the mud. Another man done in by his own self-perpetuated delusions.

The entire episode unfolded in the soft green glow of Krenshaw's night vision scope. He knew Kowalski would play the gunslinger part to the end. The kid was too young and dumb to know better. He had counted on it. Hell, he would have thrown away a hundred Kowalski kin to have a shot on his former commander.

Krenshaw whipped the muzzle towards the distant flash and fired. It was all reflex and nerves. It left him with a clenched jaw. The shot was premature. He should have waited.

"Fuck," he muttered.

The rifle was within view, but that was it. No arm. No body. No follow-up shot. Only an enormous tree filled scope.

Gnarled limbs, lit but for a moment, hung over Sherman's head. Nature's answer to the Sistine chapel. Laying on his back, under those sheltering arms, he felt like a little boy again. The one who used to go camping on his own. A precocious, solitary boy.

Pain came as memory receded. He struggled to breathe. Reaching under the vest, Sherman slowly wiggled his fingers in search of a extra hole. His hand was wet but not warm. No blood. No extra ventilation.

Grabbing the armor plate revealed a small hole pointing out away from his body. An indirect hit. The oblique angles were the only reason the tree wasn't his last sight.

Sherman looked over at the rifle and almost grabbed it out of instinct. Then he felt the hole in his vest again. The shooter was to his right, but only hit him once.

"Saved by the tree," he said to himself.

Avoiding a second round was his priority. He needed to get out of Krenshaw's field of view. That meant backtracking into the forest and outplaying a shooter at his own game. Gingerly, he rolled onto his stomach and lined up his escape route. Then Sherman hopped to his feet and ran.

Krenshaw was certain he had hit dead center mass, but less sure what his target was wearing. Jacket or vest? He tried to replay the split-second of the shot, but it was a blur. He could see that no one was reaching for M4 on the ground.

Lightning flashed overhead, and the scope flooded his retina with a blinding white light. Krenshaw grunted and switched to his left eye while the right one recovered. The gun hadn't moved.

The Captain was dead or gone. He knew the man wouldn't stay put for long. Scanning the forest didn't help. His line of sight was only good for the original shot. Trees blocked most of his view. Move or stay became the difficult choice. If Sherman was dead, he could wait it out. Once the storm cleared someone would show up and help. The alternative sent his eyes searching the horizons. His stomach tightened at the possibility.

"Fuck it," he whispered into the night.

Everything he knew about Captain Sherman screamed that the bastard was still alive. Krenshaw shook his head at the earlier missed opportunity. He could have shot him while they ran away from Barrios. Revenge impeded murder. Shooting that bitch had been a mistake. Despite his water-soaked clothes, his mouth was dry, and he swallowed hard. Suffering was his goal, but Krenshaw realized Sherman probably didn't even care about the woman. Besides, he'd gotten Tillerman, that self-righteous coward. Beating that asshole had felt good. His knuckles still remembered the broken ribs and ruptured kidneys. The memory restored his vigor. Krenshaw walked away with a menacing smile.

Thirty minutes had passed since the last gunshot. Ashley knew because she was constantly looking at her watch. Checking the time was a distraction from her shivering body. It took her mind off the numbing cold.

Fear slipped in with the rain. It built up slowly with each passing minute, but was gaining speed. Her chest tightened with dread. It hurt to breathe. The trust she had in Sherman was not absolute. It was only a few days old. Looking inward, she found some solace with Tillerman. He had trusted the man, and she trusted him. The only thing left was to find a drier place to hide.

By keeping his path unpredictable, Sherman had burned a lot of time. An hour had almost slipped by, but the rain held strong. He used a few of those minutes to swap out his front plate with the back one before turning uphill.

As the topography changed, he felt better. The landscape was familiar. He had stood at the top of the hill only a few days before. The same high ground Simpkins headed for with his long gun before Sherman put a bullet in the deputy's gut. From what he remembered, the line of sight was decent. A suitable spot for a night vision equipped rifle. His gut told him that Krenshaw would feel the same way.

The sergeant had surprised him at Barrios' house. Myopia got the upper hand, and he only saw a single threat. Overseas, he was a lone shark swimming in a sea of predators. For some semblance of normality, he dropped that frame of mind upon returning home. Trying to soften his edges and exhale the paranoia that came with deployment. He vowed not to make drop his guard again.

For all his extraordinary viciousness, Krenshaw lacked imagination. He hid in plain sight and organized things linearly. It was that sense of the man that convinced Sherman his gut was right.

As he recalled, it was the sergeant's lack of flexibility that impelled Sherman to transfer Krenshaw out of the unit. The memory was dusty, but years ago he made sure only Tillerman rotated out. Sherman didn't know what happened after that. He hadn't cared then, and nothing had changed.

When the Major asked why, Sherman told him it wasn't for lack of fighting spirit. The sergeant loved the chatter of machine guns and didn't flinch from pulling the trigger. Sherman didn't mind his violent streak or his temper. Those could be weaponized. What irritated him enough to deal with the headache paperwork caused was Krenshaw's inflexibility. The war was too gray for someone who only saw black and white. Enemies seemed to change weekly. While Krenshaw wanted to kill all of them, all the time.

The hill was nearing its saturation point. Weeks of intermittent precipitation had left little room for further absorption. Unable to drain through the soil, the rain trickled downhill. It all merged in the small drainage

Sherman was using to conceal his ascent. The climb was slow. He spent most of it watching the ridgeline and hoping a bullet wouldn't find the damaged rear plate.

Upon seeing the rifle abandoned in the pine needles, Krenshaw knew he needed higher ground. Wandering about the forest negated his advantage. Having served with the Captain, he knew Sherman was elusive. The locals used to call them all ghosts, but only the Captain could move unseen and unheard. Krenshaw had no plan to catch a bullet in the back.

He already had a spot in mind. A nice grouping of rocks on the ridge. One of those greedy cops usually took a shift up there, but they were all dead. That thought reminded him of the need to kill Reinhold. Not at that moment, but soon. The Sheriff and the Thorne girl. Krenshaw didn't like unfinished business. Better to burn the whole ball of yarn then have loose ends. The thought of smashing Reinhold's smug face kept him warm on the hike up.

Visibility was terrible, but Krenshaw could still make out shapes in the compound below. A few embers of the fire remained visible as bright green spots in the scope. Everything else was still. Corpses dotted the ground.

Methodically, he swung the scope back and forth looking for movement. Humans are excellent at identifying that which is out of place. We don't notice everything. Not all the details stick in our minds, just the incongruencies. For minutes Krenshaw saw nothing but rain drops and dead men. Then his subconscious found something different and new. The faintest flicker of white in the tree line past the fire road. He increased the zoom on the scope until a crooked grin creased his cheeks.

The distance made surety impossible, but Krenshaw swore he was looking at Ashley Thorne. With eight hundred yards between them, she was oblivious to the danger. He liked that a single trigger pull would rearrange her pretty face, but that wasn't his style. He preferred fists to bullets. There was a level of intimacy that a scope could not replicate. Yet he was a practical man. Catching her once the sun rose felt unlikely. It was better to swallow his pride and put her down than to not do the killing at all.

For all his tactical sense, Krenshaw knew that Sherman never understood his fundamental concept of war. Everyone needed to be dead. Only then would they win. The Captain's faith in people interfered with winning. The sergeant tried to convince him otherwise. To teach him a lesson worth learning. Instead, Sherman had him transferred.

The intervening years had not dampened his rage. Krenshaw's upper lip quivered as he thought about the past. All the subsequent events. All the failures. The dishonorable discharge. The time spent in military prison. He dumped everything at Sherman's feet. His body burned hot with the anger.

Pulling the trigger would have brought him some relief, but Krenshaw wanted to kill his ex-commander first. Ashley would be next. Her friends would come after that. He'd break the Sheriff somewhere in between. Taking a moment, he considered the order of the murders, and felt satisfied in the progression. Imagining it all kept the boredom away as he continued to look at corpses and trees.

Quartz studded schist boulders dotted the ridge. Angular and sharp, they looked more like coral than granite. Thick layers of green moss covered their tops. A soft natural blanket that squished under Sherman's boots. He was sure Krenshaw would be setup on an outcropping.

In the Stygian darkness he couldn't see more than a few yards. Only the occasional burst of lightning gave any illumination. With each distant flash Sherman would take in the world anew. Another group of rocks, another potential hiding spot. His was a slow progression across the ridge.

As Sherman neared the spot where he and Ashley had stood days earlier something caught his eye. It wasn't movement, or a misplaced shape, but steam rising in the frigid air. Thinking it a mirage, he tried to blink it away.

Nothing changed. He moved closer until Krenshaw's prone figure was a dozen feet away.

The thermometer had dropped into the forties and Sherman's fingers were feeling the cold as he gripped the Glock. He stood there and watched a former comrade search for a chance to kill him. Krenshaw kept scanning a wider arc, but Sherman noticed he always came back to the same spot. Beyond the road he had found a stationary target. Reinhold was gone and everyone else was dead, which left only Ashley.

A flare of white cast Sherman's shadow out over the rocks and down the hill. The rifle stopped moving.

"Captain," growled Krenshaw with his rage intact. The sudden twist of fate still loomed over the horizon, and hope lingered in his mind.

"Sergeant."

"You wrought this, Frank. All this death is your doing."

Sherman laughed at the ridiculous short sightedness of the remark. "Still missing the big picture I see. We're all in this sinking ship together. You and I just shot it full of holes after the fact, but it was always going down."

Krenshaw kept his eye on the scope while he spoke, "I enjoyed breaking Tillerman. That look of loss in his eyes. This place made him soft in the head. What's the number one rule of power, Frank?"

Sherman almost pulled the trigger but said nothing.

"You don't take. You own. Tillerman took the money, but he didn't own it. The only way to get out is by burning down the whole fucking town. Man lost his balls when he quit. Handed them back to Uncle Sam like some petty bitch."

"He found something else," said Sherman.

"Shitty furniture and that dumb bitch."

"A way out."

Krenshaw chuckled, "Listen, Captain. I'll give you a way out. Drop that gun and disappear. Do that and I won't put a bullet through her pretty little head."

"Bargaining for your life?" asked Sherman.

"Onetime offer, Frank."

"She's still ten degrees to your right asshole," replied Sherman. Then he squeezed the trigger.

Two muffled gunshots made Ashley flinch. It was an involuntary reaction of a numb mind and body. An hour had passed since she moved under the tree. The hope she started with had dwindled to a greasy residue stuck at the bottom of her mind. Like carpet in a restaurant, she was afraid to look at what remained. Twenty minutes more, she told herself, if Sherman wasn't back by then she'd leave alone.

CHAPTER TWENTY-FIVE

"You still want to catch that flight?" yelled Sherman. He was standing on the road, struggling to talk over the rain.

Ashley raised her pistol at the lone figure. Eighteen minutes had elapsed. In her mind, Frank Sherman was dead. She was summoning the will to walk back to town alone when he appeared.

"You said shoot if someone was still talking," she shouted back.

Sherman walked closer to the small pine she was hiding in, "That sounds like me."

Ashley had been sitting in the cold for too long and her knees hurt as they straightened. "Is it done?" she asked.

"He's dead," answered Sherman.

"Is it done?" she repeated.

"Not quite. We have one more thing to do."

Her body shook with exhaustion as she sighed, "What is left?"

"I'll explain on the drive."

With the feeling in her legs slowly returning, she hobbled out. "Who's fucking car?"

Sherman held up a set of keys, "His."

The dead sergeant's Jeep was parked nearby, behind a red wall of manzanita. Ashley looked at Sherman as he climbed in the front seat. The gash across the vest was obvious, but she couldn't see any blood. Otherwise he looked like a wet dog. All matted hair and lonely eyes.

She pointed at the torn fabric, "You okay?"

"Yeah. The plate stopped it."

She nodded, "I heard two shots."

"My gun jammed," he replied after starting the car.

The heat felt good, and they both sat there peeling off waterlogged layers in silence.

"Did Reinhold survive?" she asked.

Sherman shrugged, "I saw him stumble into the woods. Unless the bears get hungry, I imagine he'll make it out."

"You trust him to make the call?"

"No, but he will."

"How can you be so sure?"

"That star is all he has left," answered Sherman. "His ego can't let it go."

"It comes down to a man's ego," she said sarcastically.

"At least it's reliable."

Ashley rubbed her hands together in front of the vent. They throbbed with pain. "What is this one more thing?" she asked wearily.

"I know where the money is," he answered.

It was well after midnight when they passed the apple orchard and started climbing up out of the valley. Ashley hadn't spoken over two words on the drive down the mountain. Sherman gave her space to process his words.

The creeping fear from earlier disappeared as they parked in front of Tillerman's shack.

"I hope you're fucking wrong about this," she said as he turned off the ignition.

"Does it matter now?"

She walked away without replying.

In more ways than one, he didn't want to believe it either. The thought made little sense, and it left his mind churning, chasing a ghost in circles.

Sherman walked into the makeshift mill. It smelled of sawdust. He loved the scent. It reminded him of better days. The spruce log was still on sawhorses. Unmoved from where Tillerman had left it. It was the same log Sherman had slept under the day before.

He looked it over. Tillerman had planed the bottom flat, but the rest of the tree looked intact. The bark was still there, and sap oozed out in tiny tears. Only once he got to the end did he notice someone had carefully cut the log in half lengthwise.

Sherman scratched his beard. Going any further made his stomach churn. Some things were better left unlearned. We benefit from the mystery.

Sliding the top off revealed a hollowed-out core. Sitting there, encased in plastic sheeting, was the money. Sherman unwrapped it. There were dozens of neat stacks of random denominations wrapped in thick rubber bands.

"What have you done, Lieutenant?" he whispered.

Over his shoulder, Sherman heard Ashley sobbing. She was standing at the doorway, hands over her mouth.

"I don't believe it," she said.

Sherman didn't know what to say. Nothing he knew about Tillerman explained what was in front of them.

"Why would he do it?"

"He had his reason," said Sherman.

"All I see is betrayal. He knew what they would do," she said with a heaving chest.

"Maybe it was the only way."

"For what?" she yelled. "Only way to end up on a steel slab!"

"To get you out of this life, this place."

"All I wanted was him."

Sherman shrugged, "Isn't that usually the case. Shit just happens."

"But why didn't he tell me or leave a fucking note."

"He left a clue."

"A text to you. Forgive me, but that doesn't make me feel any better," she added.

"I doubt much will."

She nodded with an unenthusiastic jerk of the neck,

"What am I going to do now?"

"I wouldn't presume to answer that, but I know you need to get out of town."

"To where?"

"Best if I don't know," answered Sherman.

Ashley sat there, lost in the nothingness of shock. Any meaningful thought fell flat before it materialized. Sherman walked out and returned with a sleeping bag stuff sack.

She looked up, "What are you doing?"

"Making sure you get far away from here."

"I don't want that money," said Ashley.

Sherman stopped packing the cash and said, "Listen, I appreciate your stance. Believe me when I say I wish it didn't exist. But that ship has sailed. It's here. He's not. You can burn it for all I care, but after you're out."

"Why do you care?"

"Because he did," alluded Sherman.

"And look where that got us."

He sat down next to her. "I know what I'm about to say won't change anything, but for what it's worth, I think he did it for you. The timing was just off. He didn't think they'd notice so quickly, and they acted sooner than he expected."

"So, he was going to drag you into this mess?"

Sherman shrugged, "He knew I would always have his back. Shit, fewer people would have died that way."

"But why?" she said between sobs.

"Only the dead know why," answered Sherman as he resumed packing up the money.

"This fucking sucks," she moaned.

"It does."

"Take some," she said.

Sherman looked at her expression. He didn't want the money either, but there was no benefit in holding it accountable for all the death. Money wasn't the root of all evil, people were. He reached in and grabbed a few stacks.

"Thanks," she added. "Now I don't feel as icky."

He looked at his watch. It was still early, but there was

no sense in waiting around. "Come on, let's get going."

Ashley longed to wait there and take in the last vestiges of Tillerman, but the shed only held tools. Her love was gone, and it would take her years to accept his last act.

"Okay," she finally said.

The night sky was still a blazing torrent as they left down the hill and past the orchard. Not a car was in sight.

"We need to stop," she said.

The town was not yet gone, and Sherman still felt anxiousness as a growing weight on his chest. Undisturbed by Krenshaw's death, his survival instincts remained heightened. He turned to see if she was serious. She was.

"Where?" he asked.

"Brummet needs a new car."

Sherman nodded in agreement and eased the Jeep back into the small suburban neighborhood. They passed porch after porch, some dark, most lit. Uneasiness was now endemic amongst the largely retired population. The violence had cleft away any semblance of normality. A loaded gun by the bedside was common practice.

They stopped out front on the darkened street. A few blinds parted, but no one challenged their presence. Sherman still held the Glock in his hand. The threat remained until the wheels went up and he was back with the team. Then it would be another place with another threat. It was something he now accepted as an unfortunate truth. Over there or back here. The difference was smaller than he once knew.

While he watched, Ashley stashed ten stacks of bills into the coffee container in the freezer. About a hundred grand if the count held true. Maybe not life changing, but the old man deserved at least something. That cash was something. A new cab, a chunk for retirement or some nice whiskey. Ashley didn't prescribe such choices, just the option to choose.

They said nothing on the way out. The act alone carried weight. The smallest of good during an otherwise cruel few days. Sherman smiled, and not just out of habit.

Only a few cars were parked at the regional airport. A skeleton crew of janitors and a single security guard. Nothing much happened at three in the morning. No flights meant no landing lights on the runway. It screamed small town.

Checking in two hours before a flight didn't apply so the security guard looked, at a minimum, perplexed when Sherman and Ashley walked through the front doors.

"Can I help you?" asked the man. He was in his early thirties. Thin and lanky with a chipped front tooth that gave him a less than professional appearance. Not that the ill-fitting uniform and twenty-year-old revolver on his hip helped.

Sherman looked at the name tag, "Just waiting for her flight, Mr. Loeb."

"Uh, okay. You know that's not for another three hours?"

Sherman nodded.

"I mean, the counter doesn't open for another ninety minutes," continued the guard.

"We set the alarm for the wrong time," replied Ashley. "I hope that's okay."

Loeb nodded congenially, "Sure thing ma'am. Just don't see many folks at this hour."

"Thanks," she said with a smile.

"Come on," said Sherman. "I spied a coffee vending machine on the way in. I'm sure it's terrible, but I could use something hot."

"Vending machine coffee? You sure know how to treat a girl right."

"I have to beat them back with a stick," he replied while inserting a few dollars into the machine.

After a brief mechanical whirl and hiss, the machine deposited two steamy hot Styrofoam cups on a sticky tray. Sherman grabbed a little half and half container from the adjacent table and poured in the white liquid. Ashley blew on her cup.

"You know that's full of chemicals," she scolded.

He glanced at the little plastic container, "I think that is the least of my worries."

She leaned over and picked a chunk of mirror out of his hair. "Tillerman always said to watch out for the little things."

Sherman laughed, "He always had harsh words for the non-organic world."

"Industrial terrorists was the phrase."

"Ah yes. That sat well with the army boys," he added sarcastically.

When Sherman turned back, she was looking off into the wall and all the pain that lay beyond.

"What am I going to do?" she asked.

"Go live a life."

She shook her head, "No. How am I going to walk through security with a bag full of cash and not get arrested?"

The thought had occurred to Sherman on the drive over, but a simple solution had eluded him. Loeb and a black nylon cordon blocked the checkpoint. There were no TSA agents in sight. He checked his watch. Sixty minutes until the counter opened. About the same time, his boss would land unannounced.

"Hand me the bag," instructed Sherman.

Ashley held out the stuff sack while he retrieved a single ten-thousand-dollar stack.

"Bribery?" she asked.

"Bribery," he answered.

"Does that work these days?"

"That or I hurt him."

She looked over at Loeb and his innocently goofy grin, "Okay, bribery."

Ashley watched as Sherman strode over to the low-paid contract security guard with no benefits and a significant child support payment. She couldn't hear what they said, but at times it looked hostile. Loeb almost went for his revolver. Lucky for him he didn't, she thought. Sherman would beat him to the draw. The Glock stayed hidden away in his waistband.

Finally, the money changed hands and Loeb nodded sheepishly for Ashley to go ahead.

"Hide it somewhere good," said Sherman as she ducked under the security cordon.

They watched her disappear past the checkpoint, and into the darkened terminal which only had three gates. Sherman smiled at the guard, who still looked like he just stole a pack of cigarettes from the local liquor store.

"One more thing," he said. "A plane will land in a few minutes. I will need your help to exit through that side door."

Loeb looked over at the emergency door and the alarm that would ultimately go off without his code. A warning trilled loudly in the back of his mind. Run, it said, pleading to his rule bound upbringing. Then he looked at Sherman. Broken glass shimmered in his beard and blood splatters clung onto his shirt. Saying no didn't seem like an option. He did the only sensible thing and nodded.

"Thanks," replied Sherman.

No lights blinked on the Gulfstream G650 as it plowed through the clouded night sky. It came from the east, low and fast. The two pilots had a combined total of forty years behind the controls of military aircraft. A small private jet was new to their repertoire, but they were already pushing the performance envelope.

The co-pilot was busy flipping through a book of airport configurations. He had never heard of Cumbre County Regional Airport before taking off from Andrews Air Force Base.

"Two-thousand by forty-six meters. Good condition. Heading one-two-one magnetic. One-three-five true. Four light PAPI on the left side. No approach or landing lights," he informed the pilot.

"Copy that. Crossing in five."

The co-pilot turned over his shoulder to yell at the group of men lounging about on the overstuffed luxury chairs, "Touchdown in ten minutes."

"Understood," replied the Major. "Remember, we were never here. Radio silence."

"Discretion is my middle name," replied the co-pilot, who held the same rank.

Both pilots flipped down night vision goggles and closed the door. They weren't planning on using any landing lights.

The part-time aircraft controller was just coming up the stairs into the tower when the twin-engine jet roared through the clouds and onto the runway.

"What the hell," yelled the old man. He had agreed to take the gig because retirement disagreed with his constitution. Between the rowdy oil crews and the mystery plane with no lights, he was regretting his choice.

Grabbing the radio, he tried to contact the plane, but nothing was working. He picked up the phone to call Sacramento Center but got a busy signal. Convinced something was afoot, he rummaged through his bag until he found the binoculars.

"You'll pay for this," he grumbled while working the focus wheel. The controller reached for a pencil to write down the tail number required on all planes, but to his surprise the jet had none.

"A fucking ghost," he mumbled before sitting down in defeat.

Ashley and Sherman were talking to the United rep when they heard the jet land. Sherman pretended not to notice. He was busy trying to convince the woman that paying in cash would not be an issue. She, like Loeb, was just a contract employee living paycheck to paycheck and working at least two jobs.

He leaned in closer, "Get her on that plane and you can have double the ticket price."

"It's company policy to register any cash transactions."

Sherman slid over four thousand dollars, "I think you can make an exception."

The woman looked at him, then at the cash before taking it with a sigh, "Fine. Miss, where are you headed?"

"Keep it domestic so you don't have to go through security again," whispered Sherman.

Ashley smiled, "I hear Miami is nice."

The woman nodded and clacked away at the keyboard. "A one-way ticket to Miami. First class. You'll transfer in San Francisco."

"Thanks," replied Ashley as she handed over cash for the ticket price.

"Enjoy your life," said the woman.

Sherman nodded towards Loeb, who had drifted towards the side exit after the TSA agents had arrived. The guard offered a weak smile.

"My plane is here," he told Ashley.

"I know," she replied.

"I hope you find what comes next."

She smiled sadly, "You too."

Sherman jotted something down on a promotional tourism pamphlet. "If you ever need help, call this number and leave a message. I'll be in touch."

"Thanks," she said nervously, folding the paper. "Let's hope that never happens."

"Go be yourself," said Sherman.

"Stay sharp, Captain."

Sherman waved at her as Loeb opened the side door and he exited into the cold, life-affirming scent of a recent storm.

The Major was standing nearby at the base of the open cabin door.

"Captain," he said with a baritone growl.

"Major."

"You whole?"

"Yes, sir," answered Sherman.

"Are they?" asked the Major.

"Nope."

"Good, let's go."

As they climbed into the cabin Sherman stopped by the cockpit. He recognized the pilots from Jordan. "You got roped into the mess too?"

They smiled. "Should have known it was you," said the colonel. "Welcome back aboard, Captain."

Sherman took a seat next to a heap of heavy weapons and ammo. A bear of a man named Sergeant Gournsey tossed him a cold can of beer from a small fridge.

"Welcome back, Cap."

ABOUT THE AUTHOR

Joel Austin grew up in rural California under the leafy oak trees and holds an M.A. in History and International Relations. He lives in Colorado with his wife and daughter.

Find out more about upcoming releases at:

JoelAustin.online

Made in the USA
Columbia, SC
22 October 2022

69847398R00200